Maggie
Good Girls Book Seven

Christine Young

Published by Rogue Phoenix Press, LLP
Copyright © 2024

ISBN: 978-1-62420-843-0

Editor: Sherry Derr-Wille
Cover Art: Designs by Ms G

Chapter One

Glasgow 1830

Maggie sat in front of her mirror, watching as her sister fixed her hair. The long, dark blond locks were piled on top of her head with wispy little curls framing her face. She wore a lemon yellow colored gown. The bodice was cut fashionably low and was adorned with lace. The corset she wore pushed her breasts up, more than she wished to display this evening even though her mother assured her the gown was in good taste. She wasn't comfortable. Unconsciously, she continued to pull the corsage higher. The gown would never budge. Tugging the bodice to cover more of her, impossible. She didn't like the picture in front of her when she stared at her mirror.

Letting out a long, slow breath of air she turned to Nellie. Her heart in her throat, Maggie cringed at the idea of the soiree this evening. Fear pooled in her stomach. She didn't belong. The crowd of bodies all vying for attention put her off. There were young debutantes who would love to become Nelson's wife. Let any one of them have the role. Maggie didn't want the part. More than once, she told her mother she wouldn't be coerced into something so horrible she couldn't breathe thinking about it.

"I don't want to go. We all understand Mother wants to announce a marriage to Nelson this evening. I abhor the man. He believes he can have whatever he wants. Just because he's decided he wants a wife and I'm the one who will fulfill the role, he needs to understand he will never get what he wants. I'll never agree. This is a play for power. They both want more. Mother wants to have increased sway with the aristocracy. If she thinks she can gain that by throwing me to the wolf, she is terribly wrong. I refuse to be the victim in this scenario."

"Yes, all that and more is true. The problem as I see it is that Nelson wants you, Maggie," Fannie reminded her. "What can we do to change that? There must be something."

It seemed Fannie was also groping for answers.

"I could smile at the man with spinach in my front teeth. That might stop him. What do you think?"

Maggie could imagine the man's reaction to the sight. He was such a prude. He would blanche. Might cry off the engagement at that very second.

"Your powder could be caked making you look decades older. Show tons of wrinkles," Tessa added with a sly smirk. "There are any number of things you could do to scare the man."

"Such as spilling red wine on his immaculate white shirt," Nellie said, lifting her feminine shoulders in a shrug of nonchalance. "He would have apoplexy at something like that. Who would dare?"

"Smoke; take one of father's cigars then light it in front of him. Puff on it then send the smoke in his face. That would certainly dissuade the man from wishing to make you his wife."

"I would turn green if I tried to smoke the thing. Nellie, do you recall when we were fourteen and we…" Her stomach began to churn as she thought about that time. Never again. Smoking was not for her.

"Yes. Stole cigars from father's desk. Will never forget how sick we were. Haven't come close to a cigar since. Even the smell of someone else smoking one makes me sick," Nellie added with a scowl.

"You could toss your meal on him," Fannie added with a trilling laugh that warmed Maggie's heart. "He would never forgive you. A little vomit at his crotch would dissuade every man from wicked thoughts. He always appears so pristine I want to gag looking at him. For me, I don't want my husband and lover to hate the sight of a small bit of dirt. The man even brushes imaginary pieces of nonexistent dust from his shoulders."

An affectation that disgusted Maggie. Ah, Fannie and Tessa were both such dears. Always true and loyal to their older sisters. This was Tessa's first year of attending balls. The littlest sister did love to flirt as well as dance. She never failed to have a new young man panting after her. In truth she was shy. Always kept her thoughts to herself. Seemed to care too much what others thought. Maggie knew her littlest sister never cared over much for anyone's thoughts except her sisters'. Her actions at the balls were all a sham.

Maggie peered into the mirror again. Made a face of disgust. "Get me out of that ballroom if it becomes apparent mother intends to go through with this tonight. Once she sets her plans in motion, there won't be anywhere I can run. I must beat her at her game." Maggie clenched her fists tight, determined to find a means to defy her mother along with the scenario she planned for her oldest daughter. "I won't marry that man! Won't let him touch me!" Maggie cringed thinking about the one kiss Nelson forced on her. Nelson Abernathy, the Marquis of Townsend, would never have her as his wife. She'd gladly die first. Thinking about that scenario, her nails bit into the palms of her hands.

"If you don't run, you might not have a choice. We need to think of somewhere for you to go. Someone who would give you protective shelter. There are ways to force the unwilling. We cannot let that ensue." Tessa put into words what Maggie feared for the last month.

Words had been said. Promises made. Without her permission her mother planned her life. Even if she had to live in poverty, she would hide from Lord Abernathy. She knew of his cruelties. He'd never married. Nonetheless his mistresses never fared well. Some died at his hands. A few were disfigured from his cruelties. In all cases the deeds were rumored to be true. There was no proof. No concrete evidence. She wasn't about to become a victim.

"I *ken* what you're thinking, Maggie. You will, when married, have more power than the other women in his life. He wouldn't dare hurt you. If that happened, Mother would seek retaliation. I'm certain she would have spoken to the man about his inclinations before she agreed to this marriage," Nellie said but the sound of her voice lacked confidence. "He would never dare cause you discomfort. Not as he's said to treat the other inconsequential women in his life."

"Mother's retaliation would do little to help her if the man chose to inflict any type of pain. I'm not going to marry him."

"There are drugs that can make you compliant," Nellie pointed out, her voice taking on a hard edge that Maggie didn't miss. "I would that you flee while the chance exists. We will all stand beside you. Help you in any way we can."

Standing, Maggie walked to the balcony overlooking the gardens.

The air was frosty. Cold. Fog would settle in tonight. Heavy clouds would blanket the area. If she chose to run, it would be difficult for anyone searching. The streets would be cold. Maggie knew where she would go. There were a few streets where the ladies from the bakery in Glasgow supplied with leftover baked goods from the day. She wouldn't starve. Daryl Chamberlin owned the establishment. She was certain she could find safe haven in the area. Maybe even a roof over her head could be found until she could figure a way out of Glasgow.

"I see you making plans. You look as if your head spins with wild scenarios. Don't scheme anything dangerous. What is it that you're planning?" Fannie challenged her. "You can tell us. We would never betray you."

No, her sisters would never willingly give her up. They would stand with her until they couldn't. "Mother would wrest the truth from you. She has her ways. What I'm thinking can't be told even though I trust all of you. Nelson will be furious. His rage will make him a terrible enemy. If he thought any of my sisters could tell him where I am, retribution would be at the forefront of his head. Who knows what he would do to get answers. No, I have to do this on my own. Find my way by myself. Need to also protect my sisters." Maggie found she was terrified. She would leave tonight from the ball when no one was the wiser. If there was any luck to be had, no one would miss her until she was far away.

"You will send us word...?" Tessa hesitated. She stood beside her on the balcony. "If you need anything."

"If you are in trouble," Nellie continued as she too joined her sisters on the terrace. "Truly, we would tell no one. You must have a means to contact us. It's terribly cold tonight. You can't be all by yourself."

"You wouldn't intend to give me away. Come let's not speak of this. The carriage is downstairs waiting for us. We should be on our way to the soiree in a matter of minutes. Who can tell what will happen. If I'm lucky, he will fall madly in love with some unsuspecting debutante."

Maggie felt a river of cold fear bathe her. The freeze wasn't from the weather. Her body chilled thinking of the man who waited for her.

Maggie didn't understand why he chose her. There were many beautiful, more beautiful women in Glasgow. Women who would bring more to him in the way of a dowry as well as power. Hoped the rumors weren't true circulating throughout the town. She didn't understand how she knew they were true. She did. Perhaps it was the way her mother sidestepped her questions. The secretive way she held her hand to her mouth when she spoke to father so no one would hear the exchanged words.

Angus, her father, would never lift a hand to help her. He had despised her since she was born, for the simple reason she was not a son. Despised all his daughters. A man who wanted only sons had been blessed with four daughters.

Mother no longer came to his bed. She slept alone in a separate room. As far as Maggie knew there was little to nothing between them except the marriage vows. Angus left every evening to seek out entertainment. When he returned, she had no idea. She supposed it was early morning. He slept somewhere besides his home.

"I've also heard a small fortune has been offered for your hand," Nellie told her while she looked into the mirror to pinch her cheeks. "Didn't know mother and father needed funds so much they would sell you to anyone."

"Through mother's family, thought there was money along with lands," Tessa said, something they all believed was true.

Mother was always after something in addition to affluence. Wealth. Power. She scorned Angus, her husband, for not capitalizing on his daughters. Maggie knew from the moment she turned eighteen, her mother searched for the perfect match for her daughter. Anice entered into two arrangements in the two and a half years since that date trying to wed her daughter. Those two men were weak. Maggie had been able to say no to each of them with no reprisals. The men backed off, intimidated by her. This situation was different.

The first attempt at a betrothal was also to a wealthy merchant. The dowry would have been large but no title went with the consummation of the marriage. Maggie said no to the man. He decided she wasn't what he wished for in a bride. Anice didn't pursue the arrangement. She held out for better after she realized Maggie would never say yes to the marriage.

Unless her mother drugged her before walking down the aisle, she would never agree to that first union. The man not only was old enough to be her father, he'd let his body go. His jowls were large. Seemed to fill up the majority of his face. No, the nose was what she noticed first. The end was red from overindulgence of alcohol. His breath was beastly. The man loved to eat and drink. The thought of lying in bed with the man made her stomach churn. If he tried to be intimate with her, she would throw up on him.

Second time didn't work much better. While the man was an earl, Anice discovered he had gambled away the majority of his inherited wealth. He was as poor as a church mouse. Now, unable to find a woman to share his life with, he spent an inordinate amount of time with the escorts from Miss Scarlet's establishment. This man's physique was quite the opposite of the merchants. He was tall. His shoulders were broad. He possessed deep brown eyes that seemed to bore into a person as if he could read what was in that person's mind. The man gave her chills. He was cold. Not as frigid though as Lord Abernathy.

Shuddering, she turned from her cold perch on the balcony to follow her sisters down the stairs. Their mother waited at the door, impatiently tapping her foot. Her lips were pursed, a grim expression on her handsome face. They donned their capes then rushed from the warm foyer to the waiting carriage.

The ride to the Abernathy residence didn't take long. For the most part, the girls' chatter stopped once their mother joined them. Maggie tried to remain positive. Told herself her mother would never spring a betrothal on her without speaking of it to her first. In the cloak room, Anice pulled her aside. They waited until the sisters left.

Anice's whispered words to her were harsh. She held her arm, shaking her as she spoke. "You are to behave yourself tonight. A lot rests on how you act in front of the marquis. He wants you. This is the man you will marry. There is no way for you to sidestep this alliance as you have the other ones. This man has promised much for your hand in marriage. He adores you. If you do anything to mess with this contract, I'll find the oldest, fattest duke in the country to give you to. Do you understand?"

"Yes. The man doesn't adore me. The marquis doesn't know me. He can't have feelings for me. Those emotions don't exist."

"Do you understand?" Anice whispered again. "I swear you will regret it if you refuse him. Don't argue."

Maggie pulled her arm away from her mother. Turning on her, she spoke with as much determination as she could, "I won't marry that man!"

Maggie understood the moment she uttered the words they weren't heard. Nor would the refusal do a bit of good in deterring Anice from sealing an agreement made in hell. She wasn't afraid of another contract either. She found a means out of two before this one. She wasn't going to succumb to this bond. Fleeing was the only way for her to avoid an unwanted marriage.

Tonight.

It had to be done tonight.

Beneath her ribs, her heart thundered. The only question now was when to leave. She would need to watch and plan with care. If her mother was serious, the marquis would have men watching her.

She wasn't a pawn to be tossed around as if she had no say in her life. This was not the dark ages. She wouldn't allow herself to be bartered to the highest bidder. Maggie was terribly afraid her sisters might well meet the same fate. Her sisters were sweet but not biddable. Each in her own way would put up a singular fight if met with similar circumstances. It was up to her to forge the way. Make her understand that her daughters were not pawns to her schemes. Checkmate.

"You won't have a choice. The agreements have been signed as well as sealed. The documents are in a safe place...secure," her mother whispered next to her ear again. "For once, you have to do what I wish."

"Not by me! I've not signed anything. Won't agree to a marriage. At the altar I will say no. Then no. Then no again!" Maggie yanked her arm away, striding from the cloak room, noting, too, where her cloak was. She would need it soon. There was no going back. Soon she would be alone. On her own.

"Margret!" Anice's eyes flashed her anger. Her name bellowed from her mother's lips as if she didn't care who would hear. Anice's shoulders were trembling as she shook her fist at her. "You won't say no. It's too important to our family. As his wife, you will help your sisters find suitable husbands. You owe this to me. To your father. We've given you everything. Now it's your turn to give back."

I don't owe you!

She smiled sweetly. Talking more would do nothing to change her mother's simple mind. Maggie understood she'd already said too much. She should have never confronted her mother or stood up to her. Should have ignored the proposal. Pretended to go along with the suggestion. It would have been better if Anice didn't know she would rebel or refuse Lord Abernathy's suit.

The butler stood at the door waiting for them. He watched them as if he understood what was being said between mother and daughter. Another of the marquis' spies. Maggie whisked her way inside then handed her cloak to the man at the coatroom. She stood with her sisters, trembling. Her anger needed release. She drew in deep breaths hoping to ease the fury raging within.

Her heart thundered beneath her ribs. Maggie didn't think she would ever be calm again. Nothing she did seemed to help. She panted softly, willing herself to be unruffled. Eager for the fury she felt to evaporate. Her breathing softened to a more acceptable cadence even though her entire body still quivered, shaking with anger. Nelson stood across the room.

When he noticed her, his gaze shifted to her. Stared. He nodded. His eyes were cold, chilling her more than she thought possible a minute ago. His gaze traveled the length of her then back to her eyes as if he read the emotions bubbling from her.

The man was handsome. His nose long, straight. His jaw chiseled to be firm. Broad shoulders sloped to a narrow waist. Hard thighs rounded out the masculine package he presented. She kept coming back to his eyes. So fathomless. So very cold. Bleak. Distant. His cruel streak evident in the tilt of his head, the mocking slant of his lips. Shivering, she wrapped her arms around herself. No, she would never say yes to this man.

This wasn't a man she wished to be close to let alone wed. It seemed the moment her mother saw him, she walked to him. The woman smiled. Extended her hand in a warm greeting. He brought the back to his lips removing his gaze from her mother he looked at her again. The devil, he watched her as if she was his prey. In a way she was just that.

Anice would pull him to where she stood. She would have to dance. He would hold her. It was far too soon. Maggie darted away, turned to search for some place to disappear. Her heart lodged in her throat. There was nowhere to hide. A potted palm beckoned. She would be too easily found if she tried to disappear in the same room. What she needed was to find some unused room in this huge estate. Find a balcony or a way out to the gardens.

"He is coming your way," Nellie whispered, her voice soft. "Hold your ground. If Mother chooses to make an announcement, she will wait until everyone has arrived. It is still too early in the evening to make the maximum effect. There is time to plan your escape. Even if the declaration is made, nothing said here is etched in stone."

Maggie nodded, understanding the plan would need to be foolproof. Crossing her fingers, she replied. "That's true. I need something to drink. My mouth is parched, my lips dry. Can't seem to swallow."

She picked up a glass of champagne from a waiter passing by. Oh, the devil, it's champagne. They did plan this celebratory proclamation for tonight. She didn't have a chance in hell. Searching the room for an immediate escape route, she found herself in the middle of several matronly ladies. Whispering to her sisters before she tried to disappear from his view, "He is already celebrating my demise."

"Appears so," Tessa said, agreeing with her assumption.

Looking back, she gave her sister a nod to assure her the time was now. Hidden in the middle of the women she could make her escape. The women around her chatted, talked nonsense. They were turning a corner when they came to an abrupt halt.

"Ladies…"

The devil take the man, Maggie recognized the voice. The bearer of bad tidings was Nelson. He must have seen her wiggle herself into this group of ladies who must be on the way to the powder room. She intended to sneak out of the pack when they passed an empty room. She held her breath. This was still possible if he didn't see her.

"Lord Abernathy, you look so handsome tonight. Are you looking for something?" one lady asked. She giggled as if she hoped he looked for her.

"You are too perceptive by far," he smiled, giving her a wink then a nod. "Seems the lady to be honored tonight went missing a few minutes ago. With her mother's permission, I decided to look for her." He was ginning again. Tapped his finger on his chin. "Believe I've found her."

She was trying to maneuver away from the group without being noticed. So far, so good, she thought wistfully as she realized he stood in front of her, his hands on his hips, booted feet braced apart. Having noticed her, he'd been aware she was trying to put distance between herself and the ladies.

9

"Honored?" Maggie looked up at him, questioning with a shiver to her voice. "Honored? Whatever for? I'm just here at my mother's request. Would have remained at home if given a choice. Don't like these things. Never have."

"You haven't guessed? My, my, my, thought you were brighter than that. But then…your mother would not have told you. It was supposed to be a surprise. Imagine the announcement will be just that." He paused as if in thought, he stroked his chin. "I'm sorry to detain you. Were you on the way to the powder room? I will let you go see to your needs."

"Y-yes!" Maggie grasped at anything that might save her from returning to the ballroom with this man. She tilted her chin up trying to hide the trembling. "Yes, I was on my way with these fine ladies to the powder room. If you'll excuse me." She started forward leading the way.

Nelson's hands were clasped behind his back as he moved on the balls of his feet to intercept her. "No, don't believe I will do that. Imagine I should escort you." He set his hand on her arm, guiding her around the ladies. They walked for a minute or two then he stopped. "I'll wait for you here. Don't take too long. Be advised I'm not going anywhere without you."

She felt his hands on the small of her back as he gave her a tiny shove toward the door. Maggie looked over her shoulder at him as she tried to tamp down the frown of displeasure. There had to be a way out of the lady's room other than this door. A window. A balcony. They were on the third floor. Even if there was a window, she couldn't jump. Needed to avoid the marriage, not kill herself. She supposed she would have to wait for a few minutes then return to him. If she could get lucky, he might not be at the door when she left.

"Wasn't that the most romantic gesture one ever saw? He's going to wait to escort her back to the ballroom." one of the ladies asked while she smiled at her. "Do you think they will wed before the end of the year? They make such a lovely couple."

"The banns must be read first. The wedding will happen in January," someone seemed to know things Maggie didn't.

"You, my dear, are a very lucky lady to be chosen by the marquis. Not only is he handsome, the man is also rich. You should be thanking your mother for arranging such an advantageous match. He will not be hard to bed. He is so much a man."

Maggie felt her gut tighten. *Never! I won't be caught dead in that man's bed. Never!* "I have many times over. Mother is aware of my feelings," Maggie told the women while she walked to the window overlooking the street below. If she dropped herself from the window, she would die when she hit the ground below. That wouldn't do. Even if the betrothal was announced tonight, she still had time to flee. He couldn't have her watched night and day when she was still living with her mother.

Outside the door, he waited for her. She looked to the door then the window. Maggie wondered if the women would also exit in mass. He would be wary if they did. Would look for her in the middle of the group. The women would present her to him the moment they walked from the powder room. She couldn't leave with them. The sickness coursing through her stomach grew. Escalated until she tasted bile. Maggie started shaking so hard, she needed to sit. Tears sprang to her eyes. She heaved in a few deep breaths of air. Calmer now. Her legs held her upright. She searched the room. The women still chattered. There had to be a way out of this.

Both frustrated as well as angry at her circumstances, she strode the perimeter of the room. To avoid the women tattling on her, she made a few adjustments to her hair then pinched her cheeks. Maggie ran her tongue across her parched lips. Never did get something to drink, except that one drink. She attempted to raise the bodice of her gown higher.

"Now you stop that!" One of the matrons told her.

She jumped. "What?"

"The gown is in the height of fashion. Shows just enough to tempt your future husband, the marquis. He will be pleased you have breasts that will fill his hands. There is nothing wrong with a fiancé getting a tiny look at what he will own soon."

Own? Never! She was tempted to yell at the woman that she filled the bodice with scarves. She didn't. He would never own any part of her. She would always be independent. Instead, she remained silent. It would never do to antagonize any of these women. Friends here was what she was in desperate need of. Women who would understand her frantic plight to stay autonomous and not be ruled by an arrogant lord of the realm.

"Anice should be pleased she has such a beautiful daughter. Your sisters are no less fetching. She should be able to arrange profitable matches with your sweet siblings. The matches will bring great rewards.

Grandchildren in the future. Don't you think?" The lady turned her attention to the other women.

"Oh, yes, that's true. They are sweet as well as beautiful. Such perfect specimens of womanhood. Compliant women willing to obey their men. Are we all ready to leave?" The lady looked at her as if she was the one who needed to answer. "You are coming too?" she asked hopefully. "The marquis will not wish to wait overlong. A man like that doesn't wish to waste time standing at the door of the powder room."

I never asked him to wait for me.

"No, I'm going to stay here a few more minutes. Need some time to think." Maggie lifted her hands. A shrug of her shoulders, later she spoke, "This all comes as a surprise to me. Didn't know there would be an announcement this evening. Also didn't know I would have a fiancé until I walked through these doors. Would have preferred to be told in private about this arrangement."

"What better time than Christmas Eve to announce such wonderful news. It will cheer so many people," one of the ladies spoke. She did sound sincere.

"My dear, when you discover the truth, it matters not. Nothing now will change true love. If you stay in this room, your lord will come for you. You know that of course. You might gain a few minutes. No more than that. The marquis seems eager to have you by his side. If you make him wait, his good humor over the engagement might vanish. Tread with care. He is a powerful man. He could make life a living hell for you."

Unhappily, Maggie nodded. She'd been warned. "What are a few more minutes to be alone? I need the time."

Yes, she did need the seconds to get her head on straight. If she didn't get away from this man, she would have a lifetime with him.

"You enjoy these few moments of privacy. We will tell him you were feeling poorly. I'm certain that won't change his mind. Nonetheless, it will give him something to think about." The lady patted her on the hand. "You take care of yourself." All but one woman exited the room. This one seemed to wait as if she sensed there was more to her reluctance.

Maggie didn't understand the quick exchange of words. She felt as if she had a friend in this woman. Not that a friend would do her any good. Unless they could help her leave this mausoleum. Wished she knew the woman's identity. Moisture filling her eyes, liquid she tried to hold back, Maggie asked, "Who are you?"

"Lacie Stewart." The woman handed her a card. "Hide this. Don't let him see it. A woman should never have to marry a man such as that one. If you ever need anything, come to me at that address. It's not my address but my sister's. We will all help. You have friends who you wouldn't know about."

For a few seconds, her mouth gaped open. "The duke's wife? The Duke of Southcliff? Why would you help me? I'm nobody."

Her smile was sweet, generating confidence. "My husband is not only powerful but he has a wealth of contacts. Associates here as well as overseas. He could even get you out of the country if that happened to be what you wished for; France, Spain, the United States. Wherever you might like to go. Just don't let Lord Abernathy see the card. Hide it in your bosom if that might be a safe place. Don't think he will try anything of that sort tonight."

"You don't like Lord Abernathy?" Maggie asked, stunned by this beautiful woman who seemed bent on helping her from this horrid predicament. She wanted to plead with her. "You say you'll help me? Can you get me out of here tonight before I'm stood up in front of the crowd then promised to him for the rest of my life? I don't want that to happen."

"No...I can't help you leave this evening. You must find a means by yourself. Your sisters will give assistance. I'm positive Lord Abernathy is a dangerous, evil man. I cannot help you vanish. That you will need to take care of on your own. Once you find a way to escape both your mother as well as Lord Abernathy, it is then I can give aid." Lacie closed her hands over the one holding the card. "Don't lose this. Don't let him find it." With that said the woman vanished from the room.

Maggie watched the sway of The Duchess' dress before the door closed. In a second, the card disappeared into the corsage of her gown. She sat on a chair in front of the fire waiting for Lord Abernathy to invade the small private space. Flames in the fireplace danced, sending orange-gold colors into the room. Tonight. Her escape must be tonight. Choices eluded her. She couldn't wait. If she didn't make good her flight this evening, she had the feeling more guards would be set upon her. To her mother, she made her feelings clear. Anice would have told the marquis how she felt. This man wouldn't take a single chance if he understood the extent of her hatred for him. If he learned she didn't mean to say yes at the altar, the man would make certain she did. There were ways to subdue a woman.

"Miss Maggie?" Lord Abernathy stepped into the room, his expression grim. Unyielding. "Lady Stewart told me you weren't feeling well. Should I send for my carriage to take you home? I can do that after the announcement is made this evening. I will make certain you are safe."

With boldness Maggie didn't feel, she stood, smoothed the skirts of her gown. "I'm fine now. The crush of people made me hot, a bit faint. I needed a *wee* bit of space to set my mind straight. This brief interlude eased my headache. Nothing but a bit of fresh air couldn't help. Perhaps I could stand on the balcony."

"Good, then…" He stepped forward, holding out his hand. "We will attend to the guests together. I would like a dance. Perhaps some champagne will also help ease your nerves. The balcony is out of the question."

"Sir, I didn't say I was nervous."

She resented the fact the man put words in her mouth. Though he was right in assuming. Knew she wasn't nervous. Furious would be a better term to describe her thoughts.

"Your hand is shaking. To what other cause should I give this condition? I would call it by whatever name you choose. Would never intend to assume something that is untrue."

The chill in his voice sent ice down her spine. Maggie felt as if he saw into her mind. Understood her loathing of him. "Imagine you are correct. Nerves. Didn't wish to admit to them." Maggie tilted her chin.

"Don't get in the habit of lying to me. I wouldn't appreciate that." The anger in his voice was evident. "Will never tolerate mistruths from my wife."

"Never," she bit into her lip after she said the word.

Lord Abernathy ushered her from the room with nothing more said. Kept her hand on his arm. In the ballroom, he whirled her around the dance floor until he reached the front where there was a platform. At his nod, a bell sounded.

He cleared his throat. Held up her hand. Kissed the knuckles as he peered at his captive audience. "I give you my intended bride, Miss Margret MacRae."

He turned her. While a muffled chatter circled the room, he pulled her into his arms, his hand at the small of her back. His mouth captured hers, his tongue pushing inside. The kiss was brutal. His teeth tugged on her lip while his tongue ravished inside. She tasted blood. Moaned from unexpected pain. He tightened his hold upon her.

She pushed on him. Struggled. Whimpered. Felt the bulge of his sex pushing against her belly. "No…" she tried to say but the word was lost inside his mouth. His hand fell lower. Settled on her derriere. The act told all watching he owned her. Just as the woman in the powder room told her.

Nelson moved away, only a breath of air separating them. "Don't ever struggle against me or fight me. I don't like that. If you don't heed my words, you'll regret ignoring what I've told you. You are to always be willing." He set her aside then called for more champagne. "The finest France has to offer for this momentous occasion. From the city of Epernay."

Maggie felt lost now that the announcement was made. The chatter around the room varied from shock to dismay. She needed air. Gulped for oxygen. He left her standing by herself. It seemed Lord Abernathy thought her subdued. He was busy whirling another woman around the room. When she rose to walk, no one noticed her. Maggie understood he would have a man watching her. She circled the room. Searched for the best exit.

For a few minutes she wandered idly around the tables laden with food, nibbling on a few items. Nellie blocked the view of her from one of the guards she thought was assigned to her. Tessa chatted with her. Fannie handed her a plate of food. Together, they made their way from the room. Once outside, Nellie exchanged the plate of food for her cape she'd retrieved from the cloak room.

"Run, now!"

~ * ~

Jasper Kenworthy spoke with his twin brother, Jason, in their townhouse in Glasgow. They were both drinking brandy as well as smoking their favorite cigars, amusing themselves with imaginary scenarios. Challenging each other to help more with the charity that was needed in the city. The homeless seemed to increase each day. They spoke of going out tonight. The night was Christmas Eve. There were parties.

The twins were bored.

A fire blazed in the hearth. Jasper tapped the ashes of his cigar on the ashtray. Light from the flames cast glowing shadows. The sky was darkening as the sun slipped behind the hills. The two men were almost identical. Jasper, of course, was the oldest by mere minutes. Jason's eyes were so brown at times they appeared black. His brown eyes were rimmed with gold when he stood in the sunlight or next to a candle he was told. Jason was taller by the width of a finger, broader of shoulder by about the same amount.

Jason laughed.

Jasper brooded. He was after all the man to inherit everything, the title. The wealth along with all the responsibility. Though Jason had more money than he could spend in a lifetime.

"What is it you are thinking?" Jason stared into the fireplace. When he turned to speak, Jasper saw a glint of amusement in his brother's features. "Are you as wearied of all this as I am? I need something exciting to happen in my life. My day after day routine does nothing to spark enthusiasm. Life is too much the same."

"We were supposed to go to Lord Abernathy's ball. I cried off. Couldn't bring myself to witness a young woman betrothed against her will to that man," Jasper said as he swirled the amber liquid in his glass, watching firelight play off the colors. For the longest time he studied the liquid, shifting different thoughts in his head. "Everyone knew that was going to happen tonight. People who know the lady in question, understand it will be a match made in hell for her."

Jason stood, walking around the room, picking up different objects then setting them back. When he spoke, there was concern in his voice. "You don't know this engagement is against her will now, do you? The man has a title as well as serious groats. Many women would call that satisfactory, more than satisfactory. He is not difficult to look at…if one tends to be of the female persuasion. By most standards the man would be considered an excellent catch. What makes you believe a marriage to Nelson will be hell for the young woman?"

"It won't do a'tall. Not a'tall. Don't wish to witness the degradation of a beautiful woman. Never seen the chit. Though I've heard the rumors. She's unique. Flawless. Impeccable." He flicked back the remnants of brandy. Let the liquid warm his throat. "Yes, what I've heard is gossip. You are quite correct in this matter. Doesn't make the words any less true. We both know enough about the mother, Anice MacRae, to discern the truth of the rumors now, don't we? To gain more power she would betroth her daughter to the devil himself. She's an ass with no feelings."

Jason stopped his wandering mind, shrugging his broad shoulders before he hooted his laughter. "Not our business, big brother. We should…I don't know. Stay out of this?" Thinking, he pinched the bridge of his nose. "Sometimes life is a bit tedious. We should have attended the affair. Seen what was happening for ourselves. Could have judged the situation with more accuracy. Heard tell the Duke and Duchess of Southcliff would be there to lend support to the unlucky *lass* if needed. We could not have done anything else."

"Contrary to popular opinion, the lass must not be too pleasant to look on if her mother was so eager to see her wed that she would give her to Abernathy," Jasper mused. As he refilled his glass, he leaned back in the chair, thinking his life was indeed uninteresting. He needed to do something to put excitement in his days. His life here was well ordered. Nothing surprising ever knocked on his doorstep. He'd spent years making certain of that.

"On the opposite side to that story, I heard she is a real beauty. Could win the hand of just about any man she wanted. The mother, MacRae, is after more power along with wealth. Must believe that man can give her what she craves. Sold her daughter. Sold her to the highest bidder. Wonder what she got in return for the agreement concerning her oldest."

"You're right, our lives are monotonous. Here we are talking about some poor debutante's fate when we could be out doing something exciting. Don't know what that is."

He had some thoughts on that. His concerns for the less fortunate were well-known. He helped with the homeless whenever time permitted. Many of the people who were delegated to the streets simply met some type of misfortune or bad luck. He thought to change the lives of as many as possible. This was the eve before Christmas. A good God-fearing man would do something to ease the plight of his fellow man.

"You have something in mind?" Jason asked, his tone bland. "I would go to the widow I've been seeing. Celebrate Christmas Eve in her arms. Have a bit of fun tonight unless you need my company for some endeavor. Wake up Christmas morning with a warm willing woman in my arms. You should find a woman, Jasper. A man isn't meant to be alone. As we age, we need comforts. You are older. While I don't need children, you do need an heir."

Jasper tapped his fingers on the arm of the chair, thinking his brother was right. In several years, he'd not found a woman who appealed to him. On occasion, he used Miss Scarlett's escort service. Not for sex, but to enjoy a woman's company at dinner or the opera. Things he didn't wish to experience alone. "Yes, you do enjoy your widow. What's her name? Sarah something? I will venture out tonight. I would bet the lady from the bakery will be walking the freezing street with her bodyguards. Lacie Stewart might even be there. Neither the duke or Donal will allow their wives out by themselves in that part of the city."

"Thought the duke and duchess were attending the ball."

"Yes…well…how long they stay is always the question."

Jason let out a big sigh, one that sounded much like exasperation. "Sarah Russell. You need to find a woman. Stop using Miss Scarlett's place as an excuse to stay single. There is nothing wrong with commitment."

His brother had a point. Still, to marry he'd have to feel a burning need for said woman. He'd been burned once before. Perhaps he should find a woman on the streets. She would have no expectations. "Ah, yes, you should go see Sarah. Leave your older brother with nothing to do except twiddle his thumbs the night before Christmas. You're speaking of commitment as if you have a woman in mind for me. I know you aren't planning on marrying the widow. So, don't talk to me about settling down."

"Touché, big brother. You're right of course. Both of us have a great deal of time before we tie the knot. I for one will not settle for just any woman. Must have love, you know. We can't right all the wrongs of the world tonight. What we can do is make someone's life a *wee* bit better. It is the night before Christmas. We should do something to ease the plight of the homeless."

"Let's go for a walk. Perhaps we could help the ladies from the bakery hand out day old goods. It would be our good deed for the day. The hour is growing late. The women from the bakery are always happy when they have extra male company along for protection."

Jasper grinned, agreeing with the younger sibling. He did need to expend energy. Staring at the fire was not the way to accomplish the feat. Whistling, he grabbed his coat then headed for the carriage. Jason followed on his heels.

They rode to the bakery in Jasper's carriage, emblazoned with the Kenworthy seal. The sun had set. The sky was dark, clouds covering the inky blackness. The sky threatened a downpour. A brisk wind flowed from the direction of the river. The night was cold. He wondered if the temperature was low enough for snow. Jasper leaned back thinking about all the brothers talked about this evening. He meant to look closely at the women who lived on the streets. An idea simmered in his head. Would explode if he found the perfect specimen.

"I will wager," Jasper said leaning forward, his forearms resting on his thighs. He watched his brother cock his head in curiosity.

"Yes?" Jason looked as if he was going to laugh as he tapped his fingers together beneath his chin. "A wager. What do you wish to bet on? I have thoughts rolling in my head. Does this wager have something to do with these helpless women? Left with nothing. Women who need help to survive?"

"This is serious for me even though you will laugh. You do realize some of these women have been abused by husbands? They have no recourse except to flee for their lives. Yet…there is nowhere for them to go, to hide. A man possesses all rights once a woman is wed to them. I would venture that I can turn a young woman off the streets into a lady in let's say…two months' time. I would wager one hundred pounds that I can do it, by George."

Jasper felt relief. He'd thought about this for quite some time now. He knew the deed could be done. Turn a deep Scottish burr to civilized English. Take a woman who rarely bathed to adore the soft scent of perfumed water coupled with clean skin and hair.

"Make it five hundred and you have a deal." Jason laughed outright. "I'll win, you know. Such a thing isn't possible."

"Five hundred it is. I don't intend to lose."

He didn't. The right woman would present herself. If not this evening another time. He wasn't in a rush. Picking the first young woman he met would not make this doable. The woman needed to possess certain qualities. What those qualities were, he wasn't yet certain.

Jason did laugh, a big guffaw that had Jasper swearing beneath his breath. "Is that what you intend tonight? Looking for that perfect lady. What are you seeking?"

Jasper wasn't certain what he was looking for. A list. He needed to make a list in his head. That would help. "As of this moment, not entirely certain." He mulled over a few ideas in his brain. "I would say she would have to be semi-attractive. Doesn't have to be beautiful. Not hard on the eyes, might be a better definition. Would doubt if any lady straight off the streets would qualify as a beauty. Nevertheless, I can look. Pride myself in the ability to see beyond dirt smudges, the wear and tear of not knowing where the next meal is coming from. Dark circles beneath the eyes."

"What else?" Jason asked, his smile deepening as the conversation progressed. "What about intelligence? Though a brief meeting one would be hard pressed to notice intellect if one was overwhelmed with beauty. There would be more attributes to consider. If she is to succeed, she might need to be daring as well as bold. Wouldn't she need a wealth of confidence? Would you present her at a ball?"

"True to all you've pointed out." Jasper made a steeple with his fingers as he thought. "Bold or shy? What do you think would be better? Perhaps she could pretend to be timid when the move would suit. A woman is looked down on if she is too daring. Courageous in the face of complications might be a better attribute."

"Call the characteristic what you wish. I would say being bold would be necessary," Jason answered quickly…too fast. After that he paused for a few seconds in thought. "If you plan to show this lady off when you are finished with her, she cannot be shy. Cannot be the type of *lass* to jump at shadows. The men and women who she encounters will be stern. Why old Mrs. Grant would run her over the coals the moment she set her eyes on her. The woman would come out with her claws bared. This lady you are training must be able to walk among the Scottish aristocrats with her head held high, her chin in the air while snubbing her perfectly shaped nose at the men and women who would judge her."

"You do have a point." Jasper was feeling more empowered with the passing minutes. "I would hope this lady we find would be a soft combination of both characteristics. If she is overly bold, we can teach her to lower her lashes then smile sweetly. To nod in agreement even if she knows what the person is saying is perfectly false. If she is too shy, well then, we will have to teach her to show backbone. It would not do for her to agree with everything that is put in front of her. I plan to show her off as a debutante. Perhaps before the next season. She will have to be young. Cannot be over twenty in age."

"Believe she must pass the ultimate test before you escort her to her premier functions. Would like the Duke and Duchess of Southcliff to give their opinions. Perhaps introduce her at the beginning of the season. They will be the best judge of her character. We could set up an introduction. Invite the two to dinner."

"You think the Duke and Duchess of Southcliff would lower themselves to such an endeavor?"

Jasper wasn't too expectant of anyone of their status being willing to judge a woman from the streets. Though this couple was exceptional. They did loyally give to the community. He would need to see…weigh all the options.

"There they are. Look at the group, huddling together to stay warm. They are mostly women." Jason pointed out the window.

The carriage drew to a stop. Daryl, the owner of the bakery was there as was the cook. They were flanked by two men. The duke's men, Jasper felt certain of that. Might be men hired by Daryl's husband, Donal Chamberlin.

"May we join you?" Jasper asked as he strode to Daryl. He caught her hand in his and brought the back to kiss with a light touch. "We found we had nothing to do this evening so we decided to see if anyone needed more assistance than what you give with your food donations. We've brought a few blankets but can go back for more. It's the devil of a cold night."

"Jasper Kenworthy, you know you are always welcome." Daryl gave him a quick hug. "Would have thought you would attend Lord Abernathy's ball. He made such a production of a surprise announcement. Not so much a surprise. Seems he let it be known there would be an announcement of an engagement…his. Though most people attending just wanted to get a look at the girl he intends to make his wife."

"Couldn't stomach the thought of being there. Cried off at the last minute. After that found I was bored with no place to go. Thought of the homeless. Jason agreed to accompany me this evening."

Jasper searched through the women. They were all older women. The two he looked at the closest were early thirties at best. What he was looking for was a younger woman, early twenties or younger, who had fallen on hard times. Someone he could introduce as a debutante. He didn't see anyone who might qualify.

"Neither could Donal. Told me he didn't wish to support that kind of debauchery. Though it isn't corruption when betrothals such as this one still occur too often. Families make arrangements to gain power along with wealth. They use their daughters as bargaining chips." She searched through the small wagon she brought with her. "If you wish to help, hand out something to all the ladies. Talk to them if you wish. Whatever you do, don't judge. That's not our place. They are all here because where they were before was even more intolerable."

"It's cold tonight. These people are going to need fires, blankets as well as warm coats." He turned to Jason who put his hands up in supplication as if he understood what he was going to ask.

Jason's grin told him he understood what was needed. "You want me to bring wood? Build fires for these poor women to stay warm? Rummage through the attic for necessities. What else? Hmm…?"

"You sound as if you don't wish to go. I'll go then. You stay here. Hand out more food. I'll bring more blankets, too. Lord knows, we've got extras. There are trunks in the attics that are filled with clothing we no longer use." Jasper looked to the night sky. Small flakes of snow were falling. If not for the freezing conditions coupled with the state of the women he watched, the sight would have been beautiful. A sight he would enjoy sharing with a special woman if he had one.

"Warm coats?" Jason asked as if he'd given in to the notion this was how he would spend his evening. "I'll go. You seem to want to stay. Look over the women with your special project in mind." Jason was at the carriage giving directions to the driver. "We both understand there is a second reason for your concern."

Wishing Jason's words weren't true, Jasper walked along the path. The women were huddled against nearby buildings to ward off the cold winds blowing in from the river. If the weather cleared, they would freeze.

Perhaps the blanket of snow would be a godsend. If the clouds stayed, more snow would fall. In either scenario the results would not be good. Without the needed help, some might die tonight.

Grabbing a basket of bread from the cart Daryl brought, he walked, handing out food, giving comfort where he could. The night grew colder. Snow fell harder. The wail of a baby caught his attention. A woman was attempting to breastfeed the infant while trying to be modest. The baby struggled with the nipple. Jasper felt certain the woman had little breast milk. He handed her a large slice of bread.

"Thank you…" she murmured. She struggled to eat while she fed her child. "Thank you so much."

"How old is the *bairn*?" Jasper asked, wondering if this might be a candidate for his wager with his brother. This lady was too old. Too jaded. With the *wee* babe, she wasn't innocent. He reminded himself he needed a debutante. "What brought you here?"

"He is two months," she told him, her head down. "You should *nae* be lookin' at me that way. 'Tis not right."

No, what wasn't right was that this woman was alone on the streets with no one to look after her. Though he knew the duke and duchess searched for employment for those in need. "The *bairn's* father? Where is he?" Jasper blanched the moment the last question left his lips. This information was not his business.

The lady looked at him, tears sliding down her gaunt cheeks. "Doesn't have one. He does but I don't know who or where he is." Her voice was bitter as she spat out the words. "Was raped by three aristocrats who thought I was fair game. This is what came of it. The consequences none of those bastards cared about. They wanted a *wee* bit of fun at my expense. That was all. I was their plaything that night. All three of them took me throughout the evening. By the time they finished with me, I couldn't move. The three of them never looked back. Until then, I was innocent of men. When it was obvious I was increasing, my father tossed me out of the family home."

Raped. Jasper wasn't surprised. It was common practice among the young privileged men who sported titles. Women who were found alone on the streets were fair game. They thought they could take what they wanted. Something like Lord Abernathy bartering for a wife. Jasper had to admit that wasn't a very good comparison. Though both ended up forcing the woman to the man's needs.

Jasper's attention went back to the woman who was breastfeeding the infant. If he chose this woman, she would be difficult to teach. Her Scottish brogue was pronounced. Some of the words she spoke were Gaelic. Her face was fair but she was too old for his needs. Hadn't planned on a woman who already had a baby. Could never be presented as a debutante. Though this lady would prove a test to his abilities. There were other places he could introduce the woman.

He reached down to touch her shoulder. "Take care ma'am. If I can, I'll bring a blanket back for you along with the *bairn*."

Jasper wandered away from her. Stopped to talk to other women. Each had a story to relate, always a sad story. Jason arrived an hour later with the blankets along with a great deal of wood. He brought two wagons with him. Two of their servants driving the carts. Three large bonfires were the result. They stacked extra wood next to each blaze. Jasper made certain he gave the young woman with the baby a blanket. He brought her more bread along with a muffin.

A commotion near the first bonfire caught his attention. He stared, mouth agape. A woman was twirling around in what appeared to be a yellow ball gown. She was singing, cackled with delight as she threw her arms in the air. Her hair tumbled around her shoulders picking up the light of the fire. Dancing, moving through the crowd. She was crying out words. Bending low to talk to various people.

"Lookee what I got here!" She held the gown up showing bare legs, pleased with herself along with the dress. It be a real gown. A princess," she cackled anew. "I will be a fairy princess tonight." She pulled a heavy wool cape around her shoulders. "Got this for doin' nothing but sittin' by the fire, mindin' my own business. *Dinna* have to lift a finger. Me, I'm blessed tonight. Merry Christmas to me."

A few long strides brought him to the woman. Curiosity tugged at him. He eyed her critically, recognizing the fact this gown was made of silk. The cape she wore was also of fine quality. The slippers were a little small for the woman but they matched the gown.

"Where did you get that?" His voice was far too harsh. Wouldn't do to scare the lady. She backed off, moving away from him, a scowl showing between her eyes. He didn't wish to frighten her. Lifting his shoulders, he spoke. "Just interested." He searched the area for some clue. There was none. "You say you didn't do anything? This dress was given to you?"

The woman pointed a bony finger at him. Shaking it, she snapped out. "Bargained my old dress along with my shoes for this. She was eager to gift it to me. Said she *dinna* be wantin' the thing no more. Gave her my old rag. With pleasure I did. The *wee lassie* even thanked me. She gave me this for the old coarse gown. The boots I be tradin' worn…holes on the souls."

"I'm not questioning you about the validity of the exchange. Where is she? This woman?" Jason stepped up to Jasper's side. "Need to figure out what is happening here. Makes no sense a'tall. No sense a'tall," he murmured as he too searched the surrounding area.

"You say the lady exchanged gowns with you?" Jasper asked, still seeking out the possible woman who might be so desperate to not only rid herself of an expensive gown but also a solid cape in this weather. She would be freezing. "Where is she? Can you tell me that? Could you take me to her? Is she still here?" He understood he asked too many questions. A desperate need he didn't understand assailed him, struck deep into his heart.

"How would I be knowin'? Just here she was. Then she *wasnae*. *Dinna* be goin' to keep track of someone else." The woman sat down by the fire, holding her hands out to keep them warm. She pointed this time in the direction of a woman. "There she be. Over yonder."

Jasper followed the direction of the pointing finger. When he caught the lady's attention, she turned, ducking her head. She was going to run. He knew it. Dashed into the crowd. The woman dodged this way then that. She was near the carriage when he caught up to her, grabbing her arm then turning her. She started to fall. He grasped her arms. Her hands rested on his chest.

With large frightened eyes, she stared into his. Her eyes were the color of the greenest grass in the highlands. The shape of her face was almost a perfect oval. Her brows arched delicately. She pressed the soft rose color of her lips together as if trying to keep from crying out. Her nose turned up a bit on the end. The column of her neck was long white as alabaster. She was not tall nor short. Just right.

She is lovely. Mud, scratches along with the horrid dress didn't deter from her beauty. Struck by the immediate need to protect, he searched for answers.

"Who are you?"

Tugging on her arm, she tried to get away. He wasn't about to loosen his hold. If he had his way, she wasn't going anywhere. "Let me go!" Her foot came down hard on his instep. He yelped. Tried to stay focused. Hung on to her.

He wavered. His hold on her arm loosened. She managed to get away. He caught her by her hair. Tugged her back to him. Reeling from the pain she inflicted, his voice was a low growl. "I'm not going to hurt you. Even though you've hurt me."

He let go of her hair but now that he understood what this lovely little lady was capable of, he held her tighter. Protected more vulnerable parts.

"No!" She turned. Her movement was quick, surprising him. She tucked her head against his chest, burying her face beneath the lapels of his coat. "Get me out of here!" He felt the heat of her breath against him. "Please."

Stunned by the unexpected change of behavior, Jasper looked over the top of her head. He didn't see anything or anyone who should terrify her to this extreme. Still… He was more than willing to transport her away from this place. His home would be their destination. It seemed Jason anticipated his needs. The carriage was in front of them, the door stood open. Jasper helped her inside.

Once all were settled, Jasper tapped on the coach's roof. The vehicle picked up speed as they entered onto the streets. He settled back, resting his hands on his knees studying the woman. Her hair tumbled around her slender shoulders. Her eyes were wide pools of fear. She glanced out the window then immediately dropped to the floor.

Jasper turned to look. Saw nothing and no one. "Sit up," aware of the strangeness, he gritted the words. Wishing she would confide her fears.

On her hands and knees, she was shaking her head. Shivering from the cold air of the night. "No!" With fierceness surprising him, she whispered the single word. He watched her sweep air into her lungs. "I *cannae*. Not when there be a chance of him…" It seemed she caught herself in the outpouring of her truth.

Jasper was surprised to hear her talk. Until this moment, she'd been ever so quiet. He leaned back watchfully. The time would come when she would trust. Now, was not that time, obviously, she feared him. Though...not as much as the man it seemed she ran from. "Very well, suit yourself. The enfolding scenario is up to you to orchestrate." He shrugged out of his warm coat. Tucked the fabric around her. "Don't wish for you to freeze. When you decide to explain yourself, I will be a willing listener. Won't ever judge."

From her spot on the floor, she twisted her head to stare at him. "Where...where be we goin'?"

The language was so garbled with her Scottish burr then interspersed with Gaelic, Jasper could barely understand. He had to force his attention on each word. It had been so long since he spoke the old language.

"Seems you found your candidate," Jason said with a wry grin coupled with a soft chuckle. "So far, what we've seen of her, she is perfect for your experiment. I'm willing to gamble more on her than on your expertise with the language."

Jasper ignored his brother. "We're blocks away from the small camp of women. You're safe. You can sit up now. Don't expect you to remain on the floor hiding. My brother and I won't hurt you. Tell us what has you so distrustful of us."

Her wary eyes centered on his. "*Dinna* have much choice. Not afraid of the likes of you. At least not yet," she muttered while she pushed tangled hair from her face then smoothed the fabric of the ragged gown she wore.

"What's your name?"

With his questions, she panicked anew. Swept her small pink tongue across her mouth. The action mesmerized Jasper. His heart leapt. Pounded. For a few heart-stopping moments, she stared at her hands, the window again. Jasper thought if given the chance, she would leap from the carriage. He watched her breasts heave, move in then out with the air she inhaled. Again, her petite frame, the way she moved, enthralled every male part of him.

"Tessa...Tessa Stirling," she told him, her voice wavering, her eyes clouding over. "My name..."

The deep rise of crimson to her cheeks coupled with her eyes told Jasper she lied. The lady lied about her name. With a bit of investigation, he didn't think it would be difficult to find out the truth. This lass was not as she pretended. That much was obvious to anyone looking at her. He didn't have to know her to realize lies did not come easily to this woman.

Who was she? Besides the original owner of the yellow ball gown.

"Good, that's one important item out of the way. A name is very important." Jasper bent over, touched her beneath the chin to lift her face high enough he could continue to see into her eyes. "What brought you to the homeless camp, Tessa Stirling?" *In a silk gown no less.*

Her body stiffened. She grew rigid in an instant. Jasper realized in that moment if she told him anything her statement would also be a lie. He leaned back, his fingers steepled on his belly. "You find yourself on hard times? That's all I need to know. Rest assured you will be safe with me. No more questions tonight. Whatever happened to you, I'll not give your secrets away. When you are ready to tell all, you'll find me a friend, never an enemy."

Jasper almost guffawed at the look of relief that swept across her face. As if in slow motion, she sat on the seat across from him along with his brother. She rearranged her tattered skirt. Even beneath his coat, he saw the dress was about to fall from her. He thought an introduction would be nice.

Nodding he began, "Since you've given me your name, I'm Jasper Kenworthy. This is my brother, Jason. We're twins."

Her sweet yet devilish smile would have sent him to his knees if he'd been standing. His breath caught in the back of his throat. That smile could move mountains. He was far from being that strong or stalwart.

With a *wee* bit of sarcasm she spoke, "I would have never guessed. You are so the same. Though…" She gave a tiny snort. "The two of you are quite different. Have you bothered to look in a mirror?"

"How?" they spoke in unison, causing her to laugh again.

"No one has been able to tell us apart except our mother. Father always guessed." Jasper said, disbelieving her.

"To start your eyes are *verra* different. Jasper, your eyes are brown, rimmed in gold and your…twin…his eyes are so dark a brown they appear black when he questions me. I would…" she cleared her throat. "I *wouldnae* be a lookin' too well if…you be havin' two perfect dimples while Jason has one near to bein' perfect the other…be not."

Jasper didn't miss the change in diction. For a few sentences the Scottish burr disappeared entirely. He was almost disappointed thinking he would not be teaching her anything. The wager would be off. When he looked to Jason, his brother didn't appear to have noticed. Perhaps the change was a fluke. Though he wished to believe that to be the truth, he knew different. He could still continue as he planned. It was a good ruse to get to know this lady better.

Tessa did though. She flushed again. The color painting her cheeks was a beautiful shade of rosy red topped with a lighter shade down her neck. She concentrated on the window…the scenery beyond. Tilted her head upward as if to look at the nonexistent stars.

"Who are you running from?"

She blanched.

~ * ~

"What!" Lord Abernathy stormed, then whirled to confront the man he'd trusted to guard his reluctant fiancée. He expected her to bolt. She didn't disappointment. What he hadn't expected was for her to get away. When she did, he planned on the punishment when she was caught. Now, until he found his reluctant bride to be, the discipline would have to wait. Strictness was important to a relationship. A man must show the woman who controlled her.

"The girls…her sisters…blocked our view then our way when we started after her. I tripped over someone's foot. The other guard ran into a matron dumping her food down her front and into her bosom. She shrieked. Started throwing food. People gathered around to see what was happening. The mess could not be cleared in time to stop her. By the time we got past those women, she was out of sight. We both figured she would run to her home which was not so far away. We took off after her, found she was not there. After that we needed to backtrack. The trail went cold."

"Good God, you think she is witless? A fool? If she wanted to get a way, she would never run home where we could catch up to her with ease. Think, man, where would she run to?" Nelson stalked the room, cursing as he tried to think of all the possibilities. "Get Anice!" he bellowed. When both men turned to leave, "No, Angus, you stay. Where do you think she went? You been watching her for the last week. What does she do with her time? Who does she see?" Nelson wondered if there was a man, a lover in her life. If there was, he'd kill the man.

"A *lass* of her breeding, she must have run to a friend's home. Where else? I've not seen her with anyone except her sisters," his bodyguard answered.

"I don't believe that could be true. Check all the country roads leading from here. I'm thinking she might have fled into the city. She can find numerous places to hide in Glasgow. Once I speak with her mother, the two of us will take the main road into the city. On foot, she could not get very far. We'll catch her." Nelson hit a fist into his palm, his anger simmering. "By God, she will pay for this childish act of rebellion!"

The tap at the door brought Nelson back to the present. He caught his breath, schooled his emotions. Didn't wish to give his feelings away. Anice would be no more pleased than he at this sudden turn of events. He hoped she would have some ideas as to where to look. Though Anice knew little about her daughter, she would have an idea or two.

"What is it?" Anice slipped inside the door, smiling for a moment until she saw the heated look on his features. For an instant she froze as if searching his expression for a clue.

"Just as we feared, your daughter fled. It was quite the trick. I had three grown men watching her," he gritted out behind clenched teeth. Despite his efforts to stay calm, his fists clenched. "She ran! Got away from my men with the help of her sisters. You need to discipline your brood. They seem to dictate the events in your family instead of you."

"How?" Anice sounded confused by his words. Didn't seem to listen to what he told her. "She has nowhere to go. I've kept her and her sisters sheltered. Made certain they had no friends. None of my daughters have any person to turn to seeking help." She stepped into the room. So close to him the scent of her perfume filled his nostrils. "The girls have never had close friends. She must have thought to run home...but...that would do her no good."

"Knowing you would call me as soon as you found my runaway fiancée? I don't think so. One of the reasons I chose your daughter was because of her intelligence. I loathe women without brains or common sense. Maggie is worthy of becoming my countess. I want her back! This game she plays is already tiresome. She will pay. After that she will obey." This time, his palm hit the table hard, rocking the glasses of wine he poured recently. Some of the red merlot slipped down the sides of the crystal, pooling on the white linen soaking the cloth in red.

"I've no doubt you will discover her whereabouts. Until the wedding in three weeks, you may keep her with you under guard."

"I'll have to find the girl first."

"You will. Maggie is willful. However," Anice paused, tapping her well-manicured nail to her chin. She sipped in a breath of air. "If you threaten her with one of her sisters, she will comply in an instant. Obey any demand you put forth. They are close, too close since I've allowed them no friends. They've known from a tender age that their marriage would be contracted. Known they have no voice in who I choose for them. As you say this little act of defiance is already tiresome."

"Would need to catch the lady in question first," Nelson muttered beneath his breath, understanding the truth of Anice's words. "If she makes it into the city, we'll have a difficult time tracing her. I'm going to ride there myself." Nelson wasn't certain what he would do when he got his hands on her. He wanted to shake her until her teeth rattled. After that he wanted to lock her in a closet until the day of their wedding. He could do none of those things. What he was grateful for was that Anice told him what he could hold over her head. With threats to her sisters, she would comply with whatever he wished. He would mold her to be whatever he desired at whatever given time.

"Good idea. I'll take the girls home. They won't eat until they tell me Maggie's plans. They are stubborn little things. Though after a day or two without food, they will comply. The three of them have never been without."

A day or two... Nelson wasn't certain he had that long. If he didn't catch up with her soon, she might find help. People who would stand against him in this forced wedding that was planned. He caught his breath. The last lady he'd seen leaving the powder room this evening before he walked inside was the Duchess of Southcliff. The duke and duchess were powerful. He hissed in a long breath of air. The Stewarts never supported his endeavors. Always spoke out against him. If Maggie found help with Lacie Stewart, he might not ever find her. Ever. The duke had the means along with the associates to get Maggie out of the country. The devil, he could send her anywhere. He would never see her again. All his plans would be for naught.

Nelson watched Anice as she swept regally from the room, her skirts swishing around her trim ankles. She was still a beautiful and cunning woman. Through arranged matches for her girls, she meant to capitalize on her daughters, increasing her fortune in the process. She didn't care about their happiness. Only hers.

Cursing his bad luck he headed for the stables, grabbing his coat as he left the house. He leapt upon the black stallion he called Midnight. Shoved his heels into the animal's flanks then took off. Cold wind swept down from the craigs. Snow began to fall, blanketing the road. She would freeze in this weather. If that happened, she would be useless to him. After a few minutes, he eased the stallion into an easy canter. While he set his gaze on the road in front of him, he also watched the sides, stared into the ditches. Listened to the rustling of the leaves. If she walked this way, wouldn't there be footprints in the snow? Not enough snow, but soon. With the cloud coverage, it was too damn dark to see anything.

A lumbering cart loomed in front of him. A possible ride for his runaway fiancée.

Pulling up next to the driver, he peered into the back. The man was carrying grain. There were blankets along with tools beside the sacs. The man looked at him. "Sir?"

"Have you seen a *wee lass*?" Nelson motioned with his hands as to her size. "She was wearing a yellow ball gown and a dark brown cape. Her hair is light brown when the light catches the strands just right her hair appears golden. You might have seen her?"

"Believe I did. Maybe." He lifted his shoulders with a nonchalant shrug. "Maybe not. I heard some rustling of the bushes about a mile back. Thought it was deer grazing. Nothing more. You lost a lady? How can that be? How does a man lose his woman?"

Nelson didn't appreciate the sound of his snicker. "I'll find her. Mind if I look in the back of your wagon?"

Again, he lifted his shoulders, his smile broad. If the man was hiding anything, his demeanor didn't hint at it. "Suit yourself. Won't be findin' nothing but grain and some old tools. Building myself a new shed. Might

32

be a waste of your time. You should be turning that big black stallion of yours around. Go home where it's warm." The man stopped the wagon while Nelson leapt on board.

He moved the blankets. Nothing. Poked at a few of the sacks of grain with his foot. "You're right. A waste of my time. You said you heard something a few miles back? A deer?" Or a lady trying to hide herself?

"About a mile, yes. Hope you find the *lass* sometime before she freezes. There are all kinds of animals out there that could harm her if you get my drift. The worst carries himself on two legs."

Nelson was back on his horse. Tipped his hat. The city wasn't that far. He didn't intend to backtrack. Perhaps if he did miss her, he would now be ahead of her. There was one place he intended to look first. The duke and duchess were reported to help out some of the homeless at one of the parks. If they talked, this would be the place Lacie Stewart would send his wayward fiancée. The duchess' sister fed many of the homeless women who showed up there needing aid.

He wasn't wrong about her destination. Wasn't ahead of her but there she was. When he saw the yellow gown, he headed straight for the woman.

"Maggie!"

Chapter Two

Maggie felt certain she just jumped from the frying pan into the fire. The two men, Jasper and Jason, seemed nice enough. They were men. Most men acted the same. What did she know? It was obvious to her she didn't know a hell of a lot. What she did understand was that men were dangerous creatures. Ones, she now understood all too well, that she needed to be wary of. Here she was sitting in a carriage with two of the male species to avoid a third man. What the devil had she been thinking?

In the carriage she shivered, pulling Jasper's coat tight around her shoulders. Shoulders that were shaking. When he told her they were twins, she lost the Scottish burr for a blink. Caught herself but not before Jasper noticed her mistake. She didn't know if he was trying to be cute or he thought she hadn't heard.

Jasper Kenworthy was taking her to his townhouse. A residence he shared with his twin. Warming their beds was not an option she would consider. If the men thought she was an easy mark, they were mistaken. As for them being twins, she had no trouble telling them apart. Jason seemed to laugh with ease. Jasper brooded during the short carriage ride. Their eyes were slightly different shades of brown. Jasper's brown eyes were rimmed in gold.

Oh, the devil Lord Abernathy found her at the park. He didn't find her. Nonetheless, he guessed where she would head. Maggie almost fainted when she saw him accost the lady to whom she traded her ballgown. He'd been rough with the poor woman, shaking as well as yelling at her. His men must have reported back to him as soon as she vanished in the darkness. She'd known if he discovered the deceit he would be in a foul mood. Would take his anger out on anyone he found in his path. The poor lady did nothing wrong. Guilt swept through her. She'd not wished for anyone to be hurt.

The moment she saw Lord Abernathy, she fell against Jasper hiding her face against the width of his chest and behind his coat. He put his arms around her as if he knew she needed protection. His scent was pleasing. Spicy. Male. For a short flash of time, she felt protected. After that her situation crashed against her. Her heart broke rhythm then thundered. For a few seconds she couldn't grasp air. Heat flared. Maggie had never been that close to a man. While she danced with men, she'd never set her head so close to that man she could hear the steady rhythm of his heart. Feel each breath of air he stole. Never felt the warmth generated by a man's body. She didn't know what to think.

"Are you warmer now, lass?" Jasper asked, his voice soft, inquiring, jerking her from her thoughts. Brought her back with a jolt from fantasy to reality. "I would give you a blanket but we handed them all out at the park. Tell me what you would like?"

His tender look of concern rattled her nerves. Her experience with Lord Abernathy told her he wanted something. Over the last two years, Maggie learned all men wanted something from her. Oh, my what did she want? A good dose of courage along with luck. She needed daring to rail against the injustices heaped upon her. Luck to elude the man who wished to make her his pawn. Right now, the intelligence to understand what was happening to her while she stayed one step in front of him.

"Be doin' fine. *Dinna* need to *fash yerself* over the likes of me. I'll be bouncin' right back onto my feet."

This man needed to believe she was nothing more than a woman down on her luck. Must think she was from the streets of Glasgow. The fact was she was indeed down on her luck. That wasn't a lie. Understood she needed to keep her lies at a minimum. If she didn't, she wouldn't remember what she told him or didn't tell him.

"Tessa…?"

She wondered what her sisters were doing now. Making up lies to Anice she imagined. What punishment would her mother dole out to her sisters for their part in this scenario. She hoped it would not be anything more than withholding food for a few days. That was her mother's usual punishment.

"Tessa…Tessa!"

"What?" Maggie jerked to attention staring at the man. She'd been daydreaming about her sisters. "W-what is it? You sound angry. I no be doin' anythin' wrong? Just be thinkin'.'" She was confused. For a few seconds she wasn't certain what she was doing.

"I had to call your name so many times I wondered if you lied to me about it. Did you tell me the wrong name?" Jasper asked as the darkness of his gaze found its mark on her. He looked with pointed interest. Studied her as if he saw into her soul.

Flinching, she cringed back against the seat. *Lied?* True, she did tell an untruth. Wasn't going to explain anything to him even though he seemed nice. She looked out the window. Snow still fell. The night was still incredibly dark. Without street lights the night would be black. He'd gone out of his way to protect her when she was in need. The devil, if Lord Abernathy caught her tonight… This man deserved the truth. As much as she could say without fear of reprisal. That was the problem. If he knew who she was along with what happened he might take her right back to Lord Abernathy. If that happened, she would never get away from the marquis. He would guard her night and day. If rumors she heard about Nelson were true, he'd punish her. She shuddered at the thought.

Maggie didn't want to think about the consequences the truth might rain down upon her. What Lord Abernathy would do to her if he caught her. She did elude his men with the help of her sisters along with this man. She didn't know what to do accept move forward the best she could, needing to react to each moment as it came. There were no more alternatives for her.

Catching her bottom lip beneath her teeth before she replied, Maggie looked into his eyes. Said a silent prayer that this time Jasper would believe her. "Tessa is my name. Tessa Stirling," she lied again, felt heat rush to her cheeks. She hoped he couldn't see the flush on her face. If he did, he would know what she was doing.

His fingertips were tapping together. Their movement, slow mesmerizing. His fingers were long, bronzed with nails well-manicured. His expression didn't change when he replied. "I don't believe you. I will find out the truth whether or not you help me." The silence in the carriage was punctuated by the steady clomping of the horses' hooves as they clattered along the brick road…by the silence of each snowflake as it fluttered to the ground. The whistle of the wind against the vehicle. Jasper waved his hand in the air. "What I believe or not, matters not at this moment. We are home. I will see to your comfort. Perhaps once you are warmed as well as understand no harm will come to you at my hands, you will find the courage to tell me how I can help. You are in trouble. That much is obvious. Both my brother and I recognize that fact as one of your truths."

When he opened the door, his driver had already set the steps down. Was waiting for further orders by the side of the vehicle. He preceded her then held out his hand to help her negotiate the stairs. Jason followed. The driver left after Jasper spoke to him for a few minutes. Her hand still held by him, he turned it over. Studied for a few seconds. When he traced a few of the lines, her breath caught. He would read much by looking at her hands. Jasper would learn too much about her.

"No calluses," Jasper murmured, his voice soft. With his thumb he touched her wrist. Found the jeweled bracelet she'd worn to the ball. "Why is that? I wonder." He touched each stone. Focused his attention on her eyes. "Emeralds match the color of your eyes. Did you steal this? Is the bracelet yours? Ah, milady, you would tease me with curiosity. I've so many questions. None of which, I'm quite sure you care to answer." He must not have expected a response, though the hardness of his eyes staring at her pricked at her confidence. "I'm a patient man. Got all the time in the world. I wonder…do you have that much time?"

Startled, she gasped at his question. Placing her hand at the crook of his elbow, he started forward. On her fingers, his hands were warm. Unlike her, Jasper did have calluses on his strong hands. Her body heated with the touch. She felt his presence in her soul. Felt as if she'd known him forever. Maggie didn't understand why she wished she could please him by answering all his questions. If she could, she would pour out her problems…all the horrendous things her mother did to her and would continue to do.

The grounds in front of the townhouse were groomed with immaculate care even for winter. Everything she saw spoke of money. These two men were wealthy. If they chose, Maggie felt certain the Kenworthys could keep her from Lord Abernathy. She needed to do all in her power to make certain that would happen. Bushes as well as trees were trimmed. On either side of the walk, grass had been shorn, cut to the perfect length. A light lit the porch. A large gold-plated knocker was on the door. As they approached, the huge double doors were opened. A very short, very round man stood, framed in the door. He bowed, acknowledging them.

"Lord Kenworthy, Mr. Kenworthy." The man at the door smiled then nodded his head in welcome. "As your brother ordered earlier when he was collecting items tonight, I've a board with various meats and cheeses, a few other delightful tastes waiting for your dining pleasure. The food sits in the drawing room for your enjoyment. Also, the brandy is set out for your convenience." He stopped to look at her. "Should I fetch sherry for the lady? Wasn't expecting the two of you to bring company."

Jasper's gaze bore into her. Cut through all her defenses. Her hand still held by his, he smiled, an all-knowing grin. One that made her heart stutter. "Yes, I believe the lady would appreciate a sherry. She's been cold…" He paused, tapped his long slender finger against his chin. His grin grew broader. The dimple clear as he continued to peruse her. Turned her hand over as if he needed to confirm his earlier suspicions. "No, I believe a glass of mulled wine would do better for the lady. Will heat her chilled bones." Again, he looked at her. Peered into her soul. Now that she could see his eyes better, Maggie saw the amusement in the simmering gold surrounding the deep brown.

Maggie caught her breath at the heat drowning her. This wasn't the same fire that swept through her when she lied. This was different. She felt his caress in so many different parts of her. Shifting her feet, she thought of her precarious situation. Mulled wine sounded good. Maggie didn't know if she should know what that was or not. In truth what she wanted more than wine or food was a hot bath coupled with the knowledge Lord Abernathy wasn't going to find her residing in the Kenworthy household. He released her hand. Slipping out of the coat Jasper lent her for the ride, she handed it to the butler.

Jasper spoke up, amusement still resonated in his voice. "This is Keir. My…our butler. Keir, the lady tells us she is known as Tessa Stirling. We brought her here for…" He stopped then cleared his throat. "When I first saw her, it appeared she needed help. Won't tell us what that help entails. Could do better by her if I knew what I'm up against." His gaze focused with direct frankness on her eyes. "Tessa refuses to say anything about her plight. A predicament that must be dangerous since she chose to attend with us, two gentlemen, instead of remaining in the park."

Bristling at his words, she tilted her chin. Thought better of the act. Lowered her lashes so they swept against her cheeks. She didn't wish for

Jasper to get any more insights into her truths. He guessed far too much.

Keir smiled then nodded. "Lady Tessa. If you need anything, let me know. Night or day, ring the bell. Someone will be along to give assistance."

She acknowledged him with a nod of her head. In her state of dress, the man must understand she was no lady. To this lord of the realm, she was a commoner. He never spouted a title. Didn't mean he didn't have one. Keir did call him Lord Kenworthy. His title was something Jasper neglected to tell her. Perhaps he didn't take that much stock in a title. Maybe he wasn't like Lord Abernathy, who used his heading to impress people. To set himself above others with a lower rank.

"I'm going out," Jason said as he bowed to acknowledge her presence. "Appreciate the evening with my brother. Don't tell him many more lies. Jasper tends to lose patience that way. Even though he will tell everyone he possesses that trait in abundance. Whenever you can, stick to the truth. I'll see you tomorrow sometime." Turning to his brother. "Don't pursue…" He cleared his throat. "You understand what I'm trying to say."

"Yes and no. You have the subtlety of an alley cat. Enjoy your evening with your widow. We will both be here on the morrow in expectation of your stellar words of wisdom." Jasper sent his gaze once more raking over her. "Unless she doesn't wish to be here. If she asks, I'll take her anywhere she'd like to go."

She'd like to go to Lacie Stewart's residence. If not that, she'd like to visit the residence on the card Lady Stewart gave her, the lady at the bakery. She felt the paper next to her right breast. It was still there. That fact gave her confidence a boost.

Hands outstretched, searching for warmth, Maggie walked to the fire. The length of her body shivered even though the room was warm. She thought the reprieve from the questions would end now. Keir brought in two cups of mulled wine, handing her one. She drank. Thought to down the entire cup. The warmth invaded the chill surrounding her body along with her heart. Heat racing through her inside as well as outside felt so good. All this time, she continued to take solace in watching the flames dance in the grate.

Jasper was sitting in a large chair that faced the fire. His steady gaze still rested on her and seemed to absorb all that she was, everything she needed. Even though Maggie wasn't facing him, she felt the heat from his gaze on the back of her neck. "You are feeling better? I take it the warm wine is easing some of the chill about you?" he asked his voice soft, seductive in its timber. "When did you eat last? It would do you good to put something in your belly. Hmm…don't you think?"

The answer should be a few hours ago at the ball. Though that wasn't true. At the festive Christmas Eve gala her stomach wouldn't allow for food. It churned, rolled. Heaved whenever she caught the scent of food. Knowing what was intended for her was not conducive to eating. The few minutes she was at the park exchanging her gown with the lady had not been enough time to partake of the bread that was dispersed. Not that she could have eaten then either.

"This morning." Without hesitating she was able to answer. Another lie would never do. This morning she devoured a pastry with hot chocolate. *Stick with the truth whenever you can. One can never remember a lie. That's how you'll get caught.*

"You received no bread at the park? No blanket. You weren't even by a fire when the lady in yellow pointed you out to me. Why?" He pressed her for more answers. "Why did you refuse comforts?"

She wouldn't answer that question either. The why of it wasn't something he needed to learn. This man was a stranger to her. "No…" She was too busy hiding from whoever might be after her to accept food. Maggie found herself shaking her head.

Again, the man studied her. His hands forming a steeple beneath his chin, tapping, watching. Waiting for her to make a blunder. He wanted her to do his bidding. He anticipated a mistake. "There is food here. Help yourself. You can take a plate upstairs to your room if you like. Does it embarrass you to eat in front of me? Are your manners lacking? I would teach you whatever you might wish to learn. Diction. Manners. Reading along with writing. What can you do, Tessa? More than you wish for me to know?"

Awkward couldn't begin to describe what she felt. Lord Kenworthy would teach me manners? Manners had been drilled into her by her mother for the last twenty-one years. Maggie didn't believe there was anything this Lord could teach her that she didn't know. Her stomach knotted when she reached for a piece of cheese as well as bread thinking she would be able to keep it down. Instead of eating she held onto the morsel then sipped more of the wine. She drained the cup. He poured more. Closing her eyes, she let the heat from the liquid warm her again. Nibbling, she ate. The food seemed to settle the way it was supposed to. She swayed on her feet. Exhaustion seemed to be taking over her body. The potent wine dashed straight to her brain.

"Thank you," she nodded to him, looking at the carafe of wine with longing. She thought it might be easier to sleep with one more cup. "I be appreciatin' every *wee* thing you be wishin' to give. My likin' doesn't extend to findin' me in your bed. I *dinna* be that kind of *lass*."

He took a long drink of his wine. His grin showed even white teeth. She wondered what it would be like to kiss him. "You can thank me by telling me the truth. If I wished you in my bed, I'd seduce you now. You wouldn't be able to tell me no. Don't believe in wasting time with formalities."

The wine she drank sputtered from her mouth. Her eyes widened as she realized what he intimated. "Oh!" With the back of her hand, she touched the droplets. Jasper picked up a cloth napkin then touched the drops of wine on her lips and chin. She jerked with each tender contact. Her body heated again. Flames shot through her. "I do be thinkin' you be an arrogant knave. I would not be in your bed. You cannae seduce me to your evil ways."

His silent gaze unnerved her further. The challenging grin worked to her disadvantage. He waited as if he didn't have anything better to do. Perhaps he didn't. "Even your speech is a lie. Who are you? I cannot begin to help you from your plight if you don't give me a few necessary facts to go on. One must always mount a proper defense if one is to succeed at the game. As to seducing…we shall see. Before anything of that sort comes about, you do need a bath."

She bristled. Even though all he said was the truth, except the part about seduction. She wasn't about to fall into his bed because he crooked his little finger. Pompous man. Her mother did teach her to keep her virtue until the wedding night. She intended to do that. Unless the wedding was to Lord Abernathy. Perhaps the man wouldn't wish to marry a used bride. One who was less than whole. "What do you want to know? I've told you…"

"Your name!" Jasper sounded angry while he gritted out the words. The gold rimming his eyes simmered with heated intensity. There was fire in his words when he spoke. "The real name your mother and father gave you the day you were born. The name that would head your certificate of birth unless you were born in a hovel to a pauper. You weren't. I don't believe that is the type of life you have lived."

"I…" Maggie lifted her head, her manner regal, defying all she sought to deliver of her personality to this man. Her tongue stuck to the roof of her mouth. She drank more of the wine. Rubbed her temples to ease the insistent throbbing. He filled the cup. "I don't know what you mean?" Her heart stuttered as she watched his gaze roam over her, absorbing her into his brain.

"Even filthy and wearing an ill-fitting dress you are a fetching little piece of Scottish loveliness. What is your name, love? Sterling is common to the lowlands. Not here. Not in Glasgow. Not in the highlands. You must have a good highland name such as McKenzie or MacLauchlan or MacRae."

She gasped. Her eyes felt like saucers while he tossed out her surname as if he knew who she was and was playing a game he knew he would win. She turned, hiding her startled expression from him. Lowering her lashes. Maggie told herself the name was just a lucky guess. It was nothing to worry about. Jasper didn't know her name. He couldn't. If he did, he wouldn't be prodding her for answers.

"Keir said you needed me." A sweet looking older lady stood in the room. Seemed to have appeared from nowhere.

"Ah, yes, Mrs. Marshall. The *lass* is in need of a bath. See that one is heated for her. While she is a guest, give her anything she asks for. Fia, this is Tessa Sterling. Tessa, Mrs. Marshall or Fia if you'd rather call her by her first name. This sweet lady is my head housekeeper. Since we've no need of a lady's maid, she will serve as yours. Unless you say no."

"She will be fine."

Jasper grinned at her mistake. Maggie understood she would be unable to keep up this pretense for long. Might it be better for her to speak the truth to him then beg his mercy as well as his understanding. She didn't dare. One mistake after another. The man guessed the truth. She'd been in his company for a few hours. No more.

"Of course, she will do better than anyone who has served you before. Since you've had no one."

Fia's gaze darted from her to Jasper then back to her. The maid had a look of confusion about her. After a few looks, she lifted her shoulders. "I'll order the bath. Which room would you like her in?

"Oh, there are quite a few rooms to choose from. I would like her close to me. Put her in the room across the hall from mine. It is a splendid room with afternoon light. If she likes to sleep in, she won't be bothered by bright morning sunlight." As if he expected a quip or a denial of some sort he stared at her again.

If he made her nervous, that was his intent. She understood he would do all in his power to tear down the defensive shield she surrounded herself with. "What do you want from me?" Her voice was controlled when she asked. "I would rather not be compromised. It's bad enough I'm going to…"

She said too much, her words giving her away once more. A woman off the streets would not worry about finding herself seduced by a lord of the realm.

Behind her his hoot of laughter told her more than she wished to know. She felt his large hands on her shoulders. His breath feathered against the back of her neck. Maggie sucked in air as a ripple of heat swept through her. She found herself stiffening, gulping for air. He smoothed the ragged fabric of her gown on her shoulders while she sensed him watching her breasts as they moved with each desperate breath of air she tried to drag into her lungs.

His finger ran along her neck. Touched upon the pulse point at the base where her heart throbbed with a thunderous roar. "What do I want?" he mused, his voice soft, tender. His hand beneath her chin, he ran his thumb across her bottom lip.

"Y-yes…what do you want with me?" Against the power radiating from his broad shoulders, she trembled. "You can't have me. You can't know." Fighting the onslaught of his gentle hands, Maggie found herself desperate for air. Nerves already stretched, snapped.

"I will know." His lips caressed the back of her neck. The strong fingers, she watched earlier, traced a seductive path across her collarbone. She felt the calluses on his hands. "Tessa, I will learn everything about you. Already, I've employed a detective. He will bring me what he's learned tomorrow morning even though it is Christmas day. Wouldn't it be better to save me the trouble along with the time? The wasted moments could be put to better use."

"No!" Maggie turned, startled by his words. "Why?"

She drank in the sight of his dark brown eyes glimmering with golden shards. This time they didn't simmer from anger but from something else. She didn't understand the fire in his eyes. Confusion gripped her.

"Because… You intrigue me, Tessa Sterling. Fascinate my mind. Challenge when you should submit. After I teach you everything I want you to know, I wish to introduce you by your right and proper name." His hands gripped her shoulders. Squeezed. His smile held a wealth of amusement. "We know though…don't we, Tessa…there is nothing I need teach you that you haven't already learned at the hands of another tutor. Who was that tutor? A lover? A parent? Guardian? Who? Trust me, I will find out."

"I don't know what you mean." Her words wobbled from her parched lips.

"Liar." His warm breath whispered across the back of her neck. "Your scent is intriguing. Woman. Snow. Lemon. You smell like a lemon grove in the middle of a snow storm."

Stiffening, Maggie understood she was drowning. Needed to change the subject he dwelled upon. "I would take my bath now." She wanted nothing more than to escape his mesmerizing hold on her. "If you don't mind."

She lowered her lashes, trying to avoid the heat of his gaze. Again, he touched her chin, challenging her to look at him. "In the morning I'll be here waiting for you. Sleep as long as you like. I've left one of my nightshirts for you to wear. Along with a robe." He gave her an indulgent smile. "This is a bachelor abode. I've no feminine clothing for you. Tonight, while you sleep, Fia will have your gown washed. We will need to see about procuring you a few things. Believe I'll send for the modiste. What do you think, Tessa? Would you enjoy having some new gowns?"

"I don't want anything from you." Maggie didn't want him to send for the modiste. One that might recognize her. Give her away.

"Another lie. You wished for a safe place to sleep. Am I wrong? You wished to escape someone at the park. Again, I ask, am I wrong? Now, you do wish to stay here with me, because it's safer than anywhere else you have to go. Is all that I'm believing about you incorrect?" He sighed heavily, rubbing the back of his neck as if he'd had enough. "Go on. Take your bath.

Sleep. Tomorrow is another day. We'll begin anew. Perhaps with the truth. You've nothing to fear from me or my brother."

Jasper turned away from her. His hands behind his back, he gazed at the flames in the fireplace. Maggie almost stepped forward to touch him. She reached out a hand before drawing it to her side. For his help, he did deserve more than what she could give him. It wasn't as if she didn't want to trust him with her secret.

She couldn't. The consequences were too dire if he betrayed her. She would never go back. Do all in her power to stop that from occurring.

The maid stood beside her. "Lady Tessa, I'll take you to your room now. The master ordered the hot water along with more mulled wine for you. There is also a robe for you to wear. Keir lit the fire. You'll be comfortable."

"Thank you." Twinges of guilt washed through her.

The man didn't deserve what she doled out. How could she ever trust? Must think of her well-being first.

Fia led the way up the staircase then down a long hallway. She opened a door to a room then nodded. "The master's room is across the hall. Jason's room is in the other wing. If you need anything, pull the bell cord. Keir and I are not his only employees. Tonight, he gave a few people some time off since he wasn't going to be home as well as the fact this evening is Christmas Eve. No one knew he'd bring a pretty *wee lassie* home with him. It's quite unusual."

"Is it?" Maggie looked over the room.

She understood she shouldn't be here. Her reputation would be ruined. If it appeared she was ruined…Lord Abernathy might not want her. Trying not to think about her nemesis, she looked around the room. The curtains were a deep burgundy, the carpet a lighter shade. The bed was large. She thought she might get lost beneath the covers. The tub sat near the fire, water steaming, beckoning to her. After all she'd been through tonight, she did feel dirty. A large bath sheet hung near the fire to warm. Considering the evening she spent, this was heaven.

"Yes, this is different. The marquis has never brought a woman here before. For that matter, neither has his brother. Oh!" Fia brought her hand to her mouth. "It's not my place to be speakin' about them in this manner.

Please don't say anything. They are good employers. Wouldn't want to lose my job."

Her hands folded beneath her chin, a smile crinkling the corners of her mouth. "I won't say anything. Not my secret to tell. I'm certain you are not given to gossip."

"Thank you…now, there," she pointed, "on the bed is the nightshirt along with the robe. You'll be swimming in the garments. 'Twas all he had to give you."

"Thank you again. It's more than I expected. I'm grateful Jasper thought of it."

Maggie watched the sweet woman disappear all the while wondering what she got herself into now. Tonight, she would need to do some serious thinking about her future. She didn't know if she could stay here. Didn't understand how she felt when he touched her. The feelings were nothing like what she felt when the viscount touched her.

Where else will I go?

You've nowhere. You set your course with this man when you hid your face in his chest. Buried your nose against his warmth. What can you expect?

He's going to discover all my secrets. Not that there are that many. Lord Abernathy won't stop searching for me. Jasper said he has a man probing out facts. Without clues as to who I am, he won't discover anything.

If you married this man, you'd be beyond Lord Abernathy's reach. Beyond your mother's reach.

Marry! The devil take you that's a bit drastic even under these circumstances. Don't you think? I don't know the man. Don't know what he thinks or believes. Ken nothing about his character.

This man, Jasper Kenworthy was willing to take the time to help out people on Christmas Eve rather than indulge himself. Doesn't that speak to his character?

Maggie sank into the steaming water. She settled her head on the back, mulling over her thoughts. Tonight is Christmas Eve. Tomorrow would be Christmas day. She wasn't with her sisters. For the first time since she could remember she wasn't with them. Loneliness swamped her so much she thought she might drown. Mother will punish her siblings. She will refuse them food until they speak to her. The thing was, they had nothing they could tell. Because of that very reason, she kept mute about what she planned. Even if she told them she was going to hide in the city, they would never be able to tell Anice she was at Lord Kenworthy's residence. They would have never heard his name. She'd had no idea he would rescue her from Abernathy's grip. If he'd not been there, Abernathy might have caught her.

Looking at the table where Fia set the food along with the wine, guilt filled her. She would eat. Her sisters would not. They would pay for her problem. Tomorrow, on Christmas morning, her sisters would go hungry. There would be no pastries along with hot chocolate as they opened gifts. Maggie was glad she put her gift to each of her sisters beneath the tree. She wouldn't get to see them open her presents to them. Hers would remain under the tree, waiting for her. She wasn't coming home.

She didn't want to think any longer. Picking up the soap, she found it to be rose scented. One of her favorites. Unlike each of her sisters, she didn't have one favorite scent. She loved lavender. It had a soothing effect on her nerves. Citrus, orange and lemon were ones she enjoyed on a hot summer day. This time of year, vanilla always reminded her of the cookies and cakes their cook made for them. Before the ball though, she bathed in lemon scented water. Used her lemon soap to wash. The viscount didn't like the way the lemon smelled. Told her as much. She'd thought his saying so was rude. Nonetheless, the knowledge gave her a weapon she could use against the man.

Sinking into the water, she soaked her hair. Washed the long strands then rinsed. She finished, rising from the bathwater then reached for the warmed towel. Maggie wrapped it around her. Picked up a slice of cheese coupling the delicious hunk with a piece of ham. Next to the carafe of mulled wine she found a comb. Poured more wine. She was feeling drowsy as well as a *wee* bit tipsy.

Either Jasper thought of all of her needs or Fia did. Sitting on the hearth, she worked through the length of her hair, unsnarling the knots. Sipped more wine. Ate a bit more. Wondered what Jasper was doing.

Was he thinking about her? She touched her lips. His thumb brushed across the bottom one. Lord Abernathy kissed her several times. Each time was harsh, brutal, as if he meant to teach her some lesson. There was nothing gentle about that man. Maggie didn't know what that message could mean.

He told her she wasn't responsive. The devil, when Lord Abernathy touched her, she didn't feel anything except revulsion. How could she respond to that? When Jasper touched her, heat spiraled through her to places she never noticed before. Flamed to vivid life.

What was she to do?

She couldn't go backward. Forward was the only way. Would forward include Jasper in her life?

~ * ~

Jasper leaned on his thighs, his head in his hands thinking about the beguiling little liar upstairs in the room across the hall from his. He didn't lie to her about the detective. Jason would have stopped by his place on his way to see Sarah. He spent the night restless. Unable to sleep for thinking about the woman who touched him in ways he didn't understand. He wanted to both protect her and make love to her. Beneath him she would be... It was unusual for him to have a woman come with sudden force into his thoughts.

His detective, Felix Brown, was the best at what he did. He was like a dog with a bone. The detective would wrestle with every clue until he discovered what he sought. He'd growl as well as snarl at any one getting in his way. When he visited him this morning, there would be news. He was waiting for a decent hour to go about his business. Both he along with his brother had ideas about the identity of the lady. While he didn't see Lord Abernathy at the park, Jason did. If it was Tessa's yellow ball gown the woman showed off...Tessa might be hiding from Abernathy. If she was running from the Viscount, her name wasn't Tessa Sterling. It was Maggie MacRae.

Jasper didn't miss the look of shock on her exquisite face when he mentioned the MacRae surname as a highlander's name. Didn't miss the surprise on her face when she made mistakes both with her diction along with her comments. She was used to having a maid. She lied. He couldn't blame her for the deception. In her precarious position, he would also do all in his power to remain free of that man. He didn't blame her lack of trust. She would have no way of knowing he was worthy of her faith.

Last night he slept little. Most of the hours between going to bed and dawn he wrapped all the transpiring events in his brain. Before he could come to any significant conclusions, he needed hard facts. Around two in the morning, he walked into the bedroom he had assigned to Tessa. She'd thrown off her covers. Turned on her side, the exquisite view of her bared leg sucked his breath into his lungs. He liked the notion she wore his nightshirt. It was new. He'd never worn the shirt. Slept naked. The sight of her sent a reaction straight to his sex. This was another first for him. With a heavy sigh then another, he returned to his room. A few hours later, he woke, stretched. Wished he'd slept better.

A list of all he needed to accomplish this morning before he returned to the townhouse sat in his pocket. Burned a hole there. The hour was still too early to make good on his errands. Keir had orders not to allow anyone into his home while he was gone. He apprised Keir of the most prevalent fact spinning around Miss Tessa. Not that Lord Abernathy would visit before noon. Jasper was certain it would take time for the viscount to discover he'd been at the park. Even then, he didn't believe anyone saw him take the bedraggled lady under his wing then stuff her into his carriage. Well…he didn't stuff. She jumped at the chance to leave with him. If Daryl Chamberlain noticed, she would never say anything to the likes of Abernathy.

Impatient to be off as well as understanding he was going to ruffle a few feathers by requesting assistance on Christmas day, Jasper set his cloak around his shoulders before setting off to ask his first request. Christmas day was a deucedly difficult day to ask for favors. His first stop was the modiste he knew his cousin, Gracie Murray, frequented. The dressmaker was talented. He bought items there for various lady friends over the years. Thank you gifts, for fun times shared. A great deal of money was exchanged with those wonderful seamstresses. This morning he would spend even more.

Snow had been cleaned off the streets, shoveled to the sides of the road. The white flakes lining the road were no longer pristine, white; darkened by the passing vehicles and horses. The wind blew cold across his face. He pulled his muffler up to cover his mouth along with his nose. This morning Jasper opted to ride his horse instead of in the carriage. Reaching the front of the shop, he tied the horse to the hitching post.

He rang the bell, waited for an answer to his summons. Jasper knew it would take a few minutes. Madame Henderson lived upstairs above her shop. She had no family that Jasper knew of. Acknowledging she would appreciate the business, he pushed the tiny flash of guilt from bothering her on Christmas morning to the back of his mind.

Appearing at the door, eyes still a bit sleepy, her voice soft, "Lord Kenworthy, what can I do for you at this hour? On Christmas morning? Whatever you need must be important for you to be up and about."

"It is. May I come in?" Jasper asked as he stepped inside not waiting for an invitation to his request. "It's damn cold outside."

He brushed snow from his shoulders. Stamped his feet to rid his shoes of snow on the mat by the front door.

"Yes…" Madame Henderson stood back, her hands folded in front of her, waiting. "I would help with whatever you need. Not doing anything important today. Wouldn't mind a *wee* bit of company."

Madam Henderson was thin, rather tall for a woman. Her dark brown hair was turning gray at the sides. She had a long straight nose along with a firm chin. Her clothing was always modest but in the height of fashion. The singular thing about the lady was that she was always open to suggestions.

"I've a couple of things. First, I need two ready-made gowns for a lady. I don't know her size. Would you happen to be the modiste for the MacRae family?" Jasper asked, hoping his search would end here.

The modiste tapped her long finger on her chin while she thought. Shaking her head, "No…not familiar with that name. As to a ready-made gown, there are several on the racks at the back of the room. Since you don't know her size you can help me out by showing."

Jasper chuckled realizing he wasn't going to get help in that category. Using his hands was a possibility. If he'd been intimate with her, he would have a better idea of her proportions. "That's what I was hoping you could help me with. If you made the family's clothing, that would have been a godsend. You would have her measurements on file."

Last night, for this reason, he purposely touched her, circled her waist with his hands. Wished he could have cupped her breasts. He would have a much better idea of her bust size. He recalled her hips along with her little rump pushed against him. She was not very big. Estimating her hips size would not be difficult.

Clearing his throat. "The lady is petite. Her height is around here." Jasper motioned with his hand about his collarbone. Her waist." He showed her with his hands. "Small. Her breasts I believe are average size. Not so large or too small." He discovered as these statements progressed a bit of heat flushed his face. "Hips…" Again, he showed her using his hands.

"That is not a great deal to go on. I have several gowns in different sizes that might do for your lady friend. Why don't we give these a try?" Madam Henderson hustled through the store to a rack holding different gowns.

"Is there a special occasion for any of these?"

"No, day dresses will do. She won't be going anywhere. Tomorrow, if you don't mind, would you come to my townhouse? I would commission a few more items. I hate to ask this but could you come in by the back?" Jasper understood that was an unusual request.

Another flash of heat coupled with searing guilt at the strange expression on the woman's face. "I wouldn't mind." She held up her hands to halt him from speaking. "Don't need a reason. Like what you pay for my services. If you wish for me to use the back door, you have your reasons. Know enough not to talk about it or ask questions. Should I come alone? I can get the measurements along with the choice of fabrics by myself. Believe you have servants who would carry the bolts along with the fashion plates into your home. Do you have a timeline on when you wish your order to be delivered."

"I do. Thank you. As soon as possible. I would pay extra if we can do this in two days."

"Two days?" she questioned but didn't ask for a reason. "Doing so will require more seamstresses."

"What you can't finish in two days' time, you can send to my brother. He will make certain I receive the garments."

Together they selected six gowns of varying sizes. Even though he enjoyed the idea of Tessa wearing his nightshirt, he purchased a long white virginal night dress for her along with a robe of the same color. "I'll have someone return the gowns that don't work for her."

Jasper left the shop with the packages tied to his saddle. He left the purchase of undergarments for the next day. For now, she would have to make do with whatever Fia had washed for her. He assumed she didn't trade undergarments with the woman who ended up with her ballgown. Pulling out his pocket watch, he looked at the time. It was half past ten. The morning seemed to fly by. He spent more time at the modiste's than he intended. Now, he was headed to the bakery with two more things on his mind that he wished to clear up.

When he arrived, there were people inside. The scent of fresh baked bread filled the air. Once in the door and the little bell announcing his arrival stopped ringing, he hung his cloak on a peg near the front then searched out the women who were working. He hoped to see Daryl Chamberlain, the owner of this establishment. He also hoped the lady could give him a few insights as to the card Fia found among Tessa's things. Jasper felt certain Tessa would be distraught if she discovered the card with this address on it missing. He also hoped he could return it without her knowledge. On the other hand, if his guesses proved true, he might be able to use the information to draw the truth from her.

"Coffee." He ordered after he found a place to sit, a table by a window looking out on the sidewalk. "Is Mrs. Chamberlain here?"

"Mr. Kenworthy, why do you be seekin' out the owner. It's Christmas morning. Don't you have somewhere better to be? Daryl won't be in until this afternoon. Needs to spend the time with her husband as well as her children." She stepped back after pouring him a cup. "Will there be anything else I can get you?"

His grin brought a smile from the lady. "I'd like an order to go. To take with me." Jasper listed a number of items including muffins and croissants, both plain as well as chocolate. He added donuts coated in icing along with the fruit filled varieties. His cook had the day off. This would take care of breakfast. He wasn't certain about the rest of the day. The cook would have left him plates of ham and cheese, fresh bread as well as other delicious food he and Jason could eat. There would be more than enough for his new companion.

His waitress set the list on the counter for one of the employees to see to. "What else can I do for you? You did mention two things." The woman stood back, hands on her hips.

Jasper reached into his pocket to pull out the card. He set it on the table. "This…"

She looked at it for a few seconds before handing it back to him.

"No secrets. This is a standard card all her sisters carry with them in case..."

"In case of an emergency?" His left eyebrow lifted, speculating different possibilities. "You encounter a lot of emergencies?"

"If one of the sisters comes across a woman or child in need, they give them a card. Mrs. Chamberlain has a room upstairs. She allows women who need to keep their location unknown, to stay there free of charge. In exchange for the room and board, they work the floor here or clean the bakery. If they have other talents that can be put to use, she pays them. She offers protection."

"Only the sisters have cards?" Jasper tapped the card on the table before slipping it into his pocket.

"Only the sisters..." She listed off the MacTavish sisters.

"Lacie Stewart is one of them." Jasper understood this was common knowledge. He wished the duchess was here to talk to him. Certain she must have been at the Christmas Eve gala where Abernathy announced his engagement to Maggie MacRae. That ball must have been where Lacie Stewart ran across Maggie. She would have delivered the card to her?

"Yes, as is Bliss and Chelsea. Along with the sisters there is Hope. She is not a sister but a sister-in-law. She also carries cards with her."

"That's all?" He doubted any of the ladies named would have been at the fete except Lacie. He meant to pay a visit in the next few days to the Stewarts unless Tessa told him the truth. Life would be much more controllable if she could put an end to the lies. Though he did understand her fear. Pushing for the truth last night did not work in his favor. She stiffened. Pursed her lips together. Her little chin lifted into the air. Ignored his questions by asking ones of her own. When he did have a question, she ignored him. "Thanks," he said while his mind continued to churn with various scenarios.

His order was set beside him. He was ready to visit with the detective who was on retainer before he returned to his home to confront Tessa with her real name. Yes, a confrontation was in order. After that was a reconciliation to the facts he would present to her. He pulled out the card to look at it again. Perhaps he wouldn't return the information. He could use the card as a piece of evidence to draw the truth from her sweet pink lips. The thought startled him. He realized again he would like to taste her.

Unlike his other stops, Felix expected him. Opened the door with,

"What took you so long?" His preference, coffee steamed in a cup for him minutes after being admitted to his office. The man sat behind an immense desk, his hands folded on top, his mustache combed and neat, curling at the edges. His bright blue eyes rested on him.

"Well?" Jasper asked impatient to get on with the conversation so he could return home with more answers than questions.

Felix's smile gave Jasper every reason to return the grin. "The lady you inquired about is indeed Maggie MacRae. Last night at the ball after the announcement of her engagement to Lord Abernathy, Maggie made a hasty escape. With her sisters' help, she pulled off something she would have never been able to do without them running interference."

"Maggie MacRae..." He sipped the strong black coffee while he studied his fingernails. "Maggie..." A beat of his heart passed then another while he felt at a loss. "MacRae. Has a better ring to it than Tessa Sterling. I like the name. It suits her."

Jasper felt pleased, more than pleased at the first piece of information albeit something he was certain of. Now he knew what he was up against. Understood Abernathy would pursue the treasure he lost. As would any man who misplaced a woman as beautiful as Maggie MacRae. He would need be on his toes. Understood why she lied. Last night she would have believed she could trust no one.

His detective continued with more information, "Maggie has three sisters; Nellie, Fannie, and Tessa. Her mother is Anice. The mother's maiden name was Sterling. The father doesn't seem to do much except go along with Anice's dictates. He stays behind the scenes. Seems content to do nothing of value. Is rarely seen at balls. It is the mother who arranged the betrothal contract with Nelson Abernathy. From the rumors, I was able to substantiate that both Anice as well as Nelson were furious with the turn of events last night. It seems there is substantial profit for the MacRaes upon Maggie's marriage to Abernathy. I'm not certain yet what the gain for Abernathy will turn out to be. Maybe just to have a beautiful woman on his arm."

"Last night, Nelson raced after her, not leaving it to his bumbling men to find her. Left the Christmas Eve celebration that was intended to be his great pleasure. With Maggie on his arm, he made the announcement of their pending marriage. Toasted with expensive French champagne."

Jasper had the strong suspicion that it was Nelson who Maggie saw when she buried her pert little nose into his chest, when she lurched into the carriage with no invitation setting this string of events into motion. Jasper felt responsible for the young lady. If he admitted the truth to himself, he felt a whole lot more than responsible when he thought of Maggie MacRae. His body jumped to life with thoughts about the little lady who seemed to wedge into his heart with no provocation. Remembered how she felt when in his arms.

"Appears so… It won't be long before Nelson discovers it was your carriage at the park last night then shows up at your home. Need I tell you to be careful? If I were you, I would get the girl into another country as soon as humanly possible. You need to separate yourself along with Maggie from Glasgow. From Scotland. From this island. I'm not telling you to go to another city such as Edinburgh. I'm telling you to leave for London or Ireland, even Paris or Bordeaux might keep him off your scent until you can figure out what you want. Switzerland would be nice if this wasn't the beginning of winter. Damn cold there. Nonetheless, that might be the least likely place Lord Abernathy will look. From here, I will do all that I can to lead him astray. I'm positive your brother will also plant false clues. In doing so, you will be able to incorporate the necessary hours to steal away."

Since he wasn't about to marry her…yes…that was what he fully intended to do. Marriage was the only other option he could think of though a wedding didn't sound as terrible when he recalled that Maggie was a beautiful woman. The way she felt in his arms was heaven sent. He would, at some point in time, need an heir. "What part does Lady Stewart play in this scenario? She was, I assume, at the gala last night."

All Jasper needed was confirmation that it was Lacie who handed the card to Maggie then he would have more power.

"As you seem to suspect, the duke as well as the duchess were at the Christmas Eve affair. Gossip has it, they were in the powder room together, Lacie along with your Maggie. She was the last woman in that room with Miss MacRae. Once the duchess left, that was when Nelson walked in on her, hauled her out then made the announcement. Right after that, when he was entertaining another woman on the dance floor, she slipped from the room. His men weren't able to stop Miss MacRae. Her sisters, from the gossip, were adept at running interference."

"You've done well."

Jasper understood the necessity to act with speed. He penned a message to Jason before handing the short missive to Felix. Jason needed to reach out to Duncan Murray while he visited the duke and duchess. He wasn't as yet certain he needed help from the Stewarts. That remained to be seen. What he required now was to keep all options open to him. As Felix told him, not many seconds would pass before Lord Abernathy would be knocking at his door. Could be this evening or first thing in the morning.

As he entered his home, the place seemed to be in chaos. Keir rushed forward. The look on his face told Jasper they had a visitor. One he wouldn't appreciate. He didn't like that. Felt his heart slam against his ribs. Hadn't expected Abernathy to be by this morning. If it was Abernathy, his investigators were too damn good. The only way anyone would know that Maggie was here, with his protection, was if they spoke to Daryl Chamberlain. He didn't believe Daryl would tell one of Abernathy's men anything.

"The lady was here. The duchess," Keir panted out of breath from all the activities. "Just as you instructed. I didn't let her inside. I tell you though." He was wheezing then pointing a shaking finger at him. "That was the hardest thing I've ever tried. She was huffing that she would see I never worked again. Almost did what she wished at that point. The duchess knows how to throw her weight around. Did manage to intimidate the likes of me. However," Keir stopped struggling with another breath of air, "knew if I didn't do what you said, you would fire me. Her threats weren't going to sway me. Though I'm certain we will all feel her wrath."

Jasper kept the grin behind his teeth. Relief swamped him. He didn't wish to deal with Viscount Abernathy until he had a plan. Right now was far too soon. He was pleased the visitor wasn't Abernathy. "Send Fia to me. Has Tessa risen?"

"Yes…I'll do that. She is up. With nothing to wear she is still in her room. Last time Fia was up there, the *wee* little *lassie* was pacing. Swearing at you a blind streak. Would never have expected her to spout some of those words that flew from her lips. Fia wasn't certain how to handle her. She closed the door then decided to wait for more instructions. Since the *lass* wasn't going anywhere in your nightshirt and robe we weren't concerned. Hope that was fine with you. Didn't know how to deal with the *wee* one's temper."

So, his Maggie possessed a temper. "Perfect. When Fia gets down I'll be in my office. I would like a tray of hot tea brought there. I've got breakfast handled. Whether she likes it or not, she will have to appear in my nightwear or her underwear."

Jasper kept his chuckle behind his teeth. He anticipated seeing her, learning something about her temperament. From what Keir told him, he was certain she had a temper. She was definitely annoyed. A spicy little thing. Hot. Sweet. The woman would be fun. Would never prove boring. Jasper didn't think Nelson Abernathy would appreciate her temper.

A few minutes later, Fia stood in front of him shifting from one foot to the other. Her distraught was clear in the morbid lines of her face. "The *wee lassie* is swearing up a blue streak, she is. Don't know what to do. 'Tis a good thing she has no clothes to wear. If she did, she'd be high-tailin' her little rear out of here. She's mad as the dickens. Don't understand why that is so. You've been kind to her."

Jasper stared from the package of clothing to his housekeeper turned lady's maid. He intended to give the bundle to Fia to take to Maggie. Now, he thought doing so might not be wise. Needed to have an audience with her before she had something to wear. Later, after they talked, after he made a few salient points about the direction of her future, he would hand over the clothing. "Perhaps I should see her the way she is. Bring her down. I'll give her these clothes after I get a promise from her." He laughed at Fia's snort of displeasure.

Shaking her finger at him, Fia told him what she thought about this arrangement. "She's be wearin' nightclothes. Your nightclothes. Even I *ken* that's not proper. Her reputation will be ruined." Fia waved her hand in the air. "In shreds. It's be your doin.'"

"Is she fully covered?" Jasper asked even though he knew the answer. "Don't think once it is known she spent the night at a bachelor's townhouse with me that information will also sully her standing among the most elite in this city? The lady ran away from an engagement. Do believe this female doesn't care about appearances. Seems she's an independent thinker. I appreciate that concept."

Fia nodded before flushing a brilliant red. She curtsied, seeming uncertain. "It's not proper…"

57

Maggie

"You've overstepped. Bring her down. I'll talk to her as she is. What did you do with her dress?" Jasper asked, wondering if his housekeeper followed his orders. He didn't want her dressing in something so filthy as the old gown. Under his care, he would pamper her. See she had everything needed.

"Burned it like you told me. Washed her underthings."

"Give those to her. What were they like? The fabric? Was there lace and…"

This time he felt a slight twinge of heat sear his insides. That wasn't something he should be asking even though he was curious.

The flush on his housekeeper's face deepened to scarlet. "Just like a real lady would be wearin'. Tessa is pretending to be something she isn't. She's no a woman down on her luck. Well, maybe she is. It's up to you to get to the truth. If you be thinkin' you can do it easier when she's wearing your nightclothes, I'm not so certain you be thinkin' straight. More like you be thinkin' with a different… I'll bring her." She set of in a huff, her shoulders stiff.

Jasper had trouble holding back the bark of laughter bubbling up from his stomach. Never before had anyone, let alone a servant, accused him of thinking with his cock. Perhaps he should temper his thoughts to a more acceptable as well as prudent point. While his housekeeper might have an argument with the way he was going about things, he wasn't about to lower himself to that level.

He poured two cups of tea before setting out the pastries he bought at the little bakery. Ah, this time he wasn't thinking with his cock as Fia implied. He had other reasons to keep her clothed in nightwear. Fia giving him the main one. He didn't trust Miss Tessa to stay put if she was given clothing. She was flighty. So nervous she wouldn't be able to think straight. He didn't want her running away from him. What he desired was that his plan to come to fruition. The one that was still muddled in his brain. The one he hadn't yet to decide on the direction.

There were ways to secure Tessa's safety. One was to marry her. Though he was attracted to Tessa, he wasn't ready to settle down to a life with one woman. Even though she was quite beautiful. Interesting. Dynamic in ways he wasn't positive about. Didn't believe she would bore him to tears as other women of his acquaintance might. Knew at some point

58

he would need an heir. The second way was to find some place to hide her where the viscount couldn't find her. To do so, he would need to ferret her out of the country. That was a real possibility. Before he could do so, he would have to visit the Earl of Downberry, Duncan Murray. The family owned a townhouse in London. If no one was using the home at the moment, he would be happy to pay rent for a few months. He could take her to Ireland. There were beautiful places along the coastline just a skip from Glasgow. Perhaps he should take a carriage to London then sail down the Thames heading for Northern Ireland. Traveling out of Glasgow would never be prudent. It would be too easy to check passenger lists.

There were other places farther away. Paris would make a nice vacation spot. They could disappear into the countryside without leaving a trace. He did love Paris in winter. Switzerland would be too cold as his detective pointed out to him. Spain or Portugal was warm. This was turning into a whirlwind of events with too many possibilities.

"Keir," he called out, understanding the man would be close.

Just as Jasper thought, Keir stepped into the room. "Miss MacRae and I will be leaving as soon as I can get the coach ready. See to it. He wasn't going to wait to be discovered. Today, he would leave. Head for Ireland through London. That way their path would be harder to trace. He would leave a letter for Jason. He didn't require the MacMurray townhouse. Acquiring the home would take too long. Time he didn't have."

"Should I have food packed for the journey?" Keir asked while he waited for an answer.

"A nice lunch is all that is needed. Make certain the carriage has two warm blankets."

Keir turned to leave.

"Wait! Pray for an end to the snow. It will be cold enough without the white stuff." Jasper understood the next question coming from his butler would be where are you going? He couldn't tell anyone. Not even Jason would be informed. Sometimes even in homes such as his with ninety percent of the servants off duty the walls possessed ears.

"May I ask where you are off to with the *wee lassie?*"

"You can ask."

~ *. ~

"Where do you think Maggie is?" Nellie questioned as she sipped on the water their mother left in the room. Her stomach rumbled with hunger pains. She shouldn't even be that hungry. It was the idea that food would be withheld that made her stomach make those horrible noises. She'd eaten enough for three at the Christmas Eve ball.

While Anice wasn't withholding all food, they were existing on bread and water. Part of that was because Nellie felt certain her mother understood they were telling the truth. None of them knew where their sister was or what she intended.

It was Christmas morning. They usually devoured croissants along with hot chocolate. After breakfast they would open gifts then they would eat more. Their cook always made an elaborate Christmas dinner to be served early in the afternoon, roast turkey being the main course.

"I do hope she found some shelter," Fannie gave her contribution to the conversation such as it was. "It's frigid cold this morning. Last night I heard the wind howling around the eves. Thought the banshee was coming for someone. For a beat of my heart, felt certain I felt chills rushing through her."

Nellie knew there were no guarantees that Maggie was even alive. Snow fell. The temperature was glacial at best. Wind whipped down from the northern craigs. She sucked in a deep breath of air. Bread coupled with water was easy to digest knowing their oldest sibling might be existing with nothing. Not even a roof over her head. In some respects, Nellie wished Lord Abernathy would find her. On the other hand, an entire lifetime bound to that man might be worse than death at the hands of a snowstorm. She had to believe her sister was smart. Maggie wore her warmest cloak. She would take no chances. Capitalize on anything positive. Their sister was resourceful.

"Mother said to come down when we finished our bread. She wants to talk to us," Nellie told her sisters.

"That could be bad for us," Fannie added, her thoughts as morose as they were.

"She's going to try to ferret out more information…an interrogation. Facts that we don't have," Tessa said with a slight lift to her shoulders.

"If we stay true to ourselves, there is nothing to tell. Even our mother will have to understand."

As the oldest sister she was now in charge of communications. Her mother always transferred her directives to the oldest. Nellie didn't appreciate the position. Needed to be the second oldest again. No matter what happened, she would never be second in line. This was her duty now. Maggie either found a safe place or Abernathy would haul her home then marry her. Even though in Scotland the banns didn't need to be read, he went through the formality. If the viscount caught up with Maggie, he would haul her to a church then marry her before she could flee. The viscount wasn't a man who would take chances. He didn't stand for the word, no. What happened last night was unique. Something he would never understand how to deal with. Maggie would refuse him. That would be expected. There were many ways to coerce an unwilling bride.

"Are we finished eating?" Tessa asked as she set her empty cup of water on the small table in Nellie's room. "The thought of another bite of bread makes me nauseous. She didn't even give us butter."

"Will we be allowed to eat Christmas dinner?" Fannie asked, her voice wistful, her face taking on a dreamy expression as if she could taste the food.

"Remains to be seen," Nellie said, wishing she had more answers. "If I could make up something, I would do so."

"We should go see what mother wants as soon as possible. I, for one, would just as soon get this interview over with," Fannie spoke up as she watched her siblings fret over something they had no control over. "Mother will not be pleasant to us."

"Agreed. Let's go. When the interview is over, we can retire to our rooms."

Downstairs, Anice took up a regal position by the fireplace. Her long dark hair was piled high on top of her head. Unblinking, she stared at them when they walked into the drawing room. Her eyes were the exact same color as Maggie's. Startling emerald green. Her dress was of a dark green velvet that molded her curves to perfection. She arched a dark eyebrow.

The girls sat on the floor around their mother as they always did on Christmas morning. The only difference was that Maggie was missing. Nellie spread her dress out. Tucked her feet beneath her gown.

"If you are going to ask us more questions about Maggie, the time will be wasted. We don't know anything. Maggie was smart enough to keep her plan a secret. All we know is that we helped her leave the viscount's home. That's the end of our part in Maggie's departure." Nellie was tired of the second cross-examination before the questions began.

The tree was adorned with ribbons and satin balls that were many different colors. They never used candles on the tree. Too dangerous their mother always told them when they pleaded. Nellie saw the presents beneath the tree. All wrapped up and pretty. Maggie wouldn't be here to open hers. A strange loneliness swept through her. Something she'd never felt before. She closed her eyes, wondering where Maggie was. Never before had she been separated from any of her siblings. Questioned if she was cold or hungry. Had a bed to sleep in that wasn't under the stars. This would be their first Christmas without the older sister. A lone tear slipped from her eye. Not wishing any of her siblings to see the moisture or her mother, she quickly looked away so she could let the cloth from her sleeve soak the wetness.

Their butler poured eggnog for all of them. Added a touch of whiskey to each glass. Anice stood with her glass in the air, "Merry Christmas to my wonderful daughters. I prayed all last night that Maggie did not find herself in a wealth of trouble. She can be so willful. Stubborn to a fault. Hot tempered. She always wants everything her way. Tell me, why does she not wish to marry Lord Abernathy. He is good looking. Handsome. Possesses a title along with enough wealth to provide for her. Anything she would like."

"Do you have to ask? You have not bothered to look beneath the superficial? He is mean. A horrible man," Nellie whispered, her voice soft, though her words were tense. Fingers winding into the fabric of her gown. "No one likes the man. He takes advantage of every situation. Why would you hope to marry Maggie to a man who would hurt her with the littlest provocation?"

"Arrogant," came from Fannie, looking at her, eyes wide with knowledge one so young shouldn't have. Her little sister was jaded about men. "He's cold hearted. If you think Maggie wants things only her way, the viscount is far worse. They would fight. Hate each other within the first week of marriage."

"Disgusting," was Tessa's reply while she tapped her fingers on the glass of eggnog she held in her hands. "Rumors say he's responsible for the deaths of some of his mistresses. He will keep one too. Even though he is married. He sees to his comforts first. Doesn't care for others. Maggie would be miserable. She doesn't like to share."

Nellie watched her mother's face pale. She didn't like what was said. Their mother stiffened her spine. With a snort of what Nellie interpreted as distaste, Anice spoke, "Nonetheless, a lady could do worse than marrying a man such as Lord Abernathy." Anice fluffed her skirts then sipped on the Christmas drink. "I've chosen well. All of you should have someone so accomplished to be engaged to."

"One could do better? Would it be too much to ask for love?" Nellie added keeping her lashes lowered and eyes downcast. If she spoke too much, she'd find herself engaged to a man of her mother's choosing before the end of the week. She was twenty, well past the age most women wed. She wanted to find a man who would love her. Not one who wanted her for what she could give him. Needed to be able to choose the bridegroom herself.

"Perhaps, tell me…do any of you have an idea of where she would go? I'm worried about my daughter. Though, after our conversations last night, I'm certain none of you believe I care what happens to Maggie."

Nellie saw they were all shaking their heads. "She didn't tell us. That was part of the plan. Maggie knew you would ask. She wanted us to be able to speak the truth. Maggie never lies. She didn't wish us to have to make up a story to keep her safe."

"Don't believe she knew where she was headed," Fannie added her thoughts. "Everything happened so fast. There was no time for a plan. Maggie reacted to what was put in front of her."

"Maggie ran from the worst nightmare of her life. Marriage to the viscount. This is all your fault," Tessa accused, her voice heated far beyond what was normal.

Chapter Three

Maggie walked circles in the room she'd been assigned. Her temper soared, at a flashpoint. Flamed out of control. True, she was warm, sheltered, while snow swirled around the eves. Correct, he didn't feed her this morning. Her stomach grumbled. Seemed the blasted man forgot all about her. When she looked out on the snow-covered ground, she shivered, thinking about what could have been. Hugged her arms around her as if she could keep warmth inside her that way. The long breath of air sweeping from her lungs halted her musings while she thought of her siblings' opening gifts. A wave of nostalgia burst.

Christmas morning. Her sisters. Eggnog by the tree. Presents to open. Her life with no care vanished last night. She was running from a fate she wished no part of.

Her mother would punish them by withholding food. Not for long though. Once Anice figured out her sisters truly didn't know anything about her whereabouts she would renege on the punishment. They were most likely drinking that eggnog while they talked about her whereabouts. Anice would ask again if they knew what happened to her. They would tell her they didn't know.

Heat flushed Maggie's face. The devil, she swore at the poor housekeeper. Ranted as if any of this was the poor lady's fault. Even sent a pillow in her direction when she refused her the gown she'd worn last night. All she had to wear were Jasper's nightshirt and robe. The nightshirt hit her midcalf. The robe trailed along behind her threatening to trip her up. Beneath those two items she wore nothing. Nothing at all. She felt naked. Naked! She couldn't leave the room dressed this way. Where were her underthings? She had the right to them. They were hers.

Here she was in a man's home, naked. She couldn't fathom the notion that was beyond her ability to grasp. Jasper Kenworthy helped her.

Rescued her from the hands of Lord Abernathy. She buried her nose in his chest…beneath his jacket. He didn't blink. She owed him.

Hell no!

Yes.

She should thank him then ask him to take her to the address on the card the duchess handed her in the lady's room last night. Her stomach flipped over. A wave of nausea hit her. She sat on the closest chair. Felt the blood drain from her face. She made a mess of things. Everything was so…so…messy.

Where was the card? That card was precious to her. Without the written information, she would be wed to Lord Abernathy in a week. He would make sure to haul her to the nearest clergy. Because she'd run, he wouldn't trust her. He would drug her. Knew that had been done to other young women who refused.

She didn't have that piece of paper anymore. Where was it? She wouldn't have lost the blasted thing. The card was sacred to her. Close enough.

The card was with the gown, beneath her underthings, nestled against her breast. What happened to that piece of paper? To her underthings? The housekeeper, Fia, helped her undress. Took her undergarments away from her. Said she would wash them. The card would either be returned or the paper dissolved in the washing. Where?

Fia might have given the soul piece of information that might help her to Lord Kenworthy. Why was he a lord? He never told her his title. Was he higher up on the ladder of nobility than Lord Abernathy? Most likely. The only noble below a viscount was a baron. She never paid attention to the high-ranking men and women in the city. For Jasper to be titled seemed to be a huge coincidence.

Looking in the mirror, her hair was a mess. This morning after all this disorder she got herself into, she could find nothing to use on her hair. He meant to keep her here in this room as a prisoner. Naked. Almost naked. He didn't send anything for her to eat. She'd been awake for at least two hours. Didn't he tell her to pull the bell cord? After she tugged the rope, someone would see to her needs? That was a huge laugh at her expense.

Jasper Kenworthy, you are either a liar or your servants are inept. Tessa Sterling wasn't supposed to know about servants. She wasn't supposed to know about bell cords or having someone see to her needs. Last night she made two major mistakes. She couldn't afford another one. The housekeeper would tell him what she was doing. A lady off the streets wouldn't toss anything at a servant. A woman down on her luck would be sweet. Biddable. Say thank you to everything she received.

Maggie groaned; placed her hands at her temples where a headache was blossoming. Massaged. She needed to get out of this tenuous situation before her lies were discovered. She held the distinct notion it was too late for her. Events seem to be set in motion without her knowledge or input.

The light knocks on the door brought her head around. Maybe someone around here answered a summons. What an idea? The knocker was probably the housekeeper again. Maggie didn't wish to frighten her away. Feeling hesitant she answered, "Who is it?"

Behind the door, Maggie thought she felt the poor woman's fear. Caused by her. She would take sole responsibility. At this point she wanted food then clothing. The housekeeper would provide. She hoped. "Fia. It's me. The housekeeper." A beat followed then another. "Lady Tessa. Be it alright if I come inside? *Dinna* wish to talk through the door. Lord Kenworthy is requesting me to see to you."

At last someone would see to her needs. "Yes…please…I promise you won't be the recipient of any missiles. Won't throw another pillow your way. Understand you follow orders. It's Lord Kenworthy who should have to dodge pillows. What is it the…Lord Kenworthy would like? I would be happy to oblige."

As if in slow motion, the door creaked open. Fia poked her head inside the room. Just her head nothing more. "Lady Tessa…"

Maggie held up her hands to show her she didn't lie. "No pillow. Do you have food or tea? Would love something to wear. Is there a reason the lord wants to keep me naked?" Maggie smoothed the fabric of the robe that was entangled between her legs. She pushed on the unruly material, twisted, dislodged the cumbersome length. When she walked toward Fia, all her efforts were wasted. She tripped. Cursed. Her arms whirled to keep her afloat.

Fia moved back. The poor lady appeared to be holding her breath. "I wouldnae be knowin' about that. Lord Kenworthy asked me to bring you to him in the parlor. Wants to speak to you, he does." She turned as if to lead the way.

"No!"

Fia's back stiffened. When she turned the strain lines on her face were visible. It seemed the woman held her breath. "*Ye cannae* be refusin' the lord. If *ye dinna* follow me downstairs, he will come here for you. He will be yellin' at me."

Maggie thought that might indeed be a fair assessment of the situation. That was not enough to change her mind. She meant to hold her ground. Jasper, Lord Kenworthy, could give orders right and left for all she cared. She would proceed today as she meant to continue. He could not order her around. She was not his pawn. With time spent with Lord Abernathy she had her fill of arrogant, overbearing aristocratic men. Even if that man meant to save her, she wasn't going to kowtow to his every whim. "Tell him if he wishes to speak to me, he can come here."

"Oh, no, my lady. Y*e cannae* be tellin' the lord such as that. I *willnae* repeat your whim. *Ye* must be comin' with me."

Crossing her arms over her chest, Maggie stared at her more determined than a second ago. "Let him come. I'm not his to order around. I've a mind of my own. Can make decisions for myself." By the look of absolute terror on Fia's face, Maggie understood she was making a huge mistake.

Fia was shaking her head, distress showing in her body stature. She tried again to convince her into following her right into the waiting anger of Lord Kenworthy. Tried to convince her it was the right thing to do, "*Ye* must be comin' with me. You've no choice," Fia argued, desperation ringing in her voice.

"There is always a choice, Fia. I found that one must learn to make a stand in this life. I'm not interested in anything he has to say. As soon as I've something to wear, I'll make my way. Won't be staying here." Maggie tilted her chin up a notch drawing in a deep breath of air. For a fleeting second she thought she might be making a huge mistake. "Where is my underwear? I expect to get it back."

"Is that so?" The husky baritone floating through the open door gave Maggie a start. She blanched.

Speak o' the Devil!

Maggie's gaze transferred to a spot behind Fia. The man was

frowning at her. When he spoke to her his tone was gentle. She was speechless. He came here to intercede on his housekeeper's behest. The air she sucked in turned in her lungs.

"You may go, Fia. I'll take care of this little matter of disagreement myself. I understand you tried your best. She is a stubborn soul as you told me. Determined to do everything in the most difficult way possible. When you weren't down after a few minutes, I figured Tessa was giving you trouble."

He turned his attention from Fia to her. Held out his arm for her to take as if he understood she was a lady. "There is food downstairs. Hot chocolate. A gown for you to wear if you would rather not spend the rest of the day in my nightclothes."

The devil, he must have heard her stomach grumble. Heat flushed her face. Maggie meant to hold her ground, even with the promise of food as well as a dress if she obeyed his requests. "I can't." She put her wishes into simple words.

"Why?" Jasper sounded angry with her response. His eyes narrowed then one dark brow arched upward as if he didn't believe her. "Why don't you wish to eat?" He stepped farther into the room. She moved back. Her heartbeat lodged in her throat.

Jasper was just too tall, too broad of shoulder. Too… Big… Even though the room was large, he seemed to fill the space. Her breath caught in her lungs. She tried to lick her dry lips. They continued to move. She would step back. He stepped forward. The back of her legs caught on the bed. She sat. Her eyes widened. Caught. He stood over her. His arms crossed in front of his broad chest. Feet were planted wide.

"Why don't you want food? Could you be honest about that? Seems since you vaulted into my life without my consent all that I've heard from you are lies." His tone was dry. A small half-grin settled on his lips. "If we are to get along on this new journey we are about to embark on, it's time for the lies to stop."

Maggie understood the enchanting smile of his was there because her stomach was lying to him. She couldn't tell him the truth. A lady didn't walk into a man's parlor naked or wearing a nightshirt along with a robe with nothing else beneath. Something like that just wasn't done. She didn't blink. "I can't."

"If you're not hungry that's fine. You still need to meet me in the parlor. We need to talk about this afternoon." This time he held out his hand for her to take. "Among other things. Maggie MacRae…you seem to have the bad habit of telling falsehoods. It's unfortunate the lies don't help your plight. They only serve to hinder my ability to protect you."

"Y-you…you." She licked her lips. "No…hmm…my name." Maggie wished she could rush past the man, down the stairs then somewhere…anywhere.

Anywhere but here!

"Yes, you can." His voice was too calm. Too warm as well as sincere. He was looking at her with a bemused expression.

"I'm naked! I can't." Maggie knew her eyes were big. She was terrified having never been with a man when she was dressed in so little. Her body hummed to life. She recalled his scent when she pressed her nose against him. Remembered the steel hardness of his body. She found herself shaking her head. She couldn't. She just couldn't. Panicked, she sipped a good portion of oxygen. Coughed.

That little half-smile of his grew to gigantic proportions until she saw his even white teeth behind his lips. A soft chuckle followed. "You're not naked. My God, woman, you've more clothes on than…" His gaze roamed the length of her as if he was making sure his words were true. "Think I would know it if you wore nothing."

Another chuckle followed. At least that's what Maggie thought she heard before she continued to bury herself. "I've got nothing on beneath this robe of yours. It smells like you," she blurted then clamped down hard on her lower lip wishing she knew how to keep her thoughts to herself.

His hoot of laughter surprised her. Didn't expect amusement. As he did last night, he studied her. "Well, I have worn the robe. Never the nightshirt. You're wasting valuable time. Unless your most fervent wish is for Lord Abernathy to catch up to you, we, the two of us, must make haste. While I've made arrangements, it is in the end up to you to approve. I would not take no for an answer easily. Only if the place I've picked is somewhere Lord Abernathy might look for you."

I'm doaty.

You are not stupid. Maybe a little.

He knows my name. Knows about Lord Abernathy. Most likely

69

knows about the engagement I didn't agree to. No, I'm a dobber. *An idiot for assuming any man would wish to help me. He doesn't want to help me. He wants me naked. He's just like my fiancé. The fiancé I don't want to have.*

Would that be so bad? The man is a handsome devil. You might find you like him. He could become your fiancé.

No, don't need or want another man.

Jasper looked as if he was growing impatient. His hands were behind his back. He was rocking on the balls of his feet. It was something her father did when he was exasperated. "Are you coming?" A long beat later. "Do I need to carry you? As to clothing, as soon as I'm quite certain you are not going to bolt, I've purchased a few things for you to wear. I will give them to you then…after we eat, we can be on our way." When she didn't answer right away, he appeared impatient.

"I *willnae* be acceptin' anything from you!" Her nerves were stretching so tight she thought certainly they would snap. She didn't understand how to deal with this impervious man who one second was sweet then the next not so much. Maggie was far from able to handle this man or any man. She had no experience with men. To her, he was an enigma. All men were a mystery to her. She knew nothing of the opposite sex.

He spoke before she could. Clearing his throat, "Well, if that's the way you wish to play this out, you will be wearing the nightshirt along with the robe while we travel to London. The carriage will be warm enough. However, when we stop for meals or to spend the night, you will have to traipse through the lobby wearing my robe, naked as you claim. With not a stitch on beneath."

Damn the man, he was right. She clenched her teeth. "The gown I wore last night? Would that do?"

Maggie heard the clear desperation in her voice. Couldn't change the tone. This time she wished to bury her nose in the bedcovers then never come up for air. He was high handed. Bossy to the extreme. Handsome to the core.

"Burned. It was more than likely infested."

"Oh!" She fell silent. Her heart lurched. Shoulders slumping. Maggie felt defeated. "My underwear? Is that…?" She looked up, hopeful that all her garments did not find lodging in a fire to become ashes.

"Downstairs with the clothing I purchased for you. As I said a moment ago, when you convince me, you are agreeable to my plan, I'll hand over the clothing. Until then…" Jasper made it clear she would do things his way.

"Underhanded. Sneaky as well as Devious. Why can't we talk here? It's safe. I feel comfortable."

She grasped at anything to help her out of this conundrum of her making. In truth, she didn't wish to talk anywhere with this man. Jasper…Lord Jasper Kenworthy terrified her. Excited her in a way she didn't understand. Compelled her to learn more about him.

"Yes, we could. However," Jasper stroked his chin, his expression solemn. Touched upon the cleft in the middle. "However, I would believe a young lady such as yourself would prefer to speak to a man in the parlor of his home rather than a bedroom which lies across the hall from his." Jasper's eyebrow rose a notch. "So much can be implied when two people of the opposite sex are in the same bedroom. Unchaperoned. One of them naked. I would bow to your wishes in this matter. Am I wrong?"

Unable to help herself, Maggie bristled. Felt her backbone become rigid. The breath she inhaled stayed in her lungs. He was right. Damn the arrogant beast. Knew he was. Condescending. While she didn't wish to admit to anything, she was in a corner she couldn't find a means to get out of without that admission. Instead of hiding from him, she met his gaze head on. "You're right. Of course, you're right. I'll go. Besides, I am hungry. Famished," Maggie mumbled, dispirited by this second encounter with Jasper Kenworthy.

His grin was something she would like to wipe off his handsome face. "Thought you would understand my reasoning."

This time Jasper turned on his heel. Walking from the room, he headed through the door.

What Maggie saw was that all pretense of gallantry vanished. Jasper played the gentleman until she agreed with him. With a heavy demoralized sigh, Maggie pulled the long robe from between her legs. Followed the man down the steps then into the parlor. Tripped on the fabric when she stepped into the room. He caught her then righted her. The scent of pastries along with hot chocolate filled the air. A wave of hunger swept through her, drowning her. Gurgled in her stomach. Mouthwatering, she didn't wish to wait for the food. Jasper nodded for her to sit.

She wanted food. More food. More later, in that order. After her stomach was quiet, she could talk. Didn't want to wait for him to decide when as well as what was going to happen. Maggie saw that he nodded to Keir. His butler poured two cups of hot chocolate then handed one to her the other to Jasper.

"Drink up. Fill your stomach until you are satisfied. When you're finished eating, I'll explain what is happening. Talk to you about the potential of your future. Right now, the days ahead of you are not promising. We both understand the circumstances surrounding you. They are dire. Am I right or wrong?" He pointed to the package at the corner of his desk. "New clothing. Don't intend to keep you…" He looked her up and then down. Smiled. "Naked. Though if I dare say so, you don't look naked to me. I've been attempting to figure out what I'm missing in this scenario."

Heat swept up her cheeks. She pulled at the fabric of his robe. Pushed it downward over her legs. "I feel naked. Guess I'm not though. May I have one or two." Maggie knew he read all the emotions in her face. Her mother would never let her have more than one. Lord Abernathy commented with a negative vibe if she ate more than he believed reasonable for a female.

"One or two what?" Jasper smirked at her as if he didn't know what it was she wanted. "Dresses? Robes? Underwear, perchance. Might it be cups of hot chocolate? You need to be exact. If you are not precise in your wishes, I'll be left to guess. Don't appreciate guessing games. No, I don't. Not a'tall."

Throwing something at the man might relieve some of the tension in her body. Stress created by him. Instead, she cleared her throat. "Pastries."

"Oh, thought you meant gowns. You can devour as many pastries as you would like. As to the dresses, take whatever fits you. My modiste has agreed to visit within the next hour. She will take your measurements as well as bring you a few more garments to wear beneath your gowns so you won't consider yourself…naked. Is that suitable? Never wished for you to feel…unclothed. My hasty visit this morning did not garner all the necessary clothes you will need for the extended voyage."

Voyage?

I'm not going anywhere with this man.

The blasted lord of the realm thought he had everything figured out. Imagined she would agree to any underhanded dictate he would spout. He didn't. She wouldn't. Yet... Before he could change his mind, she placed one of each pastry on her plate then refilled her chocolate cup to the brim. She wasn't going to take any chances. Food was the first essential item on her list. Underwear ran a close second. For all she knew this might be her last food of the day. Beneath lowered lashes she stared at him. Bemused, he grinned at her.

"Seems you have a healthy appetite. I appreciate that in a woman. Food is good for the soul. Though...seems you do like your sugar."

"What does that mean? And...there isn't anything except sugar to choose from here."

Maggie felt on the defensive. Didn't like to defend the amount of food she ate. Lord Abernathy told her she would go to fat if she kept up her habit of eating so much. Seemed a body needed to eat to survive to the next day. Jasper was correct. She did have a healthy appetite for sugar. She loved sugar. Nonetheless, she didn't overindulge.

"You appreciate food. That's all. Why so defensive? You've no need to guard yourself against me. I've no opinion one way or the other." Jasper asked still with that silly smirk on his face.

She coughed; a flake of the croissant caught in the back of her throat. She drank chocolate. Coughed again. Before she could bring the coughing under control, he stood behind her pounding on her back.

"Stop!" She choked again then swallowed. Whatever he did seemed to have worked. Jasper became motionless. "I shouldn't have eaten quite so fast. Your comment caught me off guard."

"Did I hurt you?"

"No, well...no you didn't. It's just that..."

"I hurt you." Jasper sounded disgusted with himself. "Didn't mean to. You're too small. Used to doing that with Jason when he catches food in his throat. My brother is a lot bigger than you. I'll need to adjust if you make a habit of this choking on your food business." He sat down behind his big cherry wood desk again. "Eat. Don't mind me. I ate before you came down. Whatever you don't consume, we can take with us. Can you do more than

73

one thing at once?"

"What kind of question is that?" He put her on the defensive again. "Yes…" she changed her tune. "I can chew food as well as think. Can make comments with my mouth full, though mother would reprimand me."

"Keep eating. Eat your fill. I'll tell you what I know as well as what I'm planning for your…our future. Because of last night along with your shenanigans at the park, I find myself linked with your future. Against my will, I might add. Yours as well as mine seemed to have merged." He drummed his fingers on the arm of the chair, staring at her.

"How is that?" Maggie asked, trying to speak through a mouthful of pastry. She put her hand in front of her mouth. "I don't understand how our futures are linked. I'll go my way and you will go yours. I'll thank you for the timely save last night. You'll say you're welcome. There is nothing else."

"Where is your way?" His deadpan question unnerved her. "I'd like to understand how you can avoid the inevitable conclusion."

Maggie knew the answer she didn't like. If she left here, Lord Abernathy would find her. "I suppose you will enlighten me. I'm not certain the extent of your thoughts. I harbor no illusions that you have everything figured out. Why don't you tell me what I'm…you and I are going to be doing."

She understood she gave in to his plans much too soon. He would take her somewhere. Leave her. After that what would she do?

Jasper was sitting back in his chair looking relaxed as if he didn't have a single care in the entire world. His fingers made a steeple beneath his chin while he slowly tapped them together. He probably didn't. "Yes, you're correct. In three hours, hoping for less time, we will be on our way to London. From there we will set sail for Ireland. Haven't yet decided where I would like to set up housekeeping in that country. Have a few options at my disposal. Do you have an opinion? Is there a small town where Lord Abernathy won't think to find you." He waved his hand in the air. "Forget that. Anywhere you might suggest might be the one place the viscount will think to look. Either that or your mother will know a destination you would be familiar with."

"What, besides my name, do you know about me?"

Maggie figured once he learned her name, he would know all the pertinent truths about her life. She didn't appreciate the idea her life was such an open book for anyone to read.

"You risked your life to escape matrimony with Lord Abernathy. A courageous feat if I do say so myself. Is he such a deplorable man for you to brave a snowstorm? Wouldn't marriage be better than death?" Jasper asked.

His tone told her he did know the answer to that question.

"Yes. I'd do it again. Marriage with that man would feel as if I died then ended up in hell."

Maggie was surprised at the lift of his eyebrow. The look clearly told her he questioned her sanity.

A few moments later, he sat up. "Glad to hear it. Tells me I'm not risking my reputation for a woman who doesn't understand who this man is. From everything I've heard about him, you are correct in your assumption."

"I am?"

"The modiste will be here," Jasper pulled out his pocket watch, "in thirty minutes. As I said she will take your measurement. Whatever clothing is commissioned will be up to Jason. My brother will be the only one who knows where we are. If I deem it necessary, I'll have him send the gowns along with the other fripperies to a neutral address. We have friends in both Ireland as well England who will discreetly see to their delivery. If not…they will remain in Glasgow until we return. We will return. When is the only question."

"When we return? You think we will never be able to come home?" Panic hit. How long was she going to be with Lord Kenworthy? "My sisters…" This was her mother's fault. Anice orchestrated this match. Even touted it as a love match. She might not ever see them again. "I can't." A pause. "I have to. Don't I?"

"Not until the viscount gives up on you. When he does, he will find a more suitable…or should I say…biddable bride. When that occurs, we will be able to return. Until then we will need to remain incognito."

"That could be months…"

"Perhaps."

"What's in it for you?" Maggie questioned. "My sisters? I won't see them for months."

"Will not know if you survived this escapade until it is over. There is nothing in it for me except the fact I couldn't live with myself if I failed to take care of you."

"I can't…" she repeated. Thought she said the words to herself.

"If you don't wish to find yourself the viscount's wife, you must keep the secret from your sisters. There are no other viable options. If I knew without a doubt your mother would not discover your whereabouts if you sent your sisters details, I would allow the communication. This is something you will have to live with if you wish to remain single. Remember the alternative." Again, his steepled fingers touched each other. "I can allow you to write to them through me then through Jason. With the knowledge that I will read all your letters. You will not be able to tell them where you are at any given time."

"Oh…my…" Maggie was beyond herself, her anxieties seemed to escalate. All Lord Kenworthy told her made sense. He did understand her problems along with her fears. Seemed to understand what type of man Abernathy was. Then… She asked again, not believing his first answer. "What's in this for you? Everybody wants something for the trouble they go to. You can't be that selfless."

He sat up, forearms on his massive thighs. "Guess, I felt as if I was in need of adventure. My life was…boring."

~ * ~

Two weeks later they sailed into Dublin in County Kildare. Jasper penned off a quick note to Jason, telling him they were safe but didn't apprise him of his location. During the weeks of travel, Jasper decided that Jason didn't need to know where they were either. He sent along a letter from Maggie to go to her sisters. He read it through. She said nothing of their travels. About all that was mentioned was that she was happy. Pleased that she was not married to Lord Abernathy. Told her sisters not to worry about her. She was in good hands. Maggie didn't even mention his name. He was relieved. In another week he would apprise Jason of an address he could write to if or when Lord Abernathy gave up on his search. Jasper hoped the man would find another woman he would deem suitable to be his bride.

"We're getting in that carriage again?" Maggie whined.

Her eyes were swollen. Smudges streaked the undersides. Exhausted, she didn't want to do anything except sleep. She'd told him numerous times. He ignored her statement.

Guilt had become Jasper's middle name. He admired her. So far, Maggie had been a semi-decent traveling companion. Jasper couldn't blame her now. They'd been on the road or the Irish sea for two weeks. With a few layovers, they'd been traveling nonstop. He was tired too. Fatigued to be exact. They weren't through with their travels.

"Only a few hours. No, you cannot ride." Jasper held up his hands. "I understand. Riding in the carriage makes you sick to your stomach. If you ate something in the morning besides sugar, you might fare better."

"If you weren't such a food snob."

"I'm not a snob. I eat healthy."

"Fruit on your porridge. No honey."

He made a face. "Smart mouth," he said, his voice soft.

Maggie crinkled up her forehead. "You need to live dangerously for a change. Eat something that makes you feel good."

"Seems I am riding with danger. I am escorting you. Risking life and limb to keep you safe from the detested Lord Abernathy." Jasper was having more trouble each day keeping his hands from her and to himself. "We can't ride outside the carriage. Don't wish to be recognized. We are going to Nass. Only a few hours from Dublin. I'm hoping we won't have to go anywhere else. I've a cottage. Hired a few servants who live in a small house behind the bungalow."

"Earlier you mentioned Paris. That would be a treat. Never been to any part of France. Abernathy would never search there." She lowered her lashes before looking at him as if to see his reaction.

"Don't forget your Lord Abernathy has spies. Men who will do anything for the coin he offers. He will be looking at all the ports for us. While he might not begin with Dublin, he will, in time, look to Ireland."

Jasper felt a headache coming on. He rubbed his temples wishing Maggie didn't have an answer or a question for everything. He'd yet to tell her the ship's manifest listed them as married. They were now Justin and Maeve O'Neill. Her reaction to this bit of news was why he was putting off telling her. He didn't know how she would take the new information. To change this bit of a lie was too late.

"Is that why you registered us with false names? Are we a pretend couple? You gave us both the same last name. I looked over your shoulder. Why is that? Don't keep secrets from me." She waggled her finger at him.

As they walked to the carriage, she was eating the last few bites of her glazed donut, licking her fingers as she seemed to wait for an answer.

It was her third. He wasn't counting. Perhaps he was. He didn't intend to say anything. After he helped her into the carriage, he settled himself on the cushioned seat across from her. This was the second week in January. They'd been on the road since Christmas day. He let out a small sigh of complete exasperation.

"You've every right to complain. Promise I won't say anything again. You're tired. As am I. Tonight, we can relax. I'll explain my thinking when you're in a better mood. Maybe you should finish off the pastries. Sugar always helps your disposition."

"Together? You won't be going out for the evening? You will stay with me? Maybe we could have a glass of wine then a nice meal." Maggie rubbed her hands on her gown, smoothed the skirts along her legs.

"Can you cook?" Jasper asked while he thought the part about a nice meal in a real dining room sounded better than nice. If she couldn't cook that wouldn't happen unless he left to bring back food. His hired cook wasn't going to be at the cottage until tomorrow. He did need to visit the local pub. Information abounded with the locals.

"No. Can't cook. Can boil water for a cup of tea. Read a recipe if there is one. Never found a need to learn how to make my meals. "Can you?"

Inside he was laughing at her forlorn expression. "No but I can bring food from the local pub."

He should see what the modiste in Nass was like. If she was any good, he would buy Maggie a few new things. He was getting tired of seeing her in the three gowns that fit her. She needed more underwear. The seamstress in Glasgow brought her a high-necked virginal nightgown. He'd been disappointed when she no longer wore his nightshirt. Though…every night, she curled up in his too-big-for-her robe. He enjoyed seeing her wear the oversized robe. She always looked warm as well as comfy. He'd been tempted to join her. To bring her into his arms.

"Out for the evening?" he asked for the moment, uncertain where she was taking this. "Not tonight. Though…if he felt…she was too damn pretty. There were times he had to get away from her.

"I don't…"

He did go out when they were in London. Visited a few men's clubs. Saw some friends he'd not seen for years. Went out because he couldn't stay in her proximity without taking liberties she might not wish to give. He kept his distance, telling himself she was not his to claim. She had no idea why. Now, there was nowhere for him to go except a small pub on the outskirts of the village. The cottage they were going to was just outside the town of Nass. He would be alone with her for far too many nights.

"I won't be going out every evening." Jasper paused while he tried for a means to make his staying easier for both of them. "Did you miss me?"

He knew what answer he wished to hear. She wasn't going to stroke his ego. Many times, she told him he was far too arrogant. Maggie had a resounding point.

Maggie snorted. He loved it when she forgot her manners. The unladylike sound never failed to please him. Made her seem all the more real. He never wanted a stilted, oh so, proper woman. Needed a woman with spirit. Jasper discovered in their time together, he missed the imperfections of living. The women he'd gone out with before her were always too tied up in themselves to do anything impulsive or real. With Maggie, she was Maggie. Not some ill-conceived version of what she expected him to want. He'd never known a woman who challenged him in every conceivable way.

Maggie tested.

Questioned.

Dared him to be better…different.

"Why would I miss you? We've been together so much. I know what you're going to say before the words pour from your mouth. Can read your every thought." Maggie looked outside. The day was unseasonably warm even though there were numerous clouds in the sky.

The devil, he hoped she didn't know what he was thinking. "You do miss me. Tonight, you can tell me whatever you wish. We can talk about your sisters… I will tell you why we now have the same last name."

She waved a hand in the air stopping him. "All we've done is talk about me along with my sisters…my mother also. I want to learn about

Jasper Kenworthy. What makes him tick. You've not said a word about yourself. Who are you? What is it that has you protecting me? I still don't understand why you up and left Scotland for a woman you met a few hours before you abandoned your home. Don't get why you are still protecting me. Now when I'm safe and sound in a small cottage in Ireland, you could leave me there. Go home…or…is that what you're planning? Live the rest of your life as you wish."

He closed his eyes thinking about her questions. That night after she buried her nose beneath his jacket, he was lost. Couldn't tell her that. After a longer pause. "Imagine if I knew, I would tell you. No, Maggie, don't get anything like that in your mind. I would never leave you here alone to fend for yourself. Despite all our precautions, Lord Abernathy still might find you. Don't wish to discover you tied to that man for your life."

Jasper understood his brother left at the same time for Edinburgh hoping to lead Abernathy on a false trail. After that he was going to the continent. From there Jason hadn't decided where he would travel. Thought he'd always wanted to visit Amsterdam again. He would make up his mind when it became necessary.

From that point until they rolled up the long road to the cottage, Maggie was quiet. She alternated between closed eyes and watching the landscape. Jasper found he enjoyed silence with her. Didn't need to have a conversation all the time. He liked listening to her breathe, watching the gentle movement of her breasts. With her by his side, Jasper found he didn't brood so much. He laughed at her wit. She was, as he said earlier, a smart mouth. She didn't just criticize him with her sarcasm but also blasted herself. There was nothing about this lovely woman Nelson Abernathy would ever find enjoyable. Jasper shivered at the idea of her crazy voice along with her wit being crushed. Silenced forever. The spirit he was coming to adore vanquished. The light snuffed out. He would never allow that man close to her.

Maggie wasn't the only person who'd heard rumors of Nelson's depravities. He was not a nice man. While Jasper didn't think he would treat a wife as callously as he treated his mistresses, Jasper remembered his cousin Gracie. Her betrothed murdered his wives. Murdered them for their inheritance. Gracie was saved by Fletcher Murray. Fletcher married Gracie. They were the happiest couple he knew. Well…all the Murrays seemed content…ecstatic over their wives as long as they weren't at the family tennis courts.

Jasper wasn't ready for marriage. If he was, before they left on their way out of Scotland, he would have visited the little church where Fletcher married Gracie. Would have consummated the marriage Christmas day. Maggie would never have agreed to something so bizarre. She was still reeling from the close call with the man she detested enough to risk her life by running out into the cold of a winter's night.

Marriage to a perfect stranger.

He was arrogant enough to believe marriage to him would be far better than being wed to Lord Abernathy. He laughed, catching her attention. Unable to help himself, he grinned at her. Reached out to touch her nose with his fingertip. Her expressive features always caused a hitch in his breath. Her brows drew together. She wasn't trusting the gesture. Needed to see beyond his impulse to touch her.

"Penny for the reason you're laughing?" Maggie asked that tiny smirk on her face that showed the dimple he noticed the first night he saw her blossom. If she'd allow him the intimacy, he would brush his lips across both dimples. In order to see both, she had to have a full show of white teeth grin.

"You wouldn't think it funny. Besides, the reason is not worth so much as a penny."

"Try me." Maggie swept loose hair away from her face. "I'm all ears. Willing to listen to any nonsense. I'm bored."

She tempted him in every way a woman could tempt a man. He could never tell her how much she was beginning to mean to him. Her protection was foremost on his mind during the day as well as into the night. "Another time." Jasper dismissed her with a wave of his hand. He didn't want her to know how she got to him with just a snort.

"Coward."

"True."

He was willing to admit to fear Where Miss Maggie MacRae, now Mrs. Maeve O'Neill, was concerned he was more a coward then she would ever realize. More than he'd ever admit. Where she was concerned, he could never give her power over him. To tell her about his feelings would do just that.

They were headed up the drive to the small cottage. The building was exquisite. It wasn't a townhouse or a stately mansion though the cottage captured his imagination. Before he rented it, he saw a drawing of the exterior. Two stories with what must be an attic with windows topped it off. Jasper was eager to live there with Maggie.

When he turned back to watch Maggie, her forehead was pressed on the window, watching her new home come into view. After their conversation during the ride, he was going to disappoint her, his new bride. Wasn't going to announce that bit of news until there were glasses filled with wine along with food on the table.

Unexpected news was always better on a full stomach. With Maggie, he thought that perhaps he should serve dessert first. A little sugar for her would lighten the mood. Give him a head's up advantage. The carriage came to a stop in front of the house. His driver stood at the open door; a step placed in front. Jasper got out first then helped her down. When he turned to start up the walkway, three people walked from the interior to greet them, two women and a man.

With Maggie's hand tucked around his arm, he escorted her to meet the people he hired. He knew all their names. Just not which name belonged to which person except for Clancy. He was the butler, the only male.

"Clancy. Clancy is our butler," he motioned to him. "Would you do the introductions? I'm afraid I don't *ken* which woman is Kathleen and which is Dana."

He nodded, "Here we have Kathleen Kelly the downstairs maid and her sister, Dana Kelly. She is the upstairs maid. Tonight, she will serve as your cook. Since we knew you were arriving this afternoon, we made certain you would be treated to real Irish fare along with bottles of Guinness. In case the lady doesn't appreciate good beer, we also have a couple of bottles of Merlot. There is water steaming for baths. We've taken the pleasure to place the tub in the master suite. Even though you said you would not be sharing a room."

"Thank you. When will dinner be served? I think I hear my wife's stomach grumbling. Seems she has an insatiable appetite." He caught her look of chagrin. Threat of retaliation shone bright in her eyes. Was pleased by the crease lines on her forehead coupled with the pursing of her lips.

"I am hungry," Maggie mumbled, her voice soft as she seemed to try to read what was on his mind. "You don't have to announce it to our help," she scolded. "You know I'm most always famished."

"Come along, Maeve. A bath sounds wonderful to me after the long days on the ship then the ride here. If you're in agreement, we can share." Her grunt delighted him. He would have to remember to ruffle her innocent feathers more often. She was so much fun to tease. Though, if he thought she would share, he wouldn't waste time. He'd be in the tub with her.

The best thing for this moment was to leave her to her bath. He shouldn't step on her toes, figuratively speaking. Correspondence was waiting for him. Business that Jason sent to him and he received in London. Jason told him he'd remain in Amsterdam only long enough for Abernathy to follow his trail. If Abernathy did shadow him, he would continue south to Belgium. The papers that claimed they were married needed to be sorted through. The good reverend assured him they were in no way legal and binding. He also assured him no one looking at the papers would notice the difference. When this was over, it would be easy to claim them false. If not, an annulment could be had since the marriage would not be consummated.

The thought of either dissolving the pretend marriage or seeking an annulment twisted his stomach into a tight knot. He escorted her to the room they wouldn't be sharing. Again, he felt a strange coil to his insides. As promised the tub was in the back of the room near the fire. Dana or Kathleen must have placed two towels by the hearth to be warmed by the heat. While they were both looking around the room, all three of his new servants carried buckets of steaming water for the bath. For the duration, Jasper watched the various shades of color flitting across Maggie's face. She was embarrassed. There was nothing he could do to rectify what was happening.

He stepped up to her. Bent close so his voice would flutter close to her ear. "You've nothing to worry about. I won't be watching…or sharing. I've correspondence to see to downstairs. The hot water is all yours. When you finish come join me. I'll be in what appeared to be an office when we walked inside." Jasper felt the shiver when he brushed the tip of his tongue on her ear. He didn't know why he provoked her. He just couldn't resist. He did understand his motive. He wanted her. "You must try not to flinch when I touch you. We are a married couple. You need to act like a wife. A wife would lean into me seeking more of the same."

"Oh!"

Her eyes, wide and large with silver threads slipping through the deep green seem to flash warning signals at him. He danced away from her. His petite Maggie appeared as if she wished to punch him where the jab would hurt the most. In this environment with all three servants within listening distance, she couldn't reply.

"I'll await you downstairs. Tomorrow," he paused watching as she fiddled with the top button on her gown, "we will see to an increase in your wardrobe."

He heard the clearing of her throat while he headed for the door. "After we return, I'll see that you are reimbursed for all that you've spent. If I haven't said as much, I'm thankful for all you've done for me."

When he turned, he saw something different in her eyes. Something he didn't yet understand. Wished he could read her mind. "I will keep a running tally. Gifts, though, are not included in that count."

Jasper expected a snort at that comment or some type of loud guffaw. He didn't hear anything. She'd turned her back on him. Was shrugging out of her gown. Alabaster flesh showed above the corset. The gown hit the floor. He was frozen to the spot as she continued undressing. She thought he'd left the room.

Stuffing a huge gulp of air into his lungs, cramping him, he strode from the room. Heard the gasp from her when she realized he'd not left before she was half unclothed. His imagination didn't do her justice.

His pants were too tight.

By the time he reached his office he had his breathing along with his heart rate under control. His cock still acted on its own, throbbing beneath too tight fabric confining the blasted part of his anatomy. He sat down behind the desk. Pulled documents from his briefcase. Settled on the marriage certificate. When Maggie signed the document, she thought to be setting her name on the ledger to the hotel room they shared the first and only night in London. Instead, it was the marriage certificate. Her real birth name, Maggie MacRae was written on the line next to his name. The pretend certificate of marriage. As he stared at the certificate, the documentation appeared so real his head swam. Who would ever believe this a forgery?

If his twin knew about the reality of the document, he would call him all kinds of a fool. Jasper had seen no other way around her problems. They needed proof of marriage when Lord Abernathy found them. He would discover their whereabouts. There wasn't one doubt in Jasper's mind. When was the only question. They would not consummate the marriage. That fact would give them a good reason for an annulment. Even though he didn't appreciate the thought, Jasper had to give her a way out of a marriage that was supposed to be pretend but might not be. Again, that same strange sensation grappled his insides at the thought of an annulment.

"Sir?" It was Clancy. A bottle of Guinness sat on a tray his man held. "We are having shepherd's pie for dinner. Hope you like the meal. As you asked, Dana baked a lemon pie. The lemons came into Dublin a week ago from the Amalfi Coast. Believe your wife will enjoy the tart with the sweet."

Jasper laughed at the explanation of the lemon pie which could describe Maggie who was both tart as well as sweet. When he met her, she wore lemon scented perfume. His mind reeled back to that moment. Jasper didn't ever think he could forget the second she bounded into his arms. Stuffed her nose to his chest. He'd been smitten ever since. He'd caught the unique scent of her, now he needed to taste her.

"I'm certain Maeve will enjoy the pie more than the dinner. Her sweet tooth is remarkable, insatiable as is her appetite. How she stays so slender is beyond me. Though I'm not complaining. Maeve would be a delight no matter what form she possessed. Did you include some vegetables in the meal? Carrots or turnips would do fine. Some greens of some sort. She needs to get some balance in her diet." He needed to take care of her. See to it that she eats right. The devil, he sounded like a parent not her husband. The last role he wished for in this charade was one of father.

Hands settled behind him, Clancy bowed. "As you wish. I'll relay the message to Dana. Your cook should be here tomorrow. Though Dana would love the position if the other person doesn't work out to your liking. I'm certain she can find some greenery to add to the meal."

Jasper needed to keep his mind focused on the present. The words he would be telling Maggie after she finished with her bath stuck in his head. He tapped his fingers on the certificate of marriage. He wasn't certain how well she kept a secret. So far, she'd been untested. There had been no challenges as of yet. She seemed to except the fact she was now to be called Maeve O'Neill. When he met her, she had no trouble taking on the name of Tessa Sterling.

Time would tell.

He felt her presence before he looked up from the papers cluttering his desk. It seemed his thoughts jumbled up his mind more than the papers on his desk. He held up the beer. "Wine or beer? Clancy left an open bottle on the tray a little earlier. Said it was the best Merlot he could find in all of County Kildare."

Maggie fluffed her skirts before sitting on a chair in front of his desk. "I'd prefer wine. A big glass."

At the sideboard she found a large snifter that was used for brandy. "You can fill that up to the top. That should do for a start. I find there have been so many changes in my life, I'm having trouble dealing with the simplest. You need to tell me all the truths you've kept from me before all my nerves snap."

"You trying to get muzzled?" he asked smiling while he watched the expressions dart across her face that was now a delightful shade of rose. "Do the tops of your breasts turn the same color?"

He was delighted when the color darkened. She would have some type of retort. He should keep his thoughts behind his teeth. He had no business asking such an intimate question.

"Believe you are overstepping. Even if I knew, I would never tell you." She sipped the wine. Over the rim, her dazzling green eyes studied him. After the first taste, she gave this breathy little sigh that sent his body humming. She closed her eyes taking in another sip. "I don't know. I've never looked."

His bark of laughter made her frown. "I would look for you. That would be a delight to this man's senses."

He was waiting to feel the slosh of wine on his face. Feel the drops running downward to stain his white shirt. The tart part of her personality would never allow him to get away with saying something so provocative without retaliation.

"You're still overstepping. Though…you have put up with a lot from me. If it helps me get through this night, I might consider getting drunk. The morning after is too harsh though." She paused while putting a bit more of the wine between her lips to swallow. She closed her eyes while it seemed she rolled the liquid around in her mouth.

While he watched he didn't say anything. Couldn't, he found

himself mesmerized. Maggie looked as if she had more to say. "If this didn't taste so good and if the wine wouldn't be such a waste, I would enjoy tossing it at you. You thought that though. Didn't you? I could tell by the look in your eyes."

He leaned forward, grinning widely. "Yes, however, be assured that I would retaliate. We would both be wet with the merlot."

He groaned at his words. She wouldn't understand what he meant. He would want to taste every drop that landed on her. Sip. Savor. Devour her most fascinating, precious parts.

To his surprise, Maggie looked startled by his confession. "You would? Retaliate? Make me wet?"

Jasper groaned again.

"You are usually such a gentleman. Imagine I've gotten used to the man you wish to portray not the one you are. In truth." She sucked in a bit more of the red stuff. "I've thought you to be a bit of a prude. A killjoy would never…"

"Not a prude. Never that. Just thoughtful. I bide my time. Don't react without thought. Wait for the perfect opportunity." *The opportunity to pounce.*

"Brooding."

"Never."

"Gloomy," she retorted.

"I've been called worse by my brother. He can get away with a more decadent lifestyle. He's the heir apparent, you know. While I've all the responsibilities, he plays to his heart's content. I must work to my heart's content. Something like that." Jasper understood what he said didn't quite sound the way he meant the words.

"I'm supposed to feel sorry for you?" Instead of a snort, she let out a small giggle then a hiccup. "Oops." She covered her mouth.

"Smart mouth," he muttered under his breath smiling at her. "I'd like to see you muzzled. Enjoy the giggles. Wish to hear what will pop out of your mouth next."

"I've been called worse," Maggie spoke the words yet the shadows creeping across her face told Jasper she said the truth.

She had been called worse. He was certain the fine Lord Abernathy, her fiancé, spoke those words. He wished to change the subject. "Shall we get down to the important facts of this meeting? For now, you will listen. When I finish, you may ask all the questions you like. Don't want to be interrupted. Might forget all that I wish to tell you."

"What if I forget a question?"

He sighed. Clasped his hands together while he leaned on the desktop. "Are you going to make this more difficult? If you think you will forget to ask something, by all means stop me in my tracks. This might take longer than I intended. Would enjoy getting on with more pleasant stuff than this."

Maggie's smile lit up her face. Her twin dimples flashed. She played him. He understood that. Would always allow her to get away with teasing him. He didn't understand why, but that side of her stimulated all his senses. He did enjoy playing word games with her.

Jasper accepted the fact she would do as she pleased. "To begin," Jasper handed her the marriage certificate. "Look it over. Tell me what you see." He seemed to be holding his breath while he waited for clarification.

Her brows drew together as she read. Caught her bottom lip with her teeth. The clock ticked...ticked...ticked... another beat of time passed. Shaking her head, "I didn't sign this." Maggie handed the document back to him. "Why is my name on it?" The outrage in her voice didn't go unnoticed. "That's my real name. Not this Maeve O'Neill I'm supposed to be."

"You did." Jasper tapped on the place where he saw her name. "This is your signature. I witnessed you write your name here."

"When?" Green eyes sparked with anger. He felt as if she clobbered him with the harsh impact of her gaze. "I'm not married to you! Can't be!"

"The night we stayed in London. At the hotel when I told you your signature was required to have a separate but adjoining room." He stopped to watch her. Jasper needed her to believe the signature was real as was the document. "This paper says we are man and wife. You. Me. Married forever. I won't grant a divorce." So far, an annulment was possible. They took years and years.

"You lied to me." In a muted voice, she spoke again. "I never said I do." Unblinking, she still stared at the piece of paper. After she looked, a tiny half-smile appeared on her face the one that showed off just one of her dimples but left the other smooth. "Guess you're not such a prude after all.

What does it mean? Knowing you, I imagine this is not real. Though it does look that way. Doesn't it? What are you planning?"

It's a pretend document to keep you safe from your real fiancé. "If you recall, before you signed this," he tapped on the paper, gazing at her he needed to keep the sincerity in his tone, "the concierge asked you if you wished to have a separate room. You said I do. The concierge was a man of God I hired. This will keep you safe from Abernathy until something else can be arranged."

That piece of news left her appearing a bit dumfounded. Maggie's smile vanished. She stood up then sat down as if her legs gave out. "If it's going to keep me safe then I can go home. What would it matter? I'm married to you. He can't touch me."

"No!"

"Why not?"

"So much for the telling from the beginning to the end. You understand we've not consummated the marriage. Lord Abernathy's advocates can probably tear this document to shreds in a court of law. If we weren't living together, there would be no basis for the marriage. Those are only a couple of reasons as to…why not."

"Why go to the trouble? You don't have a reason to bed me except for this document. You kept your hands to yourself that night." The puzzled look she slanted him told him she might listen now.

"In Nass as well as the surrounding area, we will be known as the O'Neills, Maeve and Justin. No one except our three servants will know that we aren't sharing a bed. They won't say anything. I'm paying them too well. If your Lord Abernathy gets close to Nass, the different names might throw him off our scent. Maybe not. It's a chance we will have to take. When this is finished you will be able to ask for an annulment of the marriage. That might take many years. You would need to be prepared to wait."

"We sailed here under those names. I looked over your shoulder. Saw you write them down on the manifest. Thought that a brilliant move on your part. Didn't understand the breadth as well as the scope you were plotting."

"Brilliant?"

"Don't let it go to your head. Your brilliance seems to be waning. You and I don't want to be married. We hold a certificate that says we are.

What is the truth? You said a man of God wed us? Wouldn't that mean we are man and wife?"

"Smart mouth," he muttered, his voice soft. He loved her sass. "During our stay here…whenever we are out and about…we will have to appear to be a happily married newlywed couple. You will need to learn how to act the part." He paused only a moment to clear his throat. "You need to enjoy my touch. As it is now, most every time I touch you, you flinch away from me as if you abhor me."

"I get to be out and about? How novel."

"Smart…"

She held her hands out. "Sorry. That was uncalled for. I understand why you haven't allowed me outside your supervision. Though I would enjoy a bit of freedom. I'll be Maeve O'Neill gladly if I can go for a ride or talk to someone…anyone…outside this cottage. Maybe go shopping in Nass. I've never been so isolated from people. Even when Anice didn't allow us friends, we still talked to people. I had my sisters. Three of them. We were the best of friends. Now I've only you."

"With me, you can go into town. Don't want you going alone. Tomorrow we will visit the seamstress in the little village. You do need a few more things to wear."

"I can't argue with that."

~ * ~

It didn't take Nelson's sleuths long to find the trail from Glasgow to Edinburgh then on to Amsterdam. At the onset of the investigation, Nelson had been pleased with their work. Pleased until he discovered the man was Jason Kenworthy who they followed. At one time, he thought he would have his fiancée back before a week was up. True, the man traveled with a woman who matched the general description of his fiancé. Jason and Jasper were twins. Few could tell them apart. What gave the couple away was the girl he was with. She didn't act anything like Maggie. The woman was not innocent. She had the audacity to offer herself to one of his detectives. That act so stunned his man, he couldn't talk for a few seconds.

Nelson wished to strangle the incompetent people who served him. They were all idiots. *Bampots* each of them. He turned on his newest mistress. Pulled her to him. His kiss wasn't brutal for a practiced whore. Nevertheless, he thought of Maggie beneath the onslaught of his kiss. He wanted her to feel his pain. The lady in his keeping moaned softly. Her nails bit into the flesh at his neck. Scraped. Drew blood. He wanted to push inside her now! Didn't need to seduce. The woman was always ready to receive him. She was a whore.

"Is that all you've got, Nelson," she murmured against his lips, biting then licking. "I would accept a gift if you're inclined. I'll even take you into my mouth. Suck until you come all over yourself. You can spill your seed on my belly."

"You want more? I want you to pretend you're her, my Maggie. What would you like?" He questioned even though he knew he would spend the rest of the night taking her in as many different ways he could think of. Right now, he wanted her up against the wall, her lily-white legs wrapped around his flanks. "I'll give you whatever you want. Nelson ripped her gown down the front. Her breasts were bared. The tips hard pebbles that begged for him. He tugged on her legs, spread them apart. Wrapped them around his flanks. His mouth clashed against hers, devouring. Their tongues battled, lashed against each other. Rubbed. Tasted. She moaned into the dampness of his mouth.

"Hmmm…give it to me rough, sweetheart. None of this gentle stuff," she purred, her hands pushing at his frock coat until the garment fell to the floor. Tugged on his shirt until it came loose, the shirttails dangling behind him. She slipped her hands beneath his pants, holding him. Squeezing. Up then down. "Hard. Fast. Want you deep inside me now." She unfastened his britches.

He ripped at the rest of her undergarments. The pantalettes she wore split down the front. His mouth closed over her breast. Sucked. Sucked more. Harder. Bit. She arched. He held her thighs while he walked to the wall. Pushed her against the hard wood. Thrust inside her. She climaxed. He sent his seed deep inside.

"Whore."

"Bastard."

"Bitch."

He would keep her. He would need this type of release when he was married. Would never get this from Maggie.

~ *~

"It's not natural. I tell you. Those two should be spendin' their nights together," Kathleen said as she made up the bed in the master suite. Plumping the pillows she twirled around the room with one of the cushions against her breasts. Stopping by the bed to place it on the coverlet, she sighed. "They should be sleepin' together. He spends his nights in the other room. Maeve sleeps in here. What do those two think to be doin'? There won't be children if they keep this up."

"We should not be talkin' about where the master and his lady are putting their heads down for the night. Don't want to be dismissed. Where they sleep is not our affair. You've noticed the way Mr. O'Neill looks at Maeve. He's in love with her. He can't keep his eyes from following her wherever she walks. You're right about his leavin' her. She was in that bedroom one night all alone and crying." Dana pointed a finger at her sister. "He's not the type of man to leave a woman in tears. So, what's going on? Maybe we should be puttin' our heads together so as to figure this out. Those two be needin' some firm guidance in the love department."

"Yes, and while he's not ogling her, Maeve only has eyes for Justin. Why aren't they...?"

Clancy joined in with the ladies.

"We need to think of some way to get those two together. They must have had a dreadful argument. She is in tears every night. He is sleepin' without her. We haven't even seen the two newlyweds kiss. Somethin' got to be done to remedy this situation."

"We could set up a romantic dinner for them. If we had candles and wine..." Kathleen said, her eyes dreamy. "He would not want to leave her alone. Wouldn't go off to the pub for the evening."

"The two of you should not be talking about our employers that way," Clancy put in his thoughts. He was busy dusting the room. "We do wish to keep our jobs. We shouldn't be interferin' where we've not been asked." He stopped dusting for a few seconds. Touched his finger to his lips thinking. "A romantic dinner is a good idea. A right fine idea. That's not interfering. We'll be doin' them a favor."

"Mrs. O'Neill asked me to set the fire going in the outdoor patio.

She asked to eat out there tonight. Though when she made the comment, her voice sounded very wistful. I could tell she wanted the mister to eat with her. Wished for his company. She's in love with that man. He doesn't have a clue."

"Maybe she's planning a little hanky-panky with the mister. A bit of seduction here…a bit there," Kathleen said a smile bright on her face. "We can help that along. Make sure something delicious is cooking when Mr. O'Neill comes home for dinner. We'll put candles on the patio. The day is nice enough. Not too cold today. No chilling winds. No rain or snow. It's perfect for the two of them to be eatin' outside in that sheltered area. The fire in the outdoor firepit will keep it all toasty."

"Asked for wine," Clancy continued his smile growing as he seemed to have growing interest in his employer's love affair. Which was not much of a love affair. "Maeve wanted to know if we had any wine. If not, she asked me to purchase a few bottles. She does like her wine as well as her sweets."

"I'm steaming fresh fish for the meal. When you buy that wine, check the market. See if there are fresh oysters. They might need a *wee* bit of help setting the mood. A little aphrodisiac never hurt," Dana offered with a sly smirk. "I always have to make a dessert for Maeve's sweet tooth. Tonight, it's chocolate cake. Got the recipe from the owner of the pub down the road. His wife won't eat anything except chocolate."

"The mister demands we have greens, some type of vegetable. He's such a stuff shirt. She's a free spirit. No wonder they have a few problems seein' eye to eye." Dana's laugh was soft, amusing. "Mr. O'Neill wants her to eat right. Says she would eat only sugar if he allowed it. What do you all think about that?"

"That man is so in love. He would give her anything she wants including all the sugar in the world. What I still don't understand is why the empty bed. They should be working on a baby. Not sleeping in separate bedrooms. This just isn't right. There must be something going on we don't know about." Kathleen had her hands on her hips, puffing air as she finished with the bed. "Then we'd only have to make up one bed each morning."

"Yes, what we need to do is set a romantic stage for the two of them. Wine. A nice dinner. More wine. Flowers. More wine. Food. Chocolate cake. Can't forget the candles for ambiance." Dana peered out the window overlooking the patio. "Too bad there are no flowers to be had."

"Make certain the fire outside is good and hot. We can bring a large blanket for them to share. It will keep them warm. A bit of cuddling might lead to something else," Clancy added while he walked from the room. "Going to run those chores."

"See that there is only one place to sit. The swing is perfect for the two of them. One seat, one blanket, a bit of snuggling will lead to a baby. I swear it will," Dana said with a silly grin. "Those two need to put whatever argument they have with each other aside."

Kathleen grasped her hands together beneath her chin. Thinking for the first time she and her sister had a great idea. "If all goes as planned, maybe the two of them won't be sleeping alone tonight."

Chapter Four

Wistful, missing her sisters, Maggie watched the flames flit in the massive outdoor fireplace. Jasper left this afternoon. Told her he was going into Nass. She told herself not to miss the man. Though she did. Every day since they arrived was much the same. They ate breakfast together if she woke before he left. Today she was lonelier than ever. When she went downstairs to the kitchen to eat, he'd left. Jasper would tell her she should keep busy. Doing what? She always asked. He didn't want her to go anywhere by herself. He was never around to accompany her. To keep busy, she could walk up then down the stairs. How many times could she do that before she was bored to death.

She held her hands out to warm them. When Clancy first told her this afternoon they would eat outside on the patio for dinner, she slanted the butler a quizzical look. He smiled at her as if he had some secret plan. All day the maids had been dancing around her with silly smiles. When she tried to ask the reason, their answers were always vague. Kathleen brought her a glass of wine before a speedy exit. Clancy walked into the small outdoor living space setting the freshly opened bottle of wine on the table. He lit two candles then the lanterns. The patio was heated by a blazing fire. It was comfortable even though the evening would be cold.

The sun would be down in about a half hour. The night would be frigid. The month was January. Maggie could smell snow in the air. Kathleen brought a large quilt from the house along with two pillows she placed on the swing.

"It's too cold. I can't stay out here," Maggie told them, feeling distraught. She didn't wish to discourage the servants. They were so sweet. Obvious they were trying to please her. "To eat out here. I'm going to freeze." She was pouting, wishing she could ignore the food. Her stomach held a differing opinion.

95

"Justin should be home soon. He will keep you warm."

Clancy winked as if he knew something. Tonight, the butler had an answer for everything.

Jasper ignored her this morning. Why would he want to keep her warm? He left before she got downstairs to eat with him. Earlier she walked around the house then down the lane leading to the cottage. By the time she returned her nose was red from the chilling bite of the air.

When she came for dinner, she wrapped her warmest cloak around her shoulders. As she stood near the warmth of the fire, Maggie realized she didn't need the cloak. The patio was protected from the wind on three sides. Was covered by a roof. Lanterns were hung to give the small space light as well as a bit of heat. Kathleen brought several more candles. The light from the sun was growing dimmer. The servants must have brought the porch swing to the patio. Except for the table chairs, the swing was the only place to sit. It had been on the porch now the patio. What were they up to?

The servants had something planned. No doubt about that. Maggie wouldn't mind if the romantic gesture worked. Jasper had been gone all day for the last week. At night he left the cottage to go to the pub so he could drink with his friends. He told her it was to hear news. If Abernathy was anywhere close, he would learn about his presence. By now, Abernathy would have lost interest in her. They should go home so she could have a normal life. What was a normal life? She didn't know anymore.

You're feeling sorry for yourself again. Brooding. That's not your nature. Stop it.

Yes, I am. I'm tired of being by myself. Tired of being alone. Exhausted wondering where Jasper has gone off to.

You want Jasper to pay attention to you. Admit it. I'll shut up if you do. You want him to pay attention to you.

I don't know him.

You want a kiss from this man you don't know. Admit it.

All right. What if I do want a kiss? What then? It isn't like I mean anything to him. The kiss wouldn't mean anything either.

You must mean something. He gave up his regular life to keep you safe. He's still here protecting you.

He did. I should be grateful. I just don't feel all that grateful when I never see him.

Tell him you want to see him. Don't want him to leave every day. Tell him you would like to go with him when he goes off by himself.

I would like that. I can't tell him. If I did, he would think I care more about him than I do.

Damn!

Missing the man was not an emotion she wanted to feel. Maggie didn't know how to interpret her feelings. They were too new, too different. She needed to run these new unsettling emotions by her sisters. They would tell her how to act. When she was first introduced to Lord Abernathy, they had a wealth of advice. She needed a female friend to run her thoughts by. Kathleen, along with Dana while they were nice, would never give her an objective opinion. They fawned over Jasper. Believed he walked on water. Besides, they were servants. A person never aired their grievances with the hired help.

For two weeks while traveling, they'd been together both night as well as day. She placed a finger on her temple, except that one night they were in London. The night she signed her marriage certificate. He told her the document was real. They were married…for real.

It couldn't be.

It just couldn't be. She was married. All her life, she had dreams about her wedding day coupled with the very special man who would make all her wishes come true. This was not what she dreamt of. He said they were married. Jasper never touched her in a way that would claim her as his wife. They never kissed. He escorted her as a gentleman would a lady.

She didn't feel married. What did feeling married entail? A big sigh drifted from her lips. Maggie supposed she would never learn the answer to that silly question since she was already married and didn't know the solution.

Before this last week, loneliness never was a part of her life. While they traveled, they spoke of their lives. Not that much conversation. Maggie didn't have a great deal to talk about. Her sheltered life wasn't interesting until Abernathy barged into center stage. There was enough conversation to keep her from feeling sorry for herself. At home, Maggie always had a sister to talk to. Their happy chatter enlivened each day. Even her mother sometimes provided companionship.

She didn't have a lot of friends. She had her sisters.

Check that. She didn't have any friends. Her mother saw to it that the sisters were never allowed to invite friends home. The schooling they enjoyed was home based, a tutor providing the education.

Two days ago, she heard the servants talking about the fact she didn't share a bed with her husband. Hearing that conversation, a pang of regret coursed through her. What would it be like to have his big warm body sleeping next to her. Maggie enjoyed his scent when she stuck her nose on his chest the day she tried to hide from Abernathy. Liked the hardness of his body when his arms wrapped around her to hold her close. The thoughts sent a tiny rush of pleasure skittering through her. Last night, she dreamt about him kissing her. The dream wasn't very long. All she knew about kissing was a quick brush to the cheek. That wasn't quite true. She remembered Abernathy's kisses. Would rather not recall anything about that man, especially the way he kissed.

With every thought she had about Jasper, she recalled the nice way he smelled. Masculine. Fresh. Winter cold. Clean as new fallen snow. Maggie didn't think he wore a perfumed scent as Lord Abernathy did. The odor that came from Abernathy was cloying. Thick. Repugnant. Sweat based. She cringed as she recalled the few times he tugged her close for a kiss. The way he forced his tongue deep inside her mouth was terrible. She jerked back. Imagined she knew a bit more about kissing than she wanted to admit. What she'd learned at the hands of Lord Abernathy, she hated.

Maggie closed her eyes, dreaming of Jasper's eyes. Those deep brown eyes with a bit of gold rimming them. Sometimes when he stared at her those gorgeous orbs darkened, drew her to him. She thought of the way he studied her as if he couldn't get enough of her. Sometimes those eyes lingered on her breasts. Hips. Mouth. When that happened dragons sent flames pulsing into dark secret places she would just as soon ignore. An ache would well up below her belly. Wetness between her legs suffused her at those times.

On occasion he would touch her arm. Trail his finger along the length to her wrist then back. He held her hands, rubbed his thumb across the inside. Her blood raced. Sometimes he would touch the middle of her forehead when she frowned at him. Would smooth his finger along her eyebrows. Those small touches flipped her stomach. Muscles clenched. She would jerk. The flinch wasn't because she didn't enjoy the way his touch made her feel. The caress always surprised her. Took her off guard to such a degree she didn't know what to say or do. She didn't know how to behave when he became intimate in those ways. He believed her reaction was one of dislike.

It wasn't. Actually, the caress caused just the opposite.

"I see you found the fire."

His words whispered across the back of her neck. He stood behind her. So very close. Flames splintered. The insides of her body leapt to life.

She jerked. Heat from his big body enveloped her. She shivered, wondering at the opposite sensation. "It…it's warm out here. Didn't think it would be. The fire seems to heat the entire space. I," Maggie swished her tongue across parched lips. Once then twice. "I brought my cape. To stay warm. Don't need it. Didn't understand why you wanted to eat out here. You're never home for dinner. I was…surprised. This was your idea?"

She was rattling on about nothing important. Calming down was a necessity. She didn't know how to stop her nerves from splintering.

"Good." Jasper brushed a few misplaced strands of hair from her neck. His lips touched down upon the back of her neck with a butterfly caress. Soft. Intimate. Her feet moved, making her sway. She gulped for air. Her body shivered in response. "A wife would like my kisses…my touches. A wife would wish to have more from me. We spend too much time apart."

He ran his hands along her arms. Up. Down. Up again.

Apart? That was not her fault. Wasn't she just wishing for more time with him? He was always out and about doing important things. Now, he was asking to change that up. "I don't…dislike them."

"I beg to differ. You jump. Tremble. Shiver at my touch. Even now your body quakes as if you would like more distance. I would have you lean into me. Seek the warmth of my body. If I take you to the pub tomorrow, you will need to pretend better. We should practice." His voice deepened; the timbre became husky.

Tonight, she'd not expected to have to defend herself. "I…I jumped because I didn't *ken* you were behind me. Was thinking about something else… You surprised me. That's all. You're never home at this time of day. Wasn't expecting you. Never are around at dinner time." She didn't dare tell him her risqué thoughts. Mention to him she was wondering what it would be like to sleep in the same bed. What his kiss would be like if he claimed her with his mouth. If he would keep her warm in the night. How she would feel if he held her.

"What was that?" Jasper continued his assault on her neck. Touching here then there. Brushing his lips in too many different places for her to remember. His tongue flicked against her ear. Lingered. He bit with gentle finesse that sent heat pulsing within. "What was it you were thinking about? Something pleasant, I hope."

She shivered. Very pleasant. She brought her hands to her arms, wrapping herself up. Hiding from the provoking sensation. Attempted to heat herself from the outside in. Placing his hands on hers, he moved them. "N…nothing." Maggie tried to swallow the huge lump in her throat. Failed. Shivered when his teeth closed on her other ear. Was this the way he would seduce her? Charm her socks off? If so, what he did was working. She felt ready to throw all her clothes away.

"What had you so engrossed in that you didn't hear me walk onto the patio, Maggie?" Jasper turned her. Touched his forehead to hers. Felt his mint scented breath flutter across her. Wished he would kiss her not just tease her with the possibility. "I would know the truth. I find this little conversation intriguing. You had no idea I stood behind you until I touched you. What were you thinking about, Maggie? Was it me?"

Arrogant.

I'll never admit to that.

Maggie closed her eyes searching for something to tell him that might appease his curiosity. She couldn't think of one idea. Her mind was a blank slate. Nothing there except stars along with the way his hands felt on her. Moving from one place to another. Forgetting she had a glass of wine that had already been poured, Maggie asked. "Would you like wine? I would." She stepped away from him, to splash Merlot into the glass that had been set on the table. Found one full of wine. After handing him the glass, she drank deeply of hers, feeling warmth spread through her. Fuzzy. Resolve firming. "Good. This is very good."

Her hand shook when she set the glass on the table. A noise made her turn.

Behind them a smile on the butler's face, Maggie didn't understand. Clancy spoke. "Dinner will be served in a few minutes. I've left a second bottle of wine on the counter in the kitchen. We all…well…we thought the two of you might enjoy privacy tonight. Seems Mr. O'Neill won't be going anywhere. He told us he would be staying for the evening. We were all happy to hear the good news."

Maggie turned to look at Jasper, surprise in her eyes. "You're staying here? Not going out? I won't be alone?"

This was what she wished for. Was so tired of spending the evenings by herself. An uneasy feeling of doom filled her. There had to be a good reason. "Why?" she blurted as if she wished he would leave. "No...wait...I didn't mean anything. I'm happy you're staying. Want you to spend time here with me. Tired of passing the evenings by myself. Don't like being alone."

She appreciated the smile she saw on his handsome face.

"You're happy I'm going to devote the evening with you?" His hand beneath her chin, Jasper floated his thumb across her bottom lip. Once then twice. She followed the path he made with her tongue. Touched his thumb. Jumped. "In that case, I'm also happy to be here with you. We can talk about our future. There are things I need to make clear for you. Situations we need to plan for. Received a letter from Jason this afternoon. Seems your Lord Abernathy discovered the ruse. My twin took the fool all the way to the Netherlands before his detectives realized they were following the wrong man."

"Do...future." Maggie blinked, confused by both the tone of his voice along with the way he was looking at her as if he wanted to devour her. "Do we have a future? As in tomorrow or the next day?" She believed that once Lord Abernathy gave up on her then married someone else, they would return to Glasgow. Go their separate way as if they never knew each other.

"Believe so. Meaning to begin tonight to cultivate the correct deportment. We both must be convincing. I won't have any trouble pretending to covet your sweet little body. Do you want to crave mine?"

The tip of his finger rested on one of her dimples then the other. His lips touched first one then the other. Air slowly left her, rippled from her lips in a long-contented sigh of pleasure.

The brush of flesh against flesh was light, lighter than air. Butterfly soft. Maggie wondered if he did indeed touch her mouth with his. The caress so very easy. Warm. Unobtrusive. No pain. She brought her finger up to test the damp spot. Maggie gasped in a breath of air, Jasper scented air. All of her prickled with heat. Flamed on the inside.

Jasper chuckled, seeming amused by her shock, appearing to understand what she thought, or perhaps felt. "Should we sit?" Maggie asked, her breath a whisper. Eating would prove a distraction for her. Distance from the man who sent her heart to collide against her ribcage. "Don't know about you. I'm famished. Haven't eaten since this morning. Was disappointed when you were gone."

His grin showed even white teeth. He leaned close, so close she caught the wonderful scent of the man. Her breath whispered in with a stagger of longing.

"I'm hungry too." His mouth touched on a sensitive spot. Then another. "Would like to have you for a second course. Maybe the first one."

"What?"

Was this what seduction felt like? Lord Abernathy did some of the same things. She never felt…felt…as if she might jump out of her skin in a good way. Experienced flames that seared. Never felt as if she wanted to touch him in the same places. Never wanted his lips on hers. Not after that first kiss when she thought she would gag. Why did she get the sudden, startling notion Jasper wasn't speaking of food when he told her he was hungry? What was it he said? He would like to have her for a second course. What did that mean?

"More wine?" she asked even though her glass was very nearly full. She drank a huge gulp before plopping more into her glass. Nervous energy abounded. Scattered. Splintered. She always got that way when she was nervous. Didn't think she could sit. Wasn't certain now that the evening began, she wished it to continue.

"Whatever you like. Tonight is about you. Your needs. What it will take to relieve you of your fiancé. How you will respond to me when others are near? Tomorrow evening will be your first test." Jasper nodded to Clancy giving him permission to serve them. He pulled out one of the chairs to seat her.

With a deep breath of what she thought was relief, she sat, her knees knocking together as she did so. Not knowing what she should do, Maggie set her hands on the table. Played with the fork. Picked up the napkin to set the fabric on her lap. The wine she drank slid down her throat as if it had become water. Landed in the empty pit of her stomach in a swirling boil. She was hungry. The dishes were set in front of them. Despite her sudden reservations about the direction the evening was about to take, she was going to eat. From past experiences on the road, Maggie knew they didn't talk when they ate. She meant to enjoy every morsel along with every second of silence. It was what would happen when they were not eating, that sent her nerves into a tight knot.

Second course?

She was disappointed with the first serving which was comprised of green stuff she didn't know the name for. She didn't mind chasing little peas around on her plate. Nonetheless, she didn't relish eating them. January was not the season for peas. Where did they come from? He poured a bit of oil then vinegar on what he called the salad then salt as well as pepper. She did eat half just so she wouldn't need to talk. Set her fork on the table. Was tempted to play with the prongs. Through lowered lashes, she watched Jasper eat all the…greens… There must be a hot house somewhere close to get the lettuce. Maggie learned a long time ago that one did not eat all of each serving. More wine was poured. Clancy brought out a plate with oysters served with some type of seasoning.

Poking one with her fork, she looked at Jasper then back to the little sea creature. She was intrigued. It was rare she turned down new foods. This might be one of those rare times. "They look slimy. Do people eat these? This is supposed to be good for me?" Investigating, she poked one then the other.

"Try it. You're a *bricky lass*." He showed her how to eat it. Slurped the *wee* ocean animal from the shell. "Sometimes it's better not to chew. Courage now. It's dead. It won't bite you."

Watching him she shivered. Her stomach rebelled. This was so…unlike her. Unable to stop herself, Maggie grimaced then made a face at him. She'd not met a food she didn't like or wouldn't give it a try. Not yet. She let the sea animal slide down her throat. It plopped into her stomach with a bang. Stayed there. At least the food didn't squirm. "What's the point if you don't chew?" She reached for another. Did the same. The third time she chewed a bit. The flavor was fine. Enjoyable.

"Aphrodisiac." His grin lit his face. His smile blinded her with his even white teeth. "Preparing you for a few kisses. A kiss or maybe more tonight. Two kisses tomorrow night just for show when we visit the pub. Got to know how to do it properly. Kiss. Don't want people to think I didn't teach my wife how to kiss."

"Kisses?"

He meant to kiss her tonight? Tomorrow night too? Even though she wished for his kiss, a wave of panic jolted her. She didn't know how. Would embarrass herself. He would think her inept. She was incompetent. Clumsy.

"Need to be prepared for tomorrow night." He reiterated while he studied her. "If I kiss you, I don't wish to have you pulling away from me or flinching with the caress. Hope to make certain you will enjoy the experience as much as I will. What do you think? When shall we give this a try? We have all night to experiment with different ways. To practice until we get it perfect."

"Different ways?" *Practice?*

"True, lots of different ways."

"I see." Maggie didn't see anything at all. Needed to stop talking about kissing. "What's an aphrodisiac?" She returned to the first question in her mind. He said the aphrodisiac would prepare for kisses. How? "You need to explain to me how this works. If it's good for me, I should maybe try another."

"Yes, have another oyster." With a grin, Jasper held the plate up to her. Waggled his dark eyebrows at her. "The more the better."

"Jasper…!"

Maggie felt breathless, strung up tight. Nerves splintered. She knew when he wasn't going to tell her something. He let a word drop that would leave her curious then he would remain mute. She disliked that trait of his. For now, she meant to ignore him. The oysters weren't that bad. She downed a fourth.

"Very well. I don't care to know. You can have your male secrets. Probably some stupid love potion men dream up to make a woman do what they want. Bend her to his will. You won't be bending me any which way that's against what I want. Don't feel a thing. Nope. No love potion. You'll have to try to do better."

Wine sputtered from Jasper's mouth. Clear drops of the wine on the plate. On the tablecloth. On his white silk shirt. She caught one on her nose. A dribble ran down his chin. She had the strange sensation she would enjoy licking the *wee* droplet to see how the wine tasted on Jasper. Going against her first inclination, Maggie reached out with her napkin to dab at the drops.

"Was it something I said?" she asked, feeling as if she still missed the point of the oysters. "I don't quite understand what made you spit wine at me."

"Why would you say something so foolish?" he asked deadpan. As if he didn't spew a mouthful of wine across the table at her outrageous statement. "You've no idea what you're talking about. Spouting nonsense." With his napkin, he brushed drops of wine from his pristine white shirt before reaching across the table to swipe at her nose.

She giggled having had enough wine to ease her distress a tiny bit. The wine helped her relax. "When it comes to matters such as this, you're right. I don't comprehend anything. Somehow, I think I touched a nerve. A love potion...is that what oysters are?"

"No nerves here."

Seemed he wasn't going to answer her questions which told her more than a vague answer would. Maggie saw a slight tint of color on Jasper's cheeks. She was pleased she managed to embarrass him even if it was only a smidge of pink. "Foolish? It's what Lord Abernathy would do if he wished to get his way with a woman..." Maggie paused thinking long and hard before she said anything more. Wasn't about to dig a hole she couldn't climb out from "But you don't want to get your way with me. You don't want anything to do with me than is necessary to continue the ruse. The charade we are playing. Are you trying to loosen me up for a good kiss? The good Lord Abernathy tried that a time or two. Didn't get anywhere because I detest him."

"I," he choked. Took a long drink of wine. Filled both their glasses. "I didn't choose the menu." Seemed he went on the defense here.

Pointing a finger at him, she went on to ask, "Who did?"

Maggie wasn't certain. Jasper controlled everything that went on around here. He made it appear that he had his hand in every decision. Now he was claiming innocence in this matter of the aphrodisiac.

"Clancy." A knowing look shimmered in Jasper's eyes. "I'll have to have a talk with the man. Imagine he has an ulterior motive."

When Clancy stepped onto the patio again his smile was wide. Wasn't a bit put off by the frown on Jasper's face. "Rainbow trout, steamed to perfection. Will leave the two of you alone until the next course. Ring the bell when you want me." He set the plates down then made a hasty retreat.

Jasper glowered at his back. Smiled at her. Maggie smiled back. They ate. No more words were said about kissing or aphrodisiacs. Maggie enjoyed the flaky fish along with the steamed potatoes smeared with sweet butter. There were cooked carrots to go along with the meal. When she finished the plate she set her fork down, a wistful feeling. She was replete except for the lack of sugar. They needed to top off the wonderful meal with something sweet. Found she was looking at him with a wistful expression.

Jasper rang the bell as if he knew more food would be coming. Her spirits brightened when she saw the last course. Jasper slanted a bemused smile at her.

Surprising her, Clancy appeared again. Under one arm, he held onto a second bottle of wine. He held two plates of chocolate cake in both hands. "Clancy, you read my mind," he said, clinging to the idea that the butler did indeed make up the menu.

"Dessert. Know the lady of the house likes her sweets. Understand you'd rather not eat much sugar. A compromise." Clancy set the plates on the table. "I'll open the bottle then leave. If you need anything, don't forget to ring."

"We won't need you further tonight. You're excused as is Dana. Assume Kathleen went home earlier." Jasper was watching her dig into the cake with absolute delight. After the first bite, she closed her eyes, savoring the chocolate. A dreamy expression floated across her beautiful face.

"Do you want mine too?" his question was said with a small chuckle never believing she would say yes.

"Can I?" She smiled at him before waving her fork in the air. "No, you go ahead. I wouldn't want to eat your dessert. You need the sugar. Your stuffiness is in direct proportion to the lack of sweets."

The time for eating was coming to an end. She couldn't think of anything more to talk about. Jasper had an agenda she wouldn't like. Maggie was certain of that fact. Both were done eating. Once more nervous energy possessed her, rifled through her. Fiddling with the fork again, she looked across the table to see that Jasper was up and moving toward her. His hand was extended.

A catch in her throat.

Heart racing.

Knew what her hand felt like encompassed by his. Remembered kisses. Aphrodisiacs. Bend her to his will. Men wanted women to succumb. She stared at him. Ran her tongue across her mouth.

His smile was gentle. His eyes hungry. Was reminded he insinuated that he wanted to devour her, wanted her for his second course. What course were they on? Seemed to be way past the second one.

"Should we sit on the swing?" He stood behind her. His hands on her shoulders, massaging. Tickling. Waves of heat vibrated down to the tips of her toes. She was energized. Unnerved. Weak in the knees.

Maggie looked down to see her breasts heaving, moving with agitation. He would be looking there too. "Together?"

Doaty. She was stupid. So, stupid. Could she call that question back? No. He heard. She knew because the sound of his laughter rang in her ears. Of course, he would want to sit on the swing with her. It was the only place on the patio they could sit together besides this table.

"Yes, together. Side by side. Hips and legs touching. I could hold you so your back was pressed against my chest. Would you appreciate that?"

His voice had never been that gentle or deep. He never sounded whiskey smooth to her ears or gruff. "If we have to…"

This time Jasper barked his laughter. Made no move to hide his enjoyment. He bent to press a kiss to the nape of her neck. She felt her nipples tighten. He must be able to see them…almost see them. She didn't dare bend over.

"Come on, I won't bite unless you ask." His amusement was clear. Jasper was adoring her fear. No, he would never enjoy fear. It was her nervousness that amused him. She didn't want to be any man's entertainment. Didn't wish to be nervous.

"I'm just a plaything to you."

She felt outraged. Maggie turned on him, feeling as if all the color drained from her face. Her pointed finger jabbed at his chest. "You don't care about me or Lord Abernathy finding me. You leave for the afternoon. Come back to change your clothes then you're gone all night. I spend both the nights along with the days by myself. Now, you laugh at me because I don't understand what it is you want." Her voice quivered. Shook with pent up emotion. "I'm not liking this situation. Not a'tall." She found the top-lofty expression satisfying.

The appearance on his face changed. He sobered. Rubbed his big hand on the back of his neck then across his jaw. He was thinking. All signs of amusement vanished. Jasper pulled her into his arms. Held her head against his chest while she breathed in the scent of the man. Moisture clung to her eyes as well as her lashes. She sniffed. Realized how foolish she acted. They both understood she was nothing to him. Yet…he did her a great favor spiriting her away from her fiancé. Protected her at his expense. She should apologize for her outburst.

"God, I'm sorry. Thought…thought you were enjoying yourself too. You…" His hand rested on the small of her back, bringing her close. "I didn't mean to hurt your feelings. I love the way you challenge me with your words. You're always thinking one step ahead of me. You keep me on my toes. I adore that. Adore you if you must learn the truth. Want the kisses along with anything else you're willing to send my way."

"No," Maggie spoke into his chest. Her hand rested there where she heard the thunder of his heart, the depth of each breath. "I don't suppose you did. You just don't know what I've been going through. It's been awful. I…" She was still making a fool of herself. Didn't want to let him know her deep feelings. "I don't know anything about men…or relationships."

"Hush now, I mean to spend more time with you. We must show a united front. I'm sorry I haven't been here for you. I plan on changing that." His hand ran along her back, up then down. Again then again. "Hush…" He rocked her. Cradled her as he might a child. Encouraged her when she felt so inadequate.

The movement soothed. Maggie closed her eyes wishing for more contact. She didn't know when it happened. She was coming to care for this man, too deeply. Maybe it was the first time he protected her. Maybe it was the way he chased away her demon…Lord Abernathy. Maybe it was the time she signed her name to the marriage license. She wasn't sure she cared. Maggie just needed to be close to this man. She would take any scrap he wished to give her.

~* ~

Jasper didn't know how he was going to keep his hands to himself. Spend more time with her? The devil! When he looked at her, he wanted her. When he heard her voice even from a distance, he wanted to toss her skirts. When he caught the scent of her, it was all he could do to stop from thinking about all the delightful things he wanted to teach her. Kissing was just the first of many.

Maggie was innocent. If he could keep his hands away from her, she would remain in that state. If he kept his hands away from her, when all this was finished, she could ask for an annulment.

Jasper needed her in his bed. Wanted to make love to her every night for the rest of his life. She was a firestorm in his blood. Because of the distance he kept between them, Maggie believed he didn't like her or even care for her. How could he tell her he stayed away from her because he didn't trust himself to be close to her?

Every night when he sat in the pub listening to the town gossip, he agonized. After he returned home, he would stand over her sleeping form wishing he was holding her, making love to her, exploring all her sweet delectable curves. He would wake up each morning, waiting for her to come downstairs for breakfast. Night after night, sleep eluded him. Somehow, someway, he must come to terms with this infatuation of his. She was innocent. Not one of his usual women. He could not make love to her then leave her in the morning.

The gossip he heard from his servants both terrified as well as eluded him. The people he employed knew they weren't sleeping together as man and wife. If he didn't do something to remedy that, the information would reach other people. Maggie couldn't afford for that to happen. She needed the security of the marriage they pretended. Jasper understood he needed to convince Maggie he should be sleeping in the bed with her. What would happen then was not something he wished to think about.

The question arose as to how he should go about rectifying that huge problem. Sleep with her without taking what he wanted most? Without compromising her. Someday she would find a man who could return her love. He wasn't that man. What he could do was arouse her to the point she wanted him. If he did that, they would both regret his actions when he didn't finish what he started. Would also come to regret their relationship if he couldn't stop. The second choice was to talk to her, explain that they could sleep together without consequences. The notion was ridiculous. He, Jasper Kenworthy, could not be in the same bed with Maggie MacRae and not taste all her beautiful and most precious charms.

You'll have to try. There is no other way to stop tongues from wagging. The two of you cannot remain separated. You are playing a charade. A deadly game. Stop it now. Pay the price. The decision is up to you.

I need to convince her she wants me. Seduce her so she can't say no. What other choice do I have? Maggie doesn't even like me. Has kept her distance all these days. Flinches when I touch her. No other woman of his acquaintance ever flinched from his touch. It's too much to expect that she will accept me into her bed. Sleeping with her is something I must do. If I'm going to protect her, there is no other choice.

Make love to her. you know how to do it right. You'll give her so much pleasure, she'll fall into your arms every night. Teach her. In that case, you might find yourself in a real marriage. You could entertain a real marriage. This pretending is not something to be proud of. A commitment would do you a world of good. You are thirty-two. You need an heir. A man must wed sometime. She is perfect.

The certificate is fake.

She doesn't know that.

If I told her the truth, what would she do?

Perhaps understand why you've stayed away from her. Wouldn't that be better than keeping the truth of your marriage from her?

This conversation with himself was getting him nowhere. His hand firm, he lifted her chin, gazing into the biggest green eyes he'd ever seen. They were darker than usual. Her lashes were spiked with diamond teardrops. Tears he made her cry. All he wanted with her was to make her happy. At every turn he failed her. Even now, when all he wanted was to hold her, she held herself aloof.

His thumb moved with languid strokes across the line of her jaw. "We need to talk, sweetheart. I hope you will listen with an open mind." Jasper watched her flinch. Saw the silver trail of moisture down her cheek. Touched the drops with the tips of his fingers. Tasted the slight salty flavor. "Don't cry. I'll make this better. You'll see. There is no reason to cry. I won't stay away from you if that's what has you so sad."

This was unraveling into a terrible mess with knots intertwining in everything they did.

"Don't see how you can fix anything. This marriage isn't right. We both understand that fact. The biggest problem is with me. I have to be married if Lord Abernathy finds me. The next biggest problem is that you don't want to be married. At least not to me. The funny thing is, I understand," Maggie blurted with a sniff. "I've ruined your life. I'm about to ruin your shirt with my tears. The maids along with Clancy talk about the fact you're not sleeping in the same bed with me. We're not sleeping in the same bed together," she amended with another sniff. More tears fell. "I want to be strong. Don't wish to be a watering pot. Lately, when I'm by myself, I can't stop the tears from flowing. I realize they've heard. That's why this elaborate dinner."

Dear Lord, he didn't know she cried while he was absent from her life. He searched for the best words. "I know this isn't easy. The situation isn't the best for me either. For your safety, we have to make this right. Must stop the servants from their gossip. If they are to speak about us, it should be to tell people how very much in love with each other we are. We must sleep together. Show the unity to our employees that we are going to deliver to the town starting tomorrow. At every turn, we are going to be seen together. We never did go shopping for new gowns. We should start out the day at the modiste. After I purchase a brand-new wardrobe for you, we can go to lunch at the pub which is the biggest source of gossip in the town. We can eat the daily catch or something else. Whatever you would like. No more oysters unless you ask for them."

"You know I don't have funds. I can't…" Maggie was plucking at her skirt. Jasper set his hand on top of hers.

That fact was more than likely what kept them from going to the modiste the day after they arrived as he'd planned. She had no available money. "I'm your husband. Of course, I'll pay for whatever pleases you. I've more than enough groats to purchase my wife's clothing. I know you are tired of the three gowns you came here with. As my wife, you should be dressed to the status. You are a countess."

All the while he spoke, his hands roamed her sweet curves. His body came to attention with each pass of his hands. She was shivering with anticipation. He watched her tongue move across her mouth leaving an inviting trail of moisture behind. The taste, the sight of the wetness invited. His hands settled on her shoulders before exploring the sweet column of her neck. With his thumbs he braced them under her chin lifting to see into her eyes. The muscles of her neck constricted when she swallowed. Her pulse beat hard at the base of her neck. She wasn't averse to his attention.

"We should practice kissing. You know…a wife should understand what her husband likes." Jasper understood he needed to be gentle. He didn't know her experience. Though he expected what knowledge she possessed would have been at the questing mouth of Lord Abernathy. The man, from gossip, had little finesse. Abernathy was said to be rough, sometimes brutal. By the way Jasper felt at this moment, he wasn't certain he could deliver sensitivity. "What do you say? Would you like to try a kiss or two?" Or three, even more if she was acceptable. Jasper steeled himself to have discipline. He always claimed control of every situation. Now was his time to prove he could deliver.

Maggie nodded. "I imagine so. Kisses…practicing would be nice." She touched the cleft in his chin. "What are we practicing for? Is there something you have in mind?"

The answer wasn't enthusiastic at all. He wondered if she was dreading a kiss with him. Though he touched her earlier on the mouth. That kiss was hardly a kiss at all. It was a light brush of his lips against hers.

"If you cannot garner a bit more eagerness for my kiss, you'll dampen my ego. We are practicing so we can learn what each other likes best. So we don't disappoint each other or…the people who might watch us brush our lips together."

Once again, his thumb traced a path across her mouth. Enticed a soft moan from her. A whimper. After that a sigh.

"Don't believe anything can lower your self-esteem," Maggie murmured, dropping her lashes so they fluttered across her cheekbones. She appeared embarrassed by her comment. She was right though.

"Look at me, sweetheart. I want to see your beautiful eyes when I kiss you. The sight will tell me what I need to know."

He ignored her comment about his confidence. Deciding to focus on all things positive. With her, because she meant so much to him, he wasn't at all self-assured.

Her lashes fluttered open; eyes wide, dark, shimmering. The light touch he placed on her lips gifted him with another small sigh. A tiny whimper of what sounded like pleasure. Maggie's hands rose to his shoulders, pushing at his jacket as if she wanted the cloth gone. Her fingers dug into his shoulders.

He thought he might do a bit of exploring before he ended the evening. Needed to see what she would allow if she would say no to him. He would go only so far.

Jasper pulled the big quilt Clancy brought out for their use around her shoulders. He set his hands beneath. With a light touch trailed his finger along her collarbone. He pulled her onto his thighs. Her breasts pushed against him. He touched his mouth against hers again. This time he sent his tongue along the crevice between her lips. She arched. Her hands slipped beneath his jacket. The delicious response everything he dreamed of.

His hands threaded into her hair, pins flying to clatter beneath them on the floor. Her long hair fell in thick strands around her. She whimpered. Jasper was pleased with the tiny sound telling him he was doing this right. He gave her pleasure with a gentle kiss. He would deepen it. Teach her how he tasted. Learn the flavor of his Maggie. Again, then again, he brushed his lips against the softness of hers. They were damp now that he sucked with gentle pressure. Tugged the bottom into his mouth. Nibbled. Licked. Drank of her. The faint taste of wine greeted his endeavors.

"Do you like this, *Lass*? My mouth against yours." Jasper asked as he tried to hold his raging lust inside where it wouldn't get out too soon. Every step he took with this woman needed to be in the forward direction.

Didn't wish to move backward. He touched his lips upon both dimples. First the one on the right then the one on the left.

"Umm…" Her eyes possessed this dreaming dazed expression of a woman who was giving herself to the man she loved. She gazed into his. The green of her eyes reminded him of the deep green of Ireland's rolling hills. Her scent evocative, feminine and pure.

Jasper wished for a real answer. "Umm…," he repeated, his voice softening as he watched her. "What does that mean? A man needs to be positive about what his favorite lady is thinking. Needs to learn what she likes as well as what she might dislike."

Her lashes flew open. For a few beats, she looked confused. Stunned by something he told her. Maggie stared at him with a blank expression on her beautiful face. Jasper kissed the tip of her nose, distancing himself a bit, giving her space to think.

"Yes…" she nodded, her unbound hair falling around her slender shoulder. I liked the kiss. Is that all there is? The kiss was nice…"

"No, that isn't all there is. You say you want more? We can pursue that desire of yours. We are married."

Jasper intended to give this beautiful woman more than nice. She wanted more. He needed more. He meant to give her all she would be able to understand soon. Courting her might be appropriate in this situation. He could pretend there was a chaperone hovering behind him. His lips found purchase around hers. Sipped on the bottom one until the flesh began to swell from his attention. With his teeth, he tugged then teased until all of her full mouth was available. Waiting for more playtime. He ran his tongue along her teeth, touched further inside the sultry darkness. Rubbed, danced when she began to understand what he encouraged. Imitating his advances, he touched his with hers. A groan of pleasure rumbled up from the depth of him. His sex pushed against the fabric of his pants, throbbed with the arousal she brought upon him. She didn't have to do much to have him stiff and needy.

He kissed her hard. Gentle. Sipped. Took from her before giving her more. She pushed against him, her plush, rounded breast touching his chest. Long fingers fiddled with the buttons on his shirt. A few escaped their holes. Her fingers trailed between the gap of the fabric. He moved the sleeves of her dress down her arms. Pressed his fingertip along the tops of her breasts then dipped into the valley between. He needed to look at her. To see the sweet tempting jewels he could only feel.

Kissing could get out of hand too fast. Taking this slower would serve his purpose better. So far she didn't hesitate or balk at his sweet talking. He moved from her mouth to her chin. After that he licked then grazed his teeth along her throat. Stopped at the pulse point that now beat with wild abandon. Sipped on the tender spot until the place took on a rosy color. He discovered another erotic spot that seemed to make her body throb.

Jasper was pleased. He moved back to her mouth. Crashed down hard, tongue gliding inside her, receiving hers in return. This was a bit rough. She seemed to enjoy the hard force of his mouth on hers. He gentled the kiss. Little moans of passion filtered into his mouth. Whimpers. Feminine sighs, light and airy. She responded with unabandoned wildness. Before she was naked in his arms, he needed to come up for air. Needed to ease her before they could talk more.

"Kisses…? Is that all?"

Not all…she wasn't ready for all.

Her damp swollen lips invited more sightseeing. Requested he continue. Summoned his ingenuity. His thumbs ran along her neck. Stopping himself was not easy. "That's enough for now. We can pursue this at a later date." His voice faltered on the words.

They both needed more from each other. Jasper wanted to free himself then let her bring him to his climax. He wanted to show her how she could gain her pleasure by touching herself. The devil, he wished he dared taste her essence. Explore those secret intimate treasures that were meant for him. For her husband. He wasn't her husband. Cold reality slapped him in the face.

"Why? I don't wish to stop. Like the kisses." A long pause followed. She looked bemused, perplexed. Questioned? "I'm…wet?" Maggie sounded surprised at her revelation. After that she pouted, turning her head a bit to the side as if she could convince him to continue.

"If we don't stop, I'll make love to you right here on this swing. Would lower your bodice. Suck your breasts hard. Sweep your skirts around your waist so I can feel all of the most innocent parts of you. That part of you that is, yes, wet and hot, wanting something you know nothing about. I, your husband, would teach you. Would bring you a pleasure so intense it will leave your eyes glazed over," he murmured, caressing her arms, her neck. Unable to keep his hands still he pushed her gown a *wee* bit lower hoping to receive a glimpse of the rounded tops of her breasts. Like to see the color of rose that would define the tips.

"Would that be so bad? Not stopping?" she asked, sounding peevish. "We are married. We can do that. Make love? Right?" Her questions were logical. Ill-advised under the circumstance she didn't know about. "I believe I'd like you to make love to me. Don't know all that entails. You would show me?"

The biggest problem to his answer was that the document stating their marriage date wasn't legal or binding in any way. They weren't married. They weren't husband and wife. He had no lawful claim to her. If he succumbed to his desires, she wouldn't be giving herself to her husband as she thought. Instead, he would be making her his mistress. He lied to her. The lie hadn't been selfish at the time. Protecting her had been paramount in his decision. She couldn't lie worth a damn. If he told her the truth, she would give them away.

Who the devil was going to protect her from him? With every second with her, he became more enamored, more needy. He'd never taken a virgin. Never been tempted. She enticed as well as aroused every hard inch of him.

"Don't want to frighten you," he mumbled the first thought that popped into his head.

By the way Maggie responded to his kisses, Jasper didn't think anything he did would frighten her. Nonetheless, he couldn't take her virginity. If he did, he would never be able to stop with one time. There would be consequences. She didn't deserve... No, she didn't deserve to be treated as if she was his mistress or his whore as some people would name her. Didn't need to worry about conceiving a bastard child. If he had the control, he would withdraw. With Maggie MacRae, he knew control was a foreign word. He wanted to take her. To taste every part of her. Bury himself in her softness. Experience all of her. Withdrawing from the heat of her would never be plausible.

Maggie touched his lips with the soft tip of her finger. She smiled. Her white teeth were straight. Needed to run his tongue along them. Experience the smooth texture. Both dimples flashed in front of his eyes, begging to be kissed. She was shaking her head in denial. "I'm not frightened of you. I liked the kisses. Fascinated by your tongue. The way it danced over mine. Rubbed. What you did made me ache in places..." Turning her head, she cleared her throat, hesitating to say more. "*Ken* there is more to this kissing business. To this husband wife thing. We are married. I want to learn everything a wife should know about her husband."

Guilt swamped Jasper. He alone set the lie in motion. A lie he couldn't take back, at least not yet. He alone was responsible to see the lie corrected. Couldn't act on either. Would be damned forever if he couldn't stop it now. The untruth was something he thought was important...necessary at the time. If she thought they were a married couple, she would never need to act or pretend in front of others. The devil, he was besotted with her. Desired her at every turn. What the hell was he going to do now? He required his twin's presence to badger him about the stupid idiot he was. Needed Jason to guide him down the right path, the prudent one.

"Yes, but…Maggie you're an innocent. I can't just…"

He was blundering now, stumbling over his thoughts, his words, his emotions, what he wanted now versus the future. This situation with Maggie spiraled out of control so rapidly it stole his breath, his mind, stopped his heart for seconds.

"Of course, I'm innocent. I was brought up to give myself to my husband. I would never deviate from that course. Now, I'm married. I'd like to learn what it is we are supposed to be doing in bed together."

More guilt. Shame heaped upon shame. This was going from bad to worse. To drown in remorse seemed to be the direction he headed, sinking fast. He could never tell her the truth now that he lied to her. Couldn't make love to her either. When she discovered she'd done something so horrible as to give herself to a man who was not her husband, she would never forgive him. Maggie would hate him, despise the sight of him.

That very thing would happen. The inevitability boggled his mind. After this charade played out, she would discover she wasn't married to him. Maggie would view him with distaste. Loathing might be more descriptive. All her life she'd been taught that a woman only gave her body to the man who was her husband. This wasn't the way he planned the scenario. He wasn't ready for marriage, even to this beguiling woman who aroused him when he looked at her. Jasper found he was always in a state of arousal when she was near. When he caught her scent in the air. When he heard her mesmeric laughter. He scrubbed his hand down his face.

When he startled himself from his musings, he found she'd unfastened his shirt. Her soft hands rested against his chest. Swept across his flesh. A finger passed across a nipple, touched, retreated, touched again. The dark hair she found there was swirled around her fingers. The little minx pulled that hair, tested. His belly contracted at the sensual tentative contact. Her palm lay flat against him while she opened her fingers. Spread those lovely fingers wide then closed. Experimented at his expense. She bent toward him as if she meant to bury her nose in his chest again. He felt

117

the dampness of her breath whisper. The small caress of her lips. Again, her long fingers splayed across him. With the tip of her tongue, she slid the wetness down the middle all the way to his stomach. His muscles clenched, rippled. Her nails tripped across him. Sending heat straight to the most carnal parts of his body.

Damn, but if she wasn't seducing him. Charming his socks off. There was no slow sweet talking. She chased straight to the point. He groaned, setting her hands aside. "No, sweetheart. Not tonight. You can't understand what you're doing to me. I won't tell you or show you until I understand you're ready for what happens between a husband and his wife." Heat. Desire. Passion swamped him. Inundated every pour. What the devil had he been thinking? Wicked came to mind. If he ever did make love to her, she would be wicked. Naughty to her core.

"When? When will you show me more? I would…aren't you my husband? Aren't we supposed to…"

Never.

You don't mean that? Never? Give her another night of sitting on your lap. After you do that, you won't have a prayer of resisting her sweetness. Her innocent seduction. This little lady is seducing you. She doesn't even know what to do? Can you imagine what sex with her will be like when she has some idea how to proceed?

To his great misfortune, he didn't have any trouble imagining.

You have to sleep with her. One time, that's all it will take. If she's in your bed, you're in hers, no one will question the validity of the marriage. No one will know that I didn't plant myself deep inside her core. What are you going to do when she rolls over in the bed? When she is settled next to you, the heat along with her soft body pressed against you? The length of her leg thrown over yours…or…when you're spooned up tight next to her back? Your sex will be pressed against her soft, wet petals. You will be inside her before you can get your eyes open. No thought…no time to reel yourself in. The deed will be done. Jason will make certain you do the right thing.

I can't sleep with her without touching her, exploring every inch. Learning the soft wet heat between her legs. I'll not be able to control my hands or my lips. Won't be able… I've made this so messy I'll never clean it up. She'll hate me when she discovers the truth. She will. Lies never last forever. Truth has this horrible way of revealing itself. Always at the wrong time.

You told her the servants questioned your marriage. That was meant to get her into your bed. It's very obvious she is willing. If you wish to keep her away from Abernathy, there can't be questions popping up all around you. You need to make this marriage look real even if it's not. If she's not increasing soon, everyone will have more questions.

I should marry her for real.

You don't wish to be wed.

Don't remind me.

Jasper didn't know when he'd ever been more confused. His mind muddled until he couldn't think anymore and was certain his brains were made of straw. His entire adult life revolved around restraint. Since he met Maggie, he found himself spinning out of control. He'd become a whirling dervish of emotions as well as thoughts. His views changed from moment to moment. He could never settle on one notion without reconsidering then changing his mind for another time.

He was doomed.

Fated to a life and existence he didn't want. *I do want Maggie. Want to see her eyes when she climaxes. Want to spend the next days...weeks...months...years... Making her happy. Wasn't that what commitments were about?*

"What are you thinking? You drifted away from me. Am I doing something wrong?" Her soft voice tore him from his musing. Her hand rested on his belly. She was rubbing him, exploring him. Her fingers wove into the hair on his chest. "You are hard everywhere I'm soft. All of you is so different from me."

That I'm an idiot to have taken this on. What she said was so true. "You're not ready for..." What the devil was he supposed to say? By the way she returned his hot open-mouthed kisses, he could honestly say this fascinating woman must have been born ready. She was passionate. Her raw hunger for him sent ripples of heat pulsing straight to his groin. Thinking of her, wanting her, he was steel-hard. If he was honest, there would be no going back from this. After they made love, he would marry her.

"That's where you are wrong. I'm so ready. Want to be your wife in every way. Need to give all my passion to you. All you have to do is show me how. I would learn at your hands. No one else's."

Her small hands pushed on his shirt, moving the fabric down his arms. He had no will to resist. Baring him more completely to her view. If she kept this up, he wouldn't be wearing anything. He would die a happy man.

Everywhere she touched him, he heated to an inferno. When her fingers touched upon his belly, his muscles constricted. He'd never been seduced before. She didn't even know what she was doing. The lady was innocent. Inexperienced. He sat up, moving her hand away for a second time. Desperate for a quick diversion. "Aren't you thirsty? I am. We need another glass of wine."

A slowing down tactic, Jasper knew the words for what they were. Put off going to bed with her. Delay telling her what it was this conversation was supposed to be about. Damn, if he didn't remember. Seemed the necessity for a different topic was taking precedence.

"I'd like one too," she spoke softly, a smile curving her mouth. Insecurity in her voice jerked him. Reminded him he was a cad of the first order. "Yes, please, if you don't want me, another glass would help me sleep. Her eyes watered. The tiny smile could only be described as a watery smile. I'm so...don't know how to say it...so...on edge. Don't believe I'll be able to sleep a wink."

Maggie was getting the idea. Understanding he wasn't intending to make love to her tonight. Not ever. She didn't know the last part. In a few months, Maggie would thank him for his restraint if he lived a few months. Jasper never meant for this to escalate to such a degree she would beg him to make love to her. Never thought her passion would run this hot, this true, so very intense. He wished he could touch her, discover for himself if she was wet...ready for him.

He poured the wine, bringing the glasses back. Sitting down, he rested his forearms on his thighs. Jasper had no idea what to say now. She looked so lost and forlorn sipping her wine. Her eyes clouded with unshed moisture. As she moved, he caught glimpses of the rounded tops of her breasts. He'd done that. Pulled her gown lower. He was an ass. Had no right to begin a seduction that was never going to take place. However, his hands seemed to take on a mind of their own. He made excuses for himself. After all, he'd never been with an innocent...a very passionate virgin who wanted to lose her virginity. To her husband.

She thinks I'm her husband.

In the hearth the fire crackled. Flames licked upward. Needing to move, to put distance between them, he added more wood. Maggie curled up on the swing tucking her legs beneath her as she pulled the quilt around her then readjusted the bodice of her gown. There was so much he needed to say to her.

"I wish you liked me better."

His heart lurched. Recriminations slashed him.

I like her more than I should. "I like you." Liking wasn't the problem raising its ugly head between them. Liking her too much was. He needed restraint. Command of his body. Had to keep his hands along with his mouth away from her.

"When do you wish to go to the modiste tomorrow? Might as well get a few things since my husband says he can pay for them. You're right. I'm tired of wearing the same three gowns. Would love to have a few more underthings." She blushed when she looked at him. Color swept across her chest. He assumed to the tops of her breasts. If she'd kept them bared, he would have seen the rise of color.

He wasn't her husband. Never would be her husband. Telling her would hurt her. The longer he waited the worse that pain from the ugly truth he initiated would be for her. Jasper saw the emotions in the fading green of her eyes. Watched the sparkle vanish. In those few seconds, she removed herself from him.

Her sparkle vanished.

She didn't understand the difficulties he was having.

He couldn't explain. Not yet. In time, he would tell her the truth. When there was no more danger, she would be happy he didn't take her innocence. Pleased she wasn't going to have a bastard. He couldn't do that to her. Couldn't get her with child then leave her to the judgment of the women she knew. She would forever be ostracized.

"Around ten o'clock would be nice. She might have a few ready-made items for you. You can have anything you like. We can sort through fashion plates. Have a few things commissioned. Whatever you want is yours."

He would give her everything she asked for. It would be hers. No expense would be too much to make up for tonight.

"I'd like that. Afterward, will you come home with me or go to the pub without me? Will I spend the afternoon by myself? Will I be alone again?" Now that he withdrew from her, her voice was void of emotion. He watched as her breasts moved with the deep breaths of air she pulled into her lungs.

Jasper did that to her. "I don't want to hurt you," he blurted as if those few words would vanquish the last hour. Everything he did hurt her. Confused her. Frustrated her. She'd been so loving, giving of herself. He didn't know how he knew. Jasper knew sex with her would be the best he'd ever had.

"I don't understand. Guess I don't see how you can kiss me the way you did then in almost the same breath tell me you don't want me as a husband should want a wife. You don't wish to make love to me. I'm willing. Ready to experience… What more do you want? Oh, that's it, a woman you might like. Not one who has forced you into this situation." She fumbled with the blanket before she drank deep of the wine. "I'm going to bed. Imagine you will join me whenever the mood hits. You did say we needed to sleep in the same bed. I'll try not to take up too much room. Won't hog the covers. Neither will I warm my cold feet on your legs."

Warm her cold feet on my legs?

Sadness wrapped itself around her. Her eyes were blank, deep pools of endless green. With the moisture added, they reminded him of sparkling gemstones. There were silver streaks in the green he noticed again. The silver more pronounced because of the tears. He wished he could erase the misery he saw. He couldn't. Not without ruining her for the man she would someday call her husband. "I'll join you later. Not right now." If he did, he would never be able to hide his arousal. He needed to wait until she slept. Needed an hour or two to calm himself.

The devil, I sleep nude.

What was I thinking?

He was thinking about a beautiful woman waiting for him in his bed. He was thinking about a woman who thought she was his wife. Only a cad would take advantage of the situation. Or a man pushed to his limits by the woman who aroused him as no other. His mind needed to find a new place to settle besides Maggie. His Maggie. Maggie was his.

Jasper felt the only way he could ease his discomfort was to ride hard and fast. That wasn't going to happen. She would hear him leave. Would feel even more pain at his rejection. What had he gotten himself into? If he didn't care for Maggie as much as he did, he would do what she wanted. Damn the consequences. He had too much respect for her. Too much love for her. If she conceived, he would claim the child. Make the lad or lass legitimate. Give the child his name. What he couldn't do was give her his last name. That thought played over in his mind. It was all that kept him sane, kept him from making a huge mistake.

Before he walked up to join Maggie in the big bed gracing the master suite, he finished the wine. Drank straight from the bottle. From the swing on the patio, he stared out at the dark velvet sky. A few stars blinked around the clouds. He scrubbed his hands across the back of his neck. Wished he could think of some way to make this right.

The bottle was empty.

Maggie should be asleep.

With slow steps he walked the stairs to the bedroom. Imagined he was going to his execution. Saw the hangman's noose as he stepped forward. Imagined the noose around his neck. Tight. Gritted his teeth against the ensuing moments. He did this to the two of them. Dug an early grave for their relationship. She might have understood if he told her the truth from the very beginning. It was possible she could keep the secret. That was the only reason he kept the real salient facts from her. Her face was an open book. If pressed, she would give it all away. He did the right thing. Maggie could never know the truth.

Jasper knew he could tell himself that a thousand times but he'd never believe. There must have been another way to assure her safety from Abernathy. He couldn't think of one.

Standing beside the bed, just as he'd done every night since they arrived in Nass, he gazed at Maggie, wishing he dared lie down beside her. Embrace her. Make love to her. Damn the consequences. Asleep, she appeared relaxed. Fragile in her slumber. Her breathing was even, steady. Maybe she wasn't as disappointed as she'd seemed. She slept.

He hoped.

With a little groan, she turned over, presenting her back to him. That was good. Better than her front. He could curl up next to her. Hold her. Keep her warm through the night. Ease some of the guilt he felt.

Jasper's smile felt soft yet rough around the edges when he noticed she wore his nightshirt. The garment was far too big for her slight frame. The neck was pulled from her shoulder, baring the soft white flesh for him to see. Seeing wasn't enough. He wanted to touch. Kiss. The sight wasn't meant for his eyes. If possible, his body hardened more.

~ * ~

His men found the trail. Lord Abernathy understood, Lord Kenworthy fled to London. He stayed in London for a short time, no more than two nights from what his detectives could find. That was all. After that the trail went cold. Nelson understood he should go to London. Before he left, he would need to tie up a few loose ends. See to his affairs along with his mistresses.

What would he do when he found the pair? By then she would be used, no longer a virgin. Did he want Maggie MacRae if she wasn't still innocent? He still wanted what she would bring to his marriage. She could be increasing with Kenworthy's child. If that was the case, he would find someone to abort the *bairn*.

Nelson wrestled with the idea of telling Anice where her daughter hied off to. Deciding against doing so, he gave orders to his servants to pack his things for an extended stay away from Glasgow. He still wasn't positive what he would do when he found Maggie. He felt certain there would be clues for his detective to find in London. Information that would lead him to his fiancée. The question at the forefront revolved around Kenworthy's destination after London. Clues could be found on the waterfront.

"Will you take me with you?" Suzanna wrapped her arms around him, pressing her soft body against him. She ran her hand down his chest, stopping at his arousal. Pushed her knuckles along his hard sex.

Nelson held her hand still. There were pros along with cons for transporting his mistress. The first as well as the foremost to him was the fact he would never spend one night in a solitary bed. The con was that he rarely found it difficult to purchase a woman for the night. Most of the time, no money changed hands. He was adept at securing willing women. He liked the novelty of new ladies. That way he would never become bored.

"Would be best for you to stay here. Will you miss me?"

He crushed his mouth against hers before she could answer. Swept her into his arms to carry her to their bed. His hands tugged at the corsage of her gown. Pushed the fabric to her waist. Her breasts free for his carnal pleasure.

In seconds they were naked. He rammed himself into her. Thrusting upward. Pushing her legs further apart. His teeth left red marks on her breasts. Left them swollen, as he thrust again then again until he spent himself inside her channel. Nelson rolled off, leaving her heaving, panting for each breath of air. She didn't find enjoyment in that coupling. He would see to her pleasure after he returned. There was too much on his mind, for him to focus on this woman's gratification. He called out to his butler to have her removed to her home.

"I hate you!" Suzanna cried out, hitting him on the shoulder.

"No, you don't, love. I will be back. Don't worry. Until then you can remain in the beautiful home I granted you. Behave yourself. If you don't, you'll regret it. I keep what is mine. Remember that if you grow bored. If you see someone else, there will be consequences."

If she dallied with another man, he would see she never worked in Scotland again. He could ruin her. She understood him. Would remain chaste while he was out of the city. He'd been good to the woman. Given her things she enjoyed.

Suzanna made a scrunched-up face at him. "I might not be here when you get back," she shot his way.

He lifted his shoulders. "That's your choice. What will you do without my groats?" he questioned while he pulled on his clothes. "I will find someone else if you are so eager to give up the relationship we have. Makes no matter to me." He gestured with his arms. "Your elegant home."

"No, I... Nelson, you know I'm jealous. Don't like thinking of you with other women." She sat up in the bed. Her breasts moved enticingly while she spoke. She postured as if she thought he would return to her bed. "I'll be here...waiting for you."

"Good. You're in no position to be jealous of anyone."

God, he didn't like cloying women. Women were there for his use, not the other way around. Meant to be seen but never heard. Suzanna wasn't terrible when it came to clinging. She understood her place in his life even

125

though as time went on it became increasingly clear she wished for more. If she needed marriage, she would have to find another man. He wasn't about to allow her to stray from him until he was ready to move on himself.

A whore was a whore. Nothing more. She would never be more than what she was now. He left the room intent on one thing, finding Maggie then figuring out what he wanted to do with her. Before she ran off, everything was obvious. They would wed. She would bare him children. Hopefully her body could endure a child a year. He intended to keep the woman pregnant until he was satisfied with the number of children he sired. He needed an heir as well as a spare. Wanted girl children so he could find suitable husbands for them then reap the benefits. They would marry early. Maggie at twenty-one was too damn old to become a bride. He didn't understand what Anice had been thinking. The girl should have been his two years ago. If that had happened, he wouldn't have this problem today. She wouldn't be so willful.

He didn't intend to be an indulgent father. His girls as well as his sons would obey. Would be disciplined harshly if they didn't bend to his wishes. Obedience was important in children as well as a wife. Nelson let out a long dramatic sigh. His thoughts strayed too far ahead.

This trip that was not planned, would never be to his liking. He would need to find a way to make the adventure out of Glasgow more palatable. Maggie would discover he didn't take lightly to disobedience. When he caught up to her, she would be disciplined. Anice gave him *carte blanch* to punish her wayward daughter as he saw fit. Maggie's mother as much as gave her to him that day she fled. If she'd not run away, they would be married now. He might even have a child growing in her belly.

The injustices.

The trip to London went off without a hitch. He spent the evening roaming the town, scoping out a few places to gamble as well as find women who would do his bidding. By midnight, he was playing in his bed with the selected woman. She was curvaceous with striking blue eyes. Her blond hair touched her waist. He liked the way her breasts felt in his hands along with the soft whimper she gifted him with when she reached her pinnacle. Thought he might enjoy having this lady of the evening teach Maggie a thing or two about giving a man pleasure. He would enjoy watching the two women together. After that he would delight in having Maggie touch him, arouse him while the other woman watched. Stroke his member. Feeling her mouth sucking on his penis would be an interesting experience. Maybe for both of them. That little fact depended on how much she learned from Jasper Kenworthy. He should have been her soul instructor.

The morning broke with gray clouds, a heavy mist coupled with harsh winds. Rain pounded from the sky. Walking along the docks he pulled up the collar on his coat before tugging the brim of his hat down. It was too cold for man or beast. In this situation, he never intended to leave the discovery of his fiancée's whereabouts to his detective. They bumbled everything. Wasn't certain why he paid them.

"I searched the manifests of all the ships sailing to various ports in Ireland as well as France. Doubt if they went anywhere else. Nevertheless, I'll keep checking."

"You didn't find anything of importance when you asked around a few weeks ago?" Nelson asked, growing more frustrated that Maggie still eluded him. Kenworthy's money kept him from finding her.

"All I heard that comes close to what we are looking for is a couple who signed as Maeve and Justin O'Neill. The man who sold them their passage doesn't remember what they looked like. Told me they were newlyweds."

"Where did they go?" Nelson asked while he stroked his chin. The name change could be a tactical maneuver to send him off track. Could be a different couple. Didn't wish to waste time chasing false leads. "Married…" Nelson tried to remain calm. If they were married, he had lost everything he gambled on. Kenworthy would never marry a woman he met a few days past.

"Dublin. They had kin in Dublin where they wished to put down roots. Do you want to book passage? I can take care of that. Might not be a ship sailing for a few days."

A few days would please him. If they were wed, there was no rush. If this couple weren't Maggie and Jasper, they would embark on a frivolous chase. Nelson thought that perhaps settling down with someone else might be prudent. He could find a nice, young lady in Glasgow who would be biddable. He didn't think Maggie would ever be compliant no matter how much he punished her. On some level, she would continue to fight him. If she fought, it might be fun to subdue her. His plans for building his empire could wait. With any luck he would find a woman whose family held more influence than the MacRaes.

"Yes, check out the ships sailing to Dublin. Would like a few days here in London before we head out on a trip that might not give me what I want." He thought of the lady in his bed last night. The woman was enjoyable. Nothing spectacular. He could do better. Maybe he would find a lady who wouldn't mind going with him to Glasgow. Suzanna bored him. She expected too much from him. Was too clingy. It was time for him to move on to a new mistress.

"I'll let you know what I've booked."

The two parted ways. Nelson headed to the red-light district where he found last night's lady. These houses were clean. The women accomplished in many different ways. If he recalled there would be an auction tonight. A beautiful lady he could bid on. She would then be his. The situation seemed entirely too provocative to avoid.

Chapter Five

Maggie cried herself to sleep that night. She was groggy but awake when Jasper came to bed. Felt the mattress dip when he slid in next to her. He was so close, the heat of his body burned her. When she sensed him standing over her, watching her sleep, she turned her back to him. The idea he might discover she cried after she'd gone to bed would leave her far too vulnerable for her taste.

By opening up to him the way she did, she left herself exposed. Raw. Now hurt to the very marrow of her bones. Maggie wanted to be his wife in every way. He rejected that idea. Jasper couldn't have made his feelings more apparent to her. He didn't want her the same way she wanted him. She stuffed her closed fist against her mouth to keep the gulp of air from alerting him to the fact she wasn't asleep. Closed her eyes tight. Tried to close her mind from the heartache. She felt the warmth of his big body next to hers, his lips against the nape of her neck. He started the night in the same manner.

"I'm sorry I hurt you, Maggie," his whisper fluttered against her bare neck. Flames scorched her. Her long-braided hair was draped over one shoulder. "Only wished to help out. Made a mess of it. Tomorrow I'll make this *faux pas* up to you. Don't know how exactly. I'll find a way."

The sorrow in his voice was evident. Moisture clouded her eyes. Damn…double damn, she didn't want to cry again. Her emotions were too sensitive. For sticking to his feelings, he had nothing to be regretful about. She was sad she pushed him so far. If an apology would help, she would try. Though she didn't think he wished for that conversation to continue.

Jasper did help. She could tell him that tomorrow on their way to the modiste. Maggie could tell him she would never push him that way again. He didn't need to feel regret at helping her get away from her fiancé. She could speak to him in plain language. Would explain to him she would never again endeavor something so ludicrous as her attempt to seduce him was last night. She bungled everything.

What did she know about seduction? Nothing. She was a novice in that department. Though, after tonight, she did have a better idea.

His hand settled on her hip. From surprise, she jerked. Caught the startle gasp behind her teeth. She tried to tell him she didn't flinch from him because she didn't like him. Jasper always had this way of surprising her. The problem was she liked him too much. Maggie closed her eyes, thinking she would never fall asleep. His hand moved with languid slowness on her hip. He had to be awake. Why was he doing this to her?

The time between when she left him and now, her body began to calm. Now, with each gentle caress of his long fingers, each breath was a throaty gasp. Since he laid down beside her, she felt the same persistent need as before. Felt desire for him increase. Flame to life. While she knew it was wrong, she wished he would touch her breasts as well as other places that ignited when he kissed her.

Looking out the window, Maggie watched the moon. She left the curtains open so she could look at the night sky. The stars glittered, twinkling brightly in the velvet blackness. The silver light from the moon splintered into the room, casting shadows. Danced with the movement of the curtains. Maggie didn't think she would ever get to sleep. His hand moved down her leg. She pushed herself back to meet his body. Sensed him against her fanny, the hard thing between his legs she noticed earlier this evening. Her body pulsed, quickening while she tried to keep her mind focused on the stars and not his questing fingers.

The light slanting inside.

What she wished to purchase at the modiste.

The things she would say to him on the way into town.

When she felt his hand on the revealed flesh of her leg, she jerked. Her backside slammed against him. He couldn't be doing this with purpose. Again, his big hand caressed her. Sent her fist back to her mouth as she pushed down the little cry of pleasure threatening to erupt. After that, she heard long, deep breaths.

A ruffle of a snore.

Silence of the night.

Sometime before morning, Maggie drifted to sleep. When she woke, she was groggy. Her eyes didn't wish to focus. Muted sunlight bathed the room. She sighed. Heat built. Uncertain where she was. The big body behind her made her think about the night. She recalled her husband sleeping with her. The body she experienced lying next to hers was Jasper's. She remembered now. He needed to sleep with her to keep the servants from talking about their marriage.

Closing her eyes tight, she let a ripple of soft air drift from her lips, the sound sultry in the cold air that froze her nose. The room was frigid. It was winter, January. The servants should have started a fire this morning. Jasper's hand spread across her belly. Voyaged higher to surround her breast. His thumb flicked across her nipple.

Maggie sipped in a deep breath of air then another. She didn't want to cry out. He inflamed her. Caused her body to roar to life. Blood rushed through her ears. She felt him against her back, the cleft between her legs. Needed to tell him he shouldn't be touching her that way. Couldn't form words. He did things to her that seemed to melt every bone in her body. Her muscles were weak. Telling him no should be the important thought. He was her husband. She couldn't tell him no. Didn't wish to stop his drifting hands.

Was this what men and women did in bed together? Last night, Jasper made it clear to her this wasn't what he wanted to do with her. He must have changed his mind. Maggie tried to move away without waking him. He had to be asleep. If Jasper was awake, he would not be touching her this way. With thumb and finger, he twisted her nipple. She moaned. The sound was evocative. Vibrated in the cold air. It came from deep in the back of her throat. His palm flattened against the tip of her breast. Rubbed. Tested.

"You're so silky soft. Want to taste you," his whispered voice sent shivers down her spine.

Maggie wanted that too. He lifted the nightshirt she wore so it pooled against the back of her neck. His lips touched upon her shoulders, caressed the small bones running down the middle of her back. "Maggie…love."

Without warning, his hands fell away. He pushed himself from her. Frigid air surrounded her backside as Jasper leapt from the bed. She closed her eyes tight, fighting the second rejection of her person. This proved to her just as last night demonstrated, he didn't want her. She turned to him, fumbling with the covers along with the pillows. Finding the pillow, she drew it to her. Held it close for protection. Needed to shield her body from his view.

"Please go…" Maggie murmured into the pillow she held in front of her. She could still feel his hands on her naked body. The fire he created. Heat crackling as if lightning struck. She didn't want to feel this way. Hurt. Rejected. Yearning for his touch.

"I'm sorry."

There were those words again. She hated them. Never wished to hear them. She heard him dressing. The swish of his britches as he pulled them up his powerful legs. They were so long. After that Jasper shrugged into his shirt, covering his broad chest. She watched muscles ripple with each movement. Dear Lord, he'd been naked, lying next to her. In a bed. This was more than she could assimilate. More than she wished to think about. What did she do wrong this time to send him away from her when she still longed…

"Please go…" Maggie repeated even though she understood this was the last place Jasper Kenworthy, her husband, never her lover, wished to be. He didn't need to hear her next words. He was almost out the door. "Leave me be. Find someone else to torment. As far as I'm concerned, the servants can keep talking."

Jasper didn't say anything else. What could he tell her that she didn't know? By his actions he said it all. The words told her too much. Said more than she wanted to understand. *I'm sorry*. One more time her body ached, burned for something she didn't comprehend. Flamed for a man who wanted nothing more than to protect her. They were married. This was so ridiculous. No one looking at them together would ever believe they were man and wife.

Maggie didn't know how she knew this.

She just did.

How did she get herself into this mess? This disordered messed-up life was hers. It was up to her to get herself out of the situation. She couldn't rely on anyone else. Had to be her own hero. Figuring that out could come later. All she wanted now was to curl up in a tight ball. She wasn't going to cry again. Crying was for foolish women. She wasn't foolish, just an idiot.

They were going into Nass this morning to buy her a wardrobe. Maggie didn't know how she could bear riding in a carriage with this man, facing him, knowing what happened in this bed. How he touched her in more ways than she could understand. Where all her sisters were concerned, she was always the one to find trouble. Was the boldest. Sometimes took in more than she bargained for. There couldn't be more trouble than what she unearthed here with this man. Ah, but there was Lord Abernathy. How the devil did she wind up engaged to that despicable man? Now she found herself married to another. Didn't recall how exactly.

Suck in a big brash load of air, Maggie *lass*. Get over this issue you have. Move on. Tomorrow is a new day. This problem concerns both of you. Whatever you do, don't apologize. Stop that man from apologizing again too. Tell him you don't want to hear those words. *I'm sorry*. Find something else to say. Either that or he should stop doing things he needed to apologize for. She needed to tell him to keep his distance…stay far, far away.

Jasper and I need to have a good long talk. Figure out how to circumnavigate our difficulties. He can't accost me in bed then leave me without…she didn't know what that was but she felt bereft. Also…set some parameters we both can abide by. We can't sleep in the same bed if he's going to forget who he is, what he doesn't want to be. Who he doesn't wish for as a wife. Don't want to wake up with his hand on my breast, making me feel things I don't want to feel.

That's the major problem. I do wish to feel those things. I know there is more. Want to learn everything. Want Jasper to be my husband in every way.

When Jasper left a few minutes later, he didn't say anything more. No ridiculous words of apology. The door clicked with a soft sound when it closed behind him. Footsteps followed. He walked down the long hall then descended the stairs. Maggie found she'd been holding her breath all the while he'd been dressing. Didn't take her gaze off him. Couldn't bring herself to look away. As if his nudity didn't bother him, he faced her. Dared her in some way.

He slept naked.

She slept in his nightshirt.

If she was more experienced, she would know what to do. Right now, she had to do what she told herself a few minutes ago. Get over what happened. Stop thinking about the man along with what she wished for. It was inevitable. If they were to convince anyone they were wed, he would sleep with her again tonight. Every night after. She couldn't have Jasper as a real husband. Perhaps this was a charade to keep Lord Abernathy away. Her heart jolted. Kickstarted. Nausea followed. If that's what this marriage thing was to Jasper, he should have the decency to tell her. This morning's activities didn't change what she felt for him. Didn't alleviate the fact she wished to be his wife.

A charade? No, not for me. Yes, for him.

A pretense to keep me safe from Lord Abernathy. He was doing this for her. I should be grateful. Should thank the man.

The devil, what if they weren't married? She threw herself at him. Tried to seduce him. He didn't have trouble telling her no. What was he supposed to do? The hand on her breast this morning was a simple reflex to sleeping with her. He didn't know, because he was sleeping, that he didn't want anything to do with her sexually.

My mind is splintering in a million different directions. What is true? What is not true? I have to comprehend. Didn't think he would tell her the truth. She deserved to recognize what was fact as well as that which was not.

The heat of mortification painted her face. She gulped air. Once she was positive Jasper wouldn't return, she eased out of the bed they shared. Dressed, her hair combed out, she walked down the steps to the dining area. She hoped her outer appearance would seem calm while her insides seethed, rolled with each thought of the things she said, the things she did. Maggie didn't want him to know how the events of the last twelve hours left her agitated, breathless, uncertain of what she would find when she saw him again. Was surprised to see Jasper sitting at the table sipping tea and eating as if nothing untoward happened. As if he didn't have his hand on her breast a mere ten minutes ago.

After she stepped inside, he looked up. Nodded toward a chair at the table. "Good morning," he said, his voice husky. His eyes shimmered while he watched her walk to the table. He wore a half-smile coupled with one dimple.

The way he appeared was exactly how she wished she could look.

Cool. Calm. Collected in every way. For her, the sensation wasn't to be. She was the farthest away possible from calm, cool collected in every way. Her knees quaked. Her hands trembled. Picking up a tea cup without the liquid sloshing out of the rim would be impossible.

Maggie sat down. Folded her quaking fingers in front of her. Mortified, she looked at the man across from her. He grinned again. Heat rushed to her cheeks, her face flaming. Ignited places she recalled him touching. She lowered her lashes studying the plate sitting on the table. Yes, there was food. A fork. Knife. Spoon. For a few seconds, she toyed with the napkin before she set the fabric on her lap. Picked up the spoon. Put sugar in her tea. Stirred.

Jasper looked up. Smiled. Tilted his head at a roguish angle as if questioning her stability. Why was he so composed? Why was she unstable? Why did her heart beat as fast as the wings of a hummingbird? She did things she never did before. Put herself out on a limb that broke. She fell. Tumbled to the ground.

"I want to be like you?" Maggie shocked herself by saying the words she was thinking out loud to him.

The devil, this wasn't what she needed to talk about for the next few minutes. Her stomach rolled. She needed to eat. Nothing ever affected her appetite. Today was a first for her in too many ways to count.

"Like me? How so?" he queried, his voice soft, rough around the edges. Husky. The sound had a ragged edge to it. "Explain."

He leaned back, his teacup resting on his hard stomach. She recalled the way that flesh rippled with each movement of his body. She saw him naked. He touched her as a husband would caress his wife. He rejected her. Twice. Maggie understood she needed to keep reminding herself of his actions. Must stay strong. She needed to repeat herself.

He rejected me. To my mortification, more than once.

The sound of his voice forced its way to the deepest darkest secrets he revealed to her last night as well as this morning. This man touched her where, as an adult, she'd never been touched before. She forced a bite of egg into her mouth. Chewed while she used up time. The egg was cold. Congealed in her stomach. Set the fork on the table. Recalled food fights with her sisters. A bit of egg in the bowl of her spoon could send the food racing toward his face. She was a good aim. Maggie switched her attention to a scone, a blueberry scone. She dipped it into the honey on her plate. Swirled the sticky substance on the bread. Honey dripped. She set the food on her plate. Jasper tapped his fingers on the China.

"I didn't mean that...what I said...forget my words," Maggie was slow to interject her feelings.

She'd been dallying with food along with her thoughts. She looked to the plate of food she wasn't going to eat then back to him. "I...never mind." She waved her hand to put a different light on the conversation. "I don't know what I mean. Because of that, I can't explain anything to you. Don't want to talk now. Can't eat. The food is cold. Should we go?" If she could crawl in a hole then disappear this would be a great day.

She stood up then sat down. Again, her hands were folded tight in her lap. "I'm way out of my comfort here. Things happened last night as well as this morning. I don't understand any of it. Don't know...can't appreciate how to act around you now. You send too many different messages. I'm confused." Then she held her hands up to stop what she knew he would spout. "Don't...whatever you do...don't tell me you are sorry another time. Won't hear those words again."

"I am though. Even if you don't wish to hear me say the words. This, the way you are feeling now, it's all my fault."

His eyes were focused on her. He appeared intent on convincing her. "I don't usually go around... I don't make a habit of hurting people. Especially women. I don't like what I did last night as well as this morning." He cleared his throat. "Ashamed of myself."

Maggie cut in before he could further put himself down. "There is no need to explain. We both are doing things we don't wish. Acting in ways that are uncomfortable. I don't have to be experienced with a man to know you weren't comfortable kissing me or even sleeping in the same bed. You didn't wish to be there with me. You were doing it for my sake. To save me from Lord Abernathy. I welcome that gesture." Maggie paused, wondering if she should ask the foremost question on her mind. She leaned forward. "Is this whole marriage thing a charade?"

Unable to stop herself. Maggie blurted the words again without thinking. She should have considered his feelings. However, she couldn't hold back. "Is this marriage a sham? A pretense? Is that what the problem is? You can't make love to me because I'm not your wife? The marriage certificate…was it forged? I don't remember a wedding or saying the words. You said the ceremony was short. Was it so short it was nonexistent?"

Jasper paled. His face turned white right in front of her. Taking a few seconds, he looked away. Maggie's breath stopped. Her heart failed to beat. She held the uncanny opinion that what she just spouted was the truth. The words were impulsive. Didn't expect them to be true. They weren't married. All of this was a lie. She spent the night in a bed with a man she knew for such a short time. A man who wasn't her husband. Everything she believed was false.

Clearing his throat then touching his napkin to his lips, he told her. "No. Of course not. You saw the marriage certificate. Both of us signed the document. This is a real marriage. No forgery. There is no sham to this."

Powerless to help herself, Maggie found herself shaking her head. Disbelief ran rampant in her confused mind. "It's not real. There is nothing about this marriage that is real. Not unless you wanted one of convenience so when this is all over you can go your separate way with no guilt, no strings attached. No wife. Can cut your ties to me without fear of consequences. I understand you don't want me. So, that must be the truth."

Maggie was rambling now. Words tumbling from her mouth without a thought. She didn't understand where she was going with this. The direction must be somewhere. Wherever the hell that was, she had no idea.

"The marriage is real. Very real. Nothing fake about the certificate," Jasper spoke when she finished with her tirade. "We should consummate the marriage. Tonight." He stood, held out his hand. "If you're not going to eat, we should leave. Wish to introduce you to some new acquaintances. Show off my beautiful wife to the locals. We need to make friends here. Need to have their respect, their friendship as well as loyalty."

Maggie understood she spoke out of turn. By the look on his face, it was evident she offended him. Now, they would be in the carriage facing each other. Why they needed to make friends when they wouldn't be here all that long, Maggie didn't understand. She wanted to lay down a few ground rules. Instead, she spouted about things that had no bearing on them or their marriage. How this went from bad to worse in a blink, she didn't have one idea. She did though. Letting all her emotions boil over was how. She should have found a way to calm herself so her emotions would remain in check. So she wouldn't spout more words that would lead to further embarrassment.

Accepting his hand sent all her emotions into turmoil again. She found her cape. He led her to the waiting carriage. His big hands on her waist, he helped her inside. Maggie sat across from him. Stopped herself before she said the words out loud. Instead, she spoke to herself.

I'm sorry. I truly am sorry I've caused you all these problems. You don't love me. How could I think that was possible? I don't love you. We've known each other such a short amount of time. Love doesn't enter into this strange relationship we are sharing.

You've nothing to be sorry about. No regrets. Sorry because I blurted something that seemed to hurt your feelings. Sorry he now thinks we should consummate the marriage to help me feel better. All of this because they needed to convince the servants of a nonexistent marriage. The more she thought about the last few weeks the more certain she was their marriage was a pretense. A fabrication was alright with her. Why didn't he tell her the truth? Explain. She could keep a secret.

You still have to convince the servants.

That man needs to explain things to me. He's keeping secrets. Why did he seem angry with me last night when I touched him? Now he thinks we should go through that same pain again. Night after night, I'll go crazy!

You're right. You best ask him about his thoughts.

The man won't tell me the truth. So, why bother?

He interrupted her brooding. She sent him a fine scowl. "What would you like to purchase? I would hope you've a good long list in your head. You've very little to wear. Believe I need to deck you out from the top of your head to the tips of your toes." Jasper grinned as if what she spoke of was unimportant. His arms were spread across the back of his seat. He was relaxed, at ease.

"I don't care. Whatever… whatever you think I might need. It is your blunt."

She was on tenterhooks now. Didn't want this man who wasn't her husband spending money on her. if he did, it would be the same as if she was his mistress.

Filled with restless energy, she needed to pursue the conversation in more depth. "Is this a pretense for you, Lord Kenworthy? A game you are playing at my expense? A bogus marriage? Will I wake up one day with this marriage annulled? I'll be ruined. No man will wish to have anything to do with me. You will have taken my innocence. I will no longer have that to give to the man I one day marry."

His brows furrowed together. The scowl he sent her way caused ripples of fear to sink into her. "So many questions. Let me see, you will need a few day dresses, a carriage dress. Perhaps one ball gown should be commissioned. A few negligées, unless you wish to continue sleeping in my nightshirt." He ignored the real questions in her head. Disregarded that which was most important to her.

"What do I need a ballgown for? There are no balls to go to around here. I'm certain by the time the two of us return to Glasgow, we will no longer be married. I have ballgowns in my wardrobe, too many to count." Maggie leaned forward. "Will we? Are you planning on having me annulled? Is that why you didn't like what we did last night? The way I touched you? Why you left me this morning?"

"You are wrong on all counts. You will need at least two riding habits. I bought you a mare yesterday. She is in the stable behind the cottage. Do you enjoy riding?"

"Buying me. What an inventive idea. Women like things. You buy me clothes. A horse. What else, Lord Kenworthy, are you spending your groats on? I'm not your mistress. I don't care what the servants think. We will sleep in different beds!"

Her head pounded with anger. She was tired of being ignored as if her feelings were unimportant.

"My wife," he corrected her, his voice harsh, fury in his eyes. "You're not mistress material. Never will be. Keep it in your head. You are my wife!"

Maggie was shocked by the fierceness in his voice. Confused again. Bent on a path to the truth. "In so many ways but one, I might be your wife. Why don't you consummate the marriage?" Maggie didn't understand why she pressed this issue. The truth was what she needed. If he lied about the reality of the marriage, he was very good at deception. He did tell her they would do that tonight. She didn't believe a word he said on that issue.

"The truth?" His right eyebrow reached toward the ceiling of the carriage. "You want the truth?" When Jasper asked that question, he seemed nervous. Distraught.

"Only the truth," Maggie agreed, waiting to hear what that would be.

Last night she'd been ready to allow him whatever liberties he wished to take. Other than kissing, he asked for nothing. This morning he held her breast in his hand. Both times, he left her heated with desire. Left her uncomfortable. She wasn't willing to give her innocence to a man who was not her husband.

"To begin, I don't relish hurting you," Jasper said, yet seeming unwilling to meet her gaze, he looked from the carriage after he said the words. "Last night…I know I hurt you. That was never my intention. Never made love to a virgin. So, you see, this is all my fault. I'm terrified of hurting you."

That tiny moment seemed to reveal a tiny chink in his armor. Maggie had forgotten about the first pain in the marriage bed. Anice told her what might happen when she wed Lord Abernathy. That was before the announcement of the engagement. Before she ran away with Lord Kenworthy. Before he told her she signed a marriage contract she didn't recall.

"I don't relish being hurt. You must have known that when we married. You should have realized it was inevitable."

"I didn't think about it until the time came to bed you. As I told you, I'm a coward. Suppose that is a hard fact for a man to divulge. Never was the…" his huge sigh of seeming discontent unnerved her.

How to respond to this statement of his befuddled her mind. He put her into a new predicament. She had no experience to fall back on. Maggie stared out the window. Concentrated on the scenery, on the steady clop of the horses' hooves. The chilling breeze that sent bare tree branches moving. Caught the scent of winter on the air. It might snow tonight. Snow was a part of winter she adored. She pulled the cape she wore around her shoulders. A shiver coursed up her spine. She had no right to her anger. Jasper did everything for her. She should be thanking the man, not calling him a liar. Shouldn't question him or his motives.

"Should commission some warm stockings, a few pairs of shoes. Perhaps a warmer coat." He grinned when she made a face at him.

"We are back to clothing?"

"Yes."

What to purchase was the simpler of two topics. One quite annoying, the other boring. The bell chimed when they walked into the shop. Bolts of materials lined the walls. Fashion plates were set on tables. A woman stepped forward holding out her hand, "Eilinora," she told them. "What can I do for you?"

Maggie cleared her throat to speak. Jasper cut her off. "My wife needs everything from the tips of her toes to the top of her head. She has three gowns to her name. I'm growing ever tired of seeing her in the same clothing day after day. Spare no expense." Jasper went on to explain the extent of the clothing he wished to purchase for her including slippers along with a few negligées he mentioned half-heartedly.

The modiste jotted all he said down in a notebook. "If you think of anything else, let me know."

"I will pay extra to have the items finished as soon as possible."

Jasper looked through the fashion plates while Eilinora hustled her into one of the changing rooms. The woman measured her from top to bottom. She stood naked in the room except for her pantalets and chemise. She didn't have a corset to wear. Maggie rubbed her arms in an attempt to warm herself. She felt cold, inside as well as out. Even though she'd been to a modiste many times, all this seemed unreal to her. Different in every aspect. Before Jasper, her mother picked out her clothes dictated to her what was acceptable as well as what was not. Now her husband took over that role.

"Your husband is quite handsome...but then I don't need to be tellin' you that. He must be quite the lover," Eilinora spoke while she worked.

The gasp of air Maggie sucked in didn't go unnoticed. "He is...? Lover?" Maggie's voice wobbled.

She didn't know how to respond to that bit of nonsense. She heard the question in her voice as she was also certain Eilinora did. Her face flamed.

"Ah, you two be newlyweds. He is gentle with you. Is he not?" Eilinora asked as she wrote measurements in her notebook. She stepped back. "You can dress now. We'll go to the main room to see what he's picked out for you. A man such as your husband will wish to have a say in what he purchases."

"Y-yes, he d-didn't like h-hurting me that f-first time," Maggie found herself stammering out the words he'd said during the ride over here. She blurted more than she intended. The woman seemed to suck words from her. She babbled.

"Not many men do. Not the woman they love. There, love, we are all done. Get dressed and you might be able to get a word or two in about what you would like." Eilinora laughed as she left the dressing room.

Eilinora was right. By the time she joined Jasper he had fashion plates as well as bolts of fabric decided on. She'd never had much say in picking out her clothing. So, Maggie didn't care. Anice dictated what she along with her sisters were supposed to wear. They were never asked their opinion. If they managed to spout their view, they were ignored. Why should this be different?

"Mr. O'Neill has picked out quite an array of clothing for you. Are you pleased with his decisions?" Eilinora asked, seeming to watch her as she walked up to the table where Jasper sat.

Maggie lifted her shoulders unsure how to answer. "Mother always picked out my clothing. What my husband has decided on is fine with me. I've never been allowed to voice what I would like or what I would not."

She realized she held little interest in her clothing. The garments were for comfort or warmth or even to stay cool in the summers. Nothing else.

"If there is something here you don't like, please tell me. My attentiveness was meant to save time. We are due at the pub for lunch. Was told lamb stew was the special today." He stepped close to her. Brought her close so he could whisper into her ear. "We both *ken* that's one of your favorite dishes, my love."

The stew wasn't. Who was she to argue with a man so certain of himself. "I have a hankering for potato soup with some *wee* clams for taste." Maggie smiled her demeanor meant to be sweet. She tilted her head to the side, remembering Anice told her that would be flirtatious.

He grinned at her, understanding her attempt at what she thought would be flirting.

"Oh, I do love potato soup also. It's too bad it's not the special for today," Eilinora said with gusto. "I'll be sending over for a big bowl of lamb stew. Will be working into the night hours. I'll also be sending out invitations to my best seamstress to come into work. A pint of Guinness would be nice too. Some shortbread to go along with the dinner faire." The barking from the back room caught her attention. "Just a minute. Have to see to the puppies."

She rushed into the storage room then emerged holding a squirming bundle. Two puppies followed behind her along with the mother. "You wouldn't happen to want a puppy? They are ready to leave their mother."

"Yes! Can I?" Hands clasped beneath her chin, Maggie turned to Jasper seeking approval. "I'd love to have one." She knew she overstepped by the look on his face. To her surprise his expression changed.

Jasper's golden-brown eyes widened. He hesitated a moment. "If you wish…"

Maggie understood she took him by surprise. He didn't want a puppy. Jasper was going along with this to please her. She was fine with that. When he was gone during the day, she would no longer be lonely. She wrapped her arms around him. Once again, her nose was pressed to his chest. His hands settled on the small of her back. She rose on the tips of her toes. Kissed him square on the mouth. Drifting lower, his hands splayed across her backside, tucking her close. She felt his hard arousal against her belly. After the kiss ended, "Thank you."

He still held onto her waist. Jasper cleared his throat. Looked over the top of her head, to say, "Send everything when it is finished to this address." Jasper handed Eilinora a slip of paper. He paid for half then and said he'd finish the payment when the order was completed.

He slipped her arm into his as they left the shop. She leaned into him. The bell at the door chimed. She found herself whisked back to the carriage, holding the squirming puppy on her lap, wondering what was going to happen next.

~ * ~

The hell of it was, he didn't know why he lied to her about the marriage. The truth was always the best way to proceed. The devil…she might give them away if she understood she was right about the marriage. After what she told him during the ride to the dressmakers, she wouldn't sleep with him for the sake of keeping the servants quiet. He respected her for that. Didn't appreciate her decision.

What they did or didn't do for the servants, didn't make a whole lot of difference in the scheme. No matter what they did, Maggie's reputation would be ruined. They'd been together now, night and day, for almost two months. No one, not even her sisters would believe she was still chaste. If she denied sleeping with him enough times, her sisters might come to believe. Anice never would. Her mother would insist on a marriage he wouldn't be able to deny.

I should marry her.

Looking at her now, across from him, Maggie couldn't hide her emotions. She wore her heart on her sleeve. He never thought she would guess about the farce of a marriage. Thinking hard about what he would do... Damn, he told her he would consummate the marriage tonight. If he did, he would have to marry her. For him, there would be no other choice. Was that so bad? Now, when he thought about a marriage to this woman, it didn't seem to be the end of the world. She was sweet as well as funny. There was a bit of spice to her nature he would never complain about. Her body was soft, curved in all the right places. She fit him with perfection. Aroused him as no other before.

He should propose marriage to her. Explain that she deserved something she could tell her children along with her grandchildren about. Jasper often thought about children for the soul purpose as an heir. He admired his friend's children. Had always been thankful he didn't have to give up his spare time to entertain a child. Knew when he wed, the mother would do the entertaining. A child with Maggie changed all his preconceived ideas.

Here he was escorting a woman he didn't know before two months ago, protecting her from a man who meant to use her. All the while ruining her reputation. There was nothing to be done about that. They set their course when they fled Glasgow then embarked on a journey south. She agreed.

The puppy leapt from her lap then onto his. Standing on his hind feet, the pup licked his chin. He laughed, amused with the antics of the little thing. He never asked what type of dog the little creature was.

"What are you going to name this darling fellow?" Jasper asked, stroking the dog's back. "Must be something the lad can grow into."

"I don't know. Haven't thought on it. Do you have any suggestions?" She was smiling at him. Her twin dimples flashed.

That's all she needed to do to have him ready to give her anything she asked for. "Always liked the name Charlie." Jasper studied her eyes. They sparkled as if they were gemstones. So, green. The devil he wanted her.

"Is Charlie a good name for a dog? Seems like Squirmy should be his name. Though it would never be fair to name the pup something that wouldn't fit in a year or two. Blackie is too common." She smoothed her skirts. "I'll have to think on it. Is he going to be a big dog or little?"

"By the size of this one's paws, he is going to be a big dog. Might be larger than you. You are such a little mite." Jasper set the dog on the floor. "We'll have to bring him into the pub. Can't leave the tiny guy stranded and alone when he's just met us."

Maggie was laughing, shaking her head. "He might pee on the floor. Doubt if he'll behave himself. Puppies don't know right from wrong. This one isn't trained yet. He will probably chew up all your shoes."

What she told him choked him. Jasper knew nothing about dogs. "Pee on the floor…? My shoes…?"

Jasper echoed as he thought about cleaning up messes. He blanched. How were his servants going to react to the dog leaving messes behind that would need their attention?

"They do that. You know. Make messes. Pee…poop…chew… They teethe…just like human babies." Her hand was in front of her mouth. Her laughter spilled out. Rippled. Soaked into him.

"You think that's funny? Do you?" Jasper tried for a harsh tone. Could not manage it. Maggie's contagious laughter made him grin.

Nodding, she watched the puppy chase its tale. "Can we leave him in the carriage? Do you think your driver would look after him while we are inside? Perhaps we should give him a chance to pee outside the vehicle before we leave him to do damage inside. You do know that puppies chew things you don't want them to."

Jasper brought in a huge breath of air, wondering what more he was going to learn about dogs before the day ended. "What kind of damage are we talking about?" He was certain he didn't wish to learn the answer to his question.

"As I just said, they like to chew on things. Just as babies do. It makes their teeth feel better."

Maggie was still seeing a wealth of humor in his discomfort. She meant to enjoy this moment to the fullest.

Chew on things? What kind of things? Shoes? Babies liked to chew? They don't chew on shoes. Do they? Jasper thought he knew less about babies than he did dogs. "We can't take him into the pub?" Jasper hesitated for several seconds.

"Right you are." Maggie was laughing harder now.

"We could take him back to the seamstress' shop."

"No!" Maggie panicked when Jasper suggested they return the dog. Her brows came together. "I want him. Need someone to care for when you are off doing whatever it is you do. All the time you leave me alone to fend for myself. With this little pup by my side, I won't feel so alone."

"Pick him up later," Jasper amended with another long-drawn-out breath of air. She was lonely. He didn't like that thought either. "If you want the little devil, he is yours. No changing that." Jasper wasn't about to give a gift then take it back. This puppy with no real name as of yet was hers.

"He will do fine in the carriage. The little pup will fall asleep. Something else babies like to do. Sleep. We'll have to figure out what we can feed him," Maggie said as she seemed to be making a list in her head. "Should we stop somewhere for food?"

All this talk about babies was beginning to unnerve him. He felt as if he was now getting in way over his head. Sinking. Nay! Drowning! He wasn't married. He would learn about babies when he needed to do so. While he harbored intense thoughts about consummating his imaginary marriage, until now he'd not thought with any seriousness about the possible consequences. Panic swelled. The women he saw before Maggie always took precautions. Maggie wouldn't know anything about precautions so there would be no consequences. If he made love to her, he would have to think past his pleasure. Would have to take steps not to get her with child. This pretense he once thought was a great idea got stickier by the beat.

"We are here."

"Is there a blanket in here that you don't care about?" Maggie asked while he drew a blank mind.

"Why?"

"After we make sure he pees outside, we will set the blanket on the floor so he'll be comfortable. He will fall asleep," Maggie said, still grinning.

Once more he held the distinct feeling she knew something he did not.

"You know nothing about dogs, do you?"

"Or babies…" Jasper paused, realizing he said too much when her face flushed with color. He realized Maggie wasn't completely ignorant of what went on behind closed doors. She would have thought about having a child of her own someday.

"Babies…" she parroted, a new expression on her face.

Jasper could have sworn for a second or two she appeared wistful. As if she wished to have a baby. He couldn't oblige her. That wasn't going to happen. They would need to be married. They weren't. What they had wasn't legal. A bastard…good god, no! An heir was what he needed. A child to carry on the family name as well as the title.

As the puppy bounced around the yard, sniffing everything, Jasper said, "You do need to decide on a name. Can't call him "him" or "the puppy" forever. Needs a moniker befitting him." When the pup finished his business, he raced toward Maggie. Jasper had been fumbling through the storage for an old blanket which he set on the floor as per her instructions.

Maggie stroked the small dog, bent to rub her cheek against the pup's face. "You behave yourself. We'll be back shortly. If you sleep, you won't know we are gone. Know that we love you."

Realizing he'd like that gentle treatment from Maggie coupled with those words of love, he sighed. She took his arm, walking next to him as they entered the pub. Inside, a group sang. A few people danced. Most chatted and ate.

He stopped at the bar to order food and drink before escorting Maggie to a table. "What do you think?" Jasper asked as he gestured around the room. "Do you like the pub? All these people can be your friends."

"Nice. I've never been in a pub. Is this the way they all are? Is it different in Ireland? You say you learn about things by talking to the locals? What do you learn?"

"I've learned that so far, no one by the name of Lord Nelson

Abernathy has sailed into Dublin. Though he could have used a different name just as we did. Don't expect that." Jasper leaned over to point at a short rotund man with a mustache that curled on its ends. "He has been keeping watch for me as to the ships that arrive in Dublin. He will let me know when or if Lord Abernathy arrives. Forewarned, we will be better prepared. When the time comes, we will counter the attack with one of our own."

"We're married. Why can't we just go home? That shouldn't be so hard." Maggie asked, looking a bit perplexed. "With our marriage certificate, he won't have a way to object to the marriage. I miss my sisters. Can't say I miss mother."

Jasper understood. If they were well and truly married, that's exactly what they would do. Under their circumstances they could not. The document could be challenged. An expert would find it a forgery. They weren't wed.

I need to marry Maggie.

You don't want to get married until you're older, more prepared for a wife and children.

Babies…

Teething.

Chewing? What did babies chew on?

Both thoughts terrified him. A wife. Children. *Babies.* He doused himself with a long drink of air in hopes he would feel better. What he needed was a good dose of brandy. While he held the oxygen inside his lungs, the air burned. Sweat broke out on his forehead. Jasper understood in that moment Jason would laugh at him. He would inform him that in Maggie he had everything he wanted. Albeit a *wee* bit before he planned. Did that matter?

"Your missus is with you?"

"Yes. Thought it was time to show her off to my friends." He stepped back and smiled as he raised his hands. "She's beautiful."

"I'm Jackson." The man nodded acknowledging her. "You are Maeve, if I remember correctly. Your husband is besotted…and…he's right. You are beautiful."

"She is Maeve." Jasper placed her hand in his, brought it to his lips to kiss the back. "My very lovely wife, Maeve. Here to enjoy the company of my new friends."

Maggie jerked. Her eyes grew huge. "Yes, I'm his wife." Her words were spoken in a soft yet endearing cadence. Her face flushed a soft rose color as if she didn't appreciate the attention.

Jasper understood she tried. The fact remained Maggie didn't like him or love him. Perhaps she liked him a *wee* bit. The fact persisted quite prevalent in his mind. For Maggie, for any woman the idea of acting the wife in public would be impossible if they never made love. She could never know how to move forward. How to persuade.

Throughout their meal, acquaintances of his introduced themselves. He heard the chatter all around him. Listened even while he tried to give Maggie all the attention she would want. A buxom gray-haired lady brought them a second round of Guinness. Maggie appeared a bit sleepy eyed. Jasper wanted to take her home. Make love to her. His body hardened as he thought of this morning when he held her soft breast in his hand. Touched the pebbled tip.

"What are you doing? Thinking?" Maggie asked, her avid gaze drifting to his mouth. "You have this different expression on your face. I don't know what to think of it."

"It's time to go home. Want to sit with you on the back patio. Have a glass of wine. Besides, the weather seems to be turning. Heard that from the man who just stomped in here, shaking snowflakes from his coat. What do you say? Are you ready to play with that new pup of yours? Give him a name he can grow into?"

She nodded. Color rose to her face. Jasper wondered what brought the deepening pretty blush. Something he said or implied? If he asked, he didn't think she would tell him. Maybe if he was persistent, she would reveal her thoughts. He helped her into her cloak, his hands lingering in the front when he fastened it for her. His knuckles brushed against silken flesh, the tops of her breasts. From this morning, he had firsthand knowledge of the way they felt when he held them in the palms of his hands. He wanted to learn more. He was infatuated with her quiet charms. She beguiled him from the moment she first buried her pert little nose against his chest. In many ways, Maggie was bold. If not, she would have accepted her fate with Lord Abernathy.

She had not.

Now, Maggie was his responsibility.

He needed to do right by her. Ruining her reputation was not the way to go about that. Would marriage be so bad? If wed to the right woman, it might be the best thing to happen to him. Jasper had to shake his head. He was talking himself into that proposal. Renewing vows that weren't recalled was a fine idea. He would ask her tonight.

Before or after I crash through her maidenhead. Both would finalize the marriage. He would never deflower her unless he meant to wed.

When they stepped outside, snowflakes floated in a languid pattern onto the ground. Nothing stuck. Might not until later in the evening after the temperature dropped a few more degrees. Maggie shivered. He brought his arm around her. Pulled her close.

"Cold?" he asked as he bent close to her ear.

She would feel his breath. Unable to stop himself, wanting to do so much more, he nipped her ear. Touched the sensitive lobe with the tip of his tongue. This time he hoped the shiver was in response to him not the chill in the air.

"I am," she murmured, pressing herself against him.

The devil, he wanted to turn her, kiss her, push his tongue between her lips. Taste her essence. So close for the first time today, he caught the scent she bathed in. Today her scent was winter ice, a soft rose. When he closed his eyes, he imagined her petals opening for him. The sultry dampness between her legs that would invite him to search further for the woman she was. He needed to learn all her soft, dark secrets.

"Let's get home. I want to hold you on the patio wrapped up in that blanket. A glass or two of wine while we watch pup frolic around us. Fires will burn."

"We do need to feed the *laddie*," Maggie said while she leaned into him.

He'd helped her into the carriage. This time, he sat next to her. She held the sleeping pup on her lap. He was curled into a tiny ball. When she nestled against him, her eyes closing, he felt as if his world was right where it was supposed to be. He needed to marry this woman. After the real vows were said, he would take her home, back to Glasgow. Introduce her as his wife. No one to fear. No one to stand in their way.

To make certain, she would say yes to the renewal of their vows, he would make love to her tonight. In a day or two, she would be his in every way possible. Jasper felt content now that he'd come to his decision. Made up his mind to do right by Maggie. If he didn't, he wouldn't be able to live with himself.

"What are you thinking?" her voice sounded bedroom soft as if she was sated with her pleasure. Enjoyment he gave her. While she spoke, she stroked the pup.

That I'm a contented man. Now that I've made my decision, I can get on with the life I want with the woman I want.

"I love to have you close like this." Jasper understood he was falling in love with her. Hoped her feelings were the same or would grow into love. She told him that he didn't like her. The crazy statement was false. Never heard anything more ridiculous. He enjoyed everything about her from the moment she pushed her pert little nose against his chest.

"Hmm… You're warm," Maggie murmured, snuggling closer. "How long before we are home?"

"Why?" Jasper laughed before blurting the first words that popped into his head. "Are you so eager to be out of my arms?"

The moment he said the words he regretted them. Maggie stiffened. Her breath stopped for a second.

Maggie pushed away looking at him, her eyes narrowed. The earlier moment was lost to them. She moved farther away, unwilling now to rest in his arms. Pup woke. Licked her face that she now nuzzled close to the dog. He felt bereft. Stupid. His words put distance between them. Two steps forward then one back. When they reached home, he would need to move forward again. He wasn't certain how to do that.

"I cannot think of a name for the dog…" Maggie's voice trailed off.

"Give it time," he encouraged. "You will come up with a suitable moniker."

The vehicle traveled up the long drive to the cottage. Snow still fell around them. The night would be cold in more ways than one if he couldn't do something to change the tenor he set with his stupid words. After they made love, he intended to propose. She might not be receptive. He would be convincing. If she argued, he had reasons that couldn't be denied.

The ground was damp. Instead of helping her down to walk, Jasper carried her to the cottage.

"Jasper!" With her little fisted hand, she hit his shoulder. "You can't carry me!"

Unable to stop the speculative lift to his eyebrow he looked at her hard. "I can't?" Jasper continued through the house. His servants were there to greet him. Shot speculative looks at them that he couldn't describe. "Wine, along with something to eat on the outdoor patio. Is the fire burning? Water as well as something to eat for Pup." Jasper imagined Pup was a good enough name for the present.

"Yes, sir," Clancy said, staring for a moment too long at the dog that was wrestling to get down from Maggie's arms. "Ordered the wine along with a few canapes before you left. I hope today worked out the way you planned."

Not entirely, the night will be better. He set Maggie on the swing outside then lifted Pup from her arms. He set the dog outside the patio in hope he would do his business then return. Trusting tonight there would be no messy accidents.

A water bowl was set out for pup. Then another bowl with scraps of food that looked like pieces of meat. Something that looked like apple sauce was placed on the side of the meat. A few other morsels of food that Jasper couldn't identify were in the dish.

It wasn't long before pup returned. They could not keep calling the little guy by the name Pup. They could. If Maggie didn't come up with something better. Jasper wasn't going to name him. This was up to Maggie. Pup was her dog. At this interval, he'd settle for Charlie or Blackie. He wasn't good at names.

How the devil did parents find names for their children? There it was again, the notion of children…babies… He wasn't old enough to raise a child. Others far younger than he did the same. What was he thinking?

Kathleen brought a bottle of wine. He opened it then poured the wine into the glasses. Maggie was wrapped up in the blanket. Pup was devouring the dish of food as if he hadn't eaten in a year. Jasper wasn't certain how he intended to charm Maggie into his bed tonight. No matter what would ensue between then and the present, he was going to do so. In the morning, with her virgin's blood on his sheets, he would propose. She would have to accept. This time the marriage would be real in every way.

"Wine?" Jasper asked, hoping Maggie would be as receptive to this seduction tonight as she was twenty-four hours ago.

A kiss or two would help. He could loosen the buttons on her gown. Caress tender silken flesh. If he kept thinking about the next hour or so, he would end up seducing himself. He was hard…breath stealing hard. Knew he could get harder.

"Yes, please…" she said, looking at him with her huge green eyes. There were lines creased on her forehead between her eyes. He wanted to trace the small crease with the tip of his finger. Her thoughts seemed to be intense. What was she thinking?

He sat beside her. Sipped his wine for a few seconds. Studied. Postponed. Contemplated. Couldn't help forming his question into words. "What are you thinking about?" Jasper was unsure if he wanted to know the answer. If it was something negative about their relationship, he would have to do some furious backpedaling to bring the conversation into the best track.

"You told me you…" Maggie drank in a large gulp of wine. Looked up when Clancy brought food. She reached for a piece of bread then added cheese. She nibbled around the edges. Pup jumped up begging and whining for her food.

"None of that, Pup." Jasper put the dog on the floor before calling for Clancy. "Will you make a bed for the dog? Please?"

Clancy nodded. "By all means. Where do wish the dog to sleep?"

"In my bedroom." Maggie said with a smile, her dimples showing. She looked to Jasper. He hoped the look was for his approval.

"Our bedroom," Jasper corrected. "Pup will sleep in our bedroom. For now, leave him here."

Jasper was frightened, no terrified, the dog would put a twist to his lovemaking tonight. If he had his way, the dog would stay on the patio, not in his bedroom. Next thing, Maggie would want the dog in their bed. That wouldn't happen. He wasn't about to sleep with a damn dog, no matter how much Maggie might want the little devil there.

Jasper needed to get back to Maggie's question. "What were you going to tell me a few minutes ago?"

The blank look on her beautiful features told him she might have forgotten. A few moments later her eyes widened. Rose tinted her cheeks. What the devil was she remembering? Her pretty little tongue passed across her bottom lip. Jasper caught a fine drizzle of air into his lungs while he focused on her tongue. He wished to meet her tongue with his. Play. Dance. Investigate. Absorb her heat. Taste.

"You s-said you were go-going to con-consummate our marriage tonight." Maggie played with the edge of the blanket running the fabric through her fingers. "Is that true? Did you mean what you said?"

"I did. If you're still willing, I fully intend to do just that. Don't want any loopholes if Abernathy discovers where we are."

Tonight, he fully intended to make certain she was willing. A little foreplay would do nicely to set his plan in the right direction. Last night he upset her when he didn't finish the lovemaking. "Tell me now if you don't want me."

Sitting down beside her he set the plate of meats and cheeses on a small table in front of them. Thought better of it when Pup decided the snacks were more food meant for him. Jasper thumped Pup on the nose, "No!" he told the dog, who looked at him with forlorn dark brown eyes. Pup did seem to catch on by the third time he was warned about partaking of the food on the tray.

"Clancy!" Jasper called out.

His butler appeared nodding to him. A thin smile on his withered features. "Mr. O'Neill?"

"Take the dog to the master chamber. See that the bed we spoke of earlier is made up for the little guy. We'll be up soon."

Jasper had more than one negative thought about this plan. If the dog woke up at the wrong time and wanted to be part of the sensual play he intended, Pup would put a decided damper on his efforts to consummate the marriage that wasn't yet a marriage.

"Are you certain?" Clancy asked, snowy eyebrows lifting as if he thought his boss was daft. "A dog in the bedroom…" The servant shook his head. "…never heard of such a ridiculous notion."

It was as if his butler understood what tonight was all about. Jasper didn't care if everyone knew his intentions though Maggie might.

"Unless you can come up with a better plan, yes. Maggie wants Pup to sleep in our room."

Jasper looked to her, willing to give her almost anything she asked for. He expected her to say something. She didn't. Was it this awkward to have children? Would children want to sleep in their bed with them? Damn… This was something to think about. He should take precautions tonight. That thought settled like a dead weight in his stomach. No, she would question him withdrawing even though he doubted if she understood the why of it. It was perhaps possible she wouldn't notice.

Once Clancy disappeared with Pup, Maggie reached out to him. "Thank you. I want Pup to feel loved. We just took him away from his mother as well as his siblings. He's going to need our affection."

Jasper beamed, pleased with his decision. If the dog was to sleep somewhere else, the choice would need to be Maggie's. He wasn't going to thwart his plans by denying her the puppy he bought her.

"Now." He paused, still pleased with his decision making. "More wine? Food? Relax so we can enjoy what's left of the evening. See what will come…? Eh…?"

Maggie held out her glass. He splashed wine to the brim. If she were just a tiny bit fuzzy headed, this seduction of her would be easier. Though he didn't want her gone with drink. He did hope she'd be more relaxed. From his vantage point on the swing, he watched the snow fall. About fifteen minutes ago the white stuff began to stick. Jasper wondered if he would have to get up in the middle of the night to take Pup outside. He didn't cotton to that idea. Never appreciated being disturbed from a warm bed with a willing woman. Someone would have to do the job. He wouldn't allow Maggie to go out in the cold during the middle of the night.

After she finished eating and her glass was half empty, Maggie set it down. She turned to him. Silent invitation in the sparkle in her eyes, she reached out to touch his chin, trace the line of his jaw. This was heaven to him. Maggie touched him first. Initiated what he would finish later on tonight. He sucked in a breath of air as that soft caress ignited him. Quickened his pulse. Aroused. Scintillated. Didn't know if the gesture was for courage or fortitude.

He picked up her hand. Held it within his. Touched the tips of each finger with his lips then his teeth. Saw the shiver, the small quiver of her shoulders as she too flamed to life. She was a tempest in his soul. He treated her other hand in the same manner.

"Would you kiss me?" she asked, her voice quivering as she spoke the words. "I liked the way your mouth felt on mine. Would like to do that again if you don't mind too much." She paused, staring at him. "If you don't mind that is?"

Of course, he didn't mind. To have her closer to him was his intent. With amazing ease, she was falling into his plans. He pulled her toward him, turning her so she straddled him. Felt the heat of her core against his arousal. If he touched her, he felt certain she would be wet, slick with her desire. Exploring all of her would be his delight. Before he carried her upstairs to their bed, she would be ready for the consummation of the marriage. He thought of touching her legs, his hand traveling to the apex.

The consummation of their pretend wedding would be soon. He steadied himself. Braced himself against the possible repercussions of the lie. This was for a higher purpose. In this case he prayed the ends justified the means. By the time the evening ended, she would be his in almost every way. A second wedding would be all that was left to accomplish, a reaffirmation of their vows. She would never need worry about Abernathy again.

She sat on him. Her legs parted. Open for whatever he decided. Her hands rested on his shoulders, fingers moving, exploring. The blanket slipped to her waist. He wanted to see her lips swollen and damp from his devotion. View her breasts bared for his eyes only. Breath caught in the back of his throat. His hands framed her cheeks for a second. He decided on the course for the nights pleasure.

Jasper wrapped his hand around her neck, claiming her his possession. His thumb brushed across her chin. First, he tasted one dimple then the other. Touched his tongue to the slight indentations. He would do the same to the tips of her breasts. With gentle pressure, he placed his mouth on hers. Tugged on the bottom lips with his teeth. Touched the inside of her mouth, delved deeper. She met the gentle thrust of his tongue with hers. Danced. Tasted. Explored. Her flesh felt like soft silk meant for a man's pleasure. She tasted of wine and mint. Her breath sweet.

Maggie whispered his name into his mouth. He kissed her again, seeking more. Her secrets would be his tonight. By morning she would have them no more. He would learn every intimate detail of her body. Dark secrets he would delve into until she cried out her ecstasy. His hands roamed down her back. Touched upon the buttons. Flicked them open until he reached the base of her spine. Needed to feel bared flesh. She bit his lip. He sucked on her tongue, inviting her inside to taste of him, to learn of his need for her. She could explore to her heart's content. Her fingers played with the buttons on his shirt. Opened them one at a time. She spread her hands on his chest, curling her fingers in the hair she found there, tugging, stroking. She experimented by running her hands across him. He burned. His hips jerked when she readjusted herself on his thighs, pressing against his member.

Pushing the shoulders of her gown down her arms, he tugged the sleeves from her wrists. She arched against him. Her breasts thrust forward. Touched upon his chest. Titillated. Provoked. When he unlaced her chemise, with slow measured movement he pulled the blue ties from the eyelets. After he finished, he pushed the straps from her arms. Little feminine noises danced from her lips. Throaty purrs of pleasure. Palms rubbed against hardened nipples. A ripple of breath here. A long sigh there. He wanted to take those sounds into his mouth. Cherish the whimpers of desire.

His sweet Maggie.

After the kiss, the stolen moments when he was inside her, he moved back to look at the picture he revealed so far. Her mouth was damp. Lips swollen. Reddened. Wet. Moisture glimmered. Her deep green eyes glazed with pleasure. Maggie's breasts. Her breasts were works of art. They were large enough to fill his hands. The tips along with aureole a blushing shade of dusty rose. When he ran his hands along her shoulders, their movement delighted him. He enjoyed watching. Savored this experience. Committed the moment to memory.

Her eyes were fixed on his. She sucked in a long drink of air. Her chest rising then falling with the motion. The tips hardened more as cool air flowed across her. He wanted to see the sweet tips elongated. Wet. Shiny from his consideration. For several pulses of his heart, he looked into her eyes. After that he focused on her breasts. With the tip of his finger, he touched each one. Rolled the hardened crests between thumb and forefinger. Watched as they elongated, growing longer. Just as he looked at her mouth damp and swollen, he meant to see each nipple in the same way.

Keeping his gaze on her for as long as possible he bent to taste one breast. His mouth curled around the tip. Flicked his tongue. A gentle bite brought a low humming purr. When he finished the initial taste, he pulled as much of her breast as he could into his mouth. Tugged. Sucked. Drew on the tender sensitive flesh. Broke into a cavalcade of sensations leaping to his groin.

She whimpered. Arched. Writhed. Jasper switched his attention to the other breast. Played in the same manner. A sweet drone of pleasure whispered back to him.

~ * ~

Nelson was having too much fun that night to think about his wayward fiancée. He meant to have all his needs fulfilled and then some. Looking for fun, entertainment at its best, he stumbled into the right brothel. There were half-clad women everywhere. Some were naked, selling their charms. The auction he heard tell of was proceeding. Whiskey was free. Women were free until the selling of the new women was over. These were women who were said to be new to the trade. The sale was for a week's use to the lucky bidder. They would spend their time in a room upstairs. Any man's needs could be rewarded for the right price. He held no scruples. Enjoyed any type of sexual dalliance. This would be delicious. His appetite wetted. Decided he would bid whatever price was necessary. He had the coin to see to his pleasure.

Men along with the women in this brothel tonight didn't care about principles or morals. Didn't care if others saw them in the most intimate of pastimes. If they coupled with the same sex or enjoyed multiple partners of both. He'd never had sex in front of others. Perhaps this evening would be his first. Didn't believe he would mind sex in front of an audience. The mood he was in, he felt as if he could try anything. This evening, he would do whatever felt right. Men along with their women were sprawled nude everywhere. Sex rampant. This was where he was meant to be. Nelson grinned. He would buy a partner tonight. Keep her for a week. Might not leave the room even to come up for air. The devil, a week of constant sex. No complaints. The women bought as well as paid for. This was his dream of heaven.

A lady of the night set a drink on the table. She cocked her head asking if she could sit. Nelson saw the color surrounding her nipples. The dress draped low to reveal her breasts, the skirt arranged high to show off her legs. After his nod, she sat down. She sipped her drink, staring at the stage where the next woman was placed. The lady was dressed to provoke as well as tease. The sheer gown left no part of her to a man's imagination. She postured in several different delightful poses. Her large breasts swayed with each new position.

"You planning on bidding? The blond with the see through chemise, is a good catch. She will go for plenty of pounds. You have the money?" the woman asked as she continued to survey the crowds of men bartering for a woman.

Nelson perked up at the lady's words. This woman was standing on the small stage brought to the middle of the floor for the auction. "She a virgin?" Even though Nelson asked he didn't care.

What he needed most was a woman of experience to satisfy him. Virgins were overrated. A man only needed a virgin when he married. By now he should have been wed to Maggie. Would have been able to have her whenever he pleased. Teach her how he liked his sex. Instead, he had to chase after the girl. When he caught up to her, Maggie would pay. He wouldn't allow her to leave his bed for at least a month. She would know who her master was.

"Doubt it. Does it matter?" the lady asked as she sipped the drink she brought for him. "The gals all claim to be new to the business. Most aren't. Madam offers them half of what they bring in for the night. It's incentive. The prettiest show up claiming to be new to whoring. This one we all know is not. She's been at the business for several years. She will give you pleasure if you are the lucky man who outbids the others looking to experience her charms."

He lifted his glass pointing at the woman, his mouth salivating as she turned on the stage presenting herself to him. She seemed to focus on him. Appeared to ask him to bid on her. Who was he to deny himself the pleasure of this woman? "You say this lady is not a virgin? At this time, I'm not looking for a virgin. She might do…"

The lady smiled at him then winked. "Sylvie is well established here. Those who frequent my brothel understand all the woman can give. There are women who enjoy sex, relish these auctions. This is her first showing this year. This is January. I guarantee, she'll please you before you reach her room."

The lady, Sylvie, toyed with the ribbons holding her chemise together. Each one slipped through the eyelets until the chemise hung open revealing more of her ripe body. Sylvie's legs were long, very white, shapely. The tips of her breasts were soft rose. Revealed now to the crips air in the salon. Nelson raised his hand to say he was bidding. When the lady noticed, she flashed a smile at him. Turned so he could see more of her. The light hair of her mound intrigued Nelson. She positioned herself for his thoughtful perusal. He could tell she wanted him to continue bidding.

"She wants you to win her. See the other blokes raising their hands. Old. Mean as sin. Milk toast." The madam sat back to rake his gaze over him. "You, on the other hand, are nicely formed. Are you mean? Milk toast? No?" The lady tapped her long fingernail against her chin. "Imagine you will do quite nicely. Can you handle two girls at one time?"

The questions startled Nelson from his examination of the lady. There were moments he could be mean, dangerous to anyone who thwarted him, even his mistress. He wasn't going to mention those times to this woman. In the end game, what this lady knew or didn't know wouldn't matter. "Not mean. Not milk toast as I'm certain you've already decided. Never had two women at the same time. Imagine I would relish the experience. Believe I can handle two females." Nelson smiled at the woman on the dais as he raised his hand another time. The win came too easily. He wondered if he should be suspicious. If there was more to this than met the eye, he would deal with anything that happened.

"You won the lady. You will be given a room to play with her upstairs. You can come and go as you wish. The lady must remain in the room for the entirety of the week. You will have the key. If necessary, you may lock her inside. You can also dally with her in the salon before going upstairs. You can show all here what it is you won. In this, there are no rules except the ones you make up." She nodded as the blond walked toward him before pointing to the woman who now stood on the stage to be auctioned. "They come together whenever possible…a pair to delight the senses. You should bid on the second one. Constance is her name. Sylvie and Constance are not a matched pair but they do make excellent book ends. If you purchase both of them, they will show their gratitude in mouthwatering ways."

Sylvie sat on his lap. Touched his mouth with hers. Nelson's body lit up. Fired. Hardened. She played with his cravat until the fabric loosened, falling down his chest. Her nails scraped over his neck. She bit. Laved with her tongue to appease the small hurt. "That's my friend up there," she purred, touching her tongue to his earlobe before swirling it around inside. "Bid on her too. We'll both treat you right. You won't be disappointed. I promise." She brushed her knuckles along his clothed penis. "Big. Nice. You will give pleasure to two women with ease. Like my man big. Hard. You will fill us."

Nelson didn't care much about giving a woman what she wanted. He saw to his needs first. If the woman climaxed, fine; if not, that was fine too. He bid on the second lady. He'd never been with two ladies at the same time. Thought this would be a fine time for a new adventure. Sylvie unfastened his pants, pulling him free. He shuddered. Her hand wrapped around him. Squeezed. Traveled to the tip touched the moisture then back. This Sylvie was not new to the business. She knew what she was about. Sylvie was between his legs. Captured his sex in her mouth. Sucked hard. Before he knew what happened, he erupted into her mouth. He didn't realize he had won the second lady. Didn't recall raising his hand to bid. Constance sauntered toward him. Stopped. Her hands cupped her succulent breasts pushing them higher for his perusal. She was licking her lips, hips swaying one way her breasts the other. While Sylvie's bubbies were enough to sample, Constance over flowed. While Sylvie was blond, Constance's hair was black as midnight. Sylvie's eyes were a deep dark brown. Constance's eyes were China blue. The pair would make fine bookends for his entertainment.

"Connie is my name," she purred as she bent over to take his mouth in hers.

She swept her tongue across his lips. Probed. Pushed inside his open mouth. Sylvie still played with him, her hands on his chest brushing his nipples. Nelson groaned. Thought he would climax again in the salon if these two ladies kept this up. Connie brushed her nipples across his mouth. He opened. Sucked one then the other. Played their game.

"Show him to your room, ladies," the madam said, "before he's a mess. Have fun. Everything tonight is at your disposal. Nelson paid a great deal for both of you. Treat him right. I'll send up food along with drinks for the rest of the night. In the morning, your man will need to make arrangements for your further use."

The words echoed in his head. Having fun was the reason he was here. Entertainment. He never expected to have two women seeing to his needs. Two women at the same time. Nelson never thought about something such as that before. He enjoyed sharing his mistress with another man. Didn't know if he'd feel the same about Maggie. Gave thought to that. Once she was with child and he knew the brat was his, he would share. As for this evening, tonight, these two women would see to his needs, his enjoyment, imagining hands exploring him. Enticing him. He was fascinated.

As he walked by the other patrons in the bordello, he nodded. Another lady was on the stage. She was cowering from fright. Her body quivering while she tried to cover herself. Nelson thought this one must be new to the experience. A virgin. While taking a woman for her first time was gratifying, he was content with his purchase. For the next week, he might not leave the room. He would need to see how the events transpired.

He was inside the chamber where the next week would emerge. The space was large, the bed huge. Big enough to accommodate three people. He stood in the middle of the open space watching his purchases. Sylvie leaned against the door, her chemise hanging from her shoulders, her breasts bared for him. She was his for the week. Constance sat on a window sill. Her legs were crossed, naked, then she parted her thighs for him to see all of her pink sweetness. They were staring at him as if he should know what they wanted. Sylvie was the first to sweep her chemise off her body. She tossed the garment at him. The silken fabric struck him in the face. Breasts oscillating, she sauntered toward him. Her tongue touched her upper lip.

"It's my turn," Constance said in a throaty purr. She mimicked Sylvie. Her chemise landed at his feet. "I'm going to taste you. Suck you until you explode into my mouth. Would you like that? To detonate between my teeth." Her question was ridiculous. Of course, he would like what she meant to give.

Sylvie was behind him, ridding him of his shirt. Her hands, she splayed across his chest. Twisted his nipples between her fingers. Constance knelt in front of him, getting rid of his boots then his britches. Anticipating whatever she wished to deal out, he stood at attention. His rod throbbed. Ready for anything these two ladies sent his way. His fingers wound into Constance's hair. Pushed her closer to his waiting arousal. Her mouth sipped on him, pulled on him until he groaned. Her teeth scraped against his skin. His knees were weak. Didn't think he could stand much longer.

"Let's go to the bed," his words were husky. A woman never before created this incessant need in him. He required more. Wanted as much as these two ladies could give him.

Constance looked up. Nodded. Sylvie pulled him backward as Constance pushed from the front. The devil he'd never felt anything like this. He fell on the bed. Sylvie's legs straddled his head. He looked into her beautiful petals. Constance sat on his rod. Sylvie set her sweet pussy on his face. He licked. Touched inside. Devoured. Soaked in her sultry heat that covered his mouth. Tasted her nectar. His hands wrestled with Constance's breasts. Sylvie and Constance came together, their mouths touching. Kissed. She moved on him while the two women brought him higher and higher until he knew he could hold back no longer.

The woman cried out as he yelled his pleasure, exploding inside her. Felt the other lady's climax as his tongue reached inside her channel. He would die if this kept up for a week. He needed food as well as drink. A moment to recap his thoughts along with his strength. His limbs weak. All of him limp, he spread his arms along with his legs across the bed.

Sylvie bent over him, purring her lips brushing across his, still arousing. "You need more energy? This is cocaine. Ever used before?"

She was right. If this cocaine would give him more stamina, he'd use. "No…I'll try anything."

To keep this up for a week…yes…if cocaine would energize him. He'd heard about the potent effects before. Never tried the drug.

"You will love this." She showed him how to sniff the powder into his nose. "It will give you more vitality. Your energy will exceed anything you've ever known. We have a week of fun planned. Don't want you to fall asleep too soon. Before we can milk all your seed from you."

"We will have more fun than you could ever imagine," Constance said while she stroked him neck to ballocks.

Hell, he'd do anything to keep up with the ladies. Nelson sniffed the white stuff. Felt a surge of power. Energy. Vigor. His sexual drive returned. He found himself revitalized. Thought he could do anything. Strength surged.

"I'll watch this time," Constance said, sitting down on a chair near the bed, crossing her legs. "You make love to Sylvie now."

She poured him a glass of wine. He drank then set it beside the bed. Sylvie sniffed in the powder. Sat back shaking her blond hair while the strands played peek-a-boo with her dark pink nipples.

She started with his feet, licked and teased her way up his legs to his groin. Lingered there for a couple of seconds then moved upward. His fingers wound into her hair. This time he felt empowered. He was going to control the sex. He tossed her to her back before bringing her legs over his shoulders.

Thrust inside her passage. She was hot. Wet. Pulsing. Kissed his length with her body. It was over before the sex barely began. After he finished, he drank the offered wine. Ate from the plate of food that was brought in while he played with both women. Next, he viewed the two ladies as they fondled each other. Another first. He'd never seen two women make love to each other. He would remember this night forever.

The night…the week…went on in much the same manner. Nelson never left the room. The three had sex. Sometimes he watched the ladies pleasure each other. Other times he had both of them over then over again. He would pleasure one while he thrust into the other. They would exchange places. There were other moments when he had sex with them separately. They took cocaine to give energy then wine to sleep. In that entire week, Nelson didn't think he slept more than a few hours.

By the time he left the brothel he was disoriented and weak. Exhausted. The madam put him in a cab before sending him home. Once inside his rented home, Nelson slipped to the floor, his head on the back of the door. He tried to breathe, to move his muscles. He must have been on the floor for several hours. When he could move again, he crawled up the steps to his bedchamber. He slept. One of his servants woke him. Brought him food as well as wine. He didn't know how long he stayed in his bed. It must have been a day or two. Nelson had visions of returning to the brothel for a second round.

Chapter Six

She was sitting on his lap, her legs spread across his thighs. She recalled last night. Her breasts would be exposed soon for his enjoyment. He kissed her then kissed her again. Hard then soft. Ran his hands along the ladder of her ribs. Her lips were swollen from his attention. Damp from each sweep of his mouth. He pulled her lips and tongue inside him. Heat flared higher with each stroke of his tongue along with his hands. Her head fell back in a silent invitation leaving the length of her neck exposed. When he revealed her breasts, she heaved in a deep breath of air. Felt cold air. After that, she prayed this wasn't a pretend marriage. Maggie didn't think she could stop what was happening if she found out all this was fake. She needed to ignore her misgivings. Wanted to imagine everything would turn out the way she wished. He wouldn't lie to her. She trusted him.

Now, before this goes too far, I should tell him no. Right this instant, I should say the word. Before I make a colossal mistake. One I can't take back. The devil, I've already gone so far I can take nothing back.

You dinna want to do that, lass. Say no. He's making you feel things you never believed possible. You want to find out what will happen next. Where he will touch you. You could say no but you dinna want to do so. If this marriage is pretend, Jasper will do right by you. He will marry you legally. You won't be left behind.

The things he's making me feel. Ohh… I believe he knows just what to do. Why would he do right by me if I give him everything he asks for? A man will take. It's what Anice has always told us girls.

His mouth closed over her nipple. She thought she would jump out of her skin. He skimmed the throbbing crest with the tip of his tongue, again then again. Nibbled on the distended peak. She was so sensitive there. He enchanted all her senses. The man knew what he was about. Sensations flew through her. Swamped. Inundated with quicksilver speed. She arched against him. Pressed. Writhed. He turned his attention to her other breast. Tempest swept. Deep in the back of her throat she purred. Longed for more then again even more.

"Are you alright, Maggie, *lass* I would have you feel only your sweet pleasure?" Jasper asked while his hands explored the length of her leg.

She tightened her thighs against him. Higher. His fingers progressed along the insides of her legs. Touched the top of her thigh. She settled deeper onto him, feeling the press of his body against her. Felt the bulge between her thighs. "You're not afraid? Are you?" His hand splayed across her belly. Touched her hip bones as she parted her legs farther as if asking him to touch her where he had no business touching her. "I intend to see to your pleasure, love."

Words stuck in her throat. She nodded. "Pleasure, yes…" That's what he was doing now. Seeing to her pleasure. She was tingles everywhere. His taste evocative. Mint. Wine. He would do more. Anice never said anything to them apart from the kissing. Apart from the breaking through the maidenhead. That would cause pain. Her mother told her everything after that if her husband was talented the act would be ecstasy.

How would Jasper do that? Give pleasure? Ecstasy?

She wasn't supposed to allow him intimacies if she wasn't married. Jasper assured her they were wed. The ceremony was so vague she couldn't recall anything about the moments before, during or after. Did remember signing papers. He never told her what those papers were. Thought them to be…was it the hotel or the ship's manifest? Now she couldn't remember which.

Is that what he would do now? Give her pain then pleasure?

He stroked her arms. Spoke softly to her. Maggie wanted to see him, to look her fill just as he gazed at her. He would be magnificent in every way.

"Take my shirt off for me. There's a *lass*," he murmured before his lips closed over the damp tip of her breast for a second time. Her fingers fumbling, she tried to unfasten his shirt. She was getting nowhere. He chuckled the sound soft…amused.

Maggie pulled the lacing through. She saw the crisp dark hair of his chest revealed by the deep V where the shirt was open.

His voice throbbed when he spoke one more time. "That's right. You've got the idea. Lift it over my head." He held his arms in the air.

She tried to do what he said. Her hands trembled. Her body shook. Her breasts danced across his bared chest. With effort, Maggie pulled the garment over his head. Her breasts brushed against him. Sensitized tips made soft acquaintance with his exposed flesh. The contact mercuric. Raw desire pulsed through her in a tempest of hunger. Thought she might drown in the enchantment. With a heavy sigh, she let the garment drift to the ground. Fingertips against flesh. Bodies pressed together. She shuddered at the interaction. His chest pushed against her breasts. The crisp dark hair she played with earlier brushed against her nipples sending more delightful vibrations cascading into her. His hands cupped her breasts, fingers toyed with the crests. Twisted.

Maggie gulped a lungful of air. Tried to clear her head of the muddled haze of erotic sensations he orchestrated. A difficult task since all she could do was feel everything. Her body never felt so profound. So on edge. Tight. "What if the servants walk in? They would see…" Maggie whispered as she let the rest of her thoughts dangle. Cold air caressed her breasts. She dragged in another deep breath of Jasper scented air. He'd moved away from her. The gaze of his eyes roamed over her. Perused her. With gentleness, he bent to kiss one then the other nipple.

Once more he scanned her body. His thumb ran across the line of her jaw. "Your breasts are beautiful. White except for the rose crests. Firm. More than a handful. Though I don't need more. Ah, you are worried about the help. None would dare enter into our domain unless called. I gave all the night off. They would only come if one of us rings for them." After a short pause, he grinned, a wicked grin. "Is the rest of you as lovely as your breasts? I'd like to discover the truth for myself." His fingers wound into her hair, pulling her back. Her breasts thrust from her as he must have wished. Her fingers held onto his shoulders. Nails bit into flesh while he investigated more thoroughly. His lips traveled the column of her neck. He stopped laving where her pulse beat hard and fast at the base of her neck.

Outside the cold wind whistled. Inside, heat flamed with each tender caress of Jasper's mouth upon her. His lips fell upon her mouth again. Clashed. Battled with hers as she responded to the attack. Ravished. She parted for him, welcoming him inside the dark intimacy. Needing to taste as well as explore. When his tongue touched upon her, she tugged it inside. Rubbed hers against his. He kissed her everywhere. Touched upon sensitive territory while his hands and fingers sent raw craving rushing through her. Drowning. Devouring. Aching, she felt the surge of wet heat between her thighs. His fingers curved around her mound. Delved into her cleft. Touched upon her with the most tender care. Found a place that made passion flair higher. The magic of it all left her hovering in a vast land of fascination.

"We should take this upstairs," his words were whispered against her ear where he found another place that sent her body quivering with desire. "What do you say? I would make love somewhere else. This just won't do. Your first time straddled on top of me on a porch swing just isn't right. We can save this adventure for another time. Though the ambiance is romantic. Snow is falling, drifting to the ground. The scene outside is a delight to the senses."

Maggie found she was shaking her head. She didn't want to move until she discovered what was going to happen next. Was afraid he would abandon her, leave her swamped within her passion. "I…" Her lips parted. Her tongue swept across them. His hands tightened on her waist. She felt the brief touch of his kiss.

"While I'm certain no one would dare walk in on us, I'd rather have our first time together be in a bed. Private, you *ken*. This won't do a'tall. With no possibility of intrusion. What do you think? I would lay you out on your stomach first. Place tiny kisses down your spine to your sweet little butt. Want to see if your back is as lovely as your front. After that, after I thoroughly loved your back, I will turn my attention to your front. Taste every piece of silken flesh from the top of your head to the tips of your toes. Are your toes as sweet tasting at the rest of you? If you like, you can do the same to me. My body is yours to charm…my back…my front. Every part of me will be open to your passion."

"A bed…yes…nice…charm?" Maggie barely got the words out while he continued to touch as well as explore so many different parts of her. She jerked when one of his long fingers delved inside her. Moaned. Cried out. "Jasper!"

Jasper chuckled. Laughed while he continued to travel within the heat of her. Watching her eyes as he found a most erotic spot. Her insides started to pulse. Felt parts of her she never knew existed clench tight, pulsing against his invasion. She moaned again. Felt her body escalating to a place where she thought she would die if he stopped.

"Do you like that, love?" he asked as he plunged deeper his rhythm slow. Precise. Measured to gain the most. "You're so small. Tight." He groaned then stopped. A small curse left his lips.

She felt bereft once more. She'd been on a precipice of something. Wished to yell at him not to stop. Her body shuddered.

"Hoped the small barrier would not be there. Don't wish to give you pain."

Her forehead fell against his. Her voice so very soft, weak. She'd been so close to losing control. "What? Why are you swearing?" Maggie asked drawing back from him. "Did I do something wrong? I almost..."

"I'm sorry. You will...we will get to that point of no control again. Nothing...nothing is wrong. I want this to be perfect." A pause later as she listened to each of his breaths. "It's..." He didn't say anything more. She cried out as he nipped her throat. Played with lips and teeth across her collarbone. Skipped along her shoulder. Shudders wracked her body again. The building desire once more escalated. Jasper stopped. Handed her the unfinished glass of wine that had been set aside. "Drink up. We can take the glasses along with the bottle to bed with us. I want to play all night. Want you to climax in my arms a dozen times."

Climax? A dozen times?

She did as he told her while she set the glass on the table. "What now?" she murmured, feeling dazed by what he was doing to her. Her mind was in a fog filled with bliss. By what almost happened. Wished for it to become a reality. Eager as well as fascinated, she followed his directives. Ran her hands down his chest to the waistband of his pants. He sucked in air. His hard muscles contracted. Maggie tilted her head questioning. She realized the advent of power. Her touch pleasured him in some way. His lips were drawn back showing even white teeth.

His jaw tense as she explored him. Maggie tilted her head, questioning. She lowered her eyes, to see where she investigated. Witnessed the bulge below his pants. Wished she dared touch him there. Wished she could see him.

Jasper cleared his throat, his hand stilling hers. His grip tightened as he brought her hand back to his chest. "You should stop that for now, love.

You'll have time later to do what you will. For now, we go upstairs for the rest of the night." He helped her into the sleeves of her dress. Smoothed her skirts down her legs. Fastened a few of the buttons. "We'll take the bottle of wine along with the glasses. Can you carry the plate of food? Would be nice to satisfy all our appetites as we spend the night making love."

The night making love? Can two people do that?

Thought he would make love to her here…on the swing…watching the snow drift downward. Didn't want to tell him how eager she was. So fervent she didn't want to leave until he did make love to her. Maggie wanted to discover everything about this love making business. Needed to see him wearing nothing…nothing at all. Would he be naked for her?

He tapped her on the nose. His smile warmed her. Gave her the confidence she lacked. "You look disappointed. Are you?"

Her moist lips quivered. He touched the softness with his thumb and ran the base across her mouth. She responded to him with the tip of her tongue. He seemed to understand what she asked. "I…thought you would…"

"Make love to you? Yes, I have every intention of doing so. More than once if that is what you'd like? We need nourishment for that to happen. This is our wedding night. We need to celebrate with wine, food as well as ourselves. I'm going to learn everything there is to know about your sweet body. All the gentle curves. The places you wish to have me caress." He was fastening a few more buttons on her dress leaving the top buttons undone as well as a few in between. "Don't want to waste too much time getting you out of this again. Though, I could explore with infinite slowness that will have you panting for more."

It seemed he could not help but touch more sensitive places even while he attempted to dress her.

Maggie nodded. She was already breathless for more. She'd almost felt something within her body that was unparalleled. She'd been so close to magic. Jasper enchanted. Captivated. Her breasts heaved with each tender caress. Found when she tried to stand, doing so was more difficult than she anticipated. She began to fall. "Jasper…" Maggie cried out.

She clung to him. Her nose once more buried in his chest. She caught his spicey masculine scent which warmed her. Brought memories to the forefront of her mind. She dashed the thought of Abernathy from her head.

Focused on this man, her husband.

Jasper laughed as he wound his hands through her hair. More pins scattered. "Seems you like your nose right there. I enjoy that too." With a carefree motion, he flung his shirt over his shoulder before scooping her into his arms. "I will carry you. Don't want you falling for me too fast."

She held onto the wine along with the glasses. He transported her as well as the platter of food which rested across her lap. Maggie rested her head against his shoulder. Felt his steps quicken as he took the stairs two at a time. He was so strong, vibrant, and alive. She wanted him for the rest of her life. This was going to be the first real night of their marriage.

Against his chest, her nose buried in the most comfortable spot, she smiled. He was correct. She liked her nose nestled against him. The memories were almost pleasant of that night she met him. In the beginning, she'd been terrified. Her very existence had been threatened. Understood Lord Abernathy would follow. Would send his men after her to bring her back. If they found her, she would have been guarded night and day with no escape possible. Never let out of a locked door until Abernathy forced her hand in marriage. She would never say yes. There were ways though that a woman could be made to comply. Maggie understood her sisters would have been threatened. She might have been drugged. She would do anything for her sisters. Her mother understood that fact. Anice would have told Abernathy just how he could get to her.

Something about Jasper vanquished the terror rolling through her. That night, some sixth sense, an insight perhaps into the person he was, she'd known she could trust him. Could she be falling in love with the man? She hoped so. She was married to him. A woman should be in love with the man she married. At least she believed she was married. A few doubts still assailed her. He reassured her more than once the document she put her name to was legal. This marriage they embarked upon was no sham. Who was she to argue? She should trust his word of honor. From the very first, Maggie believed him to be a man of his word. Until yesterday, he'd not tried to consummate their marriage.

Last night the attempt failed.

Believing this might all be a lie, she was confused as well as angry, frustrated too. She trusted him. What if he lied? If this marriage was pretend, he did lie to her. He assured her more than once it was true as well as legally binding. She might never forgive him for the transgression if he spoke false. Forgiving him was important. She did think she was falling in love. Her emotions told her she needed to be in love before she could allow him these intimacies they rushed toward. He was the most perfect man in the world.

Except he might have lied.

At the door, he turned the knob before pushing it open with his foot. Pup met them with a bark then a leap. He whined. A whirlwind of flying feet dashed through the opening the door left. The dog headed downstairs. Jasper cursed. Swore again as he strode into the room. "The damn dog!"

"Jasper." She didn't want him angry with the animal. "He's more than likely terrified. This is all new to him. A place he's never seen and we weren't with him."

"Wait here. I'll get him. Don't worry about the dog. He'll be fine." Jasper set her on the floor then put the tray on the table. He was gone. Departed without looking back.

What did she expect? This was going to be a repeat of the night before. At least he would hold her. She would have that much. The moment Maggie had been waiting for vanished. She stood alone in the middle of the bedroom. Pup needed something. What if he got out? What if he ran away back to the modiste? It was cold outside. Pup would freeze. Jasper had to find him. She started to follow. Changed her mind. Decided the best thing to do was to stay put as he ordered. She needed to find her shoes. They were downstairs. The night was too cold. He didn't wear his shirt. He would freeze.

Maggie, he's a grown man who can take care of himself. He will bring Pup back no worse for the adventure.

They might both freeze. Did he still wear his shoes? She had no idea. He will put on a coat. Shoes too if he needs them.

She was alone with a myriad of day dreams swirling in her head. Despondent, she sat down on the bed. Poured wine into the glass she held. Drank deep. The wine was delicious. Warmed her inside as well as out. She stared at the door for too many seconds to count. Listened to the clock tick…tick…tick…. Walked to the window to look for the two males she was falling in love with. Snow, deep white snow, coupled with flakes floating to the earth was all she saw. She hoped to spy one or the other. Where the devil were they? Maggie strode to the fireplace. Held out her hands to warm them. Turned so she could warm her backside. Wondered what happened to the evening. The clock on the mantel continued to tick.

This was not as he told her how the night would go. If she could be bold, she would take the gown off. Would be naked as he told her he wanted her. All desire vanished when Jasper left the room. Well, maybe not all. The raw hunger coupled with the pulsing need no longer stormed through her with raging heat. She no longer felt intoxicated with raw passion he composed. Her body calmed to a fever pitch. With time, she would no longer feel the heat of his seduction. The charming press of his fingers within places so intimate she'd never been aware of before this man came into her life.

Sitting down on the fur rug in front of the fireplace, she sipped the wine. Stared at the clock. A few minutes passed since the last time she looked. Those minutes seemed like hours. She set her head on the back of a big chair. Closed her eyes. The next time she looked a half hour sped by. She should see if she could find them. Go outside. Freeze.

Where the devil were the two men in her life? Lost in the snow storm? Would they find their bodies in the morning light? How morbid. She closed her eyes again. Must have dozed.

A huge slurp up the front of her face jerked her awake. "Ooo..." Maggie pushed strands of hair from her eyes. Wiped the moisture away with the bottom of her skirt. *Pup?* "That's awful," she cried out, holding the squirming Pup away from her. "Don't you dare do that again!" She shook her finger at the little dog.

"Maggie, love, we're back. Pup decided he wanted to run a bit. Sorry. We've been gone an hour. Can we pick up where we left off?" His gentle hands traced the column of her neck. "I'm going to put Pup on his bed. I'll be right back to take care of you." Jasper held the dog while he strode to the corner where Clancy had set up the dog's bed.

She was still trying to figure out what happened. Jasper was back with Pup. Pup wasn't going to stay in his bed if they were awake. Maggie knew that for a fact. The dog would hope to play with them. Maybe that was what the two of them had been doing, playing in the snow. Jasper would wish to wear the little fellow out. She wasn't certain she was still in the mood for what he planned. Now, she was sleepy. Relaxed from the wine. Warmed by the heat of the fire.

To her surprise, Jasper sat down beside her minus Pup. He handed her a newly poured glass of wine along with bread and cheese. "He's sleeping. Had more exercise than he wished for. The little guy does enjoy the snow. He seemed to enjoy chasing snowflakes, biting at each one as if he tried to taste the white stuff. We've a few minutes to ourselves until he wakes. Hope that's not until dawn."

His hands were cold where he touched hers. She shivered. He held them out to the fire to warm himself. She set the bread and cheese to his lips. "Bite."

He did as she asked. Nipped the tip of one finger in the process. Maggie wasn't hungry though the wine tasted good. "Where did you go? I missed you. A couple of times, I almost went after you."

She did miss him, his warmth. The feel of his kisses. His body closed around hers.

He sat back, his arm resting on one raised knee. "I chased the little devil for about ten minutes. Pup thought it was a game I liked just as much as he did. After a time, he peed. I got him back because I tempted him with a slice of cheese. Greedy little beggar. At least we know he can be bribed with food. Believe that was why he dashed from the room. Not for cheese but to pee. Eilinora must have trained him a bit. He seems to know not to pee in the house. He raced to get outside. Whined at the door before I got there to open it for him."

Turning to him, she touched his jaw as her gaze riveted on his mouth. Once more, she wanted his kiss then one after that. "You sound proud of him. Could that be true? Are you beginning to like the little devil? At first, I didn't think you wanted him. That you agreed just to please me."

"All that is true. As to how I feel about Pup now? I don't know. I'm going to reserve judgment until the lad proves himself." He lifted his shoulders. The shrug was all masculine, muscles rippling. "Proud but annoyed as well. I'd like to get back to our night. What we planned. Just you and me. Together in the bed. Naked. You didn't take off your clothing for me. I'm disappointed."

He was sipping his wine while his fingers explored her neck. One handed, he flicked open the remaining buttons of her gown. He touched his lips upon her nape, traveled along her shoulders, nudging her gown to obey his desires. Fabric opened at his demand. Startled to feel the heat of the fire caress her breasts she discovered he never laced the chemise. His lips touched upon one breast then the other. The contact startling. The blistering, wet suck of his mouth aroused. Tempted. "Shall I continue as I explained while we watched the snow fall."

"Please…" her whispered word shimmied from her lips. She wanted him. Needed him to finish what they began.

"Since you implore with such a pretty word, I will be pleased to do your bidding." He undid all the buttons. Pushed the sleeves from her shoulders then the straps of her chemise. "Stand, love. I want the gown off."

He helped her to her feet, guiding the gown along with her other clothing to the floor. She'd never stood naked, almost naked, in front of a man. She wore only her stockings and her slippers. He ran his finger around the garter. Tugged on one ribbon then the other. So slow, the garments fell to the floor pooled around her feet. He picked up each foot to remove her slippers. She crossed her arms in front of her shivering from the contact not the air.

"Don't," Jasper told her, holding her hands to her sides. Gazing at her. "Don't wish for you to cover perfection." He carried her to the bed. Set her down on her stomach just as he told her he wished to do. A blink. A pulse of her heart. His hands caressed her with reverence. The slow glide of his hands along her body sent her heart racing. The breath she inhaled caught in her throat.

He straddled her. Felt the fabric of his pants rub against her legs. She didn't know what he wore. Heard his shirt swish to the floor. The shirt he must have donned before he chased Pup outside. His hands rested on her derriere. Stroked. Lingered as if he didn't wish to move them. After that she felt his lips at her nape, touching, nipping. His hands moved the length of her hair to the side. Felt the wetness of his tongue. Lips touched upon each bone as he enticed her body to respond to the heady feelings he furnished for her pleasure. Teeth, tongue, lips assaulted her person. Dragons deep inside her flamed to life, roaring. Inside, her muscles clasped, throbbed. Pulsed with need and wanting. He created that same magic again. Her body soared.

When he reached her legs, he came between them, his knees pushing her thighs apart, farther then farther still. He placed a pillow beneath her belly. She knew all of her was open to him. There were no secrets between them. His lips claimed a sensitive spot on the inside of her thigh. Felt the rasp of his day-old beard against her most intimate, secret parts. She gasped when he turned his head, blowing upon her hidden mysteries. Tensed. Gasped air that didn't want to find their way into her lungs.

There were more sensitive spots he claimed. Lower. Behind her knee. The arch of her foot. Each toe, he made his with the most tender attention. His hands stroked tender flesh. Ignited. Whirlwinds along with enchantment assailed her. She felt his kiss against her cleft. Her body was a quivering mesh of fire coupled with flashing tempest. He touched upon her again then again. Maggie wanted to touch him in turn. To send his body into the same raging hunger he composed in her. Needed to touch as well as explore.

"Jasper, please…I need to touch you. See you too. Don't want to be naked unless you are." He nipped her fanny. One side then the other. "Oh…!" Shuddering. Quivering with the intensity of the contact. Her body felt as if it would snap if he didn't do something else soon. He knew what he was about. He would prolong this for as long as he dared. She would ignite, burn to a cinder.

She got her wish. He flipped her over. Came down between her legs. His broad shoulders braced her thighs wide. She reached out to touch his chest. "You're not naked. Jasper, I need…" There was so very much she needed. Wanted. Wished for.

He covered her mouth with his. Entered into her with a finger as she heard his pants touch upon the floor. She realized her eyes had been closed. They flew open when she felt him against her. The sight of him awed her. He was magnificent. Broad of chest. Narrow waist and hips. His legs were well-muscled. He appeared sleek as well as powerful. This time as with the time before, when she reached out, he stopped her.

"Not yet."

"Jasper…" the moan of his name was whisper thin. A wail in the muted light of the room cast by the dying fire. She needed more…so much more. He caused her body to hum to life. Her purr of ecstasy caused a smile to form on his mouth. She recalled how she felt when he touched inside her before. A feeling that she was about to vault over some precipice to a place where all she would be able to accomplish was to feel. Her nerves stretched, contracted. Her stomach somersaulted.

His mouth framed hers. Explored inside. She touched him as she opened for him. He kissed her again and again. Moved lower, haunted her breasts. Skimmed with his tongue. Drank until her whimper drove him lower. His mouthed touched upon her belly button then lower. Explored her. Tasted her essence. Found that sensitive spot that almost sent her soaring. He nipped there. She cried out as her body clamped tight, pulsed. Entreated. She arched up begging for more. Writhed as he continued his onslaught on her most sensitive parts.

Her body seemed to remember the high he brought her to earlier. She cried out as the rolling, burning sensation took over her ability to move. Her fingers wound into his hair. He lifted her higher, his mouth seeming to devour her. All the while, he consumed her. She couldn't think. Had to hold on to him. Nails scraped. The climax he once spoke of thundered around her. With a shattering start, her body pulsed. She cried out. Pounding. Throbbing. Unable to stop the sweet painful pleasure that seared into her. Filled her. The world spun. Turned dark. Completed her. He eased, caressed with a soft touch. Moved up her body with gentle kisses.

"You are so sweet, my love. Taste yourself on my lips." His mouth crushed hers. He swept his tongue inside while his fingers dallied on her breasts, tugging, twisting until she whimpered anew. Until she felt heat. Swore again. This mercuric shattering of her body could not happen again so fast. Once more, she arched toward him, begging him. Felt the satin tip of his member where his tongue had been pressing against her.

The steel of him, eased into her, stretching her. He was too big, too hard. She tensed, knowing pain would follow.

"Relax, my love."

Maggie understood this would hurt only once. This was the moment of pain. She clung to him, biting his shoulder. He didn't seem to mind. Tried to relax as he asked. Buried her face in his chest. He thrust hard. A pulse of her heart. She screamed. Never thought the pain would be this intense.

Jasper held her. Rocked her as if she was precious. A fury bundle of growling puppy leapt on the bed. Pup, bathed her face. Licked at her tears. Turned to Jasper. Growled.

"Go to bed, Pup!" Jasper's voice was harsh. Threatened retribution.

Pup whined, seeming torn between seeing to his mistress as well as obeying the master. "Pup. Go!" He swore. Cursed at the dog. Pup slunk away from her. Leapt from the bed. Gave one last growl before he disappeared.

Before too many seconds passed the pain receded. Maggie almost giggled at the interaction between Pup and Jasper.

"Thank God, he obeyed. Didn't want to leave you to make certain he left the bed. Didn't expect the dog to jump up here to defend you."

She giggled then. "I'm fine now. Pup did obey you. You did yell. If you yelled at me that way, I would do just what you wanted."

"You would. Would you?" He smoothed damp hair from her face. "I should see to your pleasure again." He didn't wait for an answer.

There was no question. Jasper kissed her. The touch upon her mouth was gentle. Caressed with tender reserve. He didn't apologize for the pain he caused. She was thankful for that. This was making love. He was still inside her, moving. His strokes slow yet mesmerizing. Her body lurched when it seemed he touched her womb. She ran her nails down his back before changing direction then traveling toward his shoulders. Caressed each bone down to his waist then upward. She hitched in a deep breath of air when he touched upon more sensitive territory.

She realized the mounting fire he created with each plunge of his sex. His finger found that place of passion, the spot that sent her spiraling into a unique euphoria where everything soared to unimaginable heights. Spiked to the highest place a person could go. Her body understood what to expect. Maggie allowed him to bring her to that point of no return crying out his name as he thrust deep and hard. She felt the heat of his seed enter into her.

~ * ~

After she climaxed, then looked at him with dazed green eyes, Jasper knew she would be his forever. He needed to bring her pleasure every day of her life. The vague expression on her face told him she would respond with fire as well as passion. She swept her sweet pink tongue across her bottom lip. Hesitant, she reached out to him. Stroked his chest. Brought her hand back. He could still taste her. Remembered the wet sweep of her tongue.

When he hurt Maggie, he wished the first time didn't have to be that way. Jasper understood the pain would ebb. Knew he could bring her to that shattering climax again. Wanted to feel her silken sheathe kiss his length with the raw passion he composed. Know the moist heat of her mouth. Feel the searing liquid honey that would make her hot and wet, ready for his conquest. Thinking of his body within hers, his heart raced. His hands trembled.

He braced his forearms on either side of her head. Looking down on her, he saw the awe in her eyes. The love of her fingers as she touched him. Allowed his thumb to travel across her bottom lip. "How are you?"

"What?" Maggie blinked a few times. Stared at him as if he lost his mind. She crinkled her brow. "How am I?" she asked the question as if she didn't understand or she was drawing a blank. "How are you?"

Jasper barked. Hooted his amusement. She mesmerized him. Her innocence intrigued. He'd never known anyone so honest with her feelings. "I'm fine. More than fine. Quite pleased with the outcome of your first time. So far tonight, I've counted two orgasms." He still braced himself above her. Brushed her lips with his. Each corner of her mouth. The fine crease between her eyes. "Wine?" He rolled off her. Naked he sent wine into their glasses. Brought the tray of food to place at the foot of the bed. While he busied himself, she pulled covers over her. Brought them to her the tops of her breasts.

"Wine," she said softly. "I…" Maggie stopped uncertain of herself. "I'd like to put something on to cover myself."

Her gaze traveled to the gown along with her underclothing lying in a heap where he discarded them on the floor.

When he plopped down on the bed, he handed her the wine. "Why? You look ravishing the way you are now. I wouldn't change anything. I'm not intending to don clothing."

Maggie plucked at the sheets. Pulled them higher. "I'm naked." She stared at him, her eyes so wide, so very green. Still innocent. "Wish to have something to wear."

"So you are. I do like you that way. Naked, you are beautiful. If you put on a nightgown, I would have to take it off again. In my haste, might rip the fabric. A waste of time as well as clothing as I see the circumstances. Seems a bit repetitive. Put it on, take it off…" As far as he was concerned, she could do whatever pleased her. Despite the fact the process might be a waste of time, he had nothing better to do. Might be easier to arouse her while he took meticulous pain to unveil her silken skin. Suck her breasts into the depth of his mouth while they were veiled.

"We're going to do this again? Tonight? That can happen?"

A tick of the clock then another, she looked away. He smiled, pleased with the tiny bit of shyness she offered. Touched the beating of her pulse at her wrist. When she returned his perusal, she spoke with little hesitation. "I think I would like that. As long as Pup behaves himself. Stays put. Don't appreciate him growling at you. He might take a bite out of you." Maggie looked to the corner where the dog was curled into a small ball. "Didn't appreciate the attention at that specific time. Thought you would stop. Didn't want that to happen."

"Nor did I. Though I can see the humor of it all. The little devil is protective of you. He didn't like the fact I hurt you." Jasper cast his gaze in her direction. "Neither did I. Protective is a good thing." Jasper did appreciate the dog. How he acted was good. The animal's instincts were appreciated.

"He growled at you."

"Yes. That's what a good dog should do if he's going to protect his mistress. It seems to be intuitive to him. Will not take any training."

"He obeys you though."

"I'm his master. You are his mistress. We will train the animal together. Soon, he will obey you also. I will teach you what to do."

Jasper knew that wouldn't be true for long if Maggie tried her hand at training the young dog. When she did, Pup would become hers in all ways.

They both leaned against the frame of the bed. Sipped wine. Ate some of the basics Dana provided for them: Cheese, meat, bread, apple tarts for something sweet. The scene felt peaceful. He would enjoy life with his new wife. While his lifestyle had never been hectic, he appreciated the fact it would continue along the same vein. Except when Gracie was lost to them, he led a plain, simple life with his brother. Nothing would change.

Serenity encompassed the two of them. He knew snow fell from the sky. They would be isolated in this cottage. For the next few days, they would not be able to travel. The roads would be closed from the inclement weather. They were warm. The pantry was well-stocked. They had each other. No one would intrude. This would turn out to be the perfect honeymoon.

They would not need to worry about possible intrusions from the outside world. If they couldn't get out, Abernathy could not get in. Over the next few days, he meant to introduce Maggie to the world of pleasure. Everything they could share together. Different ways to give as well as receive pleasure. She was an enthusiastic pupil. He was the man in her life now. In the morning after they made love with the dawning of a new day, he would make his proposal. Jasper looked to Pup. The dog might well have a say in his plans. If Pup decided to join them in the morning, he would have to be patient as well as innovative.

When he looked at her, Maggie's eyes were closed. Her breathing was slow and even. He didn't want her to fall asleep before he made love to her one more time. Watching her aroused him. She still clung to the sheet. If he tugged… Knew she wore nothing. His imagination ran wild. The material was wound beneath her arms but not around her body. It would be child's play to pull the material to her waist. To suck each breast one at a time into the heat of his mouth. He needed to taste her silken flesh again. He'd not had enough of Maggie. The fabric would fall. He imagined she might wish to cleans herself of her maiden's blood as well as his seed. If he brought up the subject, she would be embarrassed. Perhaps mortified. He would be pleased if she allowed him. Wasn't about to force the issue with her.

Content for now, he sipped his wine. Watched her as she breathed while her breasts rose and fell. Except for the crackling of the fire along with the howl of the wind, silence surrounded them. This was serene. An evening to remember. He wished to savor the passing moments. Savor his bride. His almost bride. She would be his wife soon.

Beside him she stirred. Had not been asleep. Perhaps she also reveled in the peacefulness. She rose far enough so she could look at him. "Why were you so nice to me? That night? You didn't need to go to such lengths to help me. After you assisted me into the carriage, your entire life changed."

Jasper touched the tip of her nose with his finger tip. He watched the sheet slip a bit. The roundness of the top of her breasts intrigued. Stimulated. "Ah…good question. Changed for the better. I would add."

Sitting back, his fingers forming a steeple beneath his chin, he tapped them together. It was a moment he wondered about more than once in the last weeks. He acted on impulse. That was not in character. She spurred him to act. Especially since he had her sign the marriage certificate which wasn't real. He didn't need to go that far to secure her safety. He had the situation in hand. While she was with him, she was in no danger. Jasper wished he could tell her he fell in love with her when she pressed her pert little nose against his chest. Wished he could tell her anything except the blatant fact that the moment he felt her breasts against him, he wanted her. At that beat, what he felt was pure lust, hunger to know her better. That knowledge wasn't something Jasper was proud of feeling. He always believed when he fell in love the emotions would run deeper, more meaningful than sexual desire. Raw passion ruled him that night. Now that he was getting to know Maggie, there was more to his thoughts. More to how he felt about her. He wanted a life with her. Didn't know if he was in love with her. Though that sentiment might well come about.

At the time of their first meeting, he didn't want her for a wife. He wanted her beneath him while he thrust into her. During those first seconds of introduction, he knew she would be his one way or the other because he intended to make all his wishes come true. He wasn't proud of those thoughts. Always belittled men who fell in lust, who coveted a certain woman until they had her. He was one of them now. When he first met Maggie, he believed she came from the streets. Thought to educate her. Teach her how to be a lady. Not too much time passed in front of him before he realized there was nothing this woman needed to learn about acting a lady.

Jasper found himself caught off guard when he decided to make the marriage real. Had not intended to wed until he was much older. Acknowledged he still had a few years left to be a bachelor. Still didn't know if he loved her or coveted her body. Maggie was so damn beautiful, love didn't matter. When he saw her, he had trouble keeping his mind from meandering to sex. Wanted her all the time. Even after having her once, he needed her again. Didn't believe he'd ever grow tired of having her, making love to her. He wanted her this instant. For a virgin, this was too soon. The patience to wait might elude him.

"You don't know?" she asked, turning to him, the sheet dropping another fraction as she stared at him. Intriguing soft flesh was revealed. If the fabric dropped a wee bit more, he would see the soft color of her aureoles. "I'd like it if you could figure it out. Don't understand why. Knowing is important to me."

"I've always prided myself in helping the underdog." Jasper admitted. That much was true about him. "When I encountered you, you were most definitely a damsel in distress. Without a second look I knew that yellow dress the woman was wearing was yours. Understood trouble chased you. Watching you make your way to me, you dodged shadows. Always had your head turned in order to see what was behind you. Didn't know what the trouble could be. Why you traded that gorgeous gown for a rag confounded me too. Always liked to problem solve. You had a setback that needed resolution. I was just the man for the job. Knew whatever danger you ran from, you would find safety with me. As the depth of the issues surrounding you were unveiled, knew I had to find a means to help you weather the storm that surrounded you. Understood the man would chase you. As beautiful as you are, there is no man in this world who wouldn't wish to keep you for himself."

Jasper lifted his shoulders, shrugging, thinking he'd talked long enough. "I'm no different. Need to keep you for myself." He felt certain that by making love to her, he made the first move in that direction. While she might regret the night, if she understood she wasn't his wife, he would not.

While he spoke of how beautiful she was, she appeared stunned though she didn't comment. Instead, she downed the wine she was drinking before adding to the glass. After another long drink, she spoke, her voice soft. "You think I'm beautiful?" Maggie didn't sound as if she believed him.

Jasper wondered at the tone of her voice. Marveled, Maggie didn't see herself the way others saw her. "No one has told you that before? That you are quite lovely."

He wondered if that was the truth. Maggie was beyond beautiful. She was stunning. Unique. One of a kind. He could go on with the adjectives. Elected to stop there.

"No..." She paused as she continued to imbibe. "Lord Abernathy complained about my looks. The color of my hair...was too dark. He preferred blonds. Told me my eyes looked like dead moss. He enjoyed a *lass* with blue eyes. My breasts were too small, my legs too long. Never understood why he wished to marry me. Imagine the fact had something to do with what my mother offered him." Maggie paused again, tapping the lip of the crystal glass. "Anice always told me I was too tall. Though…"

A half-smile, he meant to finish for her. "You don't reach my collarbone. If you were any smaller, I'd lose you in the bed."

He hooted his laughter when she turned a charming shade of red. He sat back, his hands folded across his belly. Relaxed. Replete. He was in command, focused on their future. All would turn out the way fate intended. "Tell me about your sisters. Don't wish to learn anything more about Anice than you've told me." At least not now. Anice was someone he knew Maggie didn't like thinking about. She would never appreciate speaking of her now. "Start with the second oldest of your sisters. Allow me this right. Your siblings are your only friends. Am I correct in that assumption?"

The thought of her sisters put a smile on her face. "Yes, all that's true. Nellie, she is twenty. Almost one year younger to the day. She is vibrant. Alive. Her hair is blond. Seems to believe that everything will turn out perfect. Though she was worried for me the day I ran away. She and the rest of my sisters helped me leave. Blocked the man following me. Without them, I'd be his wife now." She shuddered.

Reaching out Jasper touched her hand. Brought her fingers to his lips. They were long, slender. Her nails manicured as well as buffed. He knew they were sensitive. Placed kisses across her knuckles. Touched his tongue between them. Felt her shiver of excitement. "Don't believe I've kissed the tops of your hands. By the night's end, I'd like to believe I haven't missed any part of you."

Again, Jasper felt her tremor. Enjoyed the way her small body vibrated when he caressed different parts. How she seemed to jump to life with each pass of his hands. If he read the signs right, she wouldn't mind making love again. "Tell me more."

He pulled her against his chest before handing her the wine glass she'd been sipping from.

"Nellie…my sister has big dreams. She likes to spin tales, romantic stories of a time long ago. Writing a book is something she has thought about for a very long time. Whenever she has free time, she sits down to put her imagination onto paper. I've read some of what she has written. Believe she is quite good at what she does."

"A writer...I might be able to help her with the publishing of her book. Does she have any that are finished?" Jasper asked, he would pull out all favors owed to him in order to see Nellie get her wish. He hoped Maggie didn't exaggerate her sister's talent.

"I don't know. If she finished a book, she never told me. Nellie is fanciful. Always has her head in the clouds. We are good for each other. I bring her down to earth whenever she floats too high into the clouds her feet won't touch down. She makes me understand I'm too stubborn. Cannot always have my way with everything. I always need to write the rules. Orchestrate the plan."

"Would rather be with a stubborn woman who is grounded in reality than a woman who has her head too high in the sky. The first day I met you, I recognized your stubborn nature. Saw how determined you were. You refused to tell me your name until I gave you good reason to believe I wouldn't turn you over to Lord Abernathy. While I was annoyed beyond reason, I also respected your stance."

"You knew I was hard headed and you still wanted me? Understood, I would fight you if I disagreed?" she asked, sounding as if she could never believe that for the truth. "I didn't think men liked to be challenged."

He lifted her chin. Stared into her crystalline green eyes. "Yes. Stubborn. Hard headed. Pragmatic. Shrewd. Beautiful... Never backed down from a challenge." He captured her mouth with his. Sliding his hand beneath the sheet that still covered her, he held her breast, touched upon the tight crest. Beneath his hand, he felt her leap of excitement. Smoothed his thumb along the contours of her firm rounded jewel. Delighted in the small whimper after that the purr of contentment. She responded so fast. The sheet fell to her waist as her arms wrapped around him. She pressed against him. Her fingers wound into his hair. "Not yet..." Jasper set her away from him. Despised the look of distress he saw in her beautiful eyes.

"You have changed the subject at whim. You cannot think to kiss me as you just did, touch me then put a stop to what you started." Tugging at the cover, she tried to bring it back to her armpits. He let the material go as she settled the sheet around her again.

His sigh of displeasure sent her brows together in a fierce scowl. Jasper pulled on the sheet one more time. "I would love to see you naked, Maggie. Would love to sit here next to you while we both wear nothing. As we sip our wine…eat the food. The room is warm. You would not find yourself uncomfortable."

Maggie looked down for a brief thump of her heart. He caught the drift of her downward gaze then the quick rise to stare at him. Her eyes wide. "You are…"

"Stimulated? Aroused? Excited to be with you, Maggie *lass*. Yes, all of the above. While I'd love to make love to you again. Right now. This evening is your first introduction to the ways of love. Sex. I would not hurt you for anything…are you sore?"

With his question, she flushed scarlet. Turned away from him. "I…" Maggie drank the rest of her wine. Passed her tongue across her mouth. "I…I would like to clean myself," the words blurted from her.

He wondered when she would get to that tiny problem. She would have her blood mixed with his seed on her thighs. "Would you like help?" She must have seen his sex. There was blood there too. He waited until she asked.

"Would like privacy." She tilted her chin, stubbornness rising to complicate his wishes.

Jasper couldn't keep the grunt behind his teeth. He wanted her to be his in every way. Longed for her to outgrow her innate shyness. This would take time. He couldn't help protesting. "I am your husband." Jasper almost grimaced at the blatant lie Maggie knew nothing about. "I should see to your needs."

"I can do this myself. Would you?" Maggie looked to the door. "Leave?"

Leaving her alone was not an option he would consider. Jasper strode to the basin of water Clancy left. Brought her a rag along with the basin. Wasn't at all certain how to proceed. He stepped back, crossing his arms over his chest. Thinking it would be nice if she offered to wipe the blood from his sex. His lips twitched. She wouldn't wish to touch him. Not yet. Perhaps sometime in the near future.

"I'm not leaving." He walked to the fireplace. Placed a new log on the fire. Sparks flared as the new wood caught the flames. His arm on the mantle he waited as he watched the fire. Listened to the small sound she made while she cleansed herself. Was pleased she didn't insist he vacate the room. Jasper didn't know if he could deny her anything. All he wanted, wished for, was her happiness.

After a few more minutes, he heard the rag drop into the water. Still, he waited, staring at the dance of color in front of him. Wished to hear her ask for him again.

"I'm finished," her soft words gave him reason to turn around. "You can… Oh!"

"Will you see to me?" His voice turned husky with the sudden desire spiraling within. "I would like that."

She reached out, drew her hand back. Her eyes huge pools of green. "I…" Looked away from him. "Don't think… I would touch you. Can I?"

"I would appreciate the gesture. Yes, you would need to hold me in your hand."

Jasper understood he challenged her in ways she wasn't accustomed. With slow, even steps he approached her. The water in the basin was stained pink with her virgin's blood. Her cheeks were tinted a deeper, darker shade. He watched her swallow then tilt her chin. There was his stubborn woman. She would prove herself to him.

"Alright."

She passed her tongue across her lips. Her hands trembled when she reached for the washrag.

He thought it would be ever so nice to do the same. As at this point, he was more than ready to make love to her again. When she touched him, he might explode on the spot. Embarrass himself. He would need to endeavor not to do so. All the willpower he possessed would need rise to the forefront.

Standing in front of her, watching her hands continue to shake while she dipped the cloth into the basin, he repressed his smile. With gentleness that stole his breath she touched him, held his sex in her hand. Slow strokes cleaned her blood away. She was so tender. Until now, she never touched his sex. This was… Jasper groaned. He had no idea what this was. A new experience for him as well as his Maggie. Her tenderness didn't surprise him. He wondered when Pup would come along then put an end to this moment. If possible, he would hang on to this intimate memory for the rest of his life.

After she finished, he cleared his throat then picked up the basin. Jasper set it on the counter in the privy behind the dressing room where Pup slept. He returned. Maggie settled on the bed. Her back pressed against the headboard. The sheet still wrapped around her, tucked beneath her arms. He sat on the bed beside her. Touched her hip to hip. Closed his eyes while he thought about what would happen next.

Maggie was ready to make love. He saw that in the tilt of her face, the press of her lips. The rapid pulse at the base of her neck. He might need to wait until morning. For the moment he needed a diversion. Wished to learn more about her life. "Tell me about the next sister in line."

Her eyes widened, startled. She stared at him. Tipped her head a bit to the side as she was thinking. With a deep breath of air, she began, "Fannie...her real name is Francis. Nellie is just Nellie. Don't know if Anice ever wished to call her by a different name. I don't think it is shortened."

Jasper had ideas in his head about a woman whose name was Fannie. Though he shouldn't rehash those concepts to Maggie. "Your name is Margret?"

"I don't like the name. Don't feel as if it suits. I'm not a Margret. Sometimes, when Lord Abernathy wasn't pleased with something I did, he would call me Margret. The sound from his lips made me shudder. Maybe it was just the way he said Margret. There was always this horrible tenor to his voice. Something that made my skin crawl."

"I'll remember not to call you Margret. You're Maggie to me, from the tips of your delicious little toes to the top of your pretty head. How long did you know Lord Abernathy?" For reasons he was certain, this knowledge was important to him.

"About a year...we were introduced at a ball. Mother was very pleased when he began to see me. Though I always believed she orchestrated the meeting. Planned on his courting of me."

Jasper mulled that fact over in his head. Decided to continue discovering her sisters. "So, Fannie or Francis...which does she prefer?"

Jasper ran his finger along the top of the sheet, relishing the soft round tops of her breasts. Dipped between the valley of her breasts. Heard the sifting of air.

"Fannie. No one calls her anything else. She's the shy sister. Seems to be caught between the whirlwind of her older sisters and the younger one. Fannie likes to sit back. Watch what is going on with everyone else. She is always doing her needlepoint." Maggie's hands clasped together. "You see none of us have friends. All we have is each other. Until now, we've never been away from each other except for a few hours at a time." She played with the sheet. "I miss them." When she looked to him, he saw tears in her eyes.

"You lean on each other for support. Since you don't have them now, you can lean on me," Jasper whispered, his lips close to her ear, touched upon a lobe then the sensitive spot behind. He did wish to make love to her one more time before they slept. Decided not to do so. Wished for this time to be no pain. None at all. He would wait until morning. Give her a *wee* bit more time to heal. She was so small, tight. Needed time to adjust to his size.

"We are best friends. The best ever. It's as if we know what the other is thinking before one can say the words. Tessa is vibrant. Alive in all ways. Her vitality is unequalled. She's the baby of the family. Gets her way all the time with us. We all dote on our baby sister. Anice doesn't play favorites. She dislikes us all equally."

Jasper found himself appalled at what she was telling him. He thought on his own life of privilege. His parents passed on far too soon. They should still live. Both died of the flu. When they were gone, he had Jason. They were also close. Seemed they could read each other's minds. As soon as the snow stopped and the roads cleared, he would send the letter he wrote to his brother, asking him to come to the wedding. In the missive he elaborated the fact that it no longer mattered if Abernathy learned where Maggie was. In a matter of a few days, she would be his wife. He would ask for a special license rather than wait for the reading of the banns. Even now, she might carry his child. He'd not thought of children...babies...not until they adopted Pup. Somehow the little devil started him thinking of children of an heir. A life with a family would add meaning to his existence. He would like to believe he would be a good father to his child.

"I'm having difficulty thinking of a mother disliking her children." This was something he would need to think about for more than a few minutes.

"Believe the woman wished for boys. Father didn't care one way or the other. While he doesn't seem to dislike us, he doesn't like any of us either. He's never paid us any attention. Allows Anice to dictate our lives.

Seems to have no opinion with regard to his girls." Maggie sounded so matter of fact, his heart went out to her. Bled for the emptiness of her childhood.

Jasper wished this wedding could be a real wedding. One where she had her sisters in attendance. A marriage where his brother would stand up as best man. Gracie with her husband Fletcher would have loved to witness the ceremony. He had reason to believe haste was not necessarily the best way to proceed.

Diverting her attention now might be a good idea. The rest of the evening lay in balance. His hand around the sleek column of her neck, he pulled her to him. Pressed his lips on her mouth. Thrilled she opened for him. He accepted her tongue inside his mouth. Delighted with her spontaneity. He had not even been certain they would make love again tonight. His patience as well as his decision to wait until morning was at an end. He had no idea about virgins. In his experience, if he wished to make love to the woman he was with more than once, the act was exquisite for both. Virgins were different. He hurt her. Stretched her. She was tiny.

The sheet covering her slipped. Her breast pushed against the wall of his chest. "Do you want this?" he asked, unsure of himself. He, Jasper Kenworthy, was never uncertain. He would need to be ever so gentle.

"Hmm… if you are asking me if I want you to make love to me…well…the answer is yes."

She ran her fingers into his hair. Her nails scraped his neck. "I want you, Jasper."

This moment sent him spiraling. Thinking about her taste, the soft flavor of her nipples brought heat surging. He'd never been with a woman who was so passionate. This woman was his. He heard the small woof before he registered the meaning. Looking at the clock he realized it had been several hours since he brought the dog back from his mad dash outside. He must need to pee again. Jasper understood with the best circumstance Maggie would be awake when he returned. The worst scenario, she'd be asleep.

Maybe this was for the best. In the morning, he would make love to her. Propose to her when she was sated with pleasure. She would never tell him no to the renewal of their vows since she didn't remember the first time. This would be something she would like to remember.

Pulling back, he stared down at her, regret in her eyes. Seemed she understood the difficulty. "It's Pup. He needs to go outside."

She started to rise. Pushed the covers away. He saw her naked, the sweetest movement of her breasts. Stunned by the sight along with the realization this woman was his, the breath he inhaled caught in his throat.

"Imagine this is my turn." Maggie realized she wore nothing, not even the nightshirt. Her face flushed with color.

He held her, his hands around her waist. "No. Don't cover yourself. Get back in the bed. Stay warm." He didn't want her going outside during the snowstorm. She would freeze. "I'll take the rascal outside to see to his duty. In the morning, I'll give him to Clancy to take care of. Want to have some time undisturbed with you. Before I let him into the snow, I'll have that piece of cheese he wants ready for him to devour. I won't be long."

He kissed her on the forehead understanding she would be asleep when he returned. She was barely able to keep her eyes open now.

His robe lay at the foot of the bed where he'd placed the covering in case he needed it. Didn't take the time for shoes since he was positive the scoundrel would come inside when tempted with the culinary delight he favored. Cheese, the rogue did love his cheese. Jasper decided that was what he would use to train the dog.

Pup raced ahead of him, down the steps then into the kitchen, barking, seeming to remember where he was going. He led the way. Jasper thought he would wake the household. He sat down at the door, his tail wagging with anticipation.

"Go do what you need to do," Jasper said before showing the dog the treat. "Come back then you'll have this."

He waved the cheese in front of his nose. The dog jumped trying to grab it from his hand as if he thought to get the treat before he did what he was supposed to do. Jasper held it back, motioned with his hand for the dog to go. "No treat until you've earned the morsel."

Only a few minutes passed before Pup was back devouring his small bit of cheese. Jasper scooped him into his arms heading for the room upstairs. Pup raced to his bed. Jasper sat on his. She was asleep. He lay down beside her pulling her into his arms, holding her tight. He must have dozed. When he woke, she was pressing her sweet bottom against him. His sex grew. Hardened. It was time to finish with his plans.

~ * ~

Jason read the letter once then a second time to make certain he understood what his brother was saying. He received the missive this morning. Still couldn't believe what he read for the first time this morning. Had to mull the words over in his head for a few hours before he could act on the request. Good God, he was getting married! A shock didn't come close to describing his feelings. He sat back on the comfortable chair. Stunned, he stared at the flames. Fire burned bright in the hearth warming him. Married. He shook his head wondering what bug got into Jasper's head. Neither planned to marry for some time. Not until they reached the ripe old age of thirty-five. Teased each other as to who would succumb first. He'd always told Jasper that of course it would be him because he was older.

Though...he tapped the letter on the arm of the chair. His eyes focused on nothing. He'd be delighted to go to the wedding, travel to Ireland. In winter, storms would toss the ship about. While he didn't mind sailing on smooth seas, he loathed storms, the subsequent rolling of the ship. Thinking about the movement made him nauseous.

From that one night in their home, he remembered her. Maggie was a beautiful woman. Intelligent. Stubborn came to mind. A lady in every way. In need of protection. Jasper was always the one to rescue strays. As a child he saved countless cats as well as dogs. He always found someone to give the animals to. Never kept one of his rescues.

Until now.

Jason chuckled as he recalled Jasper's mission that night. He wanted to teach this woman he plucked off the streets of Glasgow how to be a lady. Wished to prove a woman from the gutter could learn to speak good Scots English as well as learn impeccable manners. Seemed Jasper was keeping the woman far longer than expected.

Marriage. The institution was so final. Once entered into there would be no return. Jasper wanted him to go to Ireland for the wedding. Nass, a small village just outside Dublin would be the setting. It would take him a week to get there. Lord Abernathy would follow if he didn't know where Maggie was by now.

His brother wasn't worried because he had a certificate of marriage.

One that wasn't legal or binding. Jasper told him that much in a subsequent letter. Jason felt certain Jasper didn't have to marry this woman. Love…? When they left for parts unknown almost two months ago, what Jason saw in his brother's eyes was lust that stirred him to protect her. Lust wasn't love. The emotion could change to love. Time spent together with no chaperone could change the tenor of the relationship. A kiss here. A soft caress there. All could lead to deeper, more intense feelings.

Maggie MacRae could stir any man's lust. Well, he already set Keir to pack the essentials. Figured he'd be gone at least two weeks. Perhaps a bit longer. Planned to go there prepared for anything that might happen.

"What is it?" Sarah stood behind the chair. Ran her hands down his chest. Whispered close to his ear. "You look very serious."

She touched him with her tongue. The caress was light, yet reminded him of the hot suck of her tongue on strategic parts of him. Tasting her again would be delicious. Stirred his senses. He should make love to Sarah one more time.

Jason turned, pulling her onto his lap. Before tonight, he'd never brought Sarah to his home. With Jasper gone, he felt more freedom. Didn't worry about the dictates of society. No one would know she spent a night here with him in his bed. A mistress should never…ah well the Murray brothers never played by the rules. They always married the woman they brought home with them. Sarah didn't wish to be wed. Valued her independence along with the freedom that gave her. Not that he would ask. She'd done that once. Told him she would never be under any man's thumb. Not even his. Sarah enjoyed and relished her autonomy. Money was plentiful. Her husband left her wealthy. She didn't need or wish for him to provide for her. Though she did accept a gift now and then.

His lips found hers, searched inside when she opened for his exploration. Felt the tension he'd been feeling vanish. Sarah could do that to him. With his tongue he loved her sultry depths. Tasted the sweetest parts of her. Reached inside her. Caressed. Started passion flowing. She would melt pleasantly for him. Needed to make love to this woman first then explain later what had him so pensive. She was an attentive listener. Never judged.

With quick deft moves, he pulled the tiny sleeves of her gown down her arms. Her breasts were still covered by her chemise and corset. Jason didn't waste time tackling the ribbons, baring her flesh. He bent to suck on the hard crest that pouted very daintily for him. She pushed on his frock coat then opened his white silk shirt.

"Are you going to make love to me by the fire?" she asked as his shirt fell to the floor to land on top of his coat. Her fingers found the opening to his britches. Jason couldn't wait. Her small fingers inflamed him.

"After I make love to you sitting on me. Straddle me, my love. Take me into you. Hold me tight. Milk the length of me with your hot sultry channel." When he felt her moist heat, he pushed against her softness.

Sarah did as he asked. He was deep inside her with one thrust. The loving was over before he could give her more pleasure. Though he felt her climax, he delighted in hearing all her soft moans along with the feminine whimpers while he stroked her higher then higher still. Enjoyed holding back until she begged for her release. Jason picked her up. Brought her to fur rug in front of the fireplace. Finished shedding his clothing then hers. They lay together. All her soft curves pressed against him.

He spent the next minutes bringing her higher. Hearing the soft purr that told him she was ready for him. Still, he continued to caress those sensitive spots that brought her to that point she would reach for the ecstasy he could give her.

She cried out his name. Jason relished hearing the sound of his name at her climax. Her passage kissed his length. Loved him while he was deep inside. While he spent his seed. After they both climaxed, Jason held her. Stroked her back soothing her, calming the body that gave him so much pleasure. He understood someday he would marry. His wife wouldn't be Sarah. Giving this loving up would be difficult. Well, he didn't need to worry about that for quite some time. He had years with Sarah ahead of him.

Nestled in his arms, her fingers playing with the hair on his chest, she asked him again, "What is it? What bothers you? Earlier you were so pensive." She drew her finger along his forehead. "Did you know you were scowling at that harmless piece of paper. I gather it was news from your brother."

His Sarah never passed judgment. While she knew what his brother attempted, she thought the act was quite decent. It was a blink later when he spoke. "Jasper is getting married. He wants me to come to the wedding. Can't say I'm surprised. Yet, I am. Didn't expect either of us to marry for a few more years."

"Married?" She lifted up on an arm, her breasts dancing across his chest. Her smile was pensive. Delightful. "To whom? Are you going? Of course, you are. Where is your brother?" Sarah kissed his neck then across his collarbone. Touched upon sensitive places she knew by heart.

Jason held her head still. Brought her back so her cheek rested against his chest. "That's a lot of questions. You deserve answers to all. First, he is marrying a woman. Maggie MacRae is her name. I've told you a little bit about the woman. Though I doubt if I mentioned a name."

Her fist hit him hard on his chest. He responded with an oof. "Of course, a woman…" Sara giggled. "You are such a tease. So bad at times I *dinna ken* if I can trust you. Maggie MacRae…" Sarah paused in thought for a few seconds. Tapped his chin with a finger. Rubbed the tip across the day-old stubble. "The woman who fled Nelson Abernathy at their engagement party on Christmas Eve? You never mentioned anything about her when you told me Jasper was on a short vacation with a person of the opposite sex. Maggie MacRae, you say. There has been a great deal of scandal circling her name. Abernathy is said to be furious. Has mentioned quite heatedly that if she was not a virgin when she returns, he will take steps… What that means no one is certain."

"You're right about Maggie. I didn't say anything because the story wasn't mine to tell." Jason played with a strand of her hair that came loose during their activities. He wound the silken strand around his finger, let the skein glide through the sensitive insides. "Jasper found her in a homeless camp that night. She was hiding from Abernathy. Didn't know it at the time. Seems she gave away her fashionable gown. Traded it for a rag. Abernathy followed her that far. As is Jasper's nature, he sheltered her. Suppose rescued her would be a more apt description of what he did. Needless to say, the girl didn't wish to wed Abernathy. Now, it seems she has set her sights on Jasper."

Sara shuddered. "Who would want to marry that viper? The man is vile. He is scum. What are you going to do?"

"So, he is. Keir is packing my things as we speak. I will take you home. Once I've seen you safely to your place, I will take a ship to Dublin. I was lucky to find a ship ready to set sail first thing in the morning."

Chapter Seven

When Maggie woke the next morning, Jasper was behind her. Holding her breast in one hand just as he did the night before. She felt his sex against her. His hand cupping her breast stroked, teasing, loving the hardening tip. A whisper of her breath passed her lips. He kissed the nape of her neck. Roamed along her shoulders, grazed her with his teeth. She must have fallen asleep before he returned with Pup.

She didn't wish to open her eyes. The feelings he provoked in her were too new, too exhilarating. With her eyes closed all the sensation seemed more intense. She whimpered when he bit her shoulder with sweet care. Needed to absorb all the tender motions of his hands. He continued down her back. His sex prodded her, touched upon her cleft. He slipped his leg beneath hers, separating hers. She wasn't certain what he intended. His hand moved lower. Teased. Provoked sensitive spots.

"Are you ready for me, my love? I believe you are. You are hot, wet on my fingers." His sex slid across her. Touched. His fingers found the tiny spot that left her quivering and breathless. His whisper across her nape sent more flames raging inside her. One hand cupped her mound. A finger slid across sensitive folds. She swallowed air. Gulped. One long finger slid inside her. "You are hot. Wet. Prepared. You want me inside you. Want me to give you that wonderful climax you must remember from last night."

His were bold statements. She did want him just where he told her. Wished to feel herself fragment into tiny shards of pleasure.

Her gasp for air startled her. Stunned, the tip of his finger continued to massage that sensitive place she learned about yesterday. A heartbeat, a murmur of air into her lungs, he was deep inside her, holding still. Unmoving as if the clenching of her muscles was enough. "Jasper…" Her moan was soft, hoarse with the desire that seemed to consume all of her.

"Yes…do you like this? Do you like me inside you this way? He

196

moved further, easing himself inside her until she took his entire length. With his hands he roamed. Found sensual places that made her gasp anew with the mercuric flame of her passion. Her breasts. The pearl of her greatest pleasure. Her nape. Behind the earlobe. So inflamed, she quivered. Ran his fingers along her arms then touched upon her belly. She arched against him. Pushed.

"Please… You know I do." Her words broke. Shattered as he began to move harder…faster. She clung to his wrist. Knew her nails were biting into his flesh.

He made love to her. Brought her so high she lost control. Thought the world would splinter. Found her body fractured into thousands of pieces. After that he found more delightful ways to send her reaching for the heavens.

When he finished loving her the second time, he reached for the bell cord to bring Clancy up with breakfast. Maggie was surprised to find Pup missing. She half expected the dog to be on the bed with them, barking, wishing to play. She missed the little rascal. Wanted to feel the rasp of his tongue on her cheek while she cuddled him.

As if he read her mind, Jasper chuckled then spoke, "Before I made love to you, I took Pup out for his morning constitutional. When he returned, greedy beggar, for his cheese, I handed him over to Clancy. Told him he needed to see to the dog. I wanted to be left alone with you. He was to wait to bring up breakfast until I called him."

"Your butler didn't object to babysitting the puppy?" she giggled. "The poor man shouldn't have to play nursemaid to our beast. You might not believe this. I miss Pup."

"I'm certain Clancy does object. He is being paid very well, you understand. Clancy cannot articulate vigorously against the project. He might find himself out of a job. And…" He paused as if reading her mood, "I would be disappointed if you didn't miss the dog. He is yours. We should begin his training today. Though we've already a head start. We know the right treat to reward him with when he does what we wish."

The knock on the door sent her flying under the covers. She'd slept next to him the entire night, naked. Embarrassment for Jasper to see her shouldn't heat her cheeks. He understood the flush of discomfiture would take time to vanquish. Clancy was a different matter. While she still didn't want to parade around naked in front of him, she didn't seem to mind in the least if he showed off his body. She also liked to feel him close to her. Jasper understood that by the way she nestled into him.

On his way to the door, Jasper grabbed a robe off the back of the chair. Once the door was opened, Clancy stepped inside. Pup danced at his feet. Maggie ducked beneath the covers. Only her eyes along with her nose could be seen.

"Sorry, Sir, tried to keep the little animal locked in the kitchen. The scoundrel is very fast. Sped right by me. Caught my feet. Nearly fell. Here is your breakfast. Is there anything else you'd be likin'."

Clancy set the tray on the table. Lifted the lids. Eggs, ham steak along with fresh bread. "Brought tea for the missus. Coffee for you. Is there anything else you would like?"

Wagging his tail, Pup put his paws on the bed, trying to jump up.

"No, though I would wager, a piece of ham would bring Pup running to your side. The dog is easy to bribe. Seems to love his food. After that I don't wish to be bothered unless there is some type of emergency." Jasper looked to the bed, a smile forming. His little family was there. With luck Maggie would be increasing soon. A child...before meeting Maggie he never understood that he wished for a son or daughter. Both if that would be possible. Maybe one set of twins would not be too much to hope for.

"Very well, Sir. I will make certain you are not disturbed." Clancy bowed. Waited for him to give him something to bride Pup with.

Jasper cut a small piece of meat. Waved the ham in front of Pup's nose before handing the small morsel to Clancy. The dog lost interest in Maggie and the bed. Pup danced on his hind feet, jumped then followed the butler from the room.

"You are very gifted, my lord," Maggie laughed outright as she watched the scene unfold. She sat up. One more time, the covers were tucked around her. "You know the dog. I imagine you took him outside earlier this morning. Is that why your hands were so cold when you woke me? They felt as if you immersed them in ice."

"You've got the gist of it. Snow is still falling. Hope it ends soon. A little is nice, a bit romantic. A lot is horrible. Freezing. Can get tired of too much snow." Jasper sat down beside her. He needed to marry her as soon as possible. In order to do that, the snow had to stop falling. "Are you

hungry? I'd like to eat first. Afterward, I've got something to ask you."
Jasper laid out a white table cloth on the small table where they would eat.
He set plates as well as silverware down. "Would you like me to dish up a
plate for you? Pour your tea?"

"That would be nice."

What he wanted was for Maggie to relax. To come to him with no
inhibitions. That wouldn't be for a while. Shyness did become her. Jasper
understood he needed to put off more lovemaking until the question at hand
had been answered. Nonetheless she wasn't immune to him. The way she
looked at him right now as if she wished to devour him sent lightning bolts
into his limbs. Blood roared through his ears. The energy, the heat of that
look filled him with confidence that she might soon come around to his way
of thinking.

Not enough to eat naked with him though. Not yet...

While Jasper dished up a plate for her, Maggie poured the coffee
along with the tea. "What is it you wish to speak with me about?"

It seemed to him, she wanted answers to her questions now, not later.
Waving her fork in the air, she stared hard at him. Pointed the cutlery his
way. "Seems we can talk and eat at the same time. You can't do two things
at once?" Her query gave him reason to laugh.

He flashed a broad smile her way. "I can. Don't want to do so. When
we talk, I need all your attention. Don't wish for anything to get in the way
of the words." He tapped her nose with the tip of his finger. "You, my pretty
wife, will need to wait for a few more minutes. Must have a *wee* bit of
patience or I will wait until this afternoon to speak with you."

The devil, that was not his intention. He was almost as impatient as
she was. He needed her answer. Must hear the word, yes.

She was too eager to hear her answer to wait. Her snort of
displeasure made him laugh all the more. "Whatever it is you want I will
tell you no," she threatened then snorted as if she didn't care. This time after
stirring sugar into her tea she was waving her spoon at him.

He meant to bring something up she would want. He did have a flair
for the dramatic. With Maggie it was easy. "Don't believe you."

He sat back, his arms crossed over his chest chewing on his food
then sipped coffee. Realized he enjoyed himself. She wouldn't give into
anything she disagreed with. A wave of fear slipped under his skin. What if

she didn't think she needed to renew vows. What if she didn't care if she had a real wedding. Well…the wedding wouldn't be that real if they got married as soon as the snow melted. Complications might still exist depending on her answer.

As if trying to be just as dramatic, Maggie let out a long breath of air while she seemed to watch him for a reaction. He wasn't about to give into the ploy. She didn't say anything more. He imagined she decided to do what he wished. Impatience could be part of her middle name. Stubborn went along with that sentiment. She could be the opposite to those two descriptions. He liked her that way…always a surprise.

Her meal was finished before Jasper's. She rose from the cover of her sheets, naked. It seemed his lady fair decided she could be bolder than expected. Perhaps she tried to stun him into revealing his thoughts. His sharp breath of air would tell her what she needed to learn. If she continued in this manner, she could dictate to him anything she wanted. He might grovel at her naked feet.

"Little minx," he whispered.

She wasn't going to gain the upper hand. He followed her to the window where she watched the snow falling. Ran his fingertip along her back. Felt the shiver of desire escalate through her.

Didn't seem the storm would let up very soon. His hands settled on her waist. The curves of her hips. His hands smoothed along her sides. She gasped. After he turned her, Maggie discovered he'd tossed his robe to the floor. Her gaze roamed his length. Stopped at the evidence of his arousal. A small smile formed on her lips. "You want me now? I'd be happy to oblige. Perhaps it was something else you wanted? Was it something I said?"

Maggie would understand now that she tempted him with her body. To her it would appear that he would always want her. He hoped she felt the same about him. Didn't know if he'd ever get tired of her. Her breasts pushed against his chest. His hands slipped to her backside. His hard member pulsed against her belly.

She set her hands against his chest. "Jasper, I want you now. Whatever you wished to speak about can wait. I'm no longer impatient except to feel you complete me. I need for you to be part of me. One with me. Make love to me, please," she pleaded.

Pleading was something she never needed to do. "Good. Wrap your legs around my hips," he spoke next to her ear. Claimed her mouth with his as she did what he said. In seconds, he was inside her. Thrusting until she cried out. A few more moments and she climaxed. Her head settled in the hollow of his shoulder. Her nose into his chest. He caught a subtle sweet scent that was hers alone, feminine. Enticing. The soft flush of her cheek pressed against him. Felt her lashes rise then lower.

"Jasper…" she sighed. His name whispered from her lips again as he walked with her to the big arm chair sitting in front of the fire. They sat. He positioned her across him. She could straddle him later. Doing so this minute was too soon. They needed to talk. "Tell me now." Maggie needed to know. In the aftermath of their lovemaking, she couldn't stop shaking.

He ran his hands along her back, soothing, easing her. Maggie needed to be calm when he spoke. She needed to listen to his logic if she refused him. She reached for her cup of tea. He helped her by bringing the cup to her mouth. She swallowed. He sipped his coffee. Loving always stole his breath. Parched his mouth.

"Do you wish to put on your robe?" Jasper asked, seeming to be polite. His hands ran along her arms, noticing the small goose bumps. He needed to keep her warm. "Like you just the way you are." His soft murmurer made her smile. "I could put another log on the fire."

Touching his mouth with her finger she grinned back. "I would do what you like. I'm not cold. Besides, you warm me." Despite her words to the opposite, she shivered. Her discomfort was minimal. Since he liked to see her wearing nothing, who was he to insist on covering her?

"I like you naked. You know that though. Don't you?" This was a dangerous game. He might not be able to finish the conversation with her if she remained unclothed. "Perhaps we should put on our robes."

Nodding, she smiled at him, seeming to enjoy the play of their bodies as they fit together. "Enjoy feeling all the hard planes of your body. I like you naked too. Now that I've waited, will you tell me what it is that is on your mind?" She put a *wee* bit of distance between them. "I've been a good girl." Flirtatiously, she lifted her shoulder looking at him with a sly expression. "So," she licked her lips, seeming to understand he wished to do the same. "Now you can tell me what's on your mind."

"Impatient little minx," he said, his voice soft. Heated. "Yes." Jasper paused then as if he expected her to continue to ask. Waited longer.

That wasn't going to happen. Maggie appeared determined she could wait as long as he could. She ran her hands along his chest. Slipped her fingers through the short hair she found there. Stopped over the jutting of his nipples. She seemed delighted by his groan of fulfillment. She seduced with ease. It had not taken her long to learn how to stimulate all his manly parts to the point they would do whatever she wished.

"No. This won't do a'tall. Not a'tall." Jasper took her hands in his. "I understand the game you play. It's not working. I won't be swayed by a bit of feminine wiles." He kissed her knuckles, turned both hands over, placing kisses on her palms. After he finished, he set their hands on her thighs. Her flesh was soft, silken. The thought of making love to her one more time before they spoke dashed through his head with astounding speed. She had a way of making him wish for other things.

"I'm not playing any games. As to flirting? I don't know how. I'm waiting for your enlightenment. Doing my best to be patient."

On his thighs she moved, understanding that would entice him. Well…she was playing games with him as he was with her. Believed what was good for her would be better for him.

"Don't think you can ever be patient. I'm…" Jasper brought in a long deep breath of air. "I'm not usually hesitant. Seems this has me sweating buckets. Not certain of how you will answer." He sent his fingers through his hair.

"Why?"

Maggie made a face. Her brows drawing together, she suddenly seemed very concerned with the question. "You shuddered. You never give your feelings away. Are you afraid of something? I would understand what? Didn't believe you would ever fear. You don't care about Lord Abernathy. Do you? He isn't going to show up here? Today or tomorrow? Is that what has you so afraid to talk about? I would never believe that was possible. Now, you do have me worried. This isn't about Lord Abernathy? He hasn't found me?" Her body began to shake. "Has he? I would know what we are going to do? Is the marriage certificate…?"

She stopped because she didn't know if he lied to her before about its authenticity. He assured her it was legal as well as binding. More doubts assailed her. He needed to explain everything.

Jasper brought her hands to his lips. Kissed her. Smiled as if that would reassure her, vanquish all her fears. It wouldn't. "No, not to my knowledge. He's not found us. Though I'm certain by now he would have tracked us to London. We were very careful with the ship's manifest. Didn't sign our legal names. You've no need to worry about that." He paused again, brushing the back of his hand on her cheek. "I've been thinking, Maggie? I know what I want. Always been a man of strong convictions. I've come to care a great deal about you, love."

Care not, love. He did use the word, love. What does that mean?

Maggie understood she needed and wanted far more from him than care. Didn't want the type of marriage her parents had. "Thinking? Oh dear, Nellie always told me she was most frightened when I was thinking. She never knew what I would come up with. Oh…" Her hands settled on his shoulders. "You said I don't need to worry."

"You don't, my love."

The knock at the door surprised her. She jumped, startled, searching for her robe or the sheet. Whichever she could reach first. "It must be Clancy. Why would he come now?" It had to be about Pup."

"Just a minute." Jasper swore beneath his breath, setting her on the chair by herself. "You're right. Afraid this might have something to do with Pup. Wonder what the rascal has done now."

He reached the foot of the bed where their robes lay. Slipping his on, he quickly brought hers to where she sat. Waited until she belted it.

"Sir?"

"What is it?" Jasper opened the door. Pup bounded inside. His tail wagging. He didn't look as if he was in misery. No, it was most likely Clancy who was in distress. The dog was a handful. Could wreak havoc.

"Sir. The poor little guy wouldn't stop crying. He scratched at the door. Took him outside a half hour ago. Gave him his treat when he did the right thing. Made sure his water bowl was full as well as his dish filled with food. Don't know how much a puppy of his size needs to eat. He doesn't need anything except the two of you. Is it alright if I leave him here? He won't be happy in the kitchen. Dana is gone until it's time to make lunch. There are no more scraps for him to sniff out on the floor. By the way, this little scoundrel makes a fine broom for bread crumbs."

"It's fine," Maggie spoke up, talking over Jasper.

Letting her husband make this decision was not going to happen.

The poor man looked as if he was ready to cry. Jasper shot her a scowl. She shrugged off the look of displeasure. He would have said no to his butler. Serves the man right. If he'd told her what all this was about sooner, he would not be thinking now that he might be interrupted by her dog.

"Go on." Jasper waved to him to leave. "See to your other duties. My wife and I will take care of the animal. You're right. This morning we've spent little time with the dear boy. He's not very old. Needs comforting, I'm sure. Maggie is good at that."

There was only a beat between Clancy letting go of Pup and the dog ending up on her lap. He curled up with a tiny whimper. She stroked his soft fur. He snuggled against her. She felt as if she abused him by not letting him stay in the bedroom with them. Rather than spending so much time together, they should have been playing with him. Pup was a baby. He had needs beyond eating and sleeping.

Once the door shut and they heard his footsteps leaving, the room was silent. Jasper rocked on his heels, his hands behind his back. The robe he wore opened in a deep V to his waist. His crisp dark hair showed in the opening. Maggie was enthralled. Fascinated with the sight. She wished she could touch him there. Didn't wish to wake Pup up.

Jasper didn't sit down. He stood, continuing to rock on the balls of his feet, staring at her until she felt the need to look away. Even though he reassured her a nervous chill rippled down her spine. "You need to tell me before I continue to think the worst. I…"

The air in her lungs burned. Maggie wrapped her arms around herself as if that would ward off the chill he brought into the room with the escalating silence. She thought of all they'd done since leaving Glasgow. She was afraid he didn't wish to be married to her. He was going to ask for a divorce. It was too late for an annulment. That's what she thought would happen when he first told her they were wed. He did this to protect her. Afterward, they would need to dissolve the marriage.

"Yes, I've been thinking about a great deal of things over the last few days. We are married though we didn't make plans to do so. It happened out of necessity. It was the best way I knew of to protect you."

Maggie gasped for air. All her fears were coming true. She wanted to ask him why he made love to her if he didn't want her. Words would not come from her parched lips. All her life, she only intended to give herself to the man she loved, the man she was wed to. Moisture filled her eyes. She kept a sob from forming.

He cleared his throat. Began to speak again. "You are my wife. For better or worse…" Jasper cleared his throat again as if he was having trouble speaking. He held up his hands almost as if he surrendered. "Nonetheless, you never had a wedding. A woman deserves the ceremony to assure her the marriage is valid. A priest or a minister to perform the ritual. A few witnesses that we know. Someone other than the people at the hotel registry where you never knew what you signed. I thought we could wed in the church here in Nass. I'll apply for a special license. We could have the ceremony as soon as the snow has melted."

For a few beats of her frantic heart, she thought she would faint. A few seconds later, her heart was still lodged in her throat. Her hand set to her chest as if doing so she could regain her composure. Perhaps suck in a small breath of air that would sustain her. "A wedding? A real wedding." Maggie's mind skimmed over so many different ideas. Her heart swelled with the notion he would marry her a second time. He wasn't asking her for a divorce or an annulment. Maybe she could breathe again. In time her heart might beat at a normal rate. Then her mind skipped over facts, whizzed by problems that might have occurred. Her hands stroked Pup. "Why?" There were more thoughts scrambled in her head. "Did Abernathy find us? Do you think he won't believe the certificate is legal? Is there a need?"

"A renewal of vows." Jasper walked toward her. His eyes sizzled. "Thought you might like that. I never proposed to you either. A woman wants those things. I will purchase a ring in Dublin before we say the vows." Jasper was beginning to ramble.

Maggie didn't care what else he said. Didn't care if she had a ring. She had other more important things to say. To ask for. "Can I have a wedding dress?" A new gown of that magnitude would take the seamstress a week, maybe less if she had others she could pay to help. "I would pay for the dress if I had the coin. It's something I've always dreamed about. A wedding dress…" She knew she rambled just as he had been doing. "I'd like a new gown if you say it's alright. It doesn't have to be white if you object since I'm no longer a virgin. It can be off white." At his look of anguish, she ceased her blathering. "Is that alright? Just a dress. I don't…don't need anything else." She didn't think that was too much to ask for. He looked angry. Furious. His brows drew together. "Don't need a gown…"

"A wedding dress?" He asked, sounding more confused than angry. "Yes, yes, of course, a wedding gown can be yours. That would put the wedding off a few more days. You don't need to worry about money. As you must have guessed I've more than I need. You can have anything you want if it makes you happy."

"Thank you."

Maggie ran her hand across Pup's soft fur. She was glad he approved. Had something else she needed to ask. Stalled, afraid of what he might say. She just told him she didn't need anything. Perhaps it was wrong to take advantage of his generosity.

Nothing ventured nothing gained.

"The dress must be white. Why on earth would you wish to have a different color? Off white? Good God, no!"

Jasper's anger returned. She didn't understand.

Unable to stop herself she smoothed the fabric of the robe then Pups fur. Maggie wasn't at all certain she wanted to tell him. Lifting her shoulders, she shot a look at the rumpled bed. Messed up because of what they'd been doing upon it. "I'm sorry…"

"You would announce to everyone…!"

"Since we are already married…"

Her shoulders lifted a fraction. She didn't understand the protocol for something like that. She didn't wish for people to point fingers or gossip.

"You came to me a virgin. Your gown will be white!" He was roaring now. His eyes focused on her.

She'd never seen him this angry. The sensation was not pleasant. She wasn't at all certain what to do or say in this quandary. Didn't understand his obvious anger.

Jasper looked as if he just dodged the biggest boulder in the world. He pulled in a deep breath in what appeared to be an effort to calm the raging bull inside him. Jasper began to speak again. "No more talk about your white gown. As soon as the roads are cleared, we can go to the modiste. While you are consulting the seamstress, I'll ask for the special license that will be necessary to wed without the reading of the banns. Don't wish to wait any longer than necessary."

Did he have a special license the first time? There had not been enough time for the reading of the banns. Doubts. She felt as if she was drowning in uncertainties. If they were married, why did either the bans or the license matter? He would know those things. She needed to let him see to those details. Specifics she didn't know much about. She had something else on her mind. Maggie didn't know if this would be asking for too much. She had to try. "Jasper?" She found she was looking at her folded hands that rested on her lap. After she looked up, she spoke. "Can my sisters be invited? To our wedding?"

She waited for the snap of anger. Was certain Jasper would not wish to wait for the invitations to arrive in Glasgow or for her sisters to come here.

The look hurtling across his face told her he wasn't pleased with her request. He heaved in a huge sigh then placed his fingers in a steeple beneath his chin. "That would put the wedding, the renewal of our vows, off for a couple of weeks. Is that what you want? I had thought we should do this as soon as possible. I was hoping before the end of this week. As soon as your dress could be finished. If you want the truth, I was hoping it would be as soon as the snow melted. Since we are a married couple, I suppose..."

She gulped down what would be another breath of air. Seemed he might agree. Caught her lip beneath her top teeth. Afraid to ask but knowing she had to try, she blurted, "My sisters...yes. I would like them to be here. Family. A girl only has one wedding...hopefully. Well, this will be our second. You could have Jason come. We both understand we don't need to worry about Lord Abernathy finding me since we are wed. Once we are wed a second time...we renew our vows...in front of family..." She didn't know what they would do with their lives. They could return to Glasgow. They could stay here for another week or two for a honeymoon. "I can write to my sisters this morning. You can send a letter to Jason."

The look on his face was not one that Maggie could describe as pleased. She assumed her idea was a great one. Decided to run with her thoughts. Obvious that her husband wasn't content, she puffed air. For her, he seemed to hold back his anger or perhaps it was more annoyance that his plans changed. Perhaps asking him if she could have Dana bake a cake for the occasion would not be appropriate at this point. Though that would not delay the renewal of their vows.

"If you wish to wait for three weeks, we can do that. This is all for you. So you recall the ceremony. No doubt we are wed."

His words sounded stilted. They vibrated from him as if he had to say each one individually in order to extract them from his mind.

"You don't want to wait?" *Of course, you nitwit, he wouldn't be acting this way if he wished to wait the necessary time for her family to arrive.* "I'm sorry. A dress should have been enough to ask for. I'm expecting too much. Aren't I? First a dog, then a gown and now family… You must think I'm spoiled."

"That's the farthest notion from my mind." Jasper waved his hand in the air. "Don't care if you've been given many fine things in your life. I've every intention of giving you more. When I step back to peruse all you've told me, you, my dear, have not been spoiled by your mother. Believe this might be the first time in your life anyone besides your sisters have cared about you. You will have all that you want. This is your wedding. If there is more, make a list. I will see to everything."

"I shouldn't have asked for so much. It was selfish of me." She was worrying the material of her robe. Pup was wiggling, trying to get comfortable. He jumped off her lap before striding to his bed.

"You should always ask me if there is something you need or would like. I want to make you happy. Let's see." He held his finger to his chin smiling at her, "You will need a gown for the wedding. You mentioned a cake. Dana will have no trouble with that. Would you like flowers? Given the time of the year those might be harder to come by. I'll check to see if anyone in Dublin has a hothouse. There might be flowers available. What type of flowers would you like? Orchids perhaps?"

She found she was shaking her head, overwhelmed by his thoughtfulness. Maggie didn't know what to think. "What would you like? This time of year… You are right, flowers might not be available."

He hooted, seeming startled by his question. "Isn't it obvious?"

"No."

"To have the wedding done, over, as soon as possible. Come here." He motioned for her. She dashed into his arms ready to have him hold her close.

~ * ~

Jasper never understood how this situation got so far out of hand so fast. One second, he thought all he needed to do was go to the minister in Dublin and have a special license issued. They would be wed within the week. In a fraction of time, because he didn't have the ability to tell Maggie no, they would not be married officially for about three weeks. It all started with a wedding dress. Escalated from there. Got out of hand. By then this darling woman would most likely carry his child.

The babe would come early. Though…to anyone who asked, they've been wed since before they left London. By that standard the child would not come too soon. No one would question their activities before the renewal of vows.

Maggie believed they were wed.

Not yet.

"We should dress. We can discuss this with the servants. Prepare them for out-of-town guests. Explain this is a renewal, not the wedding. Don't wish for gossip. Would you like a party after the ceremony? We could invite a few more people to celebrate with us."

He was standing at the window overlooking the back of the house. While he gazed out the window, wistful, the snow fall seemed to slow. Thought they should take Pup outside to play. Wear him out so he wouldn't be such a nuisance. Didn't puppies and babies sleep a lot? That's what he heard. Thought that might be what Maggie told him.

"I can write my sisters? They will be eager. I miss them so much." Maggie sounded hesitant, almost as if she was afraid to ask him for things. "You'll write to your brother? He will come too?"

"He knows I'm planning on getting married." Jasper was quick to clear his throat. "Renewing vows. Jason will arrive here in a week or less. I assume in about five days. Sooner if possible. Didn't expect him here for the wedding. Thought…never mind." Jasper rubbed the back of his neck, thinking about the explanations. He would need to stick as close to the truth as possible. He wasn't sure what to tell the good reverend. In that case, as little as he could get away with. The pastor would wonder about the second license, the marriage certificate. He wished he could forget about the issues so he could concentrate on Maggie. "I wrote to him earlier."

Even then he mentioned to his brother how they were wed the first time. What he intended to do once they were settled. They would have the wedding in the church. This ceremony would be real. Binding them together for life. What else was there? Maggie might carry his child. Happiness surged through him.

"You did all that without asking me?" Her voice wavered. Maggie was shaking while she stood. "You could have told me. Why didn't you?"

What she said was true. Yes, he should have told her the marriage certificate was for looks only. Should have never taken her to his bed. Beneath his breath, he cursed himself along with his unruly body. In the process taking her innocence. Guilt bit him in the butt. He should have been more forthcoming with Maggie. She wore her heart on her sleeve. Was always honest in her feelings. By her standards, he deceived her. He was a man who kept his thoughts to himself. This was something he was going to need to change. He would have a wife who would also expect him to share his thoughts. In years…decades, he might be able to explain his way of thinking to her. His actions, reasons for the fake marriage.

"I didn't know if you would agree to my idea. Felt we were safe from Abernathy…but…" Those were all excuses. He should have said more to her. She should know the marriage isn't real. He couldn't tell her that bit of information. If he did, she would despise him. Might not ever forgive him. Perhaps after they'd been wed a year or two, he could speak of the deception. He kept rolling the trickery around in his head.

"You're right. We need to dress then go about our day. There is a lot to do. People to see. As soon as we play with Pup." She looked at her sleeping puppy. "Doesn't look to have much energy now. We'll get him up. After Pup is exhausted again, I will write to my sisters. Anice will look at the letter. Who knows what she will do? I don't. She might forbid my sisters from attending the wedding. The worst case would be if she insisted, they bring her along. Uninvited doesn't mean anything to my mother. She'd been known to crash a party or two. They don't have the funds in their name that they would need to pay for the trip. My sisters would need help."

"If the snow stops, I might be able to ride into Nass today. It's not that far. I'll have the minister read the banns starting this Sunday. We'll attend church. We'll need to have them read with our real names. We'll no longer be imposters." Jasper was ticking off the list of things needing to be accomplished. There was a lot to do.

Jasper watched her stiffen. Wondered about that. For the time being, he meant to let that go. Perhaps she didn't attend church. If that was true, the fact might change once they were well and truly wed. He wanted his son baptized. Needed to know they were God fearing children to grow into adults. This was all part of his legacy. A legacy he was beginning to realize was important to him. Until Maggie he'd not thought much about what he would leave behind. He and Maggie knew little about each other. It wasn't enough to know he couldn't keep his hands from her. Ah, he did understand she was stubborn. He was beginning to know bits and pieces of her. She knew less about him. Was that enough for a marriage to work? It had to be. Divorce was not something he would ever consider.

"You may take my letter with you." Her back as well as her words were stiff. "I should write the missive before I play with Pup."

There was a lot here he needed to undo. So much for him to make amends. He wasn't used to justifying or explaining his actions. There wasn't a doubt in his mind the truth would come out. Lies never lasted forever. Ah, he would deal with them when he had to do so. "When will the missive be ready?"

"Give me ten minutes. I'll write it then dress. I can meet you downstairs." Her voice was rigid. "I won't need to go to the dressmakers. She has my measurements. I'll write down what I would like. You will give that to her. It will make it easier as well as save time. In a few days, I can go into Nass for a fitting."

"Very well, if that's what you want." Jasper tried to ignore all his wildly oscillating emotions. He wasn't a man used to this type of diplomacy or negotiations. He imagined this was something he would need to become acquainted with. He was a man used to making up his mind then proceeding as he planned. Today, he gave into her wishes. Somehow, it felt good to please Maggie.

Pup followed him downstairs after he dressed. They left Maggie sitting at the desk in the room, still clad in her bathrobe. If this mission wasn't so important to him, he might have made love to her again. The one night in bed with his wife…with his wife, wasn't enough to satisfy all his needs. Morning sex held a nice ring to it. Never did that before, never stayed long enough with a woman to make love with the rising sun.

He was appalled to discover he thought of her just about every second. Maggie was a constant in his mind. Downstairs Jasper let Pup outside. Rewarded him with his morsel of cheese when he returned to the kitchen. Dana was busy making sandwiches for lunch. A tea kettle whistled.

"I'll take tea in the dining room. Bring the luncheon there when my wife comes down. We'll eat then I'm off to town." He started for the dining room before he turned. "Dana, my wife and I are going to have a real wedding after the banns are read. Maggie would like you to make a cake. It needs to be large enough to feed both our families. We'll know the number better after they arrive here sometime before the service. We haven't discussed this thoroughly but I think we would like to have a celebration after the vows are said."

"A real wedding?" she questioned then blushed understanding it wasn't her place to question. "Sorry, sir, do you know what type she likes best? I would please her."

"No. I'll ask her then let you know."

This was one more thing he didn't know about his wife. Didn't know her favorite color or flower. Didn't comprehend the types of food she liked best. How could anyone believe they were married?

You did this to protect her. In the process you wound up falling in love with her. He'd never expected to fall in love at his age. The plan was to turn thirty-five then fall in love. If not for love, he would find a suitable woman, a woman who knew her station. All his plans were going awry. He found he wasn't concerned about that. The devil with plans. They were worthless when life took charge.

When she entered the dining room, he was standing at the window. Sometimes the sun peeked its head from behind the clouds. Frozen snow glistened on the road leading from the cottage. Water dripped from melting snow off the trees. In another hour the roads might be passable.

He turned as he heard her enter the room. She was beautiful, dressed in one of the new gowns they purchased. The soft green color enhanced her eyes. Her hair was swept up in a knot on top of her head. Loose strands of hair curled about the delicate framework of her face. To him, Maggie was a vision. If the servants weren't about, he would… Perhaps Maggie wasn't ready to find herself tumbled on the dining room table. When he chuckled, she lifted her head with a puzzled expression on her face.

"Dana, our cook, would like to know what type of wedding cake you would like. I spoke to her earlier. You might give her an idea how many you think will arrive for the ceremony." His speech was brusque. He was still reeling from the change of his plans. "What is your favorite color?"

"What?"

"Don't you think a husband should know that. Mine is green." *The color of your eyes.*

She seemed inflexible. Appeared apprehensive. This was their first real conversation since she asked for a wedding gown. She had approached him with sweet sincerity. He appreciated the manner in which she spoke to him earlier. Now, Maggie handed him the postmarked letter. After that another piece of paper. "This is for the modiste. A description of what I would like for my wedding gown. Thank you. I would come into town for a fitting as soon as the roads are passable by carriage."

With a huge sigh, Maggie sat down at the table. Her hands were clenched tight in front of her. When she looked at him moisture rimmed her beautiful eyes.

He nodded. Wished he understood what brought tears to her eyes. "I will see the directions given to your seamstress. The letter will be sent to Dublin today. Is there anything else?" He pulled out a chair. Dana would bring the lunch soon.

"Just a thank you. I understand you didn't want any of this."

"You're right."

"I'm sorry…"

"Don't be. I find I like the way I feel when I see your beautiful smile light up your eyes. A man should see to a proper wedding." Jasper knew that to be the truth. "Don't think about this again. We might not have the wedding of your dreams. What I do know is that this ceremony will be far better than the first one. Which wasn't a ceremony at all. It was an exchange of words then the signing of the papers." If he could be willing to return to Glasgow for this event, the wedding would be far different. He wasn't willing. There was still the issue of her engagement to Abernathy hanging over his head.

They were still not legally wed. Every night he would take advantage of the reality she didn't comprehend that fact. If he thought he could explain away the truth that he took her innocence when they weren't wed, he would. Thinking of her reaction to that news caused a cold sweat

213

to break out.

Lunch passed far too fast. Pup was in the dining room with them. Clancy brought a bed for the rascal to stay on while they ate. He could be wrong. The thought stuttered around in his head. Jasper did believe Clancy was beginning to care for the dog.

He stood. Kissed Maggie on the forehead. Stepped back, wishing he dared take her into his arms. "Don't wear yourself out today playing with the little animal. I've plans for this evening. Want to have you all to myself. You might wish to take a nap. I'll be back as soon as possible."

On the road into town, melting snow crashed from the trees. Tumbled to the ground. The weather was warming. In a couple of days if there was no more snow or rain, he would be able to take Maggie into Nass in the carriage. He thought perhaps he should take her to Dublin. She could pick out a wedding ring for herself.

His first stop was the church. The minister met him in the rectory. Jasper would need to explain as much as he could about the situation. He would have to tell the truth. Lying to a man of God would be impossible.

"Sir, I wish to marry Maggie." He pinched the bridge of his nose, his head pounding. By the time he finished here, it was a certainty his head would be close to exploding. He stepped up to the chair in front of the desk.

"Please sit. Mr. O'Neill, I was of the belief that you and Maeve were wed. Am I wrong? Who is Maggie?" The man stared at him with an expression that made him feel as if he were still a little boy.

Jasper gasped a breath of air hoping for courage to proceed. "Maggie is…" Perhaps it wasn't time to tell the complete truth. Might be prudent to hold off for a less precipitous moment.

"Why would you wish for another wedding? One wasn't enough? You want to marry two women? Can't do that. You know…" The man sat down behind his desk, tapping the papers there looking confused.

One more time, Jasper inhaled a deep breath of air. Didn't miss the note of humor in the minister's voice. Imagining this could seem humorous to some. "We misled the town. It was not…the lie was necessary. Maeve and Maggie are the same person," Jasper blurted in a rush to expel the words. As it seemed the reverend was going to speak, Jasper held up his hands to stop him. "Let me explain more thoroughly. I would hope that as best you can, you will keep this information to yourself. This is not something we took lightly. Her life was in danger. Maggie needed my protection. Still does…"

"I don't understand."

"My name is Jasper Kenworthy the Marquis of... The woman who is with me is Maggie MacRae." Jasper went on to explain the story in its entirety. The reverend shook his head when he was finished.

"You are living in sin with the young lady. If I have this right, Miss MacRae has no idea she is not married to you. In this matter, you are correct in proceeding with all haste. The wedding must take place as soon as possible. I would have the wedding witnessed by the congregation."

Guilt once again sent a bullet into his heart. He didn't like himself much. Even with that feeling prevalent in his head, he meant to keep Maggie in his bed. He couldn't let her go even for three weeks. If he didn't continue as they did last night, without the truth Maggie would be hurt. The truth wasn't possible. "You are correct. She believes we are married. I had hoped to get this business finished within the week. As you might have guessed with her request that family be in attendance, we must wait until her sisters arrive."

"Why haven't you done so? In Dublin you could see the proper people, get a special license. I do not have the power to give you one. The matter should be cleared up. What are you waiting for?"

He scratched his eyebrow then beneath his chin. "That's the stickler, sir. Maggie asked me if she could have a wedding dress made. Well…that would only set us back a few days. I've the groats to make certain Eilinora can hire enough people to finish within a day or two. That's not all though."

"What's the problem lad? I would have that done. The sooner you get this taken care of…I don't need to explain anything to you. I will be pleased to wed the two of you with the completion of the wedding dress. Such a small thing when there is so much more at stake."

His breath exploding from his lungs, Jasper continued. "Earlier I mentioned her sisters arriving. She asked me if she could invite her sisters to her wedding. I didn't have the heart to tell her no. She deserves her family to witness her marriage. Don't you think? I've found I can't say no to anything she asks for. Need to make her happy."

"This part I do understand." The reverend's fingers made a steeple beneath his chin. He tapped them while he thought. "They live in Glasgow.

You couldn't tell her no. I'm hearing this correctly?"

The minister laughed. Laughed, roared with the humor of this conundrum until his eyes watered. He pulled out his handkerchief to dab the moisture from his cheeks where the tears slid. "You are quite the catch, Jasper Kenworthy. Maggie is a lucky lady. So, if I have this right, you risk a great deal because you want her to be happy. You love her so much…"

"That's right. You do understand what I'm up against. Don't want Lord Abernathy to get wind of this before we are truly wed. That man could cause quite a few problems for the two of us. I ran with Maggie to protect her from marriage to a man she loathed. Thought the pretend wedding was a good idea at the time. The fake ceremony was a grand idea until I burned for her. Until that moment I couldn't keep my hands from her. That was when the real trouble began. I have to make this *faux pas* up to her. Maggie believes we are renewing our vows."

"In the eyes of God, this *faux pas* you speak of is not little. I will do what I can. Though, I will not lie for you. If anyone suspects something and asks, I will have to tell the truth."

Jasper found himself nodding his head. "Yes, I understand." He couldn't expect anything different from the priest. "You will marry us? Read the banns this Sunday at church? Maggie and I will be there."

"Everyone will know your real name," the reverend told him.

"Yes."

With a gulp of air coupled with a sigh of relief, Jasper left the church then headed for the dress shop. With the reverend's agreement to marry them, a weight had been lifted from his shoulders. As he entered, the little bell rang out that Eilinora had a customer. The room smelled of fresh baked scones.

"Mr. O'Neill, how very nice to see you. We've," she motioned to the seamstress in the back of the room, "been working hard on your order. If not for the snow we would have delivered a few items today." Eilinora strode toward him, her hand extended in greeting. "Have you come in to pick up some more gowns? We've completed half the order. I'll wrap the clothing for you."

"I didn't think of that. Would be pleased to take the new gowns to my wife." He paused as she made a funny face. Jasper understood why. "I've come to order another gown. A very important one." He didn't intend to tell his story to this lady. For now, the minister was the only one who would learn who he was. In time, after the wedding, many of the people in Nass would know. Until they were married, he didn't want this situation to be common knowledge. Couldn't risk Maggie finding out. Couldn't risk Abernathy hearing then claiming his intended.

"A new gown?" Eilinora questioned with a smile of delight. "I'd be pleased to make something more for your lady. What did you have in mind?"

"There is no rush for this." He cleared his throat trying to think of the right words to say so there would be no suspicions cast Maggie's way. "It is to be a gown to celebrate the renewal of our wedding vows."

She waved her hand in the air. "Poff...never heard of such a thing. What exactly is this you're attempting to explain, young man?"

"You see..." He was going to need to tell Maggie this story. One lie always led to another. "You see..." Jasper began again, nerves beginning to twitch. "Our wedding in Scotland was in haste. As you might not *ken*, the banns *dinna* have to be read there. On our way to London, we stopped at a small church in the Scottish countryside." He wasn't certain why he didn't tell this story to the minister. He supposed he couldn't lie to a man of God.

"A hasty wedding, now the lass wishes to have something a bit more special. Am I right? You've come to the right place. I'll get it done for you. How is the puppy?"

"The rascal? He's doing quite well. Has settled in with us."

"Glad to hear."

Relief swamped him. Eilinora understood his predicament. He didn't need to tell her he had a different name as did Maggie. She still believed them to be wed. This was all good. A tiny shiver of what felt like relief passed through him. "Yes. You understand my predicament. Maggie would like a wedding dress. We are going to renew our vows to each other in three weeks. While...since we are Scotts...she doesn't care about the reading of the banns. However, she wished for her family to attend this wedding. So, the minister has agreed to do so. He will wed us in front of the congregation."

"Yes, family at weddings are nice, very important. Will you need bridesmaids' gowns?" Eilinora asked. "I will need to see Maggie in order to select the colors along with the fabrics she would wish for."

217

Her question sent a new wave of panic rushing into his head. "I'll need to ask Maggie. How would you do that? Make gowns. You don't have their measurements." Seems he traveled between relief as well as panic since he first began the conversations about this wedding…er…renewal of vows. Fear joined the emotions. Anxiety they would be discovered before the real event could take place. Abernathy still threatened.

"When I meet with Maggie about the gown, I'll ask her. Sometimes sisters are much the same size. If we get the dresses put together, a few fittings will make all perfect. How many sisters did you say she has?"

"Fittings? How long will that take?" The devil…he was shaking. This simple idea of his escalated with each conversation. He wasn't a man given to nerves. This wedding planning was all too new to him. "Three sisters."

"No more than a few days. If I have your permission to hire more help, we can get this done in a blink. What's your wife's favorite color?"

How the hell should he know? He'd known her a little over a month. He asked her this morning. She didn't answer, just gave him a quizzical look. They never discussed anything like this. He did ask her. She never answered. "I'll ask her. No, I imagine when she comes in for her fittings, you'll be able to ask her yourself." If he asked her, if he remained in this state of anxiety, he would never remember.

They might not even come. After a bit more conversation, he left the dress store. The palms of his hands were sweating. He was a mess of nerves as well as worries. Passing the pub on his way out of town, he decided to stop in for a glass of beer. Something that would calm his apprehension. The devil…

"Hello, Mr. O'Neill, glad to see you got out from beneath the snow. Would get back before the sun goes down though. Could get icy tonight." The man was wiping down the bar. "What can I get you today?"

"I will leave for home soon. Stopped in for a pint. A Guinness please." At this juncture, he needed something stronger than a beer.

"What were you doing in town? The roads are still bad," the bartender asked as he set the pint of Guinness on the table. "Must have been something important."

He blurted without thinking farther than he could toss any of these *braw* men, "Had to see to my wedding…"

He paused in shock. That was not something he meant to say. He ran a finger along his collar.

"Thought you were married to Maeve? Introduced her to us as your wife. Was that a lie?" The bartender turned to the patrons. "Justin here says he is going to get married. He be livin' in sin if he's not married now."

Quick on his feet most of the time, Jasper held up his hand. He could explain this easily. "Going to renew our vows. Got wed in a little parish church without the benefit of a wedding gown or her family. Feel guilty. We were in a hurry. That's all. Didn't wish to live in sin. Promised the little lady that I'd give her the works once we got settled. While what we have planned isn't exactly what one could describe as the works, she is pleased."

"A second wedding? Hey drinks on Mr. O'Neill. We're all going to have a pint to celebrate this second wedding. Most men think one is enough. Not our fine man here. He's a glutton for punishment he is. Has to have two weddings to keep his wife happy. There's a real gent for you. We should all take lessons from Mr. O'Neill."

"We call it the renewal of our vows, not a wedding. There is a difference. We are married."

While Jasper didn't mind paying for a celebratory drink or two to the customers tonight, he wasn't certain about the gossip that would ensue. He had no choice but to go along with these men. Keeping the affair quiet must have been a dream. Now, this was becoming a nightmare. He had no one to blame except himself. No one used thumb screws on him to get him to spout about the wedding.

"What's that? The first time wasn't good enough? Is she failing to obey? Is that what's got you going to do her bidding?" Another man chimed in. "You need to have the little lady vow to obey. After that you won't have worries."

Jasper never cared much for the obey part of the vows. He always thought when he wed, he would share his life with his mate, not command her to do and act in the way he wished. He tossed down a long delicious gulp of his beer then stood, holding the glass high in the air.

"If you fellows understand anything, it must be that it is in every man's best interest to keep his little woman happy. We married in haste. She never got a wedding gown. Her sisters didn't attend our nuptials. Wished to please her. That's all."

"Couldn't keep your hands off her. That's what I'm hearing," a man in the back of the room called out. "Maybe the two of you weren't married at all. Might be all this to do is to set your affairs in order. Dinna want a bastard to come out of the blissful nights."

There was too much truth in those words.

"Either that or he's sleeping on the couch until he gives her what she wants," the bartender chimed in with a chuckle. "Either way he's going to get his wishes. Here's to the renewal of vows."

"Drink up. When I finish, I'm going home to my bride. I'll buy another round for the rest of you before I leave."

~ * ~

Hands on her hips, a slight scowl on her face, Anice stood over Nellie after she handed her daughter the letter from Maggie. Nellie looked at her, wishing Anice would leave. She didn't want her to know what Maggie wrote. This was private for them. She might give away her location. Lord Abernathy would find her. No, Maggie was too careful to do something so stupid. Anice would stay put. All the sisters understood that for a fact.

Tapping her toe with impatience, Anice scowled at her. "Read it, Nellie. You've no other choice. I'm not going anywhere until I know what my wayward daughter has written. I would go after her then drag her back by her hair if I could. She is an embarrassment to the MacRae name. By penning this letter to you, she is giving herself away. Though Lord Abernathy is nowhere to be found. He hied off in all different directions. Seems Jason Kenworthy, the twin, led him a merry chase over half of Scotland then into the Netherlands. Who knows where the fine Lord Abernathy could be now that I might be able to tell him where to find my daughter. Still wish to see to their wedding. It was to be a fine affair."

Nellie understood Anice would go nowhere until she got what she wished for. There was no getting around this predicament. With trembling fingers, Nellie opened the envelope. Stared at the parchment, holding her breath then blinking a few times as she took in the first few words. This was it. For several more moments, she stared at the writing, her eyes clouding over as if she didn't wish to read what would be written there. Tucking in a huge breath of air, Nellie began to read.

Dear Nellie, Fannie and of course, Tessa,

Don't fret too much about the note or the address. I understand Anice will find a way to make you read this to her. Either that or she will open the letter before she gives it to you. I'm in no danger from Lord Abernathy. Even if he finds out where I am, he cannot hurt me. I'm married to Jasper Kenworthy the Marquis. I don't know his full tittle. I'm just learning about him. Though I can tell you I do believe I've fallen in love with the wonderful man. Maybe I'm not quite reciprocating that sentiment. It will happen though, sooner than later. The man, my husband, is so sweet. He let me adopt a puppy. We call him Pup. I don't believe he can tell me no. Not that it matters so much. Not that I would ever take advantage of that lack of ability. I adore him. Would never wish to change that fact by abusing his generosity. Though I do admire that quality about him after being with Lord Abernathy for almost a year. Abernathy had to have everything his way. My wishes never meant a thing to him.

I digress. Jasper and I were married in London without the benefit of family. Jasper has asked me if I'd like to renew my vows to him. To have a wedding I would be able to recount to our children. I told him, yes. He wished to marry me the next day. I asked him not to do that. I told my adorable husband I wanted a wedding dress. After that, told him I wished to have my sisters there to witness my marriage to him. He couldn't tell me no to either of my requests. If mother will allow this to happen, I would love to have the three of you with me on my special day. From the time I wrote this letter, the wedding will take place in three weeks. That leaves a little more than two for all you to find transportation here. He initiated the reading of the banns on Sunday at church. Just a formality since we are married. I hope as well as pray that all three of you can get here. Need my family to be present on the most important day of my life. Just so you know, the first time did not feel like a wedding at all. It all happened too fast. Indeed, it was to see to my protection from Lord Abernathy.

The service will be in a small white church in Nass, Ireland. Nass is a village just outside Dublin. Please, I hope the three of you can attend. Write to me. Let me know when to expect you. Don't worry about lodgings. We have enough room in the cottage for the three of you to stay. Mother, if

she comes, will need to find a place in the village. I don't have room for her.
  Love always,
  Maggie

Nellie clapped her hands together, thrilled with the news. "Can we go?" She turned to Anice witnessing the sudden defeat in her eyes while she prayed Anice would give permission. Maggie said nothing about their mother and father being invited. Well, she did mention there wasn't room at the cottage for mother.

"Not without your father and me. None of you are going anywhere. Noticed Maggie never said anything about wishing for her mother to see her wed. That seems highly unusual. Don't you all think? You would wish for me to attend your weddings? Wouldn't you?" There was a tone to Anice's voice that didn't go unnoticed. "I don't appreciate the lack of the invitation."

"You haven't been her mother or ours for years. I'm not surprised she didn't invite you. You initiated a wedding she didn't wish for. You've been nothing but despicable to all of us. Not motherly," Tessa said, her voice soft.

The moment was rare that Tessa would voice an opinion. Her usual habit was to allow the sisters to speak freely then agree with them. Nellie was silently pleased. She'd been afraid the littlest sister would be too easily manipulated. Perhaps with Maggie's departure under unusual circumstances, Tessa was developing a stiff backbone.

Anice straightened, seeming to shrug off the *faux pas*. Pointing her finger at all of them, "The three of you will not be attending the wedding without me. Take my decision or leave it." She hefted her shoulders upward. "See if I care one way or the other. Maggie can say her vows in front of all of us or none of us. In this we will stand together as a family."

"I'm of age! I don't need your permission to go to my sister's wedding," Nellie said with defiance, her heart in her throat afraid that perhaps Anice would not give them funds for the trip.

Anice had more control over her than she wished to admit. In too many ways she did need her mother's consent. She might be of age but she had no money available to her.

The smile on her mother's face sent a cringe of fear into her. Nellie found herself shivering. When she looked to her sisters, they seemed to have the same reaction. Anice understood her control over her daughters.

"You have no money," Anice didn't need to remind her. "You think to book passage on a ship out of here with your good looks alone." She gave each one a pointed stare. "Imagine you could sell your body to the captain. Spread your legs for passage. Most likely what your sister did to get Lord Kenworthy's protection."

Collectively the sisters gasped. That was crude even for her mother. Nellie found herself incensed as well as mortified at the suggestion she might consider such a thing. "Why? Why would you wish to travel all the way to Ireland to see Maggie wed? You tried to give her away to a man she loathed. No one is more aware of your feelings for her than Maggie. You despise the ground she walks on. Now, with this marriage, she will be happy. I've heard Jasper Kenworthy is very nice. By appearing there, you will ruin the wedding for her." Perhaps that was what Anice wished.

"Take it or leave it, my darlings. I stand by my decision." Anice whisked out of the room, her back stiff.

Nellie watched the door slam shut behind her mother. "I can't imagine how I would feel if my child was getting married and I wasn't invited. Do you think she is hurt by the oversight?" She stared down at the letter before she looked up again. "I didn't read this part. Jasper sent money for us to use. It's in the bank of Glasgow in my name. He had Jason put it there. Maggie doesn't even know. We can take the funds."

"Book passage," Fannie said.

"We have money." Tessa clapped her hands together. "We can go without mother?"

"All of us are of an age we can dictate our futures. We stayed here because it was comfortable. Afraid though, if we venture out leaving mother behind, she won't allow us to return home. Jasper cannot be expected to support us."

"Because, until we are married, we have nowhere else to go. We will need to include mother though we don't need to accept her money for our travel expenses," Nellie pointed out.

It was clear Anice still held sway over them. Would until they were married. What Nellie was afraid of was that she would be her next victim. Anice might offer her body to Lord Abernathy to replace Maggie."

"Would it be so terrible if mother and father joined us?" Fannie asked with a bit of nostalgia in her tone. "They would be company on the long journey. A mother along with the father should be at the wedding of their oldest daughter."

Nellie snorted her disbelief. "The journey will not be long. By ship, doubt if the voyage will last more than two or three days. Dublin is not that far. Mother creates chaos wherever she goes. She will plan something. I would not be surprised if she voiced her objection during the ceremony."

"This a second marriage...a renewal of their vows in front of family. It matters not if mother objects. Maggie and Lord Kenworthy are husband and wife."

"It's onto the Irish Sea," Tessa shared with a pleased smile. "Nass, she said their place is close by the village. We certainly could do this without parents. Especially if we have the funds."

"If Anice wishes it, she will be there."

"Something horrible will go wrong. I know it."

Chapter Eight

Maggie looked up from the letter she was reading. Pup danced around her feet barking and tugging on her skirt. Growling while he wrestled with the hem. "They are here. Arrived last night in Dublin. Nellie says mother and father came along with them. Anice gave them no choice. Mother wishes to shop for a few things. Their trip to the cottage will be delayed until tomorrow." She set the note down feeling the elation she felt vanishing. Seeing her sisters was so important to her. Seeing her mother, she dreaded.

"How do you feel?"

He stood behind her. His hands massaged her neck. She'd been so stressed the last two and a half weeks. She was worried about the wedding. Dana fretted over the cake. Had practiced with several. They settled on a simple white cake with chocolate frosting. The corsage of her dress had been cut too low. The bridesmaids' gowns were fine so far. They were hanging in Eilinora's back closet waiting for the fittings. Jasper found a man in Dublin with a hothouse. He purchased orchids for the wedding. They would be returned after the ceremony. He took her to Dublin a week ago to pick out rings. The engagement ring was a large emerald surrounded by diamonds. The ring was exquisite. Stole her breath. Her wedding band was silver with alternating emeralds and diamonds set into the gold. Jasper's ring was a simple silver band to match hers.

Jason arrived about five days ago. Except for the nights, Maggie didn't see much of Jasper. The twins kept busy with business matters that had been waiting for Japer's attention. Seemed there was correspondence that needed to be addressed. Jasper along with Jason had major holdings throughout Scotland as well as England. Had two ships that frequented the states bringing back tobacco then exchanging the cargo for tea.

He came to her in the night. They made love. He asked her silly questions he thought he should know the answer to. He was always sweet. Always loving to her. He would kiss her in the dark. She told him her favorite color was soft lavender. He said his was the color of her eyes. She told him he should have guessed because she chose that same color for the three bridesmaid dresses. He wanted to learn more about her. Told her a husband would know such things. She wasn't a person with favorites as she enjoyed so many different things.

"If you insist on three attendants, I need to find two men in the village who would stand beside me. I only have my brother Jason here. I did ask Gracie to come with her husband, Fletcher. She replied they would try. It was his turn to travel to London on business so a skip across the Irish sea might not be too difficult. He opted not to have a challenge tennis match for the privilege of staying home. Sometimes it was fun to visit London."

"What? You don't have friends at the pub? I would think the bartender might be willing to be part of our wedding. You did tell me teased you about the second ceremony."

"Hush," he told her. "I don't need three attendants. Jason would be happy to walk each of your sisters down the aisle. He's quite capable of handling that many women in almost the same breath."

Maggie hit him on the shoulder. Now that her sisters were in Dublin, she wanted to go to them as soon as possible. There were things before the wedding they could help her with. "We should take a carriage tomorrow morning. Drive to Dublin. Pick them up at the hotel where they are staying. What do you say? We could stop at the dress shop in Nass for a fitting on our return trip."

He was smiling at her. Maggie had the distinct impression he would not say *nay*. "Yes, we should. The dresses do need to be perfect. The wedding is in three days. I would not have the ceremony postponed another week because the gowns were not finished to everyone's satisfaction. It is to be held after the service on Sunday. The minister's wife will have a cake made for the members of the congregation who wish to stay. She also said there would be tea; some coffee for those who prefer. Thought that to be sweet of the woman.

"I'll send the stableboy with a message to your sisters that we will pick them up around ten o'clock in the morning. He will beat us up there but we will be close on his heels. You must rise early in the morning."

She turned. Set her hand on his cheek. Kissed him. "Thank you. I'm eager. Will Jason come with us?"

"Come where?" Jason walked into the room. His smile was broad. "Don't believe I wish to travel tomorrow. Thought I would enjoy a ride then a pint at the pub. Maybe find a willing lass…"

"To pick up my sisters in Dublin," Maggie spoke.

Now that her sisters arrived, she was happy. Giddy, if she could describe the feeling. Had been so worried Anice would not allow them the trip. In the interim she received one letter from Nellie telling her of their plans. Explaining why her mother along with her father would also show up. Told her she was certain Anice would have sent the information of her whereabouts to Lord Abernathy.

"Would love to do so. Don't you think the carriage might be a wee bit crowded if I were to go?" Jason was laughing. "Believe I'll stick to my original plans. Found a widow who seems to enjoy my attention. Will also pay her a visit this afternoon.

He was right. There would barely be enough room for the five of them. It would be crowded. She imagined no one would mind. Her sisters were not very big. Nonetheless, if Jason accompanied them, they would find themselves crushed together.

"You are right, of course."

"I will see that Dana prepares a fantastic meal when all of you make it here. Did I understand you will all stop at the modiste's place of business to have the fittings on the gowns? I'm delighted I have the chance to walk all of your sisters down the aisle." Jason had the audacity to sigh. "I'm aggrieved though I can't give the blushing bride away to my brother. Alas, her father is to be in attendance."

"Why not?"

Maggie would much rather have Jason give her to Jasper than her father. Her father had never been a part of her life. When he could have stepped in to stop the betrothal to Lord Abernathy, he said nothing. Did nothing. She remembered the day she pleaded with him to end the travesty. Her father told her to do what her mother wanted. Anice always knew best. Her decisions were sound. Logical.

"Your father will do it. He should." Jason was abrupt with his comment. Matter-of-fact in his thought.

"As far as I'm concerned, he hasn't the right to pretend he is my father. I respect you. Can you make four trips down the aisle? Would that tire you too much?" There was a touch of amusement in her voice. From what she'd seen so far of Jason Kenworthy, the man was tireless. While he sometimes put on airs of a dandy, the man was far from being one. Maggie wasn't certain why Jason pretended. She decided he tried to keep most ladies at a distance.

"If this would please you, I would be happy to oblige your wishes. Though…" He pondered the conversation for a few seconds. "What of your father? I would not wish to hurt his feelings. You are his daughter. Are you not? If I were scorned on my daughter's wedding day, I would have trouble forgiving the girl who sprang from my loins."

Maggie understood what he asked. She found herself shaking her head, denying his assumption. "As far as I know he is my real father. Though what you ask is worth thinking about. I doubt if you would hurt his feelings. For what it is worth, he doesn't care about any of us girls. Never has. Doubt if he would notice."

That was a sad statement of fact. She never before this moment doubted the man was her biological father. Now, from Jason's words, she did. Did the man sire any of her sisters? They all were similar in their looks. None favored her father, not even to eye color. They all had the look of their mother except for Tessa. Tessa didn't look like either parent. The sudden thought baffled.

Jason bowed low. "In that case, I'd be pleased to do the honors." He looked to Jasper as if he might object.

"I would also be honored. If we were home, the Murray men could serve in the other roles. We are not. As was mentioned before, I did send an invitation to Gracie and Fletcher. Fletcher might help out. Doubt if the others will attend. Gracie is my cousin. She is very dear to me."

"Perhaps," Maggie smiled at both men. "Fletcher will be here. He can attend to my sisters while you give me away to your brother. That would be wonderful in my mind. If you want to share sister duties with Fletcher Murry, you can take Nellie down the aisle then come back for me. Does that not sound like a plan?" For Maggie the details of her wedding…the renewal of her vows… were coming together. She was pleased with the results. A real wedding would be hers. This day would be one she could remember.

"A good plan if Fletcher agrees. I would be surprised if he didn't." Jason poured a cup of tea. "Shouldn't the two of you get started? Tomorrow seems to be a long day. I'll hold down the home front while the two of you are gone."

The next morning, Maggie gave Jason a huge hug then a quick kiss to his cheek. She and Jasper were in the carriage a few minutes later. Excited, she turned to him. "I can't wait to see my sisters. I'm so glad you are coming with me. For a while, I thought you might have too much business to make the trip. You've ensconced yourself with your brother every day he's been here. I was jealous. Wanted your company."

"We had a great deal to catch up on. Since he is younger, he cannot make certain decisions without my signature. Also, he does have his own affairs to look after. Jason has done well filling in for me."

"I do like your brother. He's been patient with me, with this plan that began as a ruse then ended up something so much more. I should thank him for his patience." She smoothed her skirts watching her husband. He had the devil's look in his sizzling golden eyes. She knew what that meant.

His tap to her chin caused her to tilt her head in puzzlement. He ran his thumb along her bottom lip, smoothed. "You gave my brother a hug along with a kiss. Seems I might merit something a bit more personal, intimate is what I had in mind. It's a long way to Dublin. Boring. The ride would go on and on without something to keep our minds occupied. Would be in need of entertainment over the hours. We could spend the time…" Jasper winked at her. "You understand."

Turning her head to the side again, she puzzled over what he wanted. Thought about the hidden meanings he sometimes used to say something that would be construed as outrageous. Did his thoughts follow along that vein? Something she would be scandalized by hearing. "You would like a kiss then? I don't see how a kiss would be construed as improper. Nonetheless, you would need to forestall any other actions." she said, trying to understand what new form of entertainment Jasper was speaking of. By knowing him, Maggie understood his agile mind could take on anything.

"Yes. A kiss would do for a start…a nice beginning. I was thinking even more intimate. A lot more intimate than a kiss. There are certain places on your…" he paused as if to think. Allowed his gaze to travel the length of her, lingering on her breasts. She sucked in air. He smiled then continued. "On your person that are in need of my attention. Places that pout in a very enticing manner when they receive what they need. Consideration that was not given this morning because of the very early hour we rose. We could not please ourselves before breakfast as is our usual habit."

Her husband was the very devil himself. Heat rose to stain her cheeks as well as the tops of her breasts as she began to understand what he spoke of. What he would want. There wasn't much more they could do together in a carriage. His thoughts were of the impractical variety. Though he was a clever man. "I've no idea what you are speaking about." By the shimmer of gold around the deep brown of his eyes, she was beginning to realize what he meant, and began to put his words with possible actions. She didn't see how. "We cannot…" She held out her hands while wicked thoughts flashed through her head. That was a mistake.

With a sudden jerk she found herself sitting on his thighs. His hands steadied her, moved until one cupped her breast. Over the fabric covering them, his thumb traveled. "Would have you here in the carriage. Now. Don't want to wait a moment longer, my love. Admit it. You want me deep and hard. Would you like to straddle me? That would be the easiest way to accomplish what I have in mind."

"Someone would see us?"

"How? Who?"

Shocked by his abrupt questions, she didn't have a quick or viable answer. "They…" she looked upward as if she were looking to the driver. "He would know if we were otherwise engaged in…in..."

"How?" He asked a second time with a touch of humor in his voice. "In? What…? What is it my wanton wife is thinking? If you must understand the truth, my driver cannot see through the carriage. His vision is nothing special. No one will *ken* what we do inside except the two of us. We can pursue any path that would enliven our journey."

Enliven the journey? What the devil did he intend? He couldn't be thinking? He could. Maggie found that she was quivering in her need. Even with that wicked notion in her head, she didn't wish to confess to anything of the sort. He was audacious. Cheeky. She couldn't refuse him. Though embarrassed by the thoughts, she would try. "I wouldn't know how he would know. Nonetheless he would know. When I see him again, I won't be able to look at him." She looked up again. "We can't. We just can't."

"I beg to differ." Without a by your leave, Jasper lifted her. Turned her so her thighs were on either side of his. She was open to anything and everything he was dreaming about doing. Vulnerable. "This is where I want my wife. On top of my sex. Ready for me. We won't be able to have this kind of fun once we pick up your siblings. Afraid they would be scandalized if we did what I intend in front of them." He brushed her cloak aside so it was behind her shoulders. His nimble fingers made quick work of the fasteners down the front of her bodice. She grabbed his wrists in an attempt to stop him. To no avail, he soon had the laces of her chemise through the eyelets, the corset she wore unlaced, her breasts spilling free from their confines.

Cool air wafted across the tips, making them hard. His gaze tightened them further. He didn't touch. Looked at her breasts for the longest time. Her heart thundered. Heard the surge of blood rush through her ears. A gasp of air from her. He looked up. His grin wide. She wasn't certain what he intended next. With each lurch of the carriage her breasts bobbed. She needed him to touch as he always did. Ease her. It seemed this morning, he had more patience than ever before. She burned for his caress. Longed for his attention.

"You are beautiful bathed in sunlight," he murmured.

Bathed in sunlight?

"You know, love, we've never made love in a carriage. It's been rare that I've had the light of day to drink in the sight of you. You are beautiful. The tiny blue lines on your breast hunger to be tasted. Just thinking about my lips on your nipples has hardened them. They want my thoughtfulness as much as I wish to give them the fulfillment they crave. I would see to your satisfaction then mine. What do you say? Are you ready for me? Is your body waiting, ready? Are you on fire? Pouring down rain?"

Unable to help herself, she snorted at his words. "Every morning since we arrived here. That's, let me see," She gasped when his hands touched upon her legs. She'd not noticed her skirts rising. He would know what he was about. The gentle touch of his fingers tantalized. He found the inside of her thighs. Touched higher. Not where she ignited, yearned for his touch. She tried to adjust herself so his fingers would caress her where she most needed.

"Let you see what?" he asked as he rested his hands on her bare thighs. "I would show you anything you asked. Will you show me?"

"I was going…oh!"

His large hand spread across her belly. Heated her. Moved. Pressed lower until his fingers touched her mound. Not low enough before he withdrew to perch once more on her stomach.

"Going what? What were you going to say? I would know."

His hand left her stomach. Traveled along her leg, behind her knee. Undid the garters holding her stockings up. The fabric slid to pool around her ankles.

Unable to speak, her forehead rested against his chest. She sucked in air. He seemed to hold still so she could answer his question. "To say…" Thankfully his hands remained still. "Eighteen days to be exact. Every morning, in the light for eighteen days. You cannot tell me you've only made love to me in the dark. That you've never seen me naked. You would be lying."

In true Jasper fashion, he ignored her comment. "Unfasten my shirt. The sweet tips of your breasts are a wonderful shade of rose, the aureoles a *wee* bit lighter, breathtaking. Would like to taste them. Seems unfair that I get to see your breasts in all their delight and I'm still clothed. Wouldn't you agree? Would love to feel the twin mounds pressed against me?"

Maggie found herself shaking her head. She gasped anew when his finger resumed the exploration beneath her skirt. "Jasper. We cannot do this. What if the carriage stops? We would be in a state of dishabille. A person would *ken* what we are about. They would see me naked. I know you. You wouldn't appreciate that." She knew his response would agree with her. He was a possessive man. One as he said who kept what was his. Several times he told her she was his. Well, he was hers. She didn't wish for any other person to see him in all his glory.

He lifted his masculine shoulders, sending her fingers off the button she was trying to unfasten. "True, someone might see us. True also, I would not appreciate that fact. Nonetheless, my love, I want you now. Don't wish to wait for our bed tonight. This cloak will serve as a protective shield if we do stop. In an instant you will be covered. No person would see what is mine."

"We can't…" She couldn't think when his fingers danced over her. Couldn't form words of protest when she wanted him deep inside. "Jason, not in here. I would die of mortification if anything happened."

"Again, they would see very little of you. Your cape, with one swift move will hide your pretty assets from unwanted eyes. You've nothing to worry over. I'll continue to protect you from prying eyes. All eyes except mine that is."

"You have an answer for everything," Maggie muttered beneath her breath. She arched when his fingers tested a sensitive place. Moved her legs to give him easier access. She felt the heat of his exploration. He did know how to seduce. Still, he was not investigating where she most needed him.

"Yes. Now, let me see where was I? Oh, yes, I was going to tell you…" He stopped for a moment to look at her. Once more his fingers settled on what she needed most.

"You are wicked, my lord." Maggie felt the slow glide of his hand along her legs higher then higher still. Her head was tossed back as she soaked in the warm sensations her husband elicited. He played her. Tempted as well as tormented. He would expect her to plead for him to continue while she should give protest. He taught her well a woman's pleasure. Seduced. Charmed. Knew how to make her beg.

"I am wicked? What about you?" His hand rested on her belly again, touched upon her there. The muscles of her stomach contracted. Moved down to her legs one more time. "Are you missing something? Some piece of apparel that most women wear. While that fabric shielding your dark secrets wouldn't stop me. I didn't expect a blatant invitation. You are sweet to invite me with such flagrant ease."

"Me?" Maggie feigned knowledge of what he was speaking about. "Whatever do you mean?" Her innocent act was fake as they both understood. She didn't care. This had become part of the game whenever he got audacious in the extreme. That was definitely the way he was now.

"Yes, my wicked wife. You are too naughty for the likes of this poor bloke. You tempt me to seduce me to your mischievous ways. Poor man that I am. I succumb to your wiles without putting up a fight. I'm yours to do with as you please. A pawn beneath your tiny hands."

"You are the person here who is insisting this is the thing to do. Your entertainment is what you had in mind despite my protests. You do not wish to bore yourself so you look for ways to keep your mind from succumbing to pure laziness," she argued with him, understanding she would never win. Nor did she wish to win. With his tender sweet talking, she hungered for him.

"Ah…let me see. How should I go about saying this? The information I now possess is delicate. Try to understand. Unbeknownst to me, my wife is naked beneath her gown. You keep wicked secrets milady. Your husband should be the man to have this knowledge so he can decipher the best way to proceed in the future. You, milady, are a sweet witch. I'm the poor fellow who is bedeviled by your machinations. What is a man to do when his wife advances in such a bold as well as brazen fashion?"

"I *dinna ken* what you be speakin' about milord." She squirmed. Touched down upon his sex. He pulsed against her. Despite the fabric separating them, she felt his hard arousal. She wanted to unfasten the barrier between them. In this she would need to agree with her husband. He was right, this was a wonderful way to spend the hours in the carriage that would otherwise be quite boring.

Jasper bent to sip on the tip of her breast. Touched with mercuric heat, curled his tongue around the pink bud. Nipped with a light bite of passion. Hunger ignited. She jerked, startled by the swift rise of longing. Ecstasy curled within. Raw desire spiraled. Her control of the lovemaking vanished if it was ever there. He supped on her. The heated pull of his mouth continued while she moaned her pleasure. His fingers roamed up then down her legs. Against her most secret parts she felt the pulse of his desire.

"You are no innocent of what you've orchestrated here. You mean to bedevil me. This did not happen by accident or any act of nature. I won't allow you to feign knowledge of what is happening between the two of us. You planned this. You wanted me to discover the truth of your undress. Your lack of certain strategic pieces of clothing. Not that pantalets would have stopped me from seeking all you can give. I might have ripped them in my haste to uncover your sweetest dark secrets."

His attention moved to her other breast. His hand touched upon the nakedness of her derriere. Moved to her hip. Curved around it. He squeezed. Massaged. His fingers continued their bold exploration. Her body hummed. Her heart beat faster than the wings of a hummingbird.

"I planned nothing. Never intended to be sitting on you with my breasts bared for any man to see. If you had not brought me to this position, you would not find yourself bedeviled. You, milord, set this in motion. Not I. What I didn't wear beneath my gown has nothing to do with your seduction of my person."

The hoot of laughter didn't surprise her. While he had part of this right, she never thought he would want to make love to her on their way to Dublin. "You are the wicked one, milord." She gathered in a deep breath of air. Her breasts moving with the long draught of air. Jasper smiled at her. Nipped each breast again.

"A very naughty girl is who I married. Am I displeased by that? Not even a *wee* bit. You can be as mischievous or as wicked as you like with me anytime I'm near. Why?"

Once more he sipped on her breasts. Slipped a finger through the folds that were wet and hot waiting for more deliberation. He found that place that shattered all her senses. The gentle motion aroused even more just as he intended.

"Why?" she stammered as the building sensation ripped into her through her. She skimmed her hands along his chest. Followed the trail of dark hair to his britches. Unfastened them.

"Why aren't you wearing your pantalets? I would know the truth. I'm intrigued." He kissed her lips, swept his tongue across then into her. He pulled back waiting for her answer.

"You've ripped so many in your haste. I…" She gulped at the swift invasion of her person. He was deep inside her. He held still as if he waited for the answer. Her muscles clenched around him. With no further stimulation, milked him. Enticed.

"I can afford underwear…?" His large hands gripped her waist. Stopped her from sliding along his sex. Kept her from moving. Kept her from her goal. She whimpered. Her head fell back. Soft sounds skidded from her throat. "Jasper…" The thin wail seemed to please him.

"You are ready for your climax?" Jasper asked as he thrust deep. Hard. Varied the rhythm along with the intensity.

"Yes…" she sent her tongue across her lips.

"I don't think so. You haven't paid your penance for deceiving your husband. I haven't kissed you enough. Your lips aren't swollen. You don't appear ravished. A woman needs to be…to look enraptured. Do you agree?"

Maggie nodded. Her hands ran across his shoulders. His mouth captured hers. Touched upon her lips. Pressed until she opened for him. He was deep inside her. So very still, unmoving. This was where she wished him to be. Would never tell this man no. Felt the dark crisp hair of his chest test the softness of her breasts. One of his large fingers touched upon the most sensitive spot of her entire person. Her fingers wound into his hair, tugging him closer.

He stopped his seduction. Left her feeling bereft. "Do you agree?" Jasper asked a second time. "We will go no further until you answer. A wife should always agree with her husband. Don't you think?"

"With what?" she asked, unable to think for the way he enchanted her. The magic he created. He cast a spell.

"You don't recall the question. Perhaps we should stop this seduction of yours so you can concentrate on the important questions." He began to pull out of her. "My love, you must do penance in order to receive your pleasure."

"No…" Maggie wailed, trying to keep his length inside her. With his hands he lifted her, set her away from his pulsing rod. She caught her bottom lip beneath her teeth. Her breath whimpered inside. Her body was on fire. Nerves stretched until they would shatter. "Jasper," she whispered his name. He held her face framed by his hands.

"Should a woman appear ravished when she is in her lover's arms? That is the issue here. I must have your opinion. Tell me true."

"I…" She moistened her lips again. "Don't know what you mean?"

"So, I must be more explicit. Don't mind explanations."

Once more he imprisoned her mouth with his. Taught her that he would command her attention. Brought her tongue deep inside him before exploring the depth of her. He was intimate with her. She pressed her hands along the length of him. Sought his sex. He caught her hand with his, stopping her. "Should a woman appear ravished by her lover? Tell me what you think? Don't change the subject."

"What," she gasped as he touched her even more intimately with his fingers. "What do you wish for me to say? How do you want the answer? All I want is you. Inside me. Fill me with your arousal. Please, Jasper, you started this. Cannot end it now."

"Your orgasm is what you are after. Sweet pleasure. Tell me true." He was tender. His words were unhurried. The man wasn't affected by the lovemaking. He was cold as stone.

"Yes. Need that." She brought her own fingers where he taught her to that place where she could send herself into the stars then beyond.

He stopped her. Held her hand away. His grin touched a nerve. "No, this man will see to your pleasure. Though you've my permission to do so when I'm not here to give you all that you crave. I've quite created a woman who seeks gratification at every turn. Now, if you are a good girl, I'll come inside you again. You may sit on me."

He moved just right so she could do so. Maggie closed her eyes, absorbing the wonderful pleasure she found in the length of him. She pushed on the fabric of his shirt until the cloth slid down his arms. Pressed kisses along his collarbone. Bit upon his nipple until he groaned. She would give him his pleasure while he filled her. Touched upon her womb. He thrust inside. Gave his attention to the small knot of ecstasy. She cried. Whimpered when he moved harder then faster. Sighed with a soft sound. So far inside her, he pressed the tip of his sex on her womb. She spiraled. Jerking. Unable to stop the wild sensation from rocking her body. Cried out as he continued the gentle onslaught. He continued, teasing, taunting. Holding back then giving her all she needed. Her body spasmed. Continued to pulse as he kept driving into her. Her body shattered into pieces, fragmented with the hungry sensual pleasure he gave.

When he stopped, she drifted on a silver-white cloud of euphoria. She fell against his chest, damp, slick with the exertion. Felt her lashes flutter against him. Her body shook. Hands trembled. She couldn't move. Not even to lift a hand. He didn't set her away from him. Inside her, he was still hard. Seemed even though he sent his seed inside her body he was not sated. He would mean to do this again. She needed a moment of recovery. Time to catch her breath. Would never tell him no.

While she closed her eyes, resting, calming, she heard the sound of the carriage wheels running along the road. Horse hooves pounded the dirt. Closer to her, she heard the uneven cadence of his breathing along with the steady rush of blood in his veins. The heat of his body surrounded her. A moment to regain her strength would be appreciated. Jasper often made love to her more than once. Seemed her husband was insatiable when it came to having sex with his wife. He might have been that way with all his lovers. The thought of other women enjoying this part of him sent a pang of jealousy into her heart. What happened before her he could not be held accountable to. What happened now that he was hers…

"You wish to do this again?" Maggie asked as several minutes passed by. She put a small distance between them, though he was still inside, deep inside. Hard. Her body calmed some. He'd been soothing her back. Running his hand up then down touching upon the small bones in the middle of her back.

"You *ken* the answer. Know that I want you again. Will always want you. Nothing will change my need for you." He whispered against her ear, touched the lobe with his tongue before swirling it inside.

She shuddered. Her body responded just as he planned. Her muscles clenched along his hard shaft. She moaned into his chest, once again needing him. Her fingers dug into the solid flesh of his shoulders. He aroused her with so much ease.

"Yes…" When she looked up the golden shimmer of his eyes was there. They sizzled with desire, craving. She would never refuse this man. She hungered for him. The carriage hit a rock. They bounced. His chin hit the top of her head.

"Did I hurt you?" He touched her chin, bringing her face up so he could see her answer. He would tell her the truth as it was written in her eyes.

~ * ~

After the climax, the wonder in her eyes always delighted him. Encouraged him that all he plotted was written in the stars. Even if she discovered the truth, which, at some time, she would, Maggie would forgive him. He could make love to Maggie forever. He once thought he might grow tired of a wife. Jasper understood above all else, he would never become bored with this woman. Would never seek out another to grace his bed. He chose the right woman. That wasn't quite what happened. Maggie fell into his arms quite by accident then into his heart. He did have the good sense to never let her go.

"I'm fine," she said touching upon his chin where she hit him with her head. "You? I didn't bruise you, did I? Did you bite your tongue?"

"No, but you can bite it anytime you like."

"Jasper!" She hit his shoulder with her little fist. "The truth."

"Truth," he agreed. "I will be more than fine after we make love again. Would you rather eat first? Make love this second or the other way around. Perhaps we could do both at the same time. Dana packed a snack for us to consume if hunger overtook passion. Perhaps the hunger I'm feeling is the same as the passionate fire of your kiss. What do you think?"

He found himself still overwhelmed by the notion she wore nothing beneath her gown except a few petticoats. He would have to understand her reasoning besides the fact he seemed to destroy them in his impatience. Wondered if she would continue to do so. The thought pleased him. He could toss her skirts anytime. In doing so uncover tender skin waiting for his ardent thoughtfulness. Would she keep him wondering? That would be a pleasant game.

"Let's eat," she said, her spoken words soft. "My mouth is parched. Need a long deep drink of something. What did Dana put in the basket as liquid refreshment? Is there wine?"

The little minx understood as long as he was encased inside her and she sat on him, she maintained a small measure of control. She could direct the orchestra. The little conductor. He was pleased. "But…" he wasn't about to tell her his intentions. She was as aroused as he was. Her passage, pulsed and constricted against him despite the fact she meant to deny him a second time before they ate. With his rod so deep inside her he touched her womb, she would never last long. All he needed do was stroke her breast, suck one of the hard, pebbled tips into his mouth. Stroke the pearl of her pleasure with his thumb. If he did so, she would explode, shatter into thousands of pieces in front him. He touched her lips with his thumb. "Ravished. Thoroughly enraptured. Swollen. Bee-stung. Just the way I like to see my woman."

Her mouth would be kiss swollen when they arrived in Dublin to pick up her sisters. Her mother, if she saw her, might have something to say about the pretty picture. Too bad. The sisters might notice. If they were innocent maids, they might not understand the meaning. If they did notice, might not fathom how it all came about or what else happened during the interlude. A woman's lips didn't get in this condition without serious play time with her lover.

"Is that how I look? Does it please you?" She smiled at him. Touched his lips with the tip of her finger. "You too. It also pleases me. You appear as if I ravished you. Seduced. Charmed all your manly parts." She squirmed.

Jasper did not think that pronouncement to be the truth since her lips had been inside his. He'd bitten with a light touch. Hers had been shaded by his mouth. On top… just as they usually made love though he was in favor of trying a few different positions. He'd not been so bold as to do all that he held in his mind. Thoughts of what he could do to her lovely body continued his arousal rather than diminish. In time they would experiment more meticulously.

After the marriage, they would investigate more avenues of ecstasy. She was still an incredible innocent. This interlude in the carriage shocked her to the tips of her lovely toes. He was pleased she came to do his bidding with such ease. Though once he touched her breasts, he knew she would do anything he asked. Would forget inhibitions. Her passion always accelerated, fast and blistering.

"I do not have the same look as you. Now, since you refuse to see to my needs, shall we see to the snacks. I'm certain Dana has outdone herself. There will be sweets aplenty. My cook is always thinking about your sweet tooth. I'm looking forward to nourishment so we can continue our recreation."

In the basket he discovered scones with strawberry jam. Hot tea in a special jug. Ceramic mugs to pour the steaming liquid into. When she started to remove herself from his person, he caught her waist.

"No. Stay put, my love. Don't wish for you to change your position." He grinned at her. Circled the taunt bud with the tip of his finger. "You need to keep up the persona of a wicked woman. Naughty is the perfect description. Eating while holding me inside you is wayward. We will continue this way until it is time to cover you with that cloth you call a dress."

He wondered if she carried his child. Since they began to make love, she'd not had her woman's time. Indeed, he didn't think she'd bled since they left Glasgow. He was pleased. Soon, he'd become a father. The thought never failed to send shimmers of delight into his body. He wondered how she would feel about becoming a mother.

"I am a good girl. I was until I met you, my lord husband. Of the two of us, you are the wicked one. You've changed me for the worse. Because of you, I am a wanton woman. Brazen. Beyond redemption. Where I am this instant proves the fact." She clenched her muscles against his length. "I was content to ride in the carriage, no diversion, no entertainment. Watch the scenery pass us by. Chat with my lord husband. See what you have done to me? You have transformed me. I will never be the sweet innocent maid you married."

"Never. Nor would I wish you to be. A scone, milady. Then I will pour you a cup of tea. You will be careful not to leave crumbs on my chest."

He laughed at the idea. Thought that licking up the crumbs would prove to be a delightful pastime. He imagined a dollop of strawberry jam on the tip of her breast that he could sip. The taste would be double the sweetness.

To pass the time, they ate then they made love. He would never forget this trip into Dublin. There might be more entertaining trips for them. Maggie was lovely. Evocative. Sensual in every way. She never ceased to please him. When they neared the city, he allowed her to sit on the seat opposite. Jasper straightened her hair as well the corsage of her lovely gown. He stared at her lips. They were swollen from his kisses. During the interim, she'd been well-loved.

What Jasper couldn't fix was the fact she appeared thoroughly ravished. He sat back, his arms crossed in front of his chest. While he didn't care if others understood how they spent their time, Maggie would. He hoped they didn't see her mother. Certain Anice would make some underhanded comment about her appearance or about her demeanor. None of which were Anice's business. They were, after all, wed.

In truth, Jasper didn't believe a mother would do something of that sort to embarrass her daughter. The things Maggie told him about Anice changed his mind. He couldn't do anything about that. What he could do was to keep her as far from her mother as possible.

Maggie was staring out the window watching the city trundle past. She was always so enthusiastic about new things as well as places. When she turned to look at him, her eyes were alight with eagerness. There were moments, Jasper thought, when Maggie's small body quivered with anticipation.

During the moments between watching the city pass by and looking at him, she spoke more of her sisters. Told him new details about each one. Despite the three weeks wait, he was pleased she was so happy as well as animated about the prospect of her sisters attending the wedding.

He would give this woman everything her heart desired. After they stopped then walked into the hotel, they were met by her three sisters who'd been downstairs waiting for her. The chattering grew. Escalated as all four women spoke at the same time. Jasper didn't comprehend how they heard or understood anything of which they talked about.

As if an indulgent father, he stepped back to oversee the reunion. His arms crossed over his chest. Waited. Soon Maggie took them in tow. It was time to get on with the day.

"Jasper," she began, quite breathless from the welcome. They had so many questions to be answered. She had so much to speak about. All they had been doing since they left Glasgow was left to be said. "As you know, these are my sisters." Maggie began at the top of the list. "Nellie," she curtsied. As the others were introduced, they followed suit. "Fannie and Tessa. They are not only my sisters but my best friends as well. I love them all."

"Pleased to meet you." The hour was after the normal lunch time. While he wasn't hungry and he doubted Maggie was, he felt obligated to ask his guests. "Have you eaten?" Jasper didn't wish to take time for food. He was eager to return to Nass then their cottage. The fittings needed to be done today.

"We ate. Mother wished to give us last minute instructions on our deportment. Told us we weren't to embarrass you," Nellie spoke out, her voice splintering when she ended the sentence. The small face she made reminded him of Maggie. The sisters, with the exclusion of Tessa, were very much alike.

"Don't see how any of you could embarrass me. You are all a delight to the senses," Jasper told them as they made their way from the hotel. "Don't let anything Anice says put a damper on this reunion."

Nellie, Fannie and his Maggie all looked the same. It was obvious they were family. Tessa didn't look like any of them. He tried to recall their mother and father. Couldn't. Tessa must have the appearance… Of which one, the mother or the father? Definitely not the mother.

Fannie spoke up then, seeming to realize he was staring at them too hard. She understood what he was trying to understand. "As you have guessed, except for Tessa, we appear much the same as our mother. Tessa doesn't look like either mother or father. We've always wondered about that."

Jasper found himself stroking his chin. Still studying, still thinking. Perhaps that was why the father didn't acknowledge anything about these girls. Not one of them was his. According to Maggie he could care less about any of them. "Interesting. Shall we climb into the coach. Get on our way. We've lots to accomplish before the end of the day. In Nass we will visit the dress shop first. We've your bridesmaids' dresses to see to fitting."

"Hope there is not much to do," Tessa said with a blink then a dazzling smile. The grin changed to a frown. "You said the wedding is in three days? I would that it was sooner. I've this horrible feeling of disaster."

"Tessa is known for her intuition. It is rare when she is wrong," Nellie pointed out, a somber expression in her eyes.

Jasper sucked in air catching the flower scent of all the girls combined. He also had a feeling of dread. Something untoward was bound to happen with the attendance of the mother along with the father. He half expected Nelson Abernathy to show his face soon. Was surprised they had not heard from the man in the three weeks they spent at the cottage. With the wedding soon, his life was coming to a head as was Maggie's. He had only a few more days before he was married. For real this time. After that if she discovered his lie, he could deal with the consequences. She would be angry. Of that, he was sure.

These three weeks had been too good to be true. Blissful. Idyllic. He'd gotten to know his bride so very well. She carried his child or would soon. There was little that could go wrong. Abernathy would no longer wish for Maggie to be his bride.

Rethinking the next few days, he drank in another deep breath of air. Once again was rewarded with the beautiful combined scent of the ladies. Jasper understood from experience when one became too accommodating that was when the roof would cave down upon his head. He had not become complaisant. Ever watchful, he spent time at the pub learning which men were the best source of gossip. From listening as well as asking questions he was quite certain Abernathy was not yet in Dublin. He would not be at the pub today. Time was running… The clock ticked toward their wedding day.

His sources were not foolproof. So, he would need to continue to take great care. It was possible, just as they had done, Lord Abernathy assumed a different name. He would deal with that when as well as if that happened. When thinking with logic foremost, Abernathy should be in Nass. He would be watching. Waiting for any opportunity to come his way. Anice would inform him of all their plans. No longer were there secrets.

By the time they finished at the dress shop, the girls were exhausted. They told Maggie they'd been pricked as well as prodded too many times. They described themselves as human pincushions. At home he left them to run upstairs to freshen up. With his brother, he poured them both a snifter of brandy. They were in his office. Jasper sat behind the desk, relaxing, soaking up the pleasures he found this day. Jason stood by the fireplace, one booted foot on the hearth, his arm on the mantle. To Jasper he looked ever thoughtful.

"Did you enjoy your ride today?" Jasper asked his brother. One dark eyebrow quirked toward the ceiling. "What did you do besides a short exploration of the countryside?"

Closing his eyes, Jasper sat back. His feet rested on top of the large cherry desk. He hoped his brother had gone to the pub before seeing to his entertainment of the afternoon. Information was needed as the days closed in on his wedding. Nothing could go wrong.

"You *ken* I visited the pub. I wished to listen. Remembered to introduce myself by the correct name. Told everyone there I was Jason O'Neill."

Jason sipped the brandy. His thoughts kept hidden so far.

Jasper needed to learn all his brother's thoughts. It helped when one wasn't as closely involved. "Was there news? Good or bad, it's important to be informed. Anyone heard of Nelson Abernathy?" His heart seeming to stick in his throat, he waited. Jason was usually forthright. He would continue to be that way. They shared every confidence.

"Yes, believe so. A new man in Nass booked a room at the small hotel there. His name is Nate Abbot. Matches the description of Abernathy. He's been asking questions about you as well as Maggie. He doesn't know you go by a different name just as he does. Believe our man has shown up. Seemed to have followed the MacRae family. However," Jason paused, "He came to Dublin on a ship from London. What are you going to do?"

Jasper dropped his feet to the floor. All appearances of easy composure vanished. He leaned forward, his forearms resting on his desk, the glass of brandy still between his hands. He let out a rush of air. "To begin with, Maggie is not to leave the house nor are her sisters unless one of us is with them. I will not chance a kidnapping. If that were to happen, we would be in a weakened position. Though nothing changes the fact I've a marriage certificate."

"A fake one."

"No one will be the wiser." The exchange between the brothers was clipped, fast paced.

Jason slowed the discourse. "All four of the females under your roof are willful even though the girls have been shadowed by Anice all their lives. They have a spark of defiance about them. Except perhaps Tessa, the youngest seems to follow the others. I've not seen her eyes shine with the light of battle. She watches. Waits. The girl intrigues me. She has a wealth of untapped energy. In almost every way she is vibrant. Alive with untold passion. Tessa could be a handful."

"You're right in your assessment of the *lass*. She hides her emotions well. Don't be deceived by little Tessa. She also possesses a spark. I would not wish to cross any of the girls," Jasper was thinking about the trip back to Nass. While the sisters chattered on about whatever came to mind, he studied them. Watched the way they responded to each other. While it was clear that Maggie along with Nellie seemed to dictate the conversation, all the sisters had valid opinions about things. Even little Tessa. She was a listener. That was the only difference.

Jason turned. His nonchalance evolved to a more serious nature. His brows drawing together, he spoke softly, "I'm worried if Abernathy plans are foiled with Maggie, he might try for one of the other MacRae girls. You said you thought Anice offered him something for Maggie's hand in marriage. I wonder what that could be. If the price was substantial, he would never want to lose the prize."

"That is the main reason they are not to leave the cottage without one of us. I would prefer they don't wander outside at all. If Abernathy decided to pay a visit, events could happen too fast to deal with them."

"He could take one of the girls," Jason went on to say. "Hold her for ransom? Any number of scenarios could come into play. Would not wish to see one of Maggie's sisters hurt. If he were to decide to take her by force…"

Jasper felt his stomach turn over. He wished he had wed Maggie when he planned. The day after her wedding gown was finished. Wished… What would happen if Abernathy discovered the truth? The man couldn't. The only person besides himself who knew he and Maggie weren't legally wed was Jason. The air he inhaled was fraught with disaster. All he could do until Sunday was keep his eyes wide open.

Even Maggie didn't know. She thought… He tensed with fear for their safety. Two days…two more days and he hoped they would have no more problems. They might still need to deal with Abernathy, the jilted fiancé. Would need to continue to monitor her sisters. Short of marrying all of them off to the first eligible men who they crossed paths with, he and his brother could not keep them safe from the machinations of Anice provoked by Abernathy's vile needs.

"We will keep them inside until we take them to the church for the wedding. If they wish, we can keep a fire burning on the outside patio. We can also hope for solid rain the next few days so they won't be tempted to explore the countryside." Jasper sat back and rested his brandy on his stomach.

"You realize if the girls do not wish to return to their home, you must take responsibility for their welfare. Anice will betroth them to men who are most likely undesirable. I don't believe she likes her girls. Not positive why. When I've spoken to Maggie about the situation, she doesn't know either. Though after seeing the sisters, I believe they all have a different biological father."

"Anice slept around? Cheated on her husband. Is that what you're implying?" Jason asked with a lift of his eyebrow. "The mother is a whore. The father doesn't seem to take umbrage with the fact. Perhaps the man is impotent. There are many different scenarios to this."

"That is a possibility. Why else would a man stay with a wife who is unfaithful? Not only does he stay with her, but he allows her to run his life. Seems to allow her to cheat on him at every turn."

"The reason could revolve around the fact he might like men better than women. Needs a wife for appearances sake. One who can keep her mouth shut about his preferences. He wouldn't be the first man to take a wife then see to his needs elsewhere," Jason pointed out, his tone bland. "One never knows. Perhaps the two of them also had an agreement they could both live with. Perhaps he's straight but can't stand Anice."

"What else could it be? For some reason, I cannot see Anice marrying a man you are describing unless there was something in it for her," Jasper found himself tapping his nails on the crystal decanter while he thought of all the possibilities.

"Don't suppose it would be polite of me to ask at your wedding." Jason was chuckling. "They are still to be in attendance?"

Jasper scowled. "Rude, yes," Jasper agreed.

He wondered if he could ever tell Maggie they were not wed when he took her to his bed. Could he ever tell her he suspected she was well gone with his child before the marriage. She would be devastated. Perhaps in several years she would find some humor in the tale. They could never recount the story to their children. This was something that would best stay hidden.

"By the way, big brother, are you going to tell Maggie that you are not wed to her? It might be appropriate for you to say the words before she hears the damning truth from someone else." Jason was pointing out something that would never happen.

"The only one besides me who *kens* we are not wed is you. Are you going to tell Maggie? I rather doubt you would betray me in such a manner. As to telling anyone else…you would never. Do I need worry?"

Jasper heard the anger in his voice when he spoke. True they sometimes taunted each other. This was out of the question. Nothing Jason said held humor for him.

"The man who slipped the bogus marriage certificate beneath the ledger for her to sign knows the truth," Jason pointed out as he walked to the desk. "You should tell her. She deserves to learn about everything. Truth always comes out."

"No!"

"If she comes upon Abernathy, Maggie needs to be able to defend her position. Her eyes alone would tell the man she lied. Something she seems impossible of doing. Renewing marriage vows? That in and of itself is unbelievable. If the marriage certificate was real, you would be married for somewhere around two months. Newlyweds don't renew vows they've just said. Who would believe such a travesty? Certainly not Abernathy." Jason's voice grew louder as he spoke. "Abernathy won't believe the story. I can't see Anice imagining her daughter needed to renew vows spoken so recently to a man she is supposed to love. Tell her you two are not married. Tell her before someone objects at the wedding. Her mother could denounce this as could Abernathy."

"I will not tell her we are not married!" His fist pounded hard on his desk. He knew his position was tenuous. With grave concern, he considered all the possibilities. Understood he should be upright as well as honest with the woman he loved. He did love her. Didn't know if she returned the sentiment.

"You're not married to my sister?" Nellie stood in the doorway, her face ashen as she heard the information batted around by the twins. Her hand set upon her chest as if she thought her heart might stop. "She doesn't know? How dare you take her to your bed before the vows are exchanged. Maggie would never have allowed you to do that. We've been brought up to *ken* right from wrong. What you did is immoral. Dishonest!"

"What is it?" Tessa asked as she too walked into the room. "What is all the yelling about? I would know."

"I need a brandy," Nellie said as she walked further into the room.

Jason poured her a large glass. Brought it to her. Nellie downed the contents before holding the glass out for another.

Jasper didn't think a day could ever go from the bliss he felt this morning to the end of all his dreams. The secret was out before he could command the outcome. Could never be called back. The only one to blame was himself. He should have never discussed this so openly with his brother. Hell, the door was open. "None of you are to speak of this to Maggie. It is best for my wife not to know. She will be devastated. The solution is in the wedding."

Sometime while these words were being exchanged, Fannie wandered into the room. "As of this moment Maggie is not your wife. From what I heard, never has been. I will speak to her. This is despicable. At least you endeavor to do right by her. You have planned a wedding as you should have done from the start. Why the deception?"

"Maggie will never forgive you!" Tessa pointed out, her fists held tight beside her. "I don't blame her. She should not forgive what you have done to her good name. She is no lightskirt. Not a whore or a woman of loose morals. You've deceived her! The act is unforgivable!"

Jasper felt as if he was being battered from all directions. He couldn't tell her. Drowning now in his words. Damned because he wanted the woman so much, he told her she was wed to him. He'd done so in order to protect her. That was what he told himself. Was that the real reason? "You are not to speak of this with Maggie!" he yelled as if he needed to put more force into his demand.

"I will!" Tessa yelled back. "I will tell Maggie everything she deserves to know. She must make up her mind about what she wishes for the future. If Maggie kens the truth, there might not be a wedding."

"Tell me what? What about making up my mind?" Maggie stood in the room, the light of question in her beautiful green eyes.

Sinking into the floor would be nice. He was a man damned. Everyone in this room knew that for a fact except Maggie. She would know the truth soon. Would damn him. He stood, waving his hands toward the door. "All of you out. Leave me with Maggie. We need to discuss this. Alone."

"No." Maggie's hands were on her hips. "They know what it is you are supposed to tell me. Am I right? This something that is important to me? It concerns you? And me?"

"Yes." All her sisters answered in a chorus.

"We aren't going anywhere," Nellie finished for them. "We are going to stand here. Make certain you tell her all the truth." She turned to her sister. "Maggie, when you hear what your Lord Kenworthy has to tell you, you might not wish to marry this man." Nellie turned back pointing at him.

Maggie's eyes crossed for a brief moment. After that, shaking her head she spoke. "I'm already married to him. This is just about the ceremony I missed. What more can there be? Why do you all look so angry." She turned back to gaze at him. He saw the hurt in her eyes. Felt the questions pile up around her. Saw the look of betrayal.

"The renewal of vows?" Fannie asked sweetly. She waved her hand in the air. "Bah!"

"Leave! All of you!" Jasper thundered. He wasn't about to take this inquisition from the sisters for another moment. Despite what they might think, the girls had no rights here.

Jason seemed to understand what drove his brother. He gathered the girls within his arms ushering then prodding their reluctant little behinds from the study. "You must give them time alone. Privacy is what is needed in this situation. Time to talk. Jasper will tell Maggie everything. I promise. Truly, now that the lie is out in the open, he has no choice but to do so. We will all retire to the outdoor patio. Clancy has a nice warm fire. We can speak about other things. Having something to eat as well as drink. Perhaps Pup will entertain us. He missed his mistress today. Whined most of the time she was gone."

~ * ~

"Maggie is here in Nass," Nelson gritted out to Anice who sipped a glass of wine. Anice gazed at him with a smug smile on her features. They were in the pub just outside the village. The pub was full. It was the dinner hour. Music played.

The bartender introduced himself. "So, you two are here for the wedding. Quite the affair I hear. Took us all by surprise when the man said he wished to renew vows already spoken. Said the little lady only got a quick wedding in a *wee* church in Scotland. Justin even had the banns read every Sunday just like clockwork. Justin O'Neill is marrying that little darlin' Maeve for the second time. Imagine if I had a woman who looked like that and she wanted me to marry her ten times, I'd do that for her. Would want to keep the little missus happy. Purchase a new wedding gown for her every time. What do the two of you think? Everyone is talking about the wedding on Sunday."

"Names aren't Maeve and Justin O'Neill. It's Maggie MacRae," Abernathy told him, sneering at the man. "They are frauds."

"Jasper Kenworthy is the man," Anice told the bartender. "The pair have lied to all of you. They are not who they say they are."

"Ah." The bartender wiped his hands on the dishtowel he'd had over his shoulder. "We all knew that wasn't their names. They were hiding from someone. Would that be the likes of the two of you? Well, you've found the happy couple. The way those two feel about each other is obvious. By the way they look at each other they are madly in love. Even if they aren't married, the man has had her in his bed. They were in here the other day. Couldn't keep their hands apart."

"You're right. It was me they were running from. Maggie is my fiancée," Nelson piped up, angry with his inability to find the two sooner. Furious the marquis bedded her. He'd wanted to smash through her maidenhead. Needed to see her virgin's blood on the sheets beneath him. If what the bartender said was true, that wasn't going to happen. "Dinna think the two of them are married. They are not. It's a ruse. All of it was to deceive me." Nelson understood part of the reason he wasn't in Nass sooner were the two little whores he discovered in a London brothel. While the cocaine was sweet the ladies were spectacular. Even after the week of bliss he purchased at the auction, he couldn't stay away. He spent another two weeks with the two whores. Spent money…lots of it on the pair. Every moment was worth the time. Until now. Until this instant, he'd not expected this information. Something needed to be done to stop the wedding.

"Now, I do believe Mr. O'Neil will be having something different to say about that. She's his woman. As I said, can tell by the way the little darlin' looks at him. Maeve's enamored of the man. He's swept her off her feet. Sure, as my da believes in the little people, they've been cavorting in bed for close to two months. Why, after all this time it's a certain fact she should be increasing. Mark my words, they'll soon be announcing the pregnancy. In another month the little lady might be showing."

Nelson felt his face redden. His anger escalated. Pregnant? By God she better not be! He wished Jasper were here. He'd…he'd…" He sniffed in a breath of air. He wasn't a fighter. Knew he could never win with fisticuffs where Jasper was concerned. Both Kenworthys were known to frequent the boxing gymnasium in Glasgow. He would need to deal with this on a different level. Cunning always worked well for him.

If they spent all that time in bed, maybe she wasn't worth bothering about. There was always one of her sisters. He did enjoy Tessa. She was quiet. Kept to herself, her lashes lowered. Never argued or seemed to have an opinion. Wouldn't fight him. Would do as ordered. Obey, yes, obedience was a cherished trait in a woman. Compliance…submission was the trait he needed in his woman, his wife, the younger the better. He would make a deal with Anice for the youngest daughter. They could be wed as soon as he had Tessa in his possession. This time he wouldn't wait. Would never presume the woman he chose would proceed the way he wished. Once they were wed, she would have nothing to say about how he treated her. He would have an heir at all cost. If necessary, he would keep her in his bed until she conceived. She wouldn't be allowed to go anywhere or see anyone. He would keep her bedroom door locked.

On the other side of him Anice snorted. Her smile became wicked as she studied him. "You thinking about one of my other daughters. Which one do you want? I would guess the one who is a bit more malleable than my oldest. Should have known better when you first proposed this deal. Knew Maggie would never bow down admitting defeat of any sort. That one is always a fighter."

"I want Tessa." In his mind, he imagined what the girl would look like stretched out on his big bed. Her long blond hair spread out on his white sheets. Her body naked for his enjoyment. If she didn't comply to his wishes, he would bind her hands to the bed. She would do his bidding or she would regret crossing him. The rules would be set down the first minute after they were wed.

"Well…that didn't take too long for you to decide who the most biddable of my daughters is. She is only seventeen. Of course, she would give you no grief. Tessa has always done as the others wished. I'm certain you will enjoy her timidity. The girl has a different father than the others. The man never knew he sired her. If he did, he would have objections. Ah…but that is what makes this deal so very sweet. He doesn't *ken* he has a daughter with me. I never told him. Was only in his bed one night. The conception was an accident…of sorts."

Nelson thought to ask if he knew the girl's father. Decided it was better if he had no idea. "I assume a virgin."

"I would also assume that to be true. Would be shocked if she wasn't. Hardly ever allow the girls out of my sight. Should we go from there? Maggie is out. Tessa is in. They will expect something to happen at the wedding, maybe before. We will need to be very careful."

~ * ~

Jason had his hands full keeping the sisters from tearing back into the study to confront his brother. All three ladies were yelling at him, shaking their tiny fists. Scrunching up their eyes. Sticking their pert little noses in the air. Good God, what did he fall into? A nest of vipers? His well-ordered life was in a shamble. What he heard wasn't quite yelling though their voices were raised above normal. He was beginning to take on a headache of massive proportions. He needed to herd the ladies to the backyard patio where the sound would not reverberate with such strength. His skull was vibrating. The weather warmed from the week before. With the fire, the ambiance would be quite pleasant. They could enjoy a glass of wine then perhaps a few tidbits from the kitchen.

To his surprise the littlest one, Tessa, was the most verbal as well as physical. At one point Jason thought she was going to swing her balled-up fist at him. Even with her skinny arms he would have had a bruise on his chin if she connected. He managed to duck just in time. The devil, they needn't be angry with him. He'd done nothing wrong.

"Hold it!"

Jason caught her hand before the fist could connect with his face. This was the second time she swung at him. She brought up her other fist to try to do damage. He held them both behind her back. Felt shocked when her sassy breasts pushed against his chest. Lightning dove straight to his groin. He couldn't let her go. She was intent on doing damage to his body. He liked all his parts just the way they were. "You don't wish to do that. I don't allow people to strike me." *Especially women who heretofore have been very pleasant.* He liked the way her face went from a fierce scowl to one of frustration. Her crystal blue eyes simmered and blazed with indignation. Long blond hair came loose from the chignon she fashioned. Her cheeks were red, lips full and sensual. Bloody eyes he wanted to kiss her. That wouldn't do a'tall. Not a'tall. She was too young for him. Too new to the world. Just a youngster. No experience in the art of love.

"I do! You beast! You're just like him!" Tessa cried out struggling against his hold, her body flush against his.

Jason closed his eyes for a moment soaking up the way she felt as well as the way he wasn't supposed to be feeling. Bloody hell, she was hardly out of the schoolroom. "No, you don't. You're not angry with me. Have to do what is best for my brother as well as your sister. You know that. In fact, if the three of you step back a moment and think, you'll realize the two of them need to talk things out. What they need is privacy, not three women yelling around them about things they don't understand. We don't *ken* what has gone on over the last months. Believe they do love each other."

"That man doesn't have the right to be alone with her. Her good name will be sullied even more. We cannot." Tessa was still fighting him, struggling within his arms. "Let me go! You bastard!"

Bastard? Under the circumstances the feel of her lithe feminine body pressed against him, he could forgive just about anything from this little lady.

He looked down into summer-sky blue eyes. Her dark lashes lowered to form a dark crescent against the whiteness of her skin. His voice was husky when he spoke to her. "Will you promise not to try to hit me again?" Jason was positive he couldn't trust her. If she gave her word, he would still be better off with distance between them.

Tessa looked up. There was moisture in her eyes. He hoped he didn't hurt her. She seemed defeated. "I promise."

"Good...good." He let her go. She stepped back. The glare in her eyes was noted. She didn't attack him. That put his mind at ease. "No one has a tale to tell anyone except us. If the story is spread about, the words could be detrimental to the two people we love the most. None of us want our loved ones hurt. Who is going to spread rumors that will cause pain to our siblings?"

Jason saw the look of understanding cross her pretty little face. The devil, what was he thinking? He was imagining her naked on his bed. She couldn't be older than seventeen or eighteen. He was too old, too jaded to think he'd like to kiss her. Take her into his arms. Discover the sweet tender flesh beneath her dress. Damn, things like this didn't happen to him. She was a debutante. He never dallied with virgins. He needed to remember Sarah. The way the full-grown woman felt in his arms. So responsive, so passionate, the woman made cinders out of his body. He found that when he looked at Tessa, he no longer hungered for Sarah or any other widow he'd known intimately.

He was surprised when Nellie placed a glass of sherry into Tessa's small hand, telling her to drink. Jason joined her at the sideboard pouring himself a brandy. Pup jumped around them, wagging his tail then barking for attention as if nothing was amiss. Thank his lucky stars, the room was becoming calm. The girls were no longer chattering nonstop. The sisters seemed to like their brandy. He found himself amused.

"We should adjourn to the outdoor patio. Pick up a blanket on the way out to keep warm in case there is a slight chill in the air." Jason was trying to keep his distance from the little blond with the bluest eyes he'd ever seen who caught his attention in too many ways that were all wrong for them.

Outside, Pup dashed around the yard. The snow was all melted now. It had taken several days for that to happen. Clancy brought a tray of pre-dinner appetizers. Jason wasn't certain what else to say to the ladies. Maybe they would have a few pertinent questions. What he needed to do was to keep Tessa as far from him as possible. He groaned remembering the sweet, subtle scent of her pressed against him.

Jason leaned against the brick of the fireplace watching the sisters. Crossed his ankles. How could a mother have such four lovely daughters and dislike them so intensely she was willing to give them to vile men? He felt certain the mother would choose another daughter to take Maggie's place. If he were Abernathy and expected to choose a woman who would not run from him, he would pick Tessa. From the display of a few minutes ago, none of the daughters would fall into Abernathy's plans. Tessa was no weak-minded female as others thought she was. After this, all the girls would need protection. Jasper would feel honor bound to provide that very thing. Too bad for him, Sarah would never allow him to move into her place. If Tessa lived at their brownstone, he would never be able to keep his hands to himself. He suddenly understood Jasper's problem with Maggie. After being with her for a couple of weeks, he had no recourse but to take her to his bed.

"What do you think they are talking about?" Fannie asked. She kept looking back to the main house as if there might be an explosion. "I wish we could put our ears next to the door then listen."

"How they will spend the night since they are no longer wed," Tessa pointed out. She seemed to be still seething. Though for the time being she kept her fury under control. "They cannot sleep together. It is not right!"

Jason was so shocked by her declaration brandy spewed from his mouth. He picked up a cloth napkin to pat the drops from his chin as well as his shirt. He gaped at this beautiful and surprising young woman. In an instant, he found himself mesmerized again. A distraction was needed. He had no idea what that could be. Needed to shake his head to clear the encroaching thoughts. It was just the fact he'd been too long without a woman in his bed. He reminded himself it had not been that long. Just this afternoon he'd dallied with a widow from the village.

Tessa touched him. Pressed herself against him. His body's reaction was nothing but normal. He was a man. Aroused by the contact of a beautiful woman. What could be expected from him? He should go into Nass tonight. See if the widow from this afternoon would allow him into her bed again. Better yet he could stay there until the wedding. Distance between him and Tessa was mandatory.

"Believe how our sister decides to spend her evening is not up to us," Nellie told them, searching the room for some sign of confirmation. "Though I thought much the same as the rest of you. When I heard Jasper talk about the marriage, I realized we are out of line. We cannot and will not judge my sister. She must be very much in love with Lord Kenworthy to give herself to a man who has not wed her. Though at the time she thought they were married. What she decides tonight is up to her."

Yes, Jason thought the same about his brother. Love was nasty business. Messy. Untidy. Had a way of making a man do things he shouldn't. Lust often times did the same.

Such as taking a maiden to his bed. Lie to her about a nonexistent marriage. What was his brother thinking? To his knowledge, his brother had never lied.

Lust. Lust could damn a man to everlasting hell or…heaven.

"Lord Kenworthy had good reason to lie to her," Tessa spoke up once again, surprising him. "He committed to protecting her. It was the matter of taking her to his bed *sans* wedding vows that damns him in my eyes. There had to have been another choice."

"You're right, Tessa," Fannie said murmuring as if she didn't wish to speak up. "Maggie would never have slept with him if she didn't believe they were married."

"Does that make what Lord Kenworthy did to her, right?" Nellie asked, a bit of venom in her voice. "I for one don't believe so. He needed to keep her informed of the secret. She should have been told everything every step of the way. She should have been allowed to make decisions for herself. What he did was reprehensible."

Jason cleared his throat. "Believe the two needed to do some convincing in order to prove they were wed. The servants here were asking questions. They were newlyweds sleeping in different bedrooms. What do you expect people to say? Gossip has a way of ruining lives. It was mandatory for Abernathy to believe they were married."

"Convincing? How?" Tessa asked, appearing perplexed, her eyes crossing as she tried to decipher the words. "They didn't start out sleeping together? I don't understand."

"You are too young for this conversation."

Jason reflected in an attempt to sidestep the conversation. He wasn't about to explain anything to this beautiful debutante. This was something a mother spoke of to her daughter or a husband to his new wife. Jason harbored the distinct notion Anice never said anything to these adorable ladies.

"She cannot sleep with the man tonight," Fannie pointed out, shaking her finger at him as if he would dictate what the couple did or didn't do. "They are not married."

Jason realized in order for this scenario his brother instigated to work, Maggie would need to be in his bed. If rumor got out they didn't sleep together the nights right before their wedding, Abernathy would feel empowered. While Clancy along with the other servants were loyal, there would always be gossip along with rumors. There was too much at stake here. People talked whether they were loyal or not.

"Maggie and Jasper have to sleep in the same bed." Jason breathed in deep after he said the damning words. "Must find a way to settle their differences. There are no choices here. They will be officially wed in two days. What difference will it make?"

"Leave it to a man to say something so absurd," Tessa said, staring at him as if she knew he was thinking about her in his bed.

His brandy sputtered out again.

Chapter Nine

Jasper closed the door tight. Leaned against it, the gold of his eyes shimmering. Maggie inhaled several times grasping for control. Her fury at this man had her seeing red. She thought about all they'd been doing the last months. She needed to catch her breath as well as collect her thoughts. When she recalled her behavior, she was mortified. It wasn't as if she didn't question the marriage certificate. She had done that very thing several times. After the initial question, she decided she was foolish. She dismissed the notion from her head believing in the man she married, trusting him. The same man she fell in love with. Now, she wondered if she didn't bow down too easily because she wanted him. Wanted his kisses. Needed to understand what came next.

What they did in the carriage on the way to Dublin sparked in her mind. Her cheeks heated, flamed. A tempest of insecurity swamped her. Now…at this instant…now the man didn't look the least concerned with the way he acted toward her. He seemed relaxed. Sure of himself. Again, she questioned the validity of the marriage.

"You should have a sip of brandy. I'll pour."

He started to walk to the cabinet holding the liquor. She stared at his back. His broad shoulders narrowed to lean hips. She'd seen as well as touched every part of the man. More heat flared while she recalled how she held his sex in her hands.

Incensed that he could be so very cavalier, Maggie picked up the first item she could lay a hand on. It was a book sitting on his desk. She hurled the heavy tomb at him. The projectile hit him in the back. He turned. Stared. Blinked as if baffled. For a moment in time, he appeared confused. His eyes widened. With stark clarity, he seemed to understand she wasn't just angry she was furious. He held up his hands as if offering his surrender.

"You used me! Used my body for your entertainment! How could you!" She tossed a smaller book. Missed. Found a pillow sitting on the chair in front of the desk. The object grazed his cheek. The missiles continued. Did nothing for the fury raging inside her. Jasper chose not to retaliate.

Dodging each object, he prowled toward her. Stalked. Ducked. Dipped a shoulder. His frown deepened on his forehead. His eyes darkened with what seemed to be his anger. The devil, she wanted to know why. Why did he mislead her? Why did he tell her something that held no truth? She was having feelings for the man. Thought she was in love. When he didn't touch her, she cried in her lonely bed, wondering.

Never!

Never fall in love with a man who would deceive. She was a fool. An idiot for believing in him. For trusting.

"Maggie…" Jasper stalked toward her. "Maggie put that down…" His voice was mellow. He didn't appear mellow. He looked as if he wanted to strangle her. "You don't want to throw it." The object dropped to the floor.

He was right. She needed to tackle him herself. Vent her anger. She launched herself at him. Hit his chest. Pounded on him until he caught her hands. She found herself wound tight in his arms. Her forearms pressed against him. She could no longer hit him. Tears filled her eyes. Turning her head away from him, she didn't want to see into his eyes. Moisture ran down her cheeks. Didn't want him to see the pain in her eyes. Even living with Anice all her life, she never felt so used as well as abused as she did at this moment. She would never forgive the man.

"I despise what you did. We cannot go on this way," she gritted out through clenched teeth. Her breaths were heaving. Air didn't wish to enter into her lungs. Her heart sped out of control. "You are a despicable human being. You knew how I felt about being with a man before I was married. You took my innocence while I believed you were my husband."

"I do know. God, love, I'm sorry. We had to make people believe our story," Jasper was mumbling the words. "There was no other way that I could see."

"You took advantage of me. I was…"

"Innocent. Yes, I protected you." He touched her cheek. "Took you into my home. Listened to your story. Made up my mind I would do all in my power to make sure you stayed safe from Lord Nelson Abernathy. Never intended to marry you or sleep with you. None of that was part of my plan. It just happened."

"I was your entertainment. Nothing more. I don't mean anything to you. You're worse than that…that…than Abernathy!" Maggie pushed her head against his chest, hiding. Tears were running down her cheeks, wetting his shirt. She couldn't help the wash of emotions searing her. The betrayal hurt.

"Yes. All you say is true. Though I never meant to hurt you. Was attempting to help. Again, I'm sorry. If there had been some other way. I couldn't tell you about the license. If confronted, you would have never been able to keep the secret."

If he would just tell me he loves me, I could forgive him anything. I would marry him.

You say that now.

Yes, I love the man. Want to marry him. Don't see how that can happen after all he has done. How can I ever trust him. He's taken too much from me.

You've no recourse but to marry the man. You carry his child. The bairn would be a bastard. Do you want to end up with Lord Abernathy as your husband? There is a man you should hate, despise with every breath in your body. He would despise your child.

This morning, she gave all of herself to him. The last months she'd given all of herself to this man. The things they did in the carriage. He never spoke of love. Neither did she. She was afraid to say the words. Terrified they would not be reciprocated. Could he be just as afraid? Of course not, he was a man. A man with power. A man in control. Jasper doesn't fear anything.

"You lied to me," she accused again, unable to think of anything else to say. Her accusation was weak. Her fisted hands were still against his chest. She felt the length of him pressed against her. His sex was hard. He wanted her. She wanted to feel him deep inside her body.

"If another lie would protect you, I would do it again. I have no regrets about the fake marriage certificate. If I thought you could have convincingly kept the secret, I would have told you. Could you?"

Again, then again, she was going over everything in her head. "You told me we needed the servants to see that we were married. Was that a lie too? Was it lust that drove your lies? Did you just want me in your bed?" She didn't think she knew this man. Didn't understand his motives.

"Between us, there has been only one lie. I could have had you in my bed without the fake license even though you swear you would have never slept with me. I could have seduced you." His voice was deep, husky filled with emotion. "Your passion..." he coughed. "You're a sensual passionate woman."

"How can I trust you? I would never have fallen into your arms."

Her stomach knotted then rolled, cramped. She felt consumed with distrust for this man who stole her heart. She said the words knowing them for a lie. From the first time she touched him, something inside her stirred to life. Her body hummed with excitement. Yes, she wanted his touch, his kisses.

"I'm not a man who makes a habit of telling mistruths." He spoke as if he was offended. "The lie haunted me."

Maggie looked at him. Saw the shimmer of moisture in his eyes. His lips were thinned. His brows drawn together. He set his hand beneath her chin, holding her. His thumb caught the slide of a tear. Brushed it across her bottom lip. "I want you now. Tonight, you will come to our bed. We will make love. The servants will not guess at the untruths here."

She jerked away. He let her go. Under the circumstances, Maggie couldn't bear being in his arms, feeling him aroused and wanting him too. She poured herself brandy. Drank then poured another one. The liquid burned. Warmed her where she was cold. She needed to calm herself. Needed to distance herself from the man. Her emotions coupled with her thoughts collided together.

Turning from him, staring out the window of his office, she tried to sort through all her thoughts...her feelings. What she wanted along with what she didn't. It was impossible for coherent thoughts to form in her head. All she could think or feel was the fact he lied.

Jasper lied.

All men lied.

I wanted to believe Jasper was different.

Desperate, she tried to produce logical opinions.

His presence behind her gave her a start. Maggie thought he might leave her be for a few minutes to sort out her feelings. She felt his hands on her shoulders. They moved down her arms then back. With that small touch her body flamed to life, the feelings mercuric. Maggie wished she could deny him. Rebuff how he tempted her from the right path. How he used his incredible charm to seduce.

"I had no choice but to do what I did, my love. In this case, I can see no other path forward. When you came to me, so loving…"

Jasper turned from her then. Her body chilled when the heat of his body vanished. He was no longer beside her. She felt the emptiness to the pit of her stomach.

His footsteps sounded across the floor. She heard the spill of brandy into his glass. Heard the rampant pounding of her heart. Felt the chill bite in the air. When he turned away from her, she felt frozen, her heart icing over.

Maggie dared not turn around. If she did, she would run to him. Tell him none of what he did mattered. That would be another lie. Everything he did, the choices he made for her, changed her life. Damn him, he decided things for her he had no right to do.

Finally turning to speak to him, understanding what she said was not what she wished. "I cannot marry you now, or ever. Will never be able to trust you. What is marriage without trust?" *Without love?*

Her words were stiff. She knew the minute she uttered them they were false. She was shaking. Praying he would disavow her words. Knowing if he questioned her, she would never be able to stand firm.

I love him. I have always loved this man.

Jasper's stare was hard. His lip curled upward in a small half-smile. He downed the rest of the brandy he poured. "You have to marry me."

He was so very adamant. Didn't believe anyone would defy his wishes.

It didn't seem he would take no for an answer. She was angry, furious with his determination. She had questions. "Why? Since we are already pretending to be married, I still have your protection. We can continue the ruse. We do not have to make this final." Her back was stiff. Her mind made up. Maggie understood without Jasper, she could never convince anyone the forgery was real. She would give herself away. One of her sisters would say something that would proclaim her unmarried status. Her question was not only stupid but foolish too.

"Because…"

He drank deeply. His sneer caught her off-guard. Wasn't expecting this side of him. He was a marquis. Wasn't used to having his wishes dismissed. Jasper continued.

"You carry my child. My heir. A bastard if we don't wed. For you…us…there is no choice but to forge ahead. Despise what I've done. You will marry me in two days…at the church…with your family in attendance. If you wish, hate the man who gave up his life to protect you. Marry me you will."

"I would say no." Her fingers wound together.

"Try it."

Jasper challenged every word. He stepped closer. With the back of his hand, ran his knuckles along her cheek. He seemed so different. "I recall when I set you aside in deference to what I *kenned* to be your wishes. I did not make love to you that night though I wished with all my heart to do so. Understood you were not a woman who would sleep with a man she wasn't married to."

"You did though. You slept with me. Took my innocence that you had no right to have. I gave my innocence to you without understanding the truth."

Her accusation was harsh. She wanted him all those times as much or more than he wanted her. If she tried harder…no, she believed she was wed to this man. Believed what they did together was right as well as natural.

"Do you recall how you felt when I refused to take our kissing to a deeper level? You begged me to make love to you. Those times there were tears in your eyes. You cried because you believed I rejected you. Didn't want you when that was everything but the truth. I was a man condemned. My actions those times were meant to protect. Do you believe I'm a man who can set a woman aside so easily? Even then I had strong, urgent feelings for you. Hungered for you. Your passion ran deep and hot. Told myself all I felt was lust for a beautiful woman. Suppose that was the truth of it."

Jasper threw the empty glass of brandy against the fireplace, the crystal shattering, falling in silver shards to the floor. Her breath caught and held. Petrified of what might happen next, she watched him stride from the room. Nothing was settled. Heard the door slam. Never before had she ever felt so alone. She tried to reason with him. Thought she might get through to him.

Abandoned. Jasper left before they could agree on some course of action. Some way to make all this work. Maggie wanted their lives together to work out. Wanted to find a way to forgive him. Even while she fought with herself, her emotions, she needed him. Wished to feel his warm arms around her, soothe her shattered spirits.

This was not her fault. None of this was of her design. She never orchestrated this ill-conceived plan. A plan that put her in his bed.

In the end, this was her fault. Jasper inherited her problems through no fault of his own. Jasper had been at the homeless camp distributing food along with blankets on Christmas eve. He brought wood for fires to keep the people warm. Handed out food to the needy. He was a good man.

That moment when she fell into his arms with her nose pressed against his chest, she decided to go with him. Used him to flee Lord Abernathy. Where would she be now if she didn't use this man to her own ends? Used him for her gain. She owed Jasper an apology. Going back in time wouldn't ease this situation. As he told her, he did what he thought needed to be done. She must be true to herself. How did she do that? Not now, not when she didn't know what she wanted.

If not for Jasper's kindness, she would have found herself in Lord Abernathy's bed beneath him forever. Deep in her heart she understood she would have never survived a marriage to Abernathy. She could never have endured that. She would have died. Not for a minute and least of all for the rest of her life could she live with that horrible man. While she might despise the lie perpetrated to keep her safe, she didn't not loathe Jasper. When she looked out the window, she saw him riding hard...fast as if he was a man possessed.

Jasper left her.

Would he return?

She didn't have the answer to that question. With his brother in residence, Jasper didn't need to return. Jason would do all in his power to bring her back to Scotland to her home. She could still pretend to be married. What then? When they weren't living together? The sounds of conversation entered into the room. It seemed her sisters along with Jason saw him leave in such a fury.

Race away.

He couldn't leave her fast enough.

Dazed...stunned was the way she felt while her life unraveled one tiny strand at a time. Didn't know if she'd ever feel warm again. She rubbed her hands on her arms feeling the ice settle into her bones. The entire bottle of brandy would not have the power to heat the ice that was encased inside her.

She loved the man.

Had he just run out of her life?

Left her for good?

"Maggie?"

She whirled. Felt as if she was suspended in time. This day was too much for her to comprehend. She'd begun the day obliviously happy in Jasper's arms. They made love in the carriage. Her sisters would be here for the ceremony that would unite her with the man she loved. With the night, her nerves had been shattered into thousands of pieces. On every level she was bewildered.

"Jason? What do you want? I need to be alone."

She stiffened as the man who appeared so much like Jasper strode into the room. Maggie didn't want to talk to anyone. Needed to cry out all her fears. Didn't wish to explain what went on between Jasper and her. How their lives unraveled. Jason would know part of what happened. He and his brother had been discussing this situation when her sisters walked in on them. "I would be alone with my thoughts." Her sisters stood behind Jasper's twin trying to peer around him. She saw Tessa's nose poke out beside his arm, her blue eyes large, luminous with questions.

"No, I beg to differ. You need company. Someone to talk to even if the conversation is idle chatter. Not good for you to be alone. Jasper will be back. I understand his temper. Something happened. No?" He held up his hands. "Don't expect an explanation. I'm certain what happened between the two of you is private. As soon as he has cooled off, he will return. The two of you can figure out how to go on from here. The wedding must go forth as planned."

"I can't see him again tonight." If she saw him this evening, she would splinter just as her nerves unraveled now. Maggie bent down to pick up her whining dog. Pup licked her face as if he understood she wasn't happy. Jasper bought her the dog. The dressmaker charged him for Pup. At the time, she didn't realize he paid Eilinora for her dog at the same time he paid for the gowns he ordered for her.

Agreed to a wedding gown when she asked.

Put off the wedding until her family could get her.

If he had not done those things they would be wed. The marriage would be valid. Consummated. They would not have had the argument. There would be no reason for the distance between them. She wouldn't know the first marriage was bogus.

There were too many things that got in the way of their happiness.

"Will you wait up for my brother?" Jason was speaking to her. He was expecting her to answer. "Believe he will find you wherever you decide to settle for the night. You should go to the room the two of you share. It would be best. That way the servants will have no gossip to repeat in the morning."

"Kind advice," she murmured, wondering why she felt so empty and alone. "You're right, of course. We've failed to find a solution. Told him I wouldn't marry him. He told me that I must." She set Pup on the floor. He dashed off as if he'd done his good deed for the day and was finished.

"You don't have to do anything of the sort," Tessa spoke up, walking up to her to give her a hug. "If you wish to marry him do so. If not…don't."

It seemed Tessa had to think a few minutes to come up with something else to say. "Lord Abernathy will move on to another lady. He will not want you since everyone knows you've been in Jasper's bed. Well…" she paused for thought. "They must assume that to be so. All in the town believe you to be married to the marquis. In that case, of course you were sleeping with him."

Her hands settled on her stomach. Jasper thought she carried his child as did she. He told her she would marry him. There were ways to coerce a woman into saying the vows. She didn't need to be strong armed. She was more than willing to be wed to the man. Before she could do so, she needed some type of apology.

"You are too stubborn," Nellie spoke up saying something her sisters knew to be true. "You *ken* you want the marriage. Why did you make that man who has been everything kind to you storm out of here? There was no reason for that except stubborn pride."

Fannie spoke up, "You have two days to decide. Staying in his bed is not necessary. You can sleep in my room with me."

"No, that won't be possible. As Jason said, he would find me. Jasper would put me where he wants me. That place would be in his bed. While I can't be certain, I believe he will want me with him…the same room…the same bed. I said something to him that I need to retract. Have to wait for him. Have explanations to make."

"He took you by surprise," Jason said as he seemed to study everyone. "That wasn't well done of my brother. You should go upstairs. Wait for him. I'll come with you. Make certain you are settled as well as comfortable."

The trouble was, she didn't wish to be alone with her thoughts. Jason had been right about that. Idle chatter would be better than pouring over her thoughts. "I'll take a bottle of wine. Clancy is not far away. Hot water would be appreciated." She turned to Jason. "Could you take care of that for me?"

"Anything you wish. I'll make certain you are not disturbed once the water is brought to you."

"Thank you, Jason. You're a dear. Some lucky woman will get you one day." She stood on her tiptoes to kiss his cheek.

Once in her room, she waited for the water. Maggie almost hoped Jasper would return when she was in the bath as she needed his arms around her. Since he vanished in a storm of furry, she'd been so cold.

He knew she carried his child.

She guessed but she thought it was too soon to know for certain. All the signs fell into line. She didn't think she could tell her sisters until after the wedding. Did she already mention that fact? She didn't know. She'd been so upset she spouted words that came into her head. Had no idea what she'd said.

There would be a wedding. Well…there would be one if Jasper wasn't on his way back to Glasgow. All his things were here. He wasn't a man who would abandon the woman he thought was carrying his child. Maggie felt certain she knew him that well.

The knock on the door brought her out of her musings. Jason walked inside followed by servants with steaming water. He held Pup under one arm wriggling to get loose. Despite Pups efforts, Jason held on tight.

"Do you want the dog in here? This bad boy is quite the handful. He seems to know what it is he wants. He's missing Jasper. Tried to run after him. If he didn't have such a penchant for cheese, I might not have been able to retrieve the animal. Who knows where this scamp would have ended up," he told her laughing as the adorable dog licked his face afterward and gave a small bark.

"You can put him on his bed in the closet." Maggie watched the man. He was so much like Jasper. Even though they were twins there were subtle differences. She could tell them apart by their eyes. Jason didn't have the same golden shimmer as Jasper. Though there was some gold surrounding the brown. His hair was not quite as dark. They were of the same height. Built much the same, broad shoulders, lean hips. Both commanded attention with few words. They were kind men.

Kind men. Unlike Abernathy.

After putting Pup on his bed, he set a tray on the small table in the room. Opened the bottle of wine before pouring her a glass. "Jasper will be back. I promise you. Understand you are worried. Tell him how you feel about him. Tell him you love him. I know you do. Know also my brother loves you."

"You *ken* all this how?" she asked, smiling at him, enjoying his company. She supposed one could see her love for Jasper in the way she looked at him. Maybe these moments left alone to sort out her feelings were good. She was coming to terms with how she felt about the man. Not only did she love him, she cared for him deeply.

"You need to understand my brother's point of view in this unique scenario. Why he lied to you. Jasper is not a man to tell untruths. I'm certain doing so with you cost him. Now that you know, you should look to see how the lie is tearing him apart. It's why he rushed out of here as if the hounds of hell were following on his tail."

"Oh…Jason I'm trying. It's just so hard. I feel as if he robbed me of something I held dear. He should look at my view point too. I was so hurt when I discovered what he orchestrated. It's hard to forgive."

"I believe he does understand your thoughts. Consider that as another reason he raced from here. On the other side of this situation, Abernathy is going to set his sights on one of your sisters. I'm certain of that fact. He will no longer want you. From all I've heard as well as put together over the last couple of months, your mother and Abernathy had a signed contract. Anice owes him a daughter. He will be determined to collect. Don't know yet what was promised between them with the marriage of her daughter. I'm certain the promise was monetary or involved something of value."

"Why are you telling me this? Though, I imagine I should understand. What could it be? Mother would never hesitate to sell her daughters. She's always told us that we owe her." She was curious now. Interested in what Anice would receive from Lord Abernathy upon her marriage to him. Women had been sold since time began. Even in these modern days dowries were offered.

"Worried? More than you can imagine. I'm concerned about Tessa. After your defiance, it is obvious to anyone with eyes he would decide on the one sister who he believed would not fight him."

"Tessa has more backbone than one sees at first. Maybe more than all of us put together. She would never let that man walk over her. None of my sisters would walk to the altar of their free will. Even mother doesn't know her youngest is made of sterner stuff than she ever expected. Tessa has backbone. Her head is filled with dreams. Her body is vibrant with untapped energy. She is quiet. That is all." Maggie tucked her lower lip between her teeth, staring at Jason in a new light.

"I understand your littlest sister better than most," his words were soft spoken.

"Glad to hear that. For a while this afternoon, I thought I was seeing things. She surprised me several times with her questions as well as statements. You like her. Whatever happens, don't hurt her. She has a gentle spirit."

"As I said, I understand Tessa. I would never hurt her."

"Do you care about Tessa so much?"

Maggie wondered if her sister had any idea she affected this man. He was too old for her. Some might say Jasper was too old for her. Who was she to say or judge? If the two came to care about each other, all would be good. Age should have nothing to do with love.

"I should not," Jason blanched, his fists tightening. It appeared he didn't wish to give up that piece of reserved information. "Did not intend to be so blunt or honest. Yes, I'm fond of your youngest sister. She sparks

269

something in me I've never felt before. When I see her, I don't want any other woman. I want to protect her. Imagine that is something of how my brother feels about you. I'm not the rescuing type. Jasper was always the one to bring home strays."

"You don't say?" She felt the first stirring of anger for Jason. Tamped the feelings down. She was not a stray. "I've been called many things before this by my mother. Don't ever recall being compared to a stray. Makes me think of a stray dog; muddied, dirty, under nourished." Maggie couldn't help the smile. She felt the laughter that might burst from her. With the look of chagrin on Jason's face, she lost the brewing tempest then laughed hard. The man was a dear. She supposed that when she first met Jasper, she was all that; muddied, dirty, not undernourished but disheveled.

Jason cleared his throat. It was evident he was ruffled by her comment. "Didn't mean anything negative by that. Though at the time of our meeting, you did seem to be a bit of a stray. That night when he brought you home, you needed his rescue. We both understood you were running scared. You ducked into the carriage so fast, I thought Jasper would change his mind."

She understood the tenor of Jason's apology. "Don't hurt my sister. If you feel anything for her, tell her. Act the gentleman. She needs rescuing from the likes of my mother and Lord Abernathy. Do it with my blessing. She might be angry if you are high handed." Jasper was that way. Cavalier. Autocratic. Demanding. "Don't assume she feels the same about you."

He nodded, seeming to understand the drift of her thoughts. "If possible, I will keep her apprised of everything. There will be no lies between us. Of this I promise. "I'll leave you to your bath. Will intercept Jasper before he comes here to finish your discussion. Believe we've something to discuss."

The man gave her more to think about than she needed at this time. A diversion...a departure to her troubles was welcome. Even though she now feared a bit for Tessa's virtue. If Jason wanted her in that fashion, he would have her. The men bringing the hot water had all left. She sipped on the wine as she disrobed. Thought about this morning's carriage ride. Her hands trembled at the thought of all they'd done. The searing tempest he created with ease. Remembered the nights with Jasper's warmth beside her.

The evocative way he touched her. She could never deny him. It seemed to Maggie, they were made for each other. Perfect in every way. Their thoughts coincided.

If she wished to be married to him, she needed to come to terms with his lies. Would need to forgive. Must put the one mistruth, there was only one, from her head. Her clothing was scattered along the floor. The water was hot. Closing her eyes she settled into the heated liquid.

Jason's eyes had the same way of changing color as his twin's. If she didn't miss her guess the poor man was half in love with Tessa. He would be battling their age difference. Age didn't matter if he fell in love with her sister. Might be a rocky road to travel the next few months. If she was right in her assumptions, her sisters would be spending a great deal of their time with the Kenworthy twins. There might be ample opportunity for Jason to seduce Tessa. If necessary, he would do so. If not, he would keep his lust to himself.

What did Tessa feel about Jason? Would she recognize the fact the man was besotted with her. Her sisters were all such innocents. Much as she used to be. Moonlight danced around the room. Bathed the small area with a soft glow. The fire also cast a warm reddish glow through the alcove where the tub was placed. Since the snowfall then the subsequent melting, rain fell nonstop. The earth warmed. Tonight, the sky was clear. The temperature chilly once the sun went down.

With the sponge, she ran warm water along her arms. Held it up let the steaming liquid trickle between her breasts. Rubbed the scented soap across her breasts then lower. She sighed the sound soft in the silence of the room. With her eyes closed she recalled once more the carriage ride. The mercurial touches her trembling lips when his set upon hers. The heat soaring through her with each haunting caress.

Maggie didn't hear Jasper until he knelt down behind her. His hands on her shoulders. Moved lower to cup her breasts.

"I should be furious with you."

His lips caressed the back of her neck. Thumbs traveled across the hard tips of her breasts. She quivered, trembled beneath his hands as they seduced with keen knowledge.

She should be furious with him.

Maggie

~ * ~

When he stormed out of his office he'd never before felt such anger. Maggie carried his child. Told him she couldn't, wouldn't marry him. Refused to consider anything he proposed. Refused to listen to reason. Stubborn, recalcitrant woman! Told him she would no longer share his bed. She would. After all the time they spent together, he'd come to love her. Cherish her mind along with her body. How could she deny their child its father? He would never allow such a misdeed to happen.

He wanted to both strangle her and make love to her. Shaking some iota of sense into her head was next in his thoughts. She bedeviled him. Had he done so from the very beginning, they might not be at tenterhooks now. He didn't know how she would greet him when he returned.

If he had to drug her as Fletcher did Gracie before their wedding, he would do so. They would be married officially as well as forever on Sunday. He loved her. She carried his child. He would never get over those two facts. The one fabrication should not stand between them and happiness. Abernathy along with her mother were still viable threats to her as well as her sisters. If Anice sold her once, given the chance, she would do so again. Tessa seemed to be the one sister that would be sold the easiest, put up the least fuss. Two days from now Maggie would commit to becoming his wife. In his mind, she was already his wife.

After riding for over an hour, Jasper ended up at the pub. He was brought a pint of Guinness. Sat back to think on the day's events. His mind was in a turmoil, body reeling with the remembrance of her anger. He and Jason had been foolish to talk with the door to his office open. Had not expected the sisters along with Maggie to come downstairs so soon. Thought he had the needed privacy to discuss the situation.

He was a fool.

An idiot.

By being less than careful, he put his future in jeopardy. He'd hoped to keep the secret until after their marriage, perhaps even their first anniversary. Maggie would marry him in two days. She would. He needed her to say her vows with a willing open mind. As the minutes ticked by, Jasper became less sure of that possibility. Emptiness filled him when he thought of all she meant to him. All she denied them. He would never allow her to have her way. This evening, they would finish the discussion. He would keep her awake until there was a satisfactory conclusion to their argument. There could be only one acceptable finish to this disagreement. Keeping his temper in check was necessary. Giving her a chance to speak her mind came second.

The devil, he would have a child soon. Had not thought to be married until he was thirty-five. Hell, what was three years in the scope of a man's life? Would have a wife in two days. What the hell was he doing sitting in a pub drinking beer? She must be terrified that he ran out on her. They had not solved any of their problems. There were hiccups in their lives to work out. Maggie needed to be reminded she came to him for help. She pressed her nose to his chest, rendering him helpless…at her mercy. At that moment there had been no viable choices for him. Maybe Maggie needed to figure out her feelings for him before she could make a commitment. He felt certain she loved him. He took her with care knowing she'd never been with a man. Made love to a virgin. He was the only man…lover…she'd ever known.

In his mind, for him, there were no regrets except her discovery of the falsehood. He found that he was pleased with all that had come about since he met her. She wasn't happy about all that he did. Over the months she spent with him she seemed content, not just content but happy. In some respects, he didn't blame her for the anger. Didn't have the same feelings about the events that transpired since she sought him out. Pressed her nose against his chest. From that moment he'd been smitten. Was lost. He understood he would always give her what she wanted. Except for a way out of this marriage. He would never give her that. Maggie was fire in his blood, a tempest in his soul. She wreaked havoc with his plans. She would remain his for the remainder of their lives.

"Why aren't you with your pretty wife?" the bartender asked as he set the second pint in front of him. "She getting ready for the wedding? Everybody is talking about it. Right after the Sunday service. Heard her whole family arrived today to see the blessed event. Bet all the congregation will stay after the service. The reverend's wife is baking a cake. Someone else is bringing punch. Others are bringing their favorite dishes. It's to be a celebration. Everyone in town wishes you well. Your wife too."

How did he tell the man there might not be a wedding? His fist tightened around his glass. There would be. "As we speak, Maggie is with her sisters. They've come from Glasgow. Been several months since she's seen them. The four of them are close. Thought I would give them a chance to be together. Catch up, you know on the happenings in Glasgow. Besides, I needed a *wee* bit of time to myself."

"Nice man you are. I'd want to be with my wife." With his free hand, he scratched his head. "Say, there were two people here talking about the two of you, a man and a woman. Had the wrong names for the two of you but I know it was you and Maeve they be talking about. People do sometimes want their privacy enough to give themselves different names."

"They are here then…" Jasper sucked in a long deep breath of air then let it out slow. This wasn't anything he hadn't expected. There was trouble brewing. For now, he thought all were safe at the cottage. The problems would develop after the wedding when Anice asserted her rights as their mother. She would try to take them with her. Insist on it. He and Jason would need to find a means to stop her. As Maggie told him, the girls were of age. They might have traveled here without their mother and father accompanying them but they didn't. He sent enough for travel expenses. They would not need to live with Anice. He would take on the responsibility of seeing to their needs, his sisters-in-law.

"Who?" the bartender asked, appearing a bit puzzled. "The two were huddled together in conversation, that is when they weren't asking questions about you and your wife. Who are they?"

Jasper debated telling this man anything. Though…the people in the town seemed to like him. When he brought Maggie here, they spoke to her, laughed with her. "Believe the woman was Maeve's mother, the man Maeve's betrothed. She ran from that man right into my arms. I couldn't have been more pleased."

That was the truth. Abernathy's misfortune was his to enjoy. At the cottage, Maggie would be waiting for him. He understood she would be furious he left. He had to get away. His temper soared out of control when she refused to listen to reason. Perhaps he didn't listen to her views either. Perhaps they both had some growing to do.

"Her mother along with her betrothed?" Rubbing his chin, the bartender was asking questions that would be difficult to answer. Jasper never intended to try. The less the man knew the better.

"Suffice it to say, Lord Abernathy is no longer her betrothed, since of course, Maeve is my wife. Now, that is settled. Did you overhear anything they said? It might be pertinent if I was informed. Abernathy wasn't pleased when Maeve and I were married."

"Didn't like that man. Didn't like his looks. Something about his eyes didn't ring true. The way his lips thinned as if disgusted when Maeve's name was brought up by the mother. He has this look about him. Man can't be trusted. Can always tell by looking at a man's eyes." The bartender flipped the dishtowel over his shoulder. "Could tell by his eyes," he repeated. "Yes, a man can tell by looking into the eyes. There is evil about him. That man would send his mother to hell if it was in his best interest."

That might well be true. Jasper found himself hard pressed not to laugh at the bartender's assessment of Lord Abernathy. He was right on the mark. Few people of his acquaintance in Glasgow liked Abernathy. All had the same opinion as the bartender. "Can I count on your support? Believe you've described Abernathy quite correctly. The wedding on Sunday…you will help keep the sisters away from that man. Imagine he has his eye on the youngest sister. She's the only one with blond hair."

"I'd be pleased to help out in any way. Why would he wish to have the youngest? Ah…he wants something from the mother now, doesn't he? The mother is paying him a dowry of sorts. Somehow they've formed a coalition. Maybe she's getting something from the man." The bartender paused. "More than that I assume. See what you mean. She must be selling the girl to him for her own gain. He is buying. She is selling. Keep an eye on all the lasses. Yes. That I will." He was nodding his head. "I'll do that. Don't want anything untoward to happen on the day of your vows."

"Thank you. For now, must get on my way home. Maeve and I have a few things to discuss before the evening comes to an end. I see it is getting late." Jasper finished his pint before pushing his chair back. He enjoyed this pub as well as the people who frequented here. If he wasn't in a hurry to return home then begin his new life with Maggie, he might be tempted to stay at the cottage another week or two.

The cottage belonged to his mother's family. Every summer, he and Jason visited their grandparents here. Played on the lawn in front of the house. The old oak tree used to have a rope swing attached to one of the branches. After their passing, they didn't return. The memories, she told him hurt. Until Maggie, he forgot about the place.

The cottage had been left alone over the years. Clancy, of course, stayed there. Kept the house clean. Made repairs when needed. He'd always set aside money for the upkeep. Perhaps they would return in the summer. If he could find time from his duties, the weeks might be considered a belated honeymoon.

Jasper found that he was missing Maggie. Until tonight, they spent the evenings together. Talked laughed, and explored each other. She was passionate. When he kissed her deep and hard, her lips would shiver beneath his. Her body is evocative, filled with sensuality. Her mind is curious. There was her feminine form blessed with luscious curves that filled his hands. Mercuric passion that sent him higher than he'd ever known before. Thinking of her hardened his body in an instant. Imagined she was with him tonight, at least in his mind.

His horse was tied at the hitching post. Moonlight lit the road ahead of him. No rain tonight, the drier weather was a nice change from the downpours of the last three weeks. A few wispy clouds ghosted the glow of the moon bathing the road with subtle light. Seemed to be unseasonably warm for an evening this time of the year. What did he know about southern Ireland? Not a lot...his family always visited in the summer...never January. He'd been very young then. Didn't recall much except lazy summer days. Many years passed since he'd been here.

He set the horse to a gallop. The distance wasn't far from the pub to the cottage. He needed to see Maggie as soon as possible. How she would greet him was a question in his head. Warm? Loving? No, she would be reserved no matter how she felt. She would hold back her affections. Her body would tremble with the anger he deserved.

Jason would try to soothe her. Twist her to his side, to his way of reasoning. His brother was always the mediator. Always saw both sides to an issue. Jasper didn't understand how a person could see in so much depth. Tomorrow morning, a conversation with Jason about his fears for Tessa must be in private. This time he would make certain the door was closed. Locked. There would be no eavesdropping. The two would keep their voices low.

Jasper left his horse to the stableboy. Strode to the home. Encountered Jason upon entering. Understood there would be concerns. He didn't wish to waste time speaking with his brother when there were more disturbing matters to be dealt with.

"Not now." He tried to move past his brother who blocked his way. Waved his hand as if that would dissuade Jason on whatever path he conceived.

Jason held his arm. Stopped him from moving on. To no avail, he tried to shake it off. "We need to talk before you go up there to confront Maggie if just a short conversation. There are things it's important for you to know."

The tone of his twin's voice stopped Jasper cold. In that tone the message was both concern as well as fear. Jasper stopped. Studied his brother's eyes. "Tell me. What is it that has you waylaying me?"

"Tessa is in trouble." The words were determined, frank, to the point. Jason seemed to assess him as if his stare would solve the problem.

His breath caught. He imagined Abernathy would be after one of the sisters. Anice would be selling. The man would buy. "My God, Abernathy doesn't have her! Does he?" Beneath his ribs his heart lurched to a halt.

"No, not yet. Not if I have something to say about it. I'm going to protect her. First though, I need your permission. The girls will need to live with us once we return to Glasgow. Their reputations will be in threads if I continue to live at the townhouse. There are…" Jason paused.

"You cannot protect her if you are not living in the same home. What do you need my permission for…?" Jasper's voice trailed off as he was beginning to get the drift of the conversation. He thought of that same solution earlier.

"You want her." The statement was flat. His voice still filled with the surprise of this revelation.

"The girl is too young for me but yes, I want her. Lust after her. That is not quite right. She stirs fire, a tempest blazes inside me when I'm close to her. Won't allow anything to happen to her. She is, with your permission, under my protection." Jason held up his hands, seeming to get the gist of his thoughts. "I won't hurt her."

"Not by intention. I *ken* that for a fact. Just as I vowed, I wouldn't hurt Maggie. I did. If you lust after her, find a willing woman in the village. Leave Tessa alone."

"That's the thing," Jason pinched the bridge of his nose. "I've thought about doing just exactly that. Won't help. Know it won't. Not the same. Not the same a'tall. I can't seem to extract her from my head."

Jasper watched as his brother drug in a deep breath of air. "You cannot seduce her. My God how old is she?"

"Don't know her age. She's in trouble. I'm certain Abernathy will seek her out next. Doing so makes perfect sense. Afraid for her. Believe she will turn eighteen soon." Once again, his twin was holding up his hands to stop the speech. "She will be old enough to become a wife. Old enough for Abernathy to take her. If he does, she will lose her sparkle. The vivacity that is Tessa will vanish."

"Sparkle? She is as quiet as a mouse. Though she is stunning. Her hair is nearly white it is so blond. Tessa is the only sister with blue eyes. You do have my permission to do whatever is necessary to protect her. I know you will never force the lass as Abernathy would. Try to have more restraint than I had. A little brother should learn from his big brother's mistakes."

So, his twin was interested in the youngest MacRae. He would put her wishes first. As he said, learn from his mistakes with Maggie. Jason thinks she has sparkle. Maybe for him she does. The feelings could go both ways.

"I will start tomorrow when we take them for the last fitting as well as bring the gowns home. Will you and Maggie be going with us?" Jason asked as he seemed to be making plans for the future.

"That is up to her. If I can seize the evening, I plan on keeping her up the rest of the night." Jasper looked upward. He needed to go to her. Enclose her within his arms.

Jason grinned at his brother. "She might still be in her bath. It was only about ten minutes ago I had the water brought to her along with a bottle of wine and some cheese and bread. Try to woo the girl instead of argue with her."

"I know how to seduce as well as charm my future wife. Do not need lessons from my little brother. That fact was part of the problem. I seduced too well. Couldn't stop when she pleads with me." Jasper hooted his laughter. He felt better about the night along with the marriage. She won't renege. Nonetheless, he needed to tread with care. She'd had time to think about her future.

Whistling he bounded up the stairs. Stopped in front of the door to their chambers. Inhaled deep and long. He didn't know her reaction. Prayed the time he spent away from the cottage would have calmed her. She'd been so angry. She'd thrown things at him. Knew he would sport a bruise where the book hit him. He'd also needed the time to resolve some of their issues in his mind. Assumed his brother spoke with her some of the time he was gone. Her sisters would have had a few things to say. To her…about him. He imagined that would be the way of it with sisters. Getting used to four females in his previous bachelor residence might prove to be difficult. First, she would need to agree to the upcoming proposal. He didn't think she would disagree.

The devil, since his mother passed there had been no relevant women in his home or his life. The townhouse was a bachelor pad. They had a few servants who were female. None of which lived in the brownstone. His time with Maggie had been a bit over two months. His life would never look the same.

The knob turned then the door opened without a sound. Softly closing it behind him, he leaned against the closed door. Maggie was in her bath just as Jason predicted she might be. Her damp white shoulders were above the tub with tiny droplets of water beading on top. Tendrils of hair that slipped from the bun she secured on top of her head clung to the back of her neck along with the sides of her face.

When she lifted her hands to send a cascade of water onto her breast, lightning shot straight to his groin. Despite a feeble protest, his body reacted to the sight. He held the sound of desire behind his teeth, clamping his jaw tight. He didn't wish to alert her to his presence. Thought to watch her for a few more seconds…as long as he dared.

With measured slowness, Jasper walked across the soft carpet of the room. Knelt down beside her. Placed his hands on her shoulder then moved them down to hold her breasts within his hands. Caressed the taut buds with his thumbs. She jerked at his touch. Stiffened then relaxed. Maggie didn't say anything. He imagined that could be either a good sign or a bad one. He would discover the truth soon enough.

"I should be furious with you."

His lips caressed the back of her neck. Thumbs traveled across the hard tips of her breasts. Ran his hands down the sides touching the ladder of her ribs as he explored lower. Spread a hand across her belly then lower to cup her mound with his hand.

Maggie didn't say anything as he explored. Felt the raging tempest of his need spiral higher. She would stop him soon. She didn't. A soft whimper. Small sounds escaped, rippled into the warm air inside the room. He felt the contraction of her muscles where he touched.

Brought his hands back to her breasts, held them.

"You ran out on me. I was afraid you wouldn't come back. Jason promised me you would. Wasn't certain if I should believe him." She lifted her shoulders. His hands tightened around her breasts. "You are here. Don't understand why you should be furious. I'm the one who was deceived. While you were gone, I managed to cool my anger. I also came to a few decisions."

Unable to help himself, he lifted her from the water. Pulled her against him, soaking his clothing. His lips found hers. Touched down upon them. Acknowledged the trembling within both of them. Tempest along with the flame of their hunger ignited. Seared into him. A whimper filled him then the sigh of her pleasure. He carried her to the bed. Set her down before he came over to her. Their lips met, explored, hungered for each other. The strokes were wet. Hot. Sultry. Passion swept through him. Tempest exploded.

He rose above her. Staring down at her. His fingers wove into her hair. Softer than silk. "I came back. Will always come back for you. I should be furious because you shouldn't need any more convincing that we must be wed. You are mine, Maggie. I've taken from you something that can never be replaced as well as given you my heart and soul. We are of like mind. You came to me with a willing heart."

"You are supposed to see my point of view, listen to my feelings."

Maggie tugged at his shirt, lifting the fabric from his pants. Her hands slid along his torso, explored. Discovered him. Where her fingers scraped along his back his body shuddered at the contact. Felt the tightening of his muscles where her hands rested. Her fingers played with the fastening of his pants until her small fingers closed over his erection.

"Talk to me then…tell me what is on your mind."

He didn't wish to talk. His soon to be wife was seducing him. He hungered for her more than ever before. His passion escalated, raw, pulsating with his need. She told him she would never forgive him for making love to her when they weren't married. If not forgiveness, what was this all about? This must be some form of clemency.

"You are wearing too much."

Her soft lips whispered across his chest where she'd lifted his shirt. She bit. Her small teeth scraped against his flesh. The tempest within became a wildfire of raw hunger. His fingers wove between hers. He held their hands together on either side of her head. Her emerald green eyes gazed up at him echoing her trust along with her love.

Jasper rose. Naked and stunning to his gaze, he looked upon the woman he loved who was giving to him all of herself just as she did in the carriage this morning before she discovered his lies. His boots landed hard on the floor then the rest of his clothing joined them. He came over her. She cradled him between her parted thighs. His lips found hers again. Soft moans escaped her as he discovered her body caught by his heat, alive in every way, her flesh begging to be touched. Clinching when he passed over her. Contracting where his mouth sucked. The spiral of desire within her soaring to reach into him to touch him in ways she never had before. She arched her breasts to his lips as he explored ever downward from the sultry heat of her mouth. Dug her fingers into his hair. Scraped him with her nails. Encouraged him by the sweet sounds of her pleasure. By the arching of her back while she pressed herself as close as she could against him. She gasped and writhed as he sent his fingers into the tight hot channel of her core.

Gently, tenderly, wickedly she stroked as well as teased him. Jasper sent the pins holding her hair on top of her head flying. The length fell against him. He wove his fingers through the strands. Wrapped the silken strands around his flesh, teasing him, delighting. With wild abandon she sought out erotic, evocative places on his body with the sizzling pull of her lips. The heat of her burned him. He was on fire with the honeyed dark pleasure that was Maggie. Enraptured by the woman.

He thrust inside her heat. He felt the first small kisses to his sex then the shattering pulses that swept her higher. She cried out his name then he exploded in his own climax sending his seed deep inside. For a moment, he fell upon her, spent. He braced himself above her. Moved strands of damp hair from her face. Wondered at the soft expression she graced him with. He prayed she absolved him of the guilt of his crime. They were still not wed. In her eyes, this would continue to be a sin. In his mind, love freely given was never sinful. They were lovers. They would continue to be so.

Her body was wet both from the liquid left on her from the bath as well as the exertions of these sweet moments between them. Jasper rolled to the side, bringing her with him so she lay half on top of him, half on the bed. Her nose was tucked next to his chest just the way he fell in love with her. Her unbound hair wrapped around him, floated with the slight currents of air across his sex.

He would be aroused again.

They would never talk.

Jasper was both awed as well as amazed that they came together tonight. He'd thought he would need to charm her, kiss her until she could never refuse. He wasn't certain what to say to her. Assumed that after giving herself to him this evening, she was not refusing to repeat the marriage vows. To give herself to him forever.

Women could be disconcerting. Alarming. Confusing characters in the extreme. Thought different from men. Often changed their minds. Jasper didn't know yet what to make of this conversion. He felt certain she would explain.

In his mind, they weathered the first storm of their lives together. An argument that left him sweating as well as doubting each other. There would be more storms. Maybe not between them. She had three sisters who would now play a role in his life. They would be his responsibility. He came to terms with that fact at the pub while he spoke with the bartender. An encounter at the church would be expected. That would be the next confrontation. That battle would not pit Maggie against him. They would be united in their determination to keep the sisters safe from Abernathy along with their mother.

"Did you change your mind again?" he asked, understanding with the stiffening of her body the word again was not the right word to choose even though it was true. She baffled him at every turn. They just made love. Now she was changing the scene. The scowl between her brows was meant to be erased. He touched the small crease with the tip of his finger.

Maggie pushed up, staring down at him. Her fingers drifted across his chest, touching each nipple then moved lower stilling on his belly. What the devil was she up to?

"Maggie?" he questioned, expecting an answer.

"Yes, imagine I did have a change of opinion. Is that so bad? I find I want you." Her fingertip scraped across his belly. Lower. "Though I've not forgiven you. Jason helped me understand that as you told me before you ran out on me, I've no choice. We must marry. Not certain the marriage will be for the right reasons. I always thought there should be love involved."

He did love her. At this juncture, he couldn't tell her that. Expected words of love from her before he made himself vulnerable. "Do you want to marry me?"

An emphatic yes would do wonders for his wounded ego. He didn't expect that. Though she gave herself to him, as she told him, she wasn't ready to absolve him.

She lifted her shoulder high in a shrug meant to show indifference. The hard tips of her breasts shifted across his chest. "I don't wish to give up the sex. As you said before, I enjoy the climax. The high you bring me."

She was winding the hair on his chest around her fingers, little minx.

"So, it's the sex you want for your lifetime, not the man?" Despite his vow not to let his temper ruin these moments, his irritation reached an explosive level. He should find some *wee* bit of humor in her declaration. He was having the devil's own time doing so.

"You are a nice man. Yes, I want the sex. You taught me well, Jasper. You made me crave something I was happy living without before I met you." She touched her lips to his chest. Rose up so the tips of her breasts sashayed across him. He loved the way they jiggled with her movements. "I want more too. So much more than just the pleasure you give me."

"More?" He slanted an eyebrow upward. Both pleased as well as curious as to what she would tell him next. "What more do you want? Money? Clothing? Jewels? You can have whatever you choose. By marriage to me you will gain a title. Is that what you crave?" Jasper realized she was blackmailing him. He could afford to indulge in whatever she asked for.

"Don't care about any of that. Wealth doesn't mean anything. Neither do titles. Except I do wish to keep a roof over my head along with the necessities; food, clothing, little things." She was toying with him. Her fingers traveling lower. Igniting another inferno of hunger. While she touched him, he knew the trembling of her fingers. She was not so calm as she tried to appear. What was it she intended to ask him?

Jasper needed this conversation to end before he detonated prematurely. There were more important matters at stake here. Wished to have all the issues between them out as well as in the open before she seduced him for another round. Not that he wasn't up for sex again. With her small fingers stroking him, his hard erection pulsed.

"What is it that you care about?"

Jasper gulped air when her fingers tightened around his shaft. Smoothed up then down. Working him. Toying with him. "What is it you want from life or from me if that hits closer to what you are thinking.

"My sisters need protection from mother. She will try to cut deals with more men. She tried to sell me to a horrible man. Failed. She will be ever more ruthless with the others. Please. I would give anything for their protection."

The devil, she meant to sell herself to him!

~ * ~

The next morning, Jason watched the sisters chatter nonstop. Tessa's vibrant silver-blond hair tumbled around her petite figure. True, she wasn't as animated as her sisters. True, she set herself apart, watching more than participating. This wasn't how he'd seen her the day before when she spoke up several times giving her assessment of the situation as well as her views.

Wondering why, he decided the fact was simple. She was the youngest. Nonetheless, he didn't believe her to be malleable as her family thought. A man would need to treat her with respect before she gave herself to him. He wondered about a great deal of things concerning Miss Tessa MacRae. Could see why she intrigued him past human endurance.

It was a true fact that he wanted her. Jason didn't understand the deep emotion that plagued him throughout the night as well as into this morning. He walked toward the group of women intending to walk with Tessa. In the time he meant to spend with her, he intended to get to know her better. Wished his feelings for her to be clear in his mind. Without her knowing how much he thought of her, she touched a place in his heart. The feelings he harbored for her were strong, vibrant. All encompassing. He'd never felt this particular way about any woman.

As if in a daze he walked the distance between them, stood by her chair. Watching her, a tender feeling shot through him. "Tessa?"

She looked up. The crystal-blue clarity of her eyes astonished him. When she smiled, his heart melted.

"Yes?" Tessa asked, questioning him. "Do you want something?" Her voice was soft, her tone one of curiosity.

The devil…yes, he wanted her…all of her. In every way humanly possible. Jason understood he must wait for the realization of his thoughts along with his heart. Tessa was too young. She needed time to grow up, to see the world as it truly was not through the eyes of a child. He shouldn't rush into her life while she didn't know what she wanted.

"Would you take a walk with me? It's warm outside. There is something I'd like to discuss with you. We can walk around the yard or down to the small creek that meanders behind the house. Whatever you would like." His gut constricted when she stood, nodding her head. It seemed she was agreeable to his suggestion.

"Would you like company?" Nellie asked as she seemed worried about her sister. "Might not be right for her to be alone with a man."

"We could all walk with you," Fannie spoke up as she too appeared concerned for the littlest sister. "Nellie is right."

"No," Tessa answered with a quick nod to him. The one word was firm. "We will be fine. *Dinna* think Mr. Kenworthy means to hurt me or damage my reputation. It's just a walk in the daylight. What harm could there be in that?"

That statement was true. What he wanted from Tessa might mean something different to him than it would her sisters. "If you all don't trust me with the youngest here, by all means you can accompany us. Nothing I'm going to say to her is secret. All of you will be apprised when the time is appropriate."

"No!" Her hands were fisted. Seemed she made up her mind. "I'm not a little girl though my older siblings still think of me as a child. I don't want to be guarded as if I had no wit of my own." Tessa proved her point by accepting his arm as they walked to grab coats.

Jason fastened her cloak then donned his coat. Once more he offered his arm to Tessa. She smiled at him accepting the invitation. Her smile dazzled. Sent a quickening to his loins which he was having a difficult time ignoring. While the sun was shining, the winter day was crisp. There was no breeze to make the morning seem chillier. A bank of clouds sat on the horizon. It would rain this afternoon or during the evening.

"Where would you like to walk?"

Even in silence, he enjoyed her company, the way she carried herself with elegance as well as grace. The soft flower scent that floated around her teased his senses. She leaned into him, appearing to enjoy his company.

She looked up at him, bright blue eyes meeting his gaze. "I'm not a little girl," Tessa told him, her voice firm. "I'll be eighteen in a few days. Something you should be aware of."

Looking at her, Jason didn't see a little girl. Never had. Though he knew her to be the youngest sibling, her body was that of a woman's. He snorted, laughing at himself. "Is that right? That old, huh?"

Stopping, she turned to confront him, her chin high, her shoulders rigid. Her mouth flattened into a slim line. "Are you laughing at me?"

"No, sweet one. Myself. It's myself I'm laughing at. Never wanted to think of you as anything but a grown woman. Nonetheless, you are young. Innocent. Am I wrong? Have you ever walked with a man?" He didn't wait for her answer as he continued. "I'll make it clear now. I'm old as well as jaded. I see life through narrow eyes."

Some of the stiffness left her. She still looked at him with fire in her eyes. "No. You're not wrong. Though...I'd like to learn more about men. Would you teach me?"

Damn, he might have just bitten off more than he could handle. Teach her? Didn't wish for any other man to entertain that notion. He tapped her on the nose. "You are not that old. Too young for a man to be teaching you about men."

"Eighteen is old enough to learn things. I know that sometimes women are married and have children at my age."

They continued walking after that. After a few moments of silence, Tessa spoke. "Like to go down by the creek. I love the sound of the water as it rushes to the sea. I still wish you would teach me something. Anything."

He liked that sound too. Enjoyed the sound of Tessa's voice more.

Christine Young

She probably wasn't going to give up on that notion until he caved in to her wishes. "Very well," Jason told her "We will go listen to the creek. Forget about me teaching you. It's not going to happen." With the opposite concept in his head, he thought he might give her a kiss. Wondered if it would be her first. No, most likely not. She was very beautiful. A stunning young woman. He had to take care not to kiss her.

A kiss wouldn't hurt.

It might lead to something else that would.

At the creek, they found a fallen tree trunk to sit on. Jason lifted her so she could sit. He leaned against the trunk studying the ever-changing expressions on her lovely face. Sounds of flowing water always filled his senses. The soft gurgling seemed to do the same for Tessa. She was smiling. Having wrapped her arms around her bent knees, she was rocking.

"What did you wish to talk to me about?" While his gaze met hers, she moistened her bottom lip. Tucked the pink lip gently beneath her top teeth. Watching her, his thoughts turned wicked. He wanted his teeth tugging on her lip.

Jason didn't think this was a conscious effort to seduce. Maybe all women reacted by instinct. He did like that idea. Thought he would enjoy tasting her lips. She wanted to learn about men. He wished to teach her. Begin her lessons this morning by the stream. He shouldn't until she was older. The devil, he didn't think he could wait another year until she was almost nineteen. Eighteen was old enough.

"Talk. Yes." To distract himself, he tossed a rock into the stream then another. "Your mother and father are here for the wedding. So is Lord Abernathy." That was a good beginning. He wondered if she could put together some of what he tried to tell her. It would be easier if she could come to the conclusion on her own.

"That man is here?" The little crease line formed between her eyebrows. He wanted to smooth it away. Take away her worries. "Abernathy will be after Maggie. Your brother must take care. Is that what this is all about? A warning for Maggie? Doesn't make sense."

He wished he dared run his finger along that tiny wrinkle, smooth the lines. He didn't want her to worry. He was going to be with her. Protect her if necessary. "I doubt Abernathy is still after Maggie. He believes her to be wed to Jasper. He won't wish to have a fiancée who is tainted or a wife

287

who might carry another man's child."

"Tainted! How dare you say something like that about my sister!" Her fists were tight, her lips thinned in her anger.

Jason held up his hands in hopes to sooth her fury. This was not going the way he planned. Women. "Listen. That's not what I believe or feel nor what I said. Your sister is assumed to be married to Jasper. No man would believe they didn't consummate their marriage in the two months plus they've been together. It is what married folk do. Consummate the marriage vows."

That sounded stupid. He never said stupid things. As well as some who are not wed. Didn't wish to point that fact out to her again. Once was one time too many.

"Oh." Tessa looked down to her feet. "You must think I'm not very well versed in matters of the heart. I'm not though I wish I was more experienced. Never, hardly ever talked to boys. Now that I'm allowed to go to the balls, mother makes certain I only dance with men who she deems appropriate for me. I rarely like those men. They are crude. Boring in the extreme."

Unable to keep his hands to himself, Jason touched her cheek, ran his fingers down the long column of her neck. He would never be considered one of those appropriate men. "You aren't well versed. I never would have guessed. You wanted lessons. Imagine that was the first clue. What do you think? Do you intend to take umbrage about my words? Will you understand what I'm talking about?"

"I will listen with open ears as well as my mind to everything you tell me." She smiled again…a heartwarming grin that sent more wicked ideas into his male brain. That smile could sink a thousand ships.

"Good then. Jasper and I have discussed this interesting situation we all are involved in. We both believe that since Anice sold Maggie to Abernathy, she still owes him a daughter. Abernathy will feel the same. He will mean to collect payment as soon as possible." Jason hoped she would figure this out with no more prompting.

"That would be Nellie. Wouldn't it?" Tessa asked, appearing concerned for her sister. "Nellie is the next in line to wed. She is nearly the same age as Maggie. Wouldn't he go for the next oldest? You should be with her, protecting her…not me."

Well, she didn't figure this out. He sucked in a long breath of Tessa scented air before exhaling. "You've got the wrong sister. The man didn't like the fact Maggie ran off. Defied him. Made a fool of him on Christmas Eve when he announced his engagement. A man doesn't enjoy being made a fool by a woman."

"The wrong sister?" she questioned while she stared at the water rushing by. She tilted her head as if thinking. "I don't understand. Nellie would…she thinks Anice has a man picked out for her. We just don't know who he is yet. It's not Nelson Abernathy?"

Jason scratched the side of his face, thinking about how much he didn't want to tell her that she was the one in trouble. She was the sister Abernathy would choose. He caught another long deep breath of air searching for the necessary courage. "Abernathy would be looking for a woman he believes he can control. If he watched you girls, he would be looking for the meekest. The most biddable."

Her mouth formed a perfect 'O'. He assumed at long last she figured out what he was trying to tell her. After she appeared to have digested that thought, her shoulders stiffened. Pointing a finger at him, her eyes flashed. Blazed with her indignation. She poked his chest. "Do you think I'm meek? I am not!"

The fierce look in her eyes suited her. Just as the other times she asserted herself, his body jerked in surprise. Hesitated for a few beats before he answered. "No, from the first time we spoke, I understood you would never cower in front of a man. I was surprised when Jasper explained to me that you were always the quiet one, never questioning authority. You always followed your sisters. I didn't see that when you argued with me. Attacked me. Again, I tell you, his description of you did not match what I witnessed last night. His portrayal of you came from Maggie."

"Just because I prefer to listen doesn't make my disposition meek. I'm not compliant. Just assert myself in a quiet manner. Thought my sisters understood that. I'm glad you don't see me that way." She played with the moss on the trunk. Picking at the pieces while she looked up at him.

"Doesn't matter what I think," his voice a husky whisper as he told her.

"To me, it does."

Jason rubbed the back of his neck while he thought on her words.

He was far too experienced not to realize what she was telling him. Too jaded not to want to take advantage of her feelings. He could have her right now if he let himself seduce her.

"Does your mother see you in any other role than the listener, the follower? The sister who seldom if ever questions?" He hoped the answer was yes. That answer would ease his mind.

"She does. Makes references from time to time about how insipid as well as weak I am. Anice dislikes me more than her other three daughters. I don't know why." She lifted her small shoulders. "I never cared. Believe I know her better than my sisters."

He had to be blunt. Needed to make her understand. "You are the sister Anice will hand over to Abernathy in Maggie's place. That is why I came out here to talk to you. To give warning that your future hangs in the balance. I will be here to guard you. You are not to go anywhere without me." He placed his hands on her shoulders, afraid she would never agree. "Do you understand me?"

Jason saw Tessa bristling before a soft smile curved her mouth. He had the sensation she was about to assert herself again. "Will you kiss me?"

She changed the subject with deft skill. He didn't believe she had practice. The need to shake her escalated. "Do you understand what I've been telling you?" He needed to avoid that question of a kiss. Act as if he'd not heard her request.

"I understand all that you said. Will you kiss me? A real kiss, one a man gives a woman. Not a little peck somewhere. A true kiss." Her pretty pink tongue brushed across her bottom lip in a sweet invitation. She was innocent. Had no idea what that small gesture would do to a man's libido.

Damned if he did and double damned if he didn't. The moments were rare that he ever felt caught between a rock and a hard place. This was one of those times. While he wanted to kiss her, taste her, suck her scorching tongue into his mouth, he knew he shouldn't. She wasn't even eighteen. Tessa would be soon. What did a few days matter?

I had my first sexual encounters before I turned fifteen.

It is different for the female persuasion. She's supposed to be innocent. I'm not supposed to teach her anything. That is a husband's job.

"A kiss," he murmured, the words shaky.

His knees felt weak. His hands shook. Moisture dotted his brow.

What the devil was happening to him? "Just a kiss. Nothing more."

He stood in front of her. His hands on her waist. He let them slide along her arms until his hands wrapped with possession around her neck. His thumbs held her chin high. Touched. Rubbed along her jaw. Her flesh was satin to the touch. She whimpered at the first caress. Leaned into him.

"Are you certain?"

"Oh, yes…" the words were uttered in a breathy little pant. Her eyes wide blue pools of curiosity.

His lips captured hers. He told himself he needed to be gentle. Shouldn't frighten her. Shouldn't plunge deep inside without foreplay. She said she wanted a real kiss. He would do his best. His tongue swept across the middle of her lips, pushing inside. He tugged on that lip that had been wetted for him. At that time, she didn't understand that she prepared herself for his easy entry. She sighed giving him access to her sultry dark secrets. The tip of his tongue touched upon hers. Rubbed against the velvet of hers. He tasted her. She played with his as if it was as natural as if she'd done this hundreds of times. Understood the heat building. At the base of her neck his thumb felt the hurried pulsing of her blood.

At that moment, she entered into his heart. Captured his soul. Sent a tempest of yearning flaring through him straight to his groin. His sex grew, hardened with anticipation of something that could not happen. Her hands wound around his neck, nails raking there then higher into his hair. With a groan of desperation, he pulled away. With his thumb, he touched her swollen bottom lip, still damp from his mouth. He saw her breasts heaving as she tried to collect air. He was pleased. Content that he'd been able to stop himself from ripping off her clothing then having his way with her.

When she opened her eyes, they were dazed, dreamy looking. Panting, she seemed to search for a breath of air. Jason was thankful for the cloak partially covering her breasts. The bodice of her gown would be so easy to unfasten. While it wouldn't stop further exploration if he wished to go there, he never intended to take advantage of this beautiful child-woman. His hands on her waist, he lifted her from her perch on the fallen tree.

"Another kiss?" she asked, her voice soft. The question tempted.

Another kiss would be detrimental to her innocence.

Chapter Ten

In one of the church's back rooms, Maggie watched her sisters whirl around the room doing all they could to get her ready for the wedding that would begin in fifteen minutes. Jason was going to walk Tessa down the aisle then he was going to circle around the back so he could play the father of the bride. She never asked her father to walk with her. Didn't feel right. Their father never cared whether any of his daughters lived or died. Imagined he'd hoped for a son. All men wanted a male child to carry on the family name. Maybe after four female children he was just a bitter man.

Fletcher accompanied by Gracie arrived on Saturday just after Jason returned from his walk with Tessa. Gracie along with the twins spent several hours rehashing past memories as well as how Fletcher drugged her so she would say her vows. Jasper decided Fletcher would walk Fannie as well as Nellie to the altar where Jasper would wait. To make the task easier, it was decided he would escort both women at the same time.

Nellie shook out Maggie's wedding dress, taking the gown from the package Eilinora wrapped it in. "It's so beautiful. I hope when I marry, mine will be just as gorgeous."

Nellie's eyes sparkled. They were a deeper green than hers. They all had varying shades of honey colored hair. Their eyes along with the color of their hair was from their mother. None of them looked anything like their father. For that matter, Tessa didn't resemble either parent. She was unique, one of a kind. The only one with blue eyes coupled with white-blond hair.

Maggie was dressed in white silk pantalets and her corset pushed her breasts upward. Her chemise was tied together with light green ribbons. She lifted her arms so Nellie could guide the gown downward. After that the tiny pearl buttons down the back were all fastened. Sitting in front of the mirror, Nellie fixed her hair. She wound green ribbons throughout. Maggie had to admit she had never looked as good as she did now.

Her sisters all wore lavender gowns with a simple design. The fittings went well. The dresses were lovely, the sisters more beautiful.

The girls brought the prewedding gifts to her. She received something old from Nellie. It was a bracelet that Anice gave Nellie on her thirteenth birthday. The piece of jewelry wasn't that ancient but it was the best they could do on that score. From Jasper she received a necklace with a single emerald decorated with diamond chips surrounding the stone. The garters on her stockings were blue. A handkerchief embroidered with flowers was borrowed from Fannie. This was more than she expected when Jasper posed the question three weeks ago. Of course, when he asked her to renew her vows, he had thought a special license the next day would do the trick.

She held a small bouquet made from the flowers of a hydrangea Jasper found in a hot house owned by a man living in Dublin. At the altar there were an array of lavender orchids that would be returned after the ceremony. She was certain they had all their bases covered. Her husband gave her everything she asked for. In truth he gave her more than that. She'd never felt so loved as well as cared for. He protected her from Lord Abernathy. Now was attempting to guard her sisters from the wicked designs of her mother.

While Jasper along with Gracie as well as Fletcher attended the church service, she did not, nor did her sisters. Neither did Jason. He was their ever-present shadow, haunting the door to the room where they dressed. His gaze constantly on Tessa. At the present time, he stood sentinel at the closed door while they prepared themselves for the wedding.

During the last few days, she and Jasper involved themselves in several heated discussions about her youngest sister as the situation pertained to Jason. The strangest thing about the discussions they had was they seemed to think the same way. Jason was too old for Tessa who was immature as well as naive. Tessa carried her heart on her sleeve. Maybe that was why Jason was fond of her. He was used to jaded women, women who were after whatever they could get from a man. Tessa wasn't anything like that. She looked at Jason with starstruck love in her eyes. What man could resist those crystallin blue eyes?

"Prewedding jitters?" Nellie asked while she handed over a glass of wine to her. "You deserve some for all you've been through. Drink up, the wine will make it easier for you to walk down that narrow path to your beloved." Nellie didn't seem to be able to repress a nervous giggle of her own.

Thoughtful, Maggie looked out the window thinking of the few months she and Jasper had been together. As Nellie suggested, she drank long and deep. The wine was delicious. She did hope it would ease the stress, remembering all they shared, "Yes, of course there are jitters. What bride would not have some apprehension on the day she was going to be married. My nerves are stretched tight. Feel as if they might snap at any moment." She tapped her finger on the crystal flute Jasper provided for them. For this endeavor, he spared no expense. He wanted her to have a wedding she would recall with fondness. "I'm more worried about what will happen after the wedding."

Her sisters giggled. "You do know what happens," Tessa pointed out, her finger to her lips. "I'd like to know what it's all about. Asked Jason to teach me. He refused." She sighed a long raspy breath of air slipping from her. "Men!"

"Tessa!" Her name was shouted in unison by both Nellie and Fannie once the girls realized what she told them.

Maggie found herself grinning at her sisters, looking delighted that they shared their feelings. "Not that. What you are asking of him puts too much pressure on the poor man. Have a heart." She turned to Fannie. "You are too young. What happened when you walked with Jason? Did he do something he shouldn't have? Is that why you're so suddenly curious?" Now was not the time for a lecture. If something happened between the two of them, she would need to tell Jasper. He would talk to his brother. "The man is supposed to protect you, not seduce you. You asked him to teach you things about men and women? Thank God, he refused."

"I wish he would seduce me," Tessa said, her voice soft, her eyes dreamy as if she was thinking about that very thing. She ran one finger along the stem of her glass, seeming to peruse the burgundy liquid remaining in the crystal. She spoke, a wistful expression on her lovely face. "I asked him to kiss me. A real kiss, you know. Not a peck on the cheek."

"And did he?" Nellie asked, shaking her finger at the little sister. "That was not a proper thing to ask of a man. You should know better. He is so much older than you. You should be with a man closer to your own age."

"I'm not the timid little mouse you all believe me to be!" Tessa fired back at her sisters, her blue eyes ablaze with fiery heat. "Jasper is quite a bit older than Maggie. I'm not that much younger. So, Jason should be a splendid choice. You should look at us from a different perspective. I don't wish to be courted by a boy. I think Jason is perfect for me. He is a man not a boy. That's what I wish for. A man!"

"No, I imagine you've sat back your entire life basking in the shadows of your older sisters. Jason did tell Jasper you were not as we all assumed you to be. Do you like Jason?" Maggie felt the heat of her blush. "You must since you asked for a kiss. Did he kiss you?" Maggie shook her head, "Never mind. That is not my business. Unless of course, you wish to tell us."

Tessa was nodding, hesitating for the moment to provide more information. "A lot. I like the man more than I suppose I should. He is handsome. Strong. Yes, he kissed me. I liked the kiss a lot too. He knew what he was doing. Felt as if my entire body shot up in flames. Whirlwinds of heat danced through me. I asked him again. He told me no. Suppose once was enough for him since I'm inexperienced. I do so want him to think of me as a woman…to like me."

"No…" Nellie and Fannie said together once more. "He did kiss you. That was too forward of you to ask."

"He did. A real kiss and that's all I'm going to say about what happened yesterday. Since I've shocked you by saying too much. We've got to finish getting everything ready before Jason is knocking at the door telling us you are late for your wedding. The bridesmaids still need to get dressed. Can't be going down to the altar in our underclothing." Tessa finished talking then with a swish to her hair she turned her back on them.

During her confession, Tessa's face turned a beautiful shade of rose. Maggie understood there was a lot her sister wasn't telling them. What happened between them was private. She understood that too. Maggie hoped Tessa wouldn't get into trouble by being so bold. If Jason told her no to that second kiss, she might not need to worry. She didn't think Tessa's older sisters had been kissed by a real man. Perhaps they were jealous.

Several minutes later, after a knock, Tessa opened the door. Jason turned to meet her gaze with a broad smile. Maggie saw the way his brown eyes heated when he looked upon her sister. In another year or two they would make a fine match. Maggie didn't think her sister would wait for the vows if Jason decided he wished for her to grace his bed. Just as she fell for Jasper's many charms, Tessa would fall for Jason's sweet talking. Well…she amended, her sister seemed to have already fallen. She only hoped Jason's intentions were pure. If they were, she would have no objections. If Tessa fell into his arms before they were wed, she could have nothing to say about the deed. Might be a family trait. If they were in love…

"The bride is ready," Tessa said breathlessly.

Jason bowed low, taking Tessa's hand in his then kissing the back. His eyes bore into hers. Seemed to question. Nothing more was said between them that could be construed in a way inappropriate. "The church is full to the brim. The good people from the church were eager to see the renewal of your vows. Close and lock the door behind me. I'll tell my brother it is time to proceed. Don't open the door to anyone but me. I'll announce myself. Be back in a few minutes." Tessa stood frozen in the doorway for a few moments.

"Tessa!" Nellie spoke sharply. "Close and lock the door."

She jerked then did what Nellie commanded.

Maggie thought her sisters were a bit overprotective of her as well as Tessa. On the other hand, this was Anice they dealt with, Lord Abernathy also. Anything could happen at any time. That man would believe himself entitled to take what he wanted. No one knew which sister he set his sights on now. He might just wish for revenge by taking any one of them. After the ceremony, he wouldn't be able to think of marrying her. She would be taken by Jasper. She was safe. Prayed he didn't want one of her sisters especially not Tessa. Not when Tessa seemed to have found a love of her own. Though, she wouldn't wish Lord Abernathy on any of her other sisters either. Given time they would fall in love. Jason must make certain nothing happened to the youngest MacRae.

Seemed odd that Tessa found her voice in front of Jason Kenworthy. She would have thought Tessa to be shy while talking to the first man she found attractive, not bold as well as daring. Jason was the second son. His title lesser. Some second sons claimed no inheritance unless something was left to them by a different relative. Sometimes they never claimed the lesser title. That did happen from time to time. Maggie wondered how the brothers worked those details out.

While she found herself musing about things she would soon learn, the knock sounded on the door. "It's Jason. Everything is ready."

There was no mistaking his voice. Once more Tessa opened the door, seeming eager to see him. She would be the first to walk down the aisle on Jason's arm. She would be the first of the girls to stand at the altar. Jasper needed to be wary.

"We are ready," Maggie breathed out a soft sound. Her knees felt weak. Her hands shook. She didn't know if she could manage to walk as far as the altar to meet Jasper. She would need to cling to Jason. He would be sure to steady her.

"Your mother, along with your father, sit in the front row. Lord Abernathy sits behind them. All of you will be safe during the ceremony." Jason looked at Tessa the entire time he spoke. "No one would be foolish to try something with the congregation full to the brim. Afterwards, before as well as after the cutting of the cake, I will keep Tessa by my side. Nothing is going to happen here on my watch."

"Let's go then. I for one do not want to waste any more time before I truly become Jasper's wife."

Maggie picked up her skirts, walking past Jason. She was followed by her sisters. At the opening to the sanctuary, she stopped. Her breath caught then held. Music from an organ played. Jasper stood at the altar with Fletcher by his side. Gracie sat on the opposite side of the walkway from her mother and father. A slow chill passed through her. A bad feeling that something would go terribly wrong filled her with concern.

She was amazed the church was full. Looking out on the assemblage she saw some of the people she met at the pub. The man who tended bar at the tavern sat in the third row. Eilinora was there with one of her seamstresses. They would all be witness to this marriage...this real marriage. She smiled up at Jason. He turned. With Tessa on his arm, they began the slow steady walk to the altar. Nodded to the woman sitting at the organ. The music changed.

Tessa, escorted by Jason, walked down the long red carpet leading to the platform where she would be wed. He stopped with Tessa, placing her on the bride's side. Then circled down the outer side to get back to her. She filled her lungs with air. Once then twice, it would soon be her turn.

She would be a wife. Maggie decided she would be the best wife possible.

When she first saw Jasper standing so straight and tall, her breath caught. Her heart pounded. Maggie had never seen him decked out in his finest. He must have bought the formal attire in Dublin when he purchased the rings or possibly when he sought out the owner of the hot house then procured the flowers. His cravat was tied with perfection. His tailored black pants molded his legs, showing off the muscles. He didn't need padding to fill out the shoulders of his frock coat or the calves and thighs of his formal attire. The snow-white shirt contrasted to the bronze of his skin. In her direction, he nodded. His golden-brown eyes alight, brimmed with desire.

Fletcher now stood between Nellie and Fannie. They each held an arm while he escorted them to their places. He moved to stand beside Jasper who whispered something to him. The smile on Fletcher's face was broad. She hoped she could remember to ask him later this night what he said that pleased Jasper. Would recall after the feast orchestrated by the minister's wife along with the good people at the pub Jasper seemed to enjoy.

Jason leaned close so she would be the only one to hear. "You are certain you want to marry my older brother and not me. We are not all that different. Just a few minutes makes one older. I'm much more charming. He's far too serious."

"You don't love me." Her laughter was soft. She did like both men. Loved Jasper though. "I cannot marry a man who doesn't…" She broke off with those words because she wasn't certain of Jasper's love. He never said as much nor did she. If Jasper only cared for her, she would need to love him enough for both.

"Oh, I do love you, but as a sister. I'm sorry to disappoint." Jason patted her hand, his boyish grin charming.

No wonder her youngest sister thought herself in love with this adorable man. He was a charming rake. She touched his cheek, enamored by this twin who seemed to care for her youngest sister. "Just don't hurt Tessa. Promise me you will always be honest with her. If you don't love her, don't make her think you do." She paused wondering if she should go so far as to tell him the next thing on her mind. "Don't take her innocence unless you love her." Maggie understood these two brothers could manipulate a woman, could seduce, charm until the woman could do nothing but accept whatever… He might think he was entitled to do just that. He came from a titled family along with wealth.

"I promise I would never hurt Tessa. I do care about her. Don't know if that's love. Not yet...she is young. I understand that fact. Needs time to test her wings, to grow into her beautiful body." One more time Jason patted her hand that lay on top of his arm.

Maggie reminded herself that care wasn't the same as love. Nonetheless, care could turn into love. The pair new each other for such a short time, a few days at the most.

"I will make do with that promise. Appreciate you telling me even though we both understand you did not need to do so." The music changed again to the traditional wedding march. She brought in a drink of air before gulping the oxygen down.

"Think this our cue to begin the walk," Jason said, bending close so he could whisper to her. "Don't be nervous. My brother's a fine upstanding fellow. He will be a good husband and father when the time comes."

"Yes, he is." Maggie stood straight watching Jasper as she approached him. The path to the altar seemed to go on forever. Jasper's hands were behind his back as he waited for her. They stopped in front of the minister.

"Who gives this woman..." he began.

Jason cleared his throat while the minister continued speaking. "I do, Jason Kenworthy gives Maggie MacRae to my twin Jasper Kenworthy."

It was not traditional. The father of the bride usually spoke the words. Maggie didn't feel she had a father. Never had. A commotion behind her caught her attention. She turned...

Her father stood in the middle of the aisle. His face, beet red, livid with anger. "That man has no right to give Maggie to any man. She is a bastard! All her sisters are bastards!" He was shaking his fist at her. "If she follows in her mother's footsteps, you will have bastards for children. She is a whore just like her mother." He paused for air, sucking in gulps. "Tell the truth. You slept with her before you were married." Spittle flew from his mouth. He shook his fists at Anice. Then back to Maggie. "You aren't going to marry her! She's no a MacRae."

"Get him out of here!" Jasper turned for help from both Fletcher along with his brother. His fists were tight. The muscle at his jaw clenched. Jasper turned to the minister. Seemed he intended to take care of this matter

299

by himself. "You will wait. I'm going to marry this woman." He stepped forward, seeming to take the initiative.

His brother along with Fletcher started forward. Maggie felt her world tumbling down around her.

Seemed the entire congregation gave a gasp at the man's words then stilled into what appeared to be an eerie silence.

"Wait!" Jason said, his voice calm. "I'll take care of this. I'll have him out of here in a moment. Don't stall this for me. Go on with the ceremony. The wedding must take place." Towering over the man, Jason grabbed him by the collar escorting him from the sanctuary.

During that time all seemed to freeze. Nothing was said. The people attending were chattering. Maggie couldn't see what happened after that. Jason must have taken her father to the front door before heaving him from the church. When Jason returned, he had a solemn expression on his face. He nodded at the minister then he stood beside his brother as his best man. Fletcher was next to him.

This was unexpected. While she thought her father didn't care about her, she never assumed that he wasn't her real father. He always lived in the house. Anice and he went their separate ways. That's the way her family always acted. Seemed content with that. Neither were ever home in the evenings.

She was caught up in her thoughts, heedless of the words being spoken around her. The minister droned on. She should have thought to tell him to make the service short. Her legs itched from standing still for so long. Once again, she thought her knees would buckle. Didn't like standing. Jasper squeezed her hand. She wished they'd gotten that special license. Done this with no fanfare. She didn't need her family by her side. Nor did she need a special wedding gown. All she wished for were the vows to be said.

"Does anyone object to the marriage of Maggie MacRae and Jasper Ken…"

Another rustle of sound had everyone staring at Anice. She stood. Her eyes blazing. Her fist shaking at them. "I object. Object a thousand times. Maggie was engaged to be wed to Lord Abernathy. Promised to be his wife. If she cannot follow direct orders from her mother, she is not fit to be any man's wife. She will make a horrible life partner to the marquis. She doesn't abide by rules. Always doing what she wishes without concern for another living soul. I will never allow her to marry this poor man."

Dazed by the accusations, Maggie thought her heart was in her throat. Thought she would faint. Nothing was going as it should.

Jasper turned to Fletcher. "Get Anice out of here." Then to the minister. "Please continue. I'd like to have the I dos said so we can celebrate. Their objections mean nothing to me or to Maggie." He looked at Maggie. Touched her gently beneath the chin. "Are you alright?" he asked, his voice so tender she didn't think she'd ever heard him like this.

A gasp from the congregation carried to her shattered nerves. When she saw the man who rushed toward them, she jerked. Trembled. "No!"

Her father shook his hands at them. His strides were long as he closed the distance between them. "Maggie won't marry this man. She is to be the wife of Lord Abernathy. He is here to witness this travesty. He should step up to the altar. That's who Maggie should be marrying."

Her father was walking toward them with a gun in his hand. He was waving it at different people. His hand shook. He stopped. Pointed the gun. "She won't marry Lord Kenworthy because he is not going to live to say I do. I'm going to kill the man this instant!"

Her father fired the gun. Maggie had been moving, anticipating he would shoot her. His gun was pointing at Jasper. When she heard his words, she understood the bullet wasn't meant for her. Maggie didn't intend to let anyone kill Jasper. She lunged in front of Jasper just as she heard the sound of the gun firing. Felt the bullet hit her. Jasper's hands were on her arms, holding her up. Heard him swear.

"No!" When he turned her to look at him, she saw the golden simmer of his eyes. His anger. He held onto her. Cradled her in his arms. "Get a doctor!"

The assembly was breathless for a few minutes. Her head lay against his chest. Everything was turning, swirling in shades of gray. Lights shimmered then darkened. Her head pounded. Blackness swamped her though she heard voices. Her sisters... Jasper giving orders. He was swearing. She passed in and out of consciousness.

"My God, that bullet was meant for me. Little fool, why did you jump in front of the bullet? I had it handled. The bartender from the pub was behind him. The congregation..."

Maggie didn't hear anymore.

~ * ~

Jasper's hand was soaked in her blood. Blood stained his shirt. He was bent over her. Holding her hand. She breathed…weak breaths. Her pulse was quick. The doctor pronounced that she would be fine. Sweat beaded across his brow. Didn't think he'd ever been so terrified in his entire life.

The bullet grazed her head. The wound was superficial. So, why didn't she wake up? Why were her eyes still closed? Her father had been taken away. Anice had visibly paled then sunk to the ground in a dead faint. While the woman didn't care for her daughters, it appeared she didn't wish them dead. Anice had other uses for her girls. She was handing them over, he assumed to whoever offered her the most incentive.

The minister showed them the way to his home which was behind the church. Jasper set her down on the sofa in the living room. The minister's wife bustled around clucking about what happened. Brought back a pitcher of water along with soft clean cloths. Jasper stepped back to allow the doctor access to Maggie. He rubbed his hand on the back of his neck. They were still stained with Maggie's blood.

Jason stood next to him, his hand on his shoulder. "She's going to be fine. There is always a great deal of blood from head wounds. You know that. In the morning, the light will shine. We'll have to figure out how to get the two of you married."

Jasper understood Jason tried to humor him. Attempted to ease his mind. Nothing would ease him until Maggie sat up with her eyes wide open. He needed to hear her voice. He found his entire body shook with fear for Maggie.

The village doctor who had been at the wedding touched Jasper's shoulder. "I'll take it from here, sir. You need to let me get to her. I'm going to clean up the wound. See if she needs a few stitches then bind it. After I'm finished, you can take her home. She will need rest. Though I doubt if she will wake up soon. Maybe tomorrow morning."

Fletcher left to retrieve the carriage that would take them to the cottage home. Soon, he would bring her home to his townhouse in Glasgow.

For now, he would put her in their bed. He would stand guard over her until she woke. Nothing more was going to happen to her.

He didn't wish to leave her side. Stepping back, he held very still. Her hair was moved from the wound. Her head cleaned. Once the blood was gone, he could see the crease of the bullet along her scalp. The doctor shaved part of her head.

"I will need to put in a few stitches. She's going to be fine." The doctor continued to repeat himself. "Get her home. Rest is what she needs. If she wakes up, make her stay awake. Talk to her. Don't want her to go back to sleep until I see her again. When she wakes, send for me. I'll be at the cottage as soon as I can get there."

Jasper found himself nodding his head at the directions. Wasn't certain if he would remember anything. All he heard was common sense. He had Jason to help if he forgot. His frame shook again as the images collided inside his head. Her father holding the gun. Maggie terrified beside him. Anice standing up shouting at them. He couldn't rid himself of the sight of Maggie jumping in front of him as her father, who was not her father, shot the pistol.

He was surprised at the revelation that the girls were not his. Yet he was not. He expected the three oldest were his but not Tessa. The mother seemed as astonished at the revelation as the rest of the people in attendance. Though she would be certain to comprehend who the father of her children was or was not.

Maggie was a bastard. That didn't matter to him, not a'tall. Made her more real to him. He hoped she didn't care. Nothing would change the fact he needed her to be his wife. Wanted her to stay with him forever. God, how he loved her.

After she was stitched up, the ride home was somber. For the entirety of the trip, he held Maggie in his arms with her head resting against the hollow of his shoulder. Even though he tried to clean as much as possible, her beautiful white gown was soaked in her blood. He'd been able to wash his hands as well as his face but he was still bathed in red. What a travesty of a day. He was supposed to be a married man.

He should never have agreed to all this fanfare. Should have obtained that special license. If he had not given in to her wishes, they'd be married now. If he had there would never have been a place for her mother and father to showcase their fury. Anice was left alone in the church. Under the circumstances none of the girls wanted to stay with her. He hoped some good Samaritan had seen to her. The last he saw, she fell to the floor in a dead faint. Anice might still be lying on the church's floor. He didn't care what happened to the ugly woman. She orchestrated part of the horrific drama in the church this afternoon.

Jasper carried Maggie upstairs where Clancy had a steaming tub of water waiting for them. After laying her out on their bed, he undressed her. Washed her with some of the warm water. She never woke. He left the gown on the floor where it fell. He found a soft white nightgown for her to wear. Dressed her. When she was covered with blankets, he undressed then slipped into the tub.

He was eager to rid himself of her blood, of the reminder she could have died today. He set his head on the rim of the tub. Soaked. Tried to relax. His muscles were still tense. His nerves stretched taut. To a small degree, the water soothed. He needed to finish with his bath, certain he would have company soon. The sisters would be hoping to see their sister. Would come by to see if she woke. None would sleep tonight. The girls couldn't stay in his room. He needed to be alone with Maggie...only Maggie.

The devil, she leapt in front of a bullet to save his miserable hide. If he had any doubts about her feelings for him, they were laid to rest today. Maggie loved him. He found himself overwhelmed by those thoughts. Wished...

Maggie loved him. That was all he needed to know. The thought brought a smile to his heart. It seemed strange that in the middle of all this chaos, he could smile. As soon as he could, after she woke, he would tell her he loved her. Would make love to her with the sweet tenderness she deserved. She needed to hear the words he'd felt for so long but never spoke. He'd been a damn fool. Afraid to let the woman know how vulnerable he became when she was near. He would give her anything she wished for.

Pup whined around her small body, sniffed. Spoke to him with a bark that accused. After that he curled up beside her, his head resting near her head. The white bandage the doctor wrapped around her head was a stark reminder of the day's events. He learned a great deal today. Learned how one small woman could change his heart forever. Learned no matter what he did or the precautions he took, he might not always be able to protect her.

Even though they prepared for events that might not be to their liking, they'd not been able to comprehend the depth of loathing in the MacRae family. Tessa was still at risk as were Nellie along with Fannie. Who the devil was their father? Who was Tessa's father? It might be prudent to discover the identity of those people. Doubted if that would be possible. Anice would never divulge the fathers if she even knew.

They would travel back to Glasgow as soon as Maggie was pronounced healthy enough to make the journey. The girls would live in his townhouse. They would go nowhere without protection. If he thought Anice would give up guardianship, he would appeal to her. Perhaps with the events of today, a judge would be on his side. Gracie's father was a judge, Judge Seymour. He could point him in the direction of a man who might be willing to go against a mother in favor of him. Maybe none of that needed to be done. All the girls were of age. In that case it wouldn't matter. They wouldn't need a guardian.

He sunk down. Moved lower into the steaming liquid. The hot water calmed him, eased the tension that radiated from him since he grasped what happened. Since he held Maggie in his arms. Since he realized she'd been shot.

The devil, they still weren't legally wed. He found his eyes closing. Jerked up splashing water onto the floor. Pup jumped up startled by his unexpected reaction. He reached for the glass of brandy he set on the stool. Drank. Closed his eyes as the liquid burned down his throat.

Sometime while he slept in the tub, Clancy brought in a towel to warm by the fire. Rising, water sluicing around him, he stepped from the tub. He wrapped the heated material around him then padded to the bed where Maggie slept. Kneeling down beside her, he touched her cheek with his hand. Moved her hair. Kissed her forehead. Longed for her to open her eyes. Ran his finger along the length of her nose. Touched the bandage. Wondered if she was aware of him by her side.

Murmuring, he continued the gentle touch down the long white column of her throat. "You sweet little fool. You jumped in front of the bullet that was meant for me. Never ever do that again. Your action was foolish. Could have gotten you killed." He let out a slow breath of air trying to purge the resurgence of fear. "You must love me. How I love you, Maggie. Loved you the moment you set your sassy little nose on my chest. Knew you hid from someone. In that instant, I needed to protect you from whoever you ran from."

She moaned, a soft sound in the deepening twilight. The sound of pain disturbed him. The doctor left laudanum for him to give her when she woke if she needed something to curb the pain. She would wake with a pounding headache.

He looked to the window. Moonlight filtered in through the glass panes casting shadows across her face. Her face was beautiful bathed in moonlight. If she opened her eyes, he would be able to see the deep green color.

He touched her lips. Cast in moonglow, they were a soft pink hue. He knew their taste, the feel of them beneath his. Remembered when she learned to return his kisses. When she first let him enter into her. "Open your eyes, sweet Maggie. Let me see them. The green vibrant coloring when you are aroused. When your passion ignites my body."

She'd come so close to having her life extinguished today. He reflected on random thoughts, jumping from one place to another. His mind didn't work well right now. Once again, he touched her, trailed a fingertip along the line of her jaw. His thumb traced a path across her bottom lip.

"Wake up. Let me look into your eyes. Want to hold you. Cradle you in my arms. Pup misses you. Doesn't understand why you are sleeping and not playing with him. The rogue is going to be a little hellion by tomorrow morning if his mum doesn't wake and pay a *wee* bit of attention to him. Hmm…what do you say? Open those sooty long lashes so you can look at me. So, you can tell me how you are feeling."

The day had been exceptionally warm. With little to no cloud cover. The evening was chilly. He'd thought tonight he would be drinking wine with his wife as well as making love. Instead, he had a brandy sitting on the nearby table and he was praying for his wife to open her eyes then smile at him. She wasn't his wife. He didn't enjoy the reminder. The minister agreed to stop by tomorrow afternoon if she was awake to finish the ceremony. Seemed the vows kept getting put off.

Under these circumstances, he didn't want to wait any longer than necessary. Lord Abernathy still roamed free to initiate any plan he concocted. Jason kept a steady watch on Tessa. Unfortunately, he couldn't sleep with her. Jasper gave a small chuckle. Jason might use that as an excuse though Jasper didn't think his brother would take advantage of that situation. Perhaps it was for the best. If he found time to speak with his brother in privacy, he would suggest that he plan on sleeping on the floor of Tessa's bedroom until they knew she would be safe. The youngest MacRae wouldn't be secure until she was wed to Jason…or some other lucky man. Somehow Jasper didn't think there would be another man besides Jason for Tessa.

Jasper donned his robe. Poured a second glass of brandy then sat down beside Maggie. Just as Pup needed to be close to her, he did too. He rested against the headboard of the bed. For several seconds, he closed his eyes. Silence surrounded him. Silence except for Maggie's deep breathing, soft and even in her sleep.

Still thinking.

Still remembering.

The silence didn't last long. Nellie poked her head inside the room. Fannie stood behind her peering over her shoulder. Light from the hallway filled the space behind the two girls. He'd been expecting them. Knew he would need to share this time with her sisters. They loved her too. The two girls would need to know how she fared.

"Can we come in? We need to see her. Is she…?" Nellie's words thinned into nothing. If she said more, he didn't hear.

They hovered in the doorway. Nellie shifted from one foot to the other. Fannie stepped forward now as if she meant to walk inside this instant. He didn't know what they wanted to hear. The truth was always the best way to proceed. "Where is Tessa?" he asked then realized they wanted to know about Maggie.

"Close, she is coming with your brother. He hasn't let her out of his sight since we returned from the church. Well, he did long enough for her to change her gown. He's concerned but won't tell us why he is hovering. It would be nice to understand." Nellie inched her way inside the room.

Fannie stepped from behind her sisters, answering his question. "We thought it might be because Lord Abernathy is out there somewhere. The bartender from your pub sent a message saying Lord Abernathy is at the pub drinking as well as talking about what he is intending to do as soon as he gets the chance. Said he always wanted Tessa more than Maggie. Says she wouldn't argue with him. Is that why Jason is hovering around our little sister? Seems a bit too protective."

At Fannie's words, he stiffened. If his brother heard the message, he would never leave her side. He needed to give the sisters information, scant as it was. "Maggie is not awake, if that is what you are asking? The doctor told me she might stay asleep until tomorrow. Both of you, you need to get some rest. The day was long as well as exhausting. Tomorrow might not be any better. No one knows what will ensue. Doctor said he didn't expect her to wake up until tomorrow. The injury was traumatic. Maggie needs the time to heal. Waiting in our bedchamber will not make her open her eyes sooner." The glass of brandy he held rested on his stomach. He expected Jason to be in here soon.

"We don't want to wait until the morning. She needs to wake up now," Fannie protested. "She can't keep sleeping. What if she dies?"

Jasper's breath whistled through his teeth. "Maggie is not going to die. Where are Tessa and Jason? I need to talk to my brother as well as your sister as soon as possible. Imagine the two of you also need to hear what we speak about."

He didn't wish to alarm the girls but there was still so much at risk. Abernathy would not give up on this new quest of his.

Nellie and Fannie walked close to the bed. Stood over their sister for several seconds. Nellie spoke, her voice soft, filled with so much emotion. Jasper, once again, realized how very close the siblings were to each other. "I don't understand how she got shot. Father…not father was shooting at you…" she broke off realizing what she implied. "He meant to kill you. I don't understand any of this."

"Neither does anyone else. I'm glad he didn't want to kill Maggie. Though my being the target doesn't please me either." Maggie was no longer the man's daughter. He told the world all the girls were bastards. While disgracing the children, Jasper felt certain he meant only to disgrace Anice.

"Don't see how a man who pretended to be our father for so long could want to kill her," Fannie said, her voice soft.

"It's alright. I wish she didn't jump in front of me also. Never would have wished she take a bullet meant for me. I knew the bullet would never hit me. His aim was off. Could tell by the way he was holding the gun." The thing was…Maggie didn't jump in front of him. When she was hit, she was on his right. He'd been watching the pistol. Saw the potential trajectory. The bullet would have never found its mark. It was aimed to the right of him. Jasper believed it might have grazed his arm. Might not have hit him a'tall.

"I'm glad he's not our father," Fannie said in her soft voice. "Mother could have told us. She never implied anything. The man never cared whether we lived or died. I always thought he hated us. In the evening, he disappeared. Was never around on holidays or birthdays."

"So did mother," Nellie pointed out. "They never went anywhere together though. Disappeared in different directions."

That she was a whore? No, Jasper didn't believe Anice would ever admit to that. Though he understood that wasn't what Fannie was speaking about. If Anice claimed the man wasn't their father, that fact would lead to the conclusion she cheated on the man she wed. He would be surprised if Anice didn't denounce her husband's words. As to the validity of the father's words there was no confirmation, no proof. It would come down to his word against hers.

By his actions in the church, the man proved himself to be touched in the head. Though at this point nothing would surprise him. They would need to stay here until there was a trial. Though there was an entire congregation of witnesses. Maybe they would not need to remain. All he wanted was for Maggie to open her eyes then marry him. After that he needed to get her to a place where there would be no more trauma. Maybe he could rent that little cottage where Fletcher kept Gracie as his mistress.

The movement at his door caught his attention. He smiled. Knew the two would be here soon. Jason held her hand as he tugged her forward. He let go after they stepped into the room. His twin appeared besotted with her. His brother would indeed spend the night with Tessa. The floor or the bed was yet to be determined.

Jason and Tessa walked in through the open door. Jason's hand was at the small of her back. With that small protective gesture, Jasper understood he claimed the girl as his.

"How is she? Jason asked his hand moving along Tessa's back to be placed on her shoulder.

"Much the same. She rests peacefully. Sleeping, the doctor told me until tomorrow. There is no need for everyone to stay much longer now that we all know she is fine. Maggie will recover. As soon as she is awake as well as feeling herself, I'll send for the minister." At long last they will be wed.

"Good, good," Jason said, as his hand ran the length of Tessa's back then back to her waist. "Maggie will wake soon? You will call us when she does?"

Jason would do all in his power to protect Tessa as he would do everything to keep guard over Maggie as well as the other girls. Lord Abernathy was still out in the Irish countryside somewhere. The man still needed a wife. Anice was still offering her girls for something in return. Jasper didn't believe she needed money. What the devil was she getting in return? They were all at risk. Nothing was going to change in the near future.

"Not unless she opens her eyes at a decent hour. After today's chaos, I'm not going to disturb anyone's night of sleep. The doctor has assured me she will be fine. In the morning or tomorrow at some time Maggie will open her eyes. When that happens, I'll let everyone know. You'll probably hear my holler of joy."

Jasper understood none of them were pleased with what he announced. They would have to accept his decision. No one except him would stay here for the remainder of the night. He wished for privacy. Needed time to think about their future together.

His twin was smitten with the youngest. Jasper could tell by his posture. By the way he looked at her. The protective as well as possessive nature of the man who never showed that quality before. They also stood by the bed looking at his sleeping bride. Tessa leaned her back into Jason. His hands were around her, beneath her breasts. Jason's head rested at the top of her head. The sight was poignant. He never expected to see his brother fall in love. Just as he never expected to fall in love himself. He believed he would marry a woman who he was attracted to. A lady who would grace his arm as well as bear his children. He knew he would care about the woman.

Love?

Never love for him. For others, yes. Gracie found love with Fletcher Murray. He'd been happy for her. Never thought love was something that could exist for him. When he met Maggie…ah Maggie was so different

310

from any other woman of his acquaintance. She became a part of his soul. So fast he was struck unaware.

Love was not something he anticipated. Love was some abstract thought that a poet invented. Love had always been something to avoid.

He'd been wrong. Love was potent. All-consuming. Love was something a person would give his life to protect. Love was how he felt about Maggie. How Jason, he was positive, felt about Tessa. He wondered if they would have an easy or a difficult journey. Abernathy threatened their existence. He needed to get on with the necessary conversation. Wished to sleep with his almost wife. The devil, she'd been his almost as well as his pretend wife for what now seemed like forever. This scenario must end.

"Everyone find a chair, a place to sit. Come by the bedside. I know Jason understands what I wish to speak to all of you about." Jasper felt as if he needed this conversation to be finished.

His hands clasped together on his stomach Jasper waited. Beside him, Maggie moaned softly then readjusted her position. Jasper rested his hand on her hip. Once all were vacated from the room, he would pull her into his arms. He didn't think he could sleep if she wasn't in his arms. He also needed to speak to his brother without Tessa hearing his words.

"What is it?" Jason had pulled up both of the big overstuffed chairs that sat by the fire. "You need to explain our thoughts about Abernathy?"

Fannie and Nellie sat in one chair while Jason held Tessa on his lap in the other. They all appeared exhausted.

"Jason and I discussed this earlier. We believe your mother tried to sell Maggie to Abernathy. Offered her for something…if not monetary gain what? She was quite put out when that didn't work. I've a feeling she lost a great deal of something in the transaction though I could be wrong."

"Selling our sister?" Nellie asked as she seemed to think over the situation. "Doesn't surprise me. As we've said before, mother never liked us. We understood the engagement would be beneficial to her in some way."

"Anice will wish to recoup her loss," Jason pointed out while his hand stroked Tessa's arm. "If our thinking is correct, she will wish to sell one of the three of you to Abernathy to replace Maggie since the oldest is now beyond her reach."

Jasper continued for his brother. "In lieu of the fact Maggie proved most unbiddable as well as costing a great deal of time not to mention energy in pursuing her, the two of them will be planning that nothing like that will occur a second time."

"Anice will sell him the most biddable of creatures. The daughter who seems to never have an original thought of her own. The one who follows," Jason spoke softly, gazing down at Tessa.

Jasper watched Tessa stiffen then turn to look at his brother. Jason grinned at her. Set his hand on her shoulder. "Don't scowl like that. The look doesn't become your sweetness." He ran his thumb across her brows. "Anice has no clue what a little hellion you are, my love. I do though. I understand that you are far from biddable or meek. You have an independent mind that seems to work nonstop."

It was clear to Jasper Tessa wasn't certain how to respond to his comments. "From what Maggie tells me, Tessa, you don't voice your opinion often. You never initiate a solution to a problem."

Tessa's eyes flashed hot blue sparks. She snorted. "I'm an avid listener. Just because I don't spout out words willy-nilly doesn't mean I can't think for myself. I'm a quiet listener." Tessa seemed bent on defending her position. "Others do not need to know what I'm thinking. It's not important."

"As we've all discovered," Jason said with a smirk. "Now what all this means is that you are the one sister who we believe to be at the greatest risk. I'm not about to let anything happen to you."

Tessa tossed her hair. Jason caught a few strands in the stubble of his beard. Grinned then swept them away. "You are going to stay by my side."

"That's not necessary! I can take care of myself!"

Before all was settled, there would be a skirmish between these two, hopefully not a war.

~ * ~

Jason stood outside Tessa's door while she changed her clothing. He was puzzled by the sudden distance she put between them. When she claimed she didn't need him, her eyes flashed her anger. As soon as the words were uttered, she walked away, her small slender back stiff. She didn't speak to him before she opened the door to her bedroom then marched inside. He caught the door with his foot before she could slam it shut. Didn't have any idea what turned her against him. One moment she'd been relying on him, resting comfortably in his arms. Next she put distance between them.

While he stood in the doorway, Clancy brought a cot from storage for his use in her room. He wasn't going to leave Tessa alone for more than a few seconds even if she was furious with him. The reason for that anger, he wasn't able to fathom. When he did leave her side, he meant to know where she was as well as what she was doing. He would need to stand guard over her until they could marry. In his mind that would be the day after she turned eighteen. In her mind…after the last few minutes he had no idea.

While they sat in Jasper's bedroom listening to the story, he felt a change in Tessa. Not just the stiffening of her small body when she was described as weak as well as biddable. He sensed other small changes. Hoped she would talk to him so they could figure this out. He was ready to marry her to keep her safe the moment their feet touched down on Scottish soil.

Tessa didn't open the door for him after she finished donning her nightgown. He'd expected her to let him know when it was safe for him to enter. Understood she should be dressed as well as in bed by now. Something that was said in the Jasper's room put a bug in her. His guess would be accurate.

Pulling in a deep breath of air, he nudged the door open with his shoulder, peeking around the corner to see where she was. Sure enough, she was in her bed the covers pulled to her chin as if she needed protection from him. He was the least of her worries. Seducing her before she became his wife was not in his plans. Unlike his brother, he intended to wait to make love to her until the vows were said and done. Until after the ceremony as well as the celebration of their nuptials.

"Tessa? You would have left me to stand at your door for the night?" Jason asked as he sat down on the cot to rid himself of his boots. While he intended to sleep in his pants, he wasn't going to wear anything else. Comfort on a damn cot…? Clothing wouldn't help. Sleeping so close to Tessa not being able to hold her wasn't going to improve his disposition.

She snorted. Rose up on her elbows. Light from the moon spattering into the room cast a golden glow across her face and hair. He saw the hard crests of her breasts pushing against the soft white fabric. The sight was one that pleased him. "I don't want you in here. Don't need to be protected from Lord Abernathy. The bartender told us all in that message he said that the man was drinking hard. He won't be around tonight. If I'm going to continue to speak my mind, rather than be meek as well as biddable, I believe Lord Abernathy will return to Glasgow to regroup."

Only a few minutes ago, Tessa was leaning into him, absorbing his strength, relying on him. Earlier she asked for a kiss. What the devil was going on here? He needed to be firm. "A drunk can cause unforeseen problems. Act without logic or rational thought." Again, Jason didn't understand what bee got into her bonnet. "I need to make certain you are not abducted from your bed in the middle of the night. Can't do that from my bedroom." He hated to admit to the fact he was growing angry with her. She was being stubborn. Seemed as if she intended to change everyone's impression of her tonight. He didn't need convincing. Knew already she wasn't biddable. The girl would never bore.

"Are you going to sleep in my room every night for the rest of my life?" She sounded petulant as well as annoyed. "I would think...I want privacy."

Damn right. "Until we are all certain Lord Abernathy has moved on to a new victim. Hoping that won't be one of your sisters. If he marries elsewhere, I'll feel you are safe." By then we will share a room because I've married you."

"Jason, I don't...I want to have a season. Go to a ball or two. Will that happen if you and your brother keep us behind the walls of your townhouse. I'm too young to..." Tessa cut her words off. "Don't want to anger you. I've never danced with a man. Only been kissed by you. I..." Tessa caught her lip beneath her teeth. "There is so much life to live. I want to have...a life before I become a wife."

After that he watched her pass her sweet tongue across her lips. Remembered the taste of her. Knew she was young with a wealth of living to do. Didn't want her to kiss another man. During a season he would get in the way. Be under foot while she flirted with young men wishing to toss her skirts. Knew he would be judgmental. Protective. Damn!

With the last of his thoughts harboring on denying her all she asked for he bit back the sharp reply that was on the tip of his tongue. He would give her whatever she asked for. "We will see. If it's a season you would like, then you shall have one."

His stomach cramped at that loathsome thought.

Epilogue

One week later they were in Glasgow. The small entourage settled into the townhouse. She and Jasper married two days later. She balked at the idea of the wedding taking place when she woke the next morning. The doctor visited. Pronounced her fine.

They heard Lord Abernathy accompanied by Anice left Dublin. Headed, they all assumed for Glasgow. They made no attempt to kidnap any of the three girls. Once they heard that Abernathy was no threat, Tessa insisted that Jason keep to his own bedroom.

Maggie watched the interplay between the new couple with fascination. Tessa refused to talk about the altercation. Overnight she seemed to become a different woman changing in front of everyone. She told her sisters no one would walk over her. Intending to assert her will, she began with Jason.

A year passed. Maggie had indeed been pregnant. She gave birth to a boy. Jasper was thrilled with his heir. Tonight they left the little one with Keir, Jasper's butler and the sweet housekeeper Fia Marshall to attend a ball. All three of her sisters were there along with Jason.

"What do you suppose my brother is thinking?" Jasper asked as he watched Tessa dance around the ballroom with one dandy after another. Jason stood on the sidelines as he'd done for the past year. Watching. Always with his hands behind his back, rocking on his heels. Always with a scowl on his face. One would think that frown would be enough to keep all her possible suitors off her dance card.

"Giving her space as well as time to grow up," Maggie said with a small giggle. "Tessa has managed to bedevil him. She has him beneath her thumb. Wrapped around her fingers. Sometimes he needs to make her see reason. Tessa does want him. Now that she's asserted her independence, she doesn't *ken* how to get Jason back. Tessa has set a path she doesn't know how to get away from."

"I agree. Jason has had incredible patience all this time. I've seen him several times swear beneath his breath. He wants to shake her until she sees things his way. After the end of the day, he wants to take her to his bed. Show her how he feels about her. He is smitten. In love with your sister. He doesn't know what to do about it."

"True and maybe, he should do just that. With his silent permission my sister is treading all over him. Testing her wiles. Making him jealous and enjoying what she is doing to him. She never before had a chance to flirt." Maggie leaned into him thinking they should go home soon. She needed to nurse the *wee* bairn. Was tired. Wanted Jasper to hold her in his arms. Required lovemaking to fall asleep.

"How long do you think this will go on? Another year? Two years? Jason will be insufferable if this lasts another week." Jasper didn't seem to be able to keep his laughter behind his teeth. My brother is on tenterhooks. Exasperated beyond all reason. Wouldn't surprise me if he took a page out of Fletcher's book.

Kidnap her.

Drug her.

Marry her.

"It's been more than a year," Maggie commented. She pointed a finger at Jason. "Look, seems he's headed for the couple. Look at his face. Something is going to happen now. I hope he doesn't embarrass himself."

"Don't think he cares."

"What is he doing?"

"He means to cut in," Jasper said laughing now as he watched the scene unfold. "Appears he's had enough watching. His patience is now over. He's going to create a scene everyone will be talking about for weeks."

"This will be his second dance. Seems Jason is going to make a statement that everyone will understand. He means to tell the world Tessa is his."

Maggie watched as her brother-in-law whirled Tessa toward the terrace. It was cold outside. Another January in Scotland. It didn't seem Jason cared about any of that. A scandal might just bring about the marriage Jason wished for.

"No, look over there." Jasper pointed toward the opposite side of the ballroom. "There is Lord Abernathy."

"Something is going to happen. I don't like this," Maggie's voice trembled. "Does Jason know Abernathy is here?"

"Doubt it."

"You've got to tell him."

"Lord Abernathy hasn't been in the picture since we returned. Heard he was in London seeing to affairs," Jasper watched Abernathy then allowed his gaze to shift to his brother's departing back.

"Wonder what those affairs were. Appears now he has returned," Jasper said. "It's time we brought the sisters home. Maybe lay out a few rules for the ensuing months. Where Tessa is concerned, Jason will take care of her."

Only a few minutes passed before they were settled into two carriages. Alone without her sisters, Maggie leaned into Jasper's arms.

"Can't believe it's been more than a year since we met then married. I love you, Jasper Kenworthy."

"I love you too," he whispered, pulling her onto his lap. "Want to have a little fun in the carriage before we get home. Do you recall our trip into Nass to pick up your sisters? We could recreate the moments."

"You're still a devil. A handsome rogue who will never cease stealing my heart."

"You will always be my Maggie. I love you."

The ride home was much the same as the one they both recalled so vividly.

Coming Soon

Tessa
Good Girls Book Eight

Glasgow 1832

Rain pelted the window. Eerie wind howled around the eaves of the two-story home while lightening slashed in blue-white streaks electrifying the night air. Thunder pounded jarring the stillness. Rain fell from the sky in torrents. The weather fit his turbulent mood, the conflicting emotions raging within.

Jason Kenworthy watched her slight form in the bed he shared at their convenience. He'd been with her the last four years. Ever since her husband passed. The woman lying naked in the bed gave him pleasure. She was sweet. Sincere. Loyal. Sarah was always ready to take him into his arms when he came around to see her. Jason understood he used her to assuage his needs. She never complained. Took unholy advantaged of her giving nature. Depended on her to right his sinking ship this last year. He found he was drowning in the depth of misery. The melancholy was of his own making. He didn't know how to go about changing that. Sarah told him he needed to take the bull by the horns. His huff of air told him he didn't *ken* how to do that. Sarah told him to make it clear how he felt toward the love of his life who danced around him, leading him on by the nose.

Jason reached over to brush a slow caress on Sarah's arm. She shivered as if she was awake and responding to his touch. Toward Sarah there existed a deep tenderness in his heart. His Sarah was a woman he would always care about. If she ever needed him, he would be there for her.

He stepped back. Sarah was beautiful. Her dark brown hair glistened in the candlelight bathing her form, highlighting golden strands that had been bleached by the sun. She defied custom, seldom donning a hat to shade her features while she tended to her flower beds. Gardening was her joy. Her blue eyes were banded around the outside with silver. Her bottom lip a bit too full to be considered fashionable. She possessed a stubborn streak that got her into trouble from time to time.

Earlier this evening she told him he was no longer welcome to see her in the evenings or to entertain her in this big bed. Tonight was the last one they would have together. The lovemaking was bittersweet. In this they were of a like mind. He was ready to cut the entanglement between them. Before he visited Sarah this evening, he knew he was leaving her. This dalliance in her big bed was their last one together.

She told him he sulked. Well, he did. After spending his days at his home, he needed a bright spot in the evenings. Sarah provided to be that tiny bit of light that brought him out of the depression his life had become. Jason understood he couldn't hide behind her skirts any longer. He needed to face his future. Tessa MacRae was that future. He just didn't know how to go about doing convincing Tessa it was time for her to make a decision concerning them. What he saw in Sarah's eyes told him he might well be in for a lecture on his behavior. He didn't need anyone to expound on his misconduct.

Sarah pushed hair behind her ears while she brought it a deep breath of air. "It's been more than a year, Jason. You've done nothing to right the matter that has you befuddled. Are you going to allow another year to pass you by before you do something about the *wee tendre* you have for the lass? You cannot continue in this vein. I will no longer support what you are doing to yourself. You've become less of a person. You do not belong in my bed when your heart is elsewhere."

"…and…" Jason pulled on his boots while he debated with himself over the necessity to tell her the truth. "What am I doing to myself?" The *tendre* was far from little. He was head-over-heels smitten with Tessa MacRae. Sometime in the last year, the little flirt withdrew into herself. She changed. He didn't know how to reach her. After the first few weeks with her here in Glasgow, he thought he would be wed to her by the year's end.

"Sulking," she replied so quick the word stole his breath. She reached for a full glass of wine sitting on her nightstand. Before they made love, she'd not tasted the drink seeming to understand this time would be the last time. She sipped now, closed her eyes as she let the red burgundy slide down her throat, seeming to savor the slow glide. "You have been brooding for the last year. Take the lass by the hand then explain your feelings. Lay down the law. She might well be thankful. Perhaps she is in as much a quandary as you."

Unable to help himself, he snorted his aversion. *Sulking?* No matter his thoughts to the contrary, what she said was true. He would have called his mood brooding. No matter, the words presented the right picture as to his frame of mind. "If you must know, I asked Tessa to marry me." He found himself hoping for sympathy or empathy at the least. From Sarah, he wasn't likely to get any type of emotion. She always called the situation as she saw it.

As she smiled, the small dimple on the left side of her mouth deepened. While she tapped the crystal with the tip of her nail, she seemed to be thinking. Before Sarah spoke, she set her head to a slight angle. Pursed her lips before she spoke, "Let me get this right. Tessa said no to your proposal. Was it romantic? I daresay, knowing you the request was anything but. Blurted the words out, did you? Ah, I see by the glint in your eyes that's what happened. You gave up with one try. Correct me if I'm wrong. Over a year ago she fancied herself in love with you. How long ago was the question popped?" Sara sat up pulling the sheet around her, tucking the fabric beneath her arms to cover her generous breasts. He'd miss burying himself in her bosom. Ah, but there was always Tessa's if he could changer her way of thinking.

For a tick of the clock on the mantle, Jason was surprised by Sarah's actions. In his presence, she never covered herself. He supposed that was another sign this relationship had seen its last days. "Six months, give or take a week or two." He didn't understand why he told her. Four years of sharing confidences was most likely the reason behind his confession.

"That long? You are resigned to remaining a bachelor. Hmm... I would not have expected that after you returned from Ireland. Why haven't you asked her again? Seems that half a year ago, she was in the midst of her season. Of course, she wouldn't agree." The rest of her wine disappeared down her throat. She set the glass on the table. Touched a small drop that was heading down the glass. Brought that bit of wine to her mouth.

"Suppose I am, at least for the time being. Tessa spends her free time alone. If I seek her out to talk with her, she tells me she's busy. Need to find some means to coax the Tessa that I know from her hidey-hole. She's pouting about something." He tied his cravat then tucked his shirt into his britches. "Tessa is so quiet. Reserved. Never fails to surprise me when she asserts herself. I'm of the opinion all she wishes to do is curl up by the fire with a good book. From earlier experiences with her, I know she is vibrant. Alive with curiosity. Don't understand where that woman has disappeared."

"Are you giving up on Tessa? Is the young lady not worth a bit more effort? As you just said, coax her from her hiding place. Find out the truth. Tell her how you feel. If you don't, I've a mind to pay her a visit. Someone or something needs to shake the two of you out of the hole that's been dug." Sarah smoothed the big quilt that was covering her with her hands. Her nails were well-manicured. Buffed to shine. Without closing his eyes, he knew in detail what Sarah now hid from his view. The thought of her naked beneath the covering did nothing to arouse. With this new discovery, he turned a major hurdle in his life. Thinking of Tessa set him on fire.

While he looked for his frock coat, he turned to Sarah. He felt the need to defend himself. Waved his hand through the air. Unable to understand the direction of his anger, "You don't understand anything."

Her hefty laugh caught him off guard. To Jason there was nothing humorous about his relationship with the disagreeing woman who bedeviled his life. Sarah's brows drew together as she spoke all humor cast aside. She cleared her throat before continuing with her lecture, "On the contrary, I understand all you've told me. It's what you don't say that I can't comprehend. There is much you are keeping to yourself. Which is your right." She lowered her lashes before opening them. "You should…"

Sarah was going to tell him to leave. The discussion would go nowhere. "Yes…well…" He thought of the way he saw Tessa the other night. Past midnight she showed up in the library wearing her night clothing. He'd wanted to pull her into his arms. Kiss her. Fighting for control at the time, he did nothing. "Some thoughts are private. Restricted to the two participants involved. You know more than you should."

"Have you kissed the *wee* lass?"

Jason choked on her question. Over the year, he'd thought of little else. A purpose, Sarah pushed his patience. "You are prying, madam. I would never kiss and tell." He'd kissed her, yes. Not enough times to suit him. It wasn't that she shied away. The reason was…hell if he kissed her again, he might not stop with a brush of the lips or even a deep taste of her. When he saw her, he ached for what he couldn't have until they wed. She refused him. When she was near, he felt the need to test the curve of her hip. Wished to hold her breasts in his hands. Feel the humid softness between her legs.

Sarah lifted her shoulders in a feminine gesture that used to make him hard. "Make love to her. Get her with child. That would set events in motion that could never be stopped." Sarah sent him a sly smile. "You are a nice man. You deserve some measure of happiness. For some unbeknownst reason, she is playing you for a fool. Find out what keeps her from committing. In that way, you'll be able to fight. Until you know the truth about what hold her back, you are at a disadvantage."

"I've considered your proposal. Getting her with child. Considering then doing are far different scenarios. Good God, she is living beneath my roof." Jason rubbed his hand on his chin thinking. He could never impregnate the lass in order to get her to the alter. To force her was repulsive to him. He did want her in his bed. Damn tired of waiting for her to grow up. Now that she seemed to reach that state, she didn't want anything to do with him.

"You won't act on it though. Too much the gentleman. You should forget that fact about your nature. Your twin did…forget. Seems the bedding came before the wedding. They are in love. Aren't they?"

His waistcoat went over his shirt. Yes, Maggie and Jasper were in love. The baby, conceived from their stay in Ireland, learning to sit was comical. He was more determined to do right by Tessa. "I won't compromise Tessa for my own ends. Can't do that to her. Don't wish to force her hand. If she walks down the aisle to me, she must be willing."

Jason bent over to brush a gentle kiss across her lips. "Good bye, Sarah. I'd send you a parting gift if you won't yell at me." Jason found himself grinning at her. He understood how she'd reply to his outrageous suggestion. Over the four years he'd been seeing her, she'd accepted gifts only on her birthday along with Christmas.

Her stiffening shoulders along with the tightening of her brows told him she was not agreeable to a goodbye present. "I'm not under your protection. Not your mistress. Never have been. I make my own way. You *ken* that."

The long whisper of air that left his lungs didn't make him feel any better. Her scowl left him winded then wishing for something that could never be. Perhaps he would send her something anyway. A gift might put a smile on her face. If nothing else, the small present might serve to remind her of him. Jason settled on that idea as being perfect. Tomorrow afternoon, he would search for the perfect gift. She didn't need jewelry. Something to remember him by. Something she couldn't send back to him. He would figure it out.

"Will you be at the Laughton's ball?" Needed a change of subject after speaking of presents. Though he wasn't looking to a future with Sarah, he would miss her company. A dance might ease his mind. If he saw her with another man, he might not feel such a cad for his desertion from her bed.

"Of course. I would not miss the event. That ball was a favorite of my late husband. Lady Laughton is a dear friend of mine."

This time she sounded indignant. Sarah was drawing into herself as they finished the conversation. The time had come for him to let himself out the door.

"I'll find the door for myself. No need to get up," Jason told her as he bowed in the open doorway before leaving the room. "Take care of yourself, Sarah."

A few minutes later, Jason stepped into the cold night air. The weather was not so cold, just stormy. The rain that pelted the windows earlier died to a thin mist. The storm seemed to have moved on to different territory. During his conversation with Sarah, a weight seemed to be lifted off his shoulders. He felt lighter. Figuring out Tessa's change of heart would be his sole purpose until the knowledge came to him. Maybe he should kidnap her. Take her to Ireland. The cottage was still there. The ploy worked for his brother.

Jason motioned for his driver to follow him. He needed to walk for a time while he cleared his thoughts. Wasn't about to walk the miles to his home. He had to think about Tessa. A plan of action might be nice. Jasper, his twin, talked about moving to the country for the summer months. A respite in the clear air away from the city would be welcome. A change of scenery might distance Tessa from whatever was troubling her. The travel would take the girls away from their summer entertainments, the soirees they disliked. None of the girls enjoyed the crush of the season. During the summer months the number of entertainments diminished. Jason didn't think any of them would be devastated by that.

If Jasper moved Maggie and the baby, he would follow. Since Maggie's sisters were under the guardianship of Jasper, they would have no choice. Though Nellie along with Fannie were old enough to not need a guardian, the protection was the necessary catalyst. Even in the country, there would be activities to contend with. The nice thing most would be during the early morning hours when the weather was not too hot. They could visit with the Murrays. Play some lawn tennis. He wondered if any of the girls ever played before. He enjoyed the game. The Murray men took the game to a different level.

Tessa would come along. Yes, a move to the country would be nice, very nice indeed. He would find the time to get to know her better. Jason felt less out of sorts now that he plotted a course of action. There would be extra moments where he could walk with Tessa. If she enjoyed riding, there were numerous trails to explore. Perhaps steal a kiss or two away from the curious eyes of her sisters.

During their strolls, she would open up to him about whatever it was that was troubling her. Something was bothering her. He had no doubts about that. Getting to the bottom of her difficulties would be his mission this summer. He didn't appreciate feeling as if he was on tenterhooks. While he wasn't the serious twin by far, he did possess a smidgeon of that singular attribute. Knowing why Tessa was acting the way she was took up a major portion of his thoughts during the day as well as the nights. An end to this scenario was a necessity. He was ready for a wife.

Knowing he needed to get home, he signaled for his driver to stop so he could climb into the carriage. He did so just as the wind changed and a gust of rain showered down on them. Perfect timing if he did say so himself. For the rest of the journey home, Jason set his head on the back of the seat then closed his eyes. He meant to relax. The hour was not that late. He could settle in the library with a snifter of brandy. If he got lucky, Tessa might join him. The plan could begin tonight.

During the next ten minutes, Jason listened to the sounds

surrounding him. Heard the steady beat of the rain on the roof. The clip clop of the horses' hooves on the cobblestone street. Waited for the carriage to turn into the drive leading to the townhouse.

After he entered the house, he made his way to the library half hoping Tessa would be curled up on the big overstuffed chair she favored. Half hoping she would be sound asleep in her bed so he could wait for the inevitable encounter. In her room she wouldn't serve as a temptation for his lust. If he didn't see her, he wouldn't want her in the most elemental ways.

That was part and parcel the problem. Jason needed to know if what he felt for Tessa went deeper than lust. Had to know if Tess had a *tendre* for him. A year ago, he thought she did. She'd been curious about kissing. About him. Believed that by the end of the year they would be engaged. A wedding would be planned. In the present, he was farther away from her in spirit than he'd been on their first meeting.

In the library, he splashed two fingers of brandy into a snifter. Sipped. Swallowed. Felt the heat of the drink rush down his throat. Sipped again before walking to Tessa's favorite chair. She was not sitting in it, waiting for him. Looking up toward her room, he thought perhaps she'd retired for the night.

Just as well. It would never do for the two of them to be together alone at this time of night. He still needed to figure out his plans. Stay in the city or go to the country? What a conundrum? Going to the country seemed to be his preference. What if she refused? He couldn't leave her here to fend for herself. She still needed protection from Lord Nelson Abernathy.

He heard the rustle of footsteps outside the door. Reached for the knife he kept tucked into his boot. With silent footsteps he made his way to the door. Whoever was out there was not wasting time on trying to hide the fact they were intruding. The door creaked open. When he recognized the wealth of light blond hair, he sucked in his air.

"What are you doing?" Under the circumstance, his voice sounded harsher than he wished. With as much aplomb as possible he placed the knife back into his boot.

When she looked up at him her blue eyes were clouded over. He saw no sparkle in the depth. Hadn't seen that sly semi-mischievous look that Tessa used to toss his way for a very long time. Who stole her vivacity. These last month's Tessa became a shadow of herself. Did he do this to her?

"I could ask you the same. It's late." Tessa took the crystal glass from him then drank. She closed her eyes as the liquid slid down her throat. When she opened them again, he was certain she wished to tell him something of importance. Instead, she turned away, shuttering her expression.

"You went out without a chaperone?" The accusation was there. His gut clenched at his question, at the realization she was alone. Lord Nelson Abernathy was still a threat to her. She needed to take care every time she ventured from her home. Tessa was not a prisoner. She could still come and go as she pleased. Both he and his twin warned her of the dangers awaiting her with one slip up.

She seemed to take umbrage with his question. Sent him a fierce little scowl. Tessa would do the same with his thoughts if he spoke them. "My mother sent her driver for me. I was safe." She unfastened her cloak then shook it out sending a pattern of tiny raindrops on the floor. After that she walked to the sideboard, filled his glass then poured one for herself. Turning she leaned against the wood, watching him. Seeming to wait for more words to sputter from his lips. That wasn't going to happen. She had every right to her opinion, even though he understood it to be wrong.

Strands of Tessa's thick blond hair loosened from the chignon tumbled down her back to reach her waist. She was slim, not coltish as she was a year ago. Her body filled out over the past months. Curved in all the right places for a man's hands to enjoy. What Jason liked best about her was the vibrancy in her eyes. Now, when he looked at her, hunted for what he'd come to admire, the life was gone. Vanished. He needed to discover the reason. Needed to know how the spark was stolen.

Several questions about her whereabouts this evening rambled through his head. The first one being why did she venture out in this storm to see a woman she disliked? None of the girls held good feelings for their mother. The second being, why the devil did she believe herself to be safe? That was the farthest notion from the truth he could think of. Lord Abernathy made it clear he was no longer interested in any of the MacRae girls as a wife. That didn't mean he lost interest in them as a conquest.

Not about to argue with her this evening or any other one, "If you say." Jason wasn't agreeing with her. He was giving her the right to a different opinion than his own. "However, next time, I would suggest you tell either Jasper or myself when you intend to leave as well as your destination. Even if it's seeing your mother." He paused as he watched the change of expressions across her face. "Especially if it's to see Anice. We both understand the woman cannot be trusted." His gut clenched at the thought of Tessa falling victim to the woman.

"You don't trust my mother." Her small voice held an accusing edge to the tone. She rubbed the back of her neck as if tension knots settled there.

If he could, he'd ease those muscles. Jason felt side-swiped by her statement. After all that had gone on over the last year, Tessa should never put her faith in that woman. Again, no reason to raise his voice or put forth his sentiments on the ghastly topic. Confronting her with her feelings for the woman seemed important.

"Do you? You know as well as I that she is a pariah." Anice was a man eater. Did seem to hold a tender spot in her heart for her daughters. A very tiny tender spot. She was willing to hand them over to any man for her personal gain. That fact was repellent. A great distance from what could be termed motherly love. Anice had no redeeming qualities as far as he was concerned.

A small breathy sigh waffled from Tessa's lips. Her shoulders slumped as if in defeat. "I don't either. Trust her." Tessa took a moment to drink more of the brandy she poured. "She is my mother. If she asks to see me, I can't refuse her. There are times I miss her. She can be nice. Last year, Christmas morning, after she figured out none of us knew where Maggie ran off too, she relented. She let us eat more than bread and water. We opened the presents under the tree."

At that never previously divulged bit of information the air he sucked into his lungs served to choke him. Anice punished the girls by not allowing them food, a basic need. "If she is getting what she wants," Jason sat down again. Studied the woman who bedeviled him for more than a year now. "Let me get this straight just to clarify. If Anice is getting what she wants then the woman is nice."

"Mother almost always gets what she wants. That doesn't ever make her nice. Makes her arrogant. Mean. What are you doing here?" Tessa looked on her hands resting in her lap then through the flutter of her lashes peered his way. "Thought you would be with your friend, Sarah. Did something happen?"

Little minx, she was flirting with him. Even heard what might be a smidgeon of jealousy in her tone. For the beat of his racing heart, he was taken aback by her question. She shouldn't know anything about his lady friend or her name. Jasper never would have mentioned Sarah. He sure as hell didn't. "What do you know about my...friend?" The fact Tessa asked questions about Sarah terrified. He never mentioned her. What she was doing was plying him for more information.

Tessa lifted her lily white shoulders in an indifferent gesture. With quiet confidence, she sipped he brandy. "Nothing much. Is she pretty?" The question was stated once more beneath the flutter of her dark lashes.

Jason wasn't certain if he was about to dig his grave where Tessa's feelings for him were concerned. Treading with light footsteps would be his best advice to himself. He wasn't about to lie to her. Neither was he going to tell her anything she didn't ask. He supposed she did deserve answers. If she agreed to marriage, he wouldn't hold anything back. Now, his relationship with her was tentative at best. Nonexistent at its worst. At times they spoke. In the present, that was all there was between them. To get to the depth of his relationship with Sarah, she would need to ask him things she would not feel comfortable asking. He hoped she would confide in him also.

"Very lovely."

Her lashes jerked up telling him his answer surprised her. She must not have expected a response. The widening of her eyes confirmed his conjecture. On the way to her mouth to sip a portion of her drink, her hand trembled. Beneath those fluttering lashes there were more questions.

"You are seeing a woman?" With her hands, she pressed the fabric of her gown. "Never mind, I don't..."

True, she might not want to know the answer. In this case, she might. If she cared anything for him, she would appreciate what he was about to say. "No." He wouldn't offer her the information that this was the last night he would visit Sarah. She would have to be more explicit in her questions.

She appeared stunned by his answer. "Do you lie?" The crease lines in the middle of her forehead deepened.

Jason thought it would be nice to pass his finger along them, soften them until she had no more concerns. "No." He found himself shaking his head at the statement a small smile forming. "No, Tessa, I do not lie."

"You were seeing a woman. A lovely woman." Her voice was a whisper thing exhale of air quivering on the last words.

For a blink his heart stopped. This was a question he didn't wish to answer. He could ignore. Discounting would be too close to a lie to suit. "Yes."

Tessa face turned ashen. Her eyes narrowed. She sent her tongue across her lips, moistening them before she sipped more of the potent brandy. The pause was long, tiresome. "Like…like that…way?"

Jason kept the amused chuckle stuck in his throat. Tessa wanted to know if they had sex. Didn't quite know how to ask the imposing question. She probably wanted to know more. She was innocent. He wasn't going to change that fact this evening. He fiddled with his glass, rolled the crystal between his hands while he watched the amber liquid play with the light from the fire. When he felt in control of his emotions, he spoke his heart. "Ask me what you wish to know. Be specific. Don't hedge when you have the words. Cannot guarantee you'll appreciate the answer. While we are discussing my past, don't forget I asked you to marry me. I'll be honest with you. Promise." His voice was gruffer than he wished. She was delving into his personal life. One that just this evening he put an end to. Sarah was a fond memory. Nothing more. Tessa was his future if she would allow that to happen.

One more time she whetted her mouth while she tried to drum up courage, lips glistening with the moisture her tongue left behind. Her eyes wide, "Did you fornicate with her?" Tessa did blurt the words that shocked him to the tips of his toes.

Brandy flew from his mouth. Drops splattered on his white silk shirt. He tried to wipe them away with the palms of his hands. Had never expected such a question. To his surprise Tessa stood behind him, pounding him on the back with her tiny hands. She thumped him a couple of times before he stopped wheezing. Jason grabbed her hand. She was stronger than expected. Her little fist packed a wallop. "I'm fine."

"You don't look fine."

"Trust me. I'm just dandy." *Did he fornicate with Sarah?* Well, that was one way to put what they did. The words seemed crude. What they did together never reached the level of fornication. Between them there was tenderness along with caring. He cared for Sarah. Would never hurt her even though he did admit he took advantage of her. They both had physical needs.

Tessa seemed to be over her concern for his wellbeing. She faced him, her chin tilted upward while she demanded the answer. "Well? Did you?" She persisted with this line of questioning. "Fornicate?"

"Can you not come up with a different way of putting the act of making love? I would not wish to put what was done together in that obscene vein." Sexual games were many and varied. Sarah was a sensual passionate woman. There intimate relationship shouldn't be brought down to that level.

"Well?" Tessa persisted, her voice taking on an edge he didn't recognize. She persisted. "Did you?"

If he didn't misunderstand the emotion, Tessa was angry. He cleared his throat more than one time before he could speak. "We were intimate, yes." Jason held up his hands either in surrender or in hopes she wouldn't ask for details. Good God, the word she used for something very special. Who gave her that word? The only person who came to mind was her mother, Anice. It would be just like Anice to call the intimate act of making love fornicating.

Her face turned a mottled shade of red. That was good. A true innocent could never use that word without becoming flushed. Maybe she had nothing else in her arsenal she could substitute. What the devil was he going to say if she asked him anything else?

"So...so you did do it...fornicate." Tessa was studying her hands which were wrapped together in such a tight clasp that her knuckles were turning white before his eyes. Now, it didn't seem she would look up. He wanted to step closer to her. Put his fingers beneath her chin to tilt her head higher. Wished he could see into her eyes.

Needing to clarify, he began, "We are done. I won't bed her again. Tonight, we both decided we would no longer see each other. We don't suit. The decision was mutual. This is more than I should tell you. More than you should know. If you agreed to my proposal six months ago, I would have ceased my nightly visits." To his surprise, Jason felt his own flush of embarrassment at the revelation. His face heated. Something unusual for him. Couldn't recall the last time he blushed. He never considered what he did in bed with a woman as fornicating. With women, he had a slow hand. Never left his lover unsatisfied. His touch was easy, gentle. He always saw to their pleasure first. Thought of himself as a considerate lover.

This woman, the one standing in front of him, drinking his brandy, was the woman he wanted in his bed as well as his life. Just as he could have done a year ago, he could take her into his arms. Kiss her until she wanted what he wanted. Make love to her. He pushed the promiscuous lock of hair from his eyes instead of ridding himself of wayward thoughts.

"Why?" Tessa downed what was left of the brandy. She sat down in a plop as if she didn't have the energy to remain standing.

The question was blunt as well as to the point. Why? Why did he call off the relationship or why did he make love to her? Because Sarah wasn't the woman he needed in his bed. Sarah served her purpose. Earlier, he admitted to the fact he used her. Sarah used him also. She needed him to warm her bed in the lonely nights that stretched in front of her after her husband's death.

"She was willing."

"Is that all that is needed? A woman to be willing?" Tessa questioned while she continued to direct her frown his way.

Not wishing to continue in that vein, he didn't answer with a direct word of yes or no. "Sarah is a sweet woman. I cared for her. She is still important to me. We filled a need for each other that was left vacant." More than most would ever know. Only his brother understood what Sarah meant to him. Tessa would never understand what he was saying. There was a time he wished he loved Sarah enough to marry her. The fact he thought of marrying her never mattered. Sarah was adamant in her denials of marriage. She'd told him she was independent now, a free woman. Needed for her life to remain that way. All the wealth from her deceased husband was hers. Even though he had more at his disposal than she, Sarah didn't want marriage even to increase her wealth. One husband, for her, was enough. Didn't need or want anything she didn't have.

"I'm willing." Tessa stepped forward. Her finger wrestled with the buttons on her blouse. One popped free then another. "I want you to fornicate with me." She continued unfastening her blouse until a creamy expanse of skin was revealed. Her silk chemise did little to cover her breasts.

Struck wordless by her actions, he coughed. Clutched at his mind for something to say he wouldn't come to regret in the morning. He wasn't about to do her bidding. She wasn't ready for sex. Someone put her up to this. Anice came to mind. He didn't understand what bug got into her. Good God, did she understand what she was asking. No, Tessa wasn't asking. She was showing.

The stubborn glint he'd come to know over the course of the year he'd been with her was shining crystal clear in her sky-blue eyes that were no longer vacant. More buttons were coming unfastened. This wasn't the time for her to disrobe. He had no intention of carrying out Sarah's wicked thoughts of getting Tessa with child so she would have to marry him. A forced marriage was not in his plans. He wanted her willing compliance, yes. Nothing less would do. This evening, he didn't understand her intent.

Stepping forward, he clasped her hands in his. Held them away from her, behind her back. That was a mistake. Her breasts pushed forward. The softness against his chest beckoned to a starving man. "No, not tonight. Not like this."

The soft sheen of moisture in her eyes terrified him. Something else was at play here. He wondered again if it had anything to do with her visit to her mother. "No, Tessa. I'm not going to let you hurt yourself. Won't use you like this. Despite your actions, I know you don't want to have sex without benefit of marriage. You've always maintained that you would hold your innocence close to your heart. You need a real wedding night. Not a dalliance." He caught another glimpse of tender white flesh. Through her silk chemise he saw the rosy tips of her nipples. Her breasts were round, firm. Bigger than he thought they would be. She was so slender.

A tear slipped down her cheek. With his thumb he whisked the silver droplet away. "I've been…" The words that she didn't finish caught in her throat.

"Why the sudden need to…?" He couldn't say the word she used. When he let go of her hands they moved to the buttons. This time she fastened them.

"Believe I'll go to my room." Her voice was harsh. He saw her mortification. The emotion was etched in her expression.

Jason wasn't ready to let her run from him. Answers were needed. "What did your mother say to you?" He reached out to stop her. Caught her elbow. Turned her so she faced him again. The need to know why all this was happening threatened his calm exterior. Anice must have said something that had Tessa reeling. The facts pointed to something unnerving her. She had never started to disrobe in front of him. Never spoke of intimate acts between a man and a woman.

"N-nothing."

Under the circumstances and with the softest voice he could manage, he spoke to her, "Little liar. Anice told you to do this. I know. What is she holding over your head? Whatever she wants, together we will fight your mother." He held his breath while he waited for an answer that wasn't going to appease him. Anice didn't deserve such beautiful daughters.

"N-nothing."

"That's not an answer. Why don't you sit. Drink another brandy. Think about telling me what happened that has you acting so out of character." With each unsteady breath Tessa inhaled, his determination to remain calm faltered.

"No, I don't want another drink. Don't wish to sit. I'm leaving." She whirled. Stumbled on legs that appeared to wobble. She grasped for the back of a chair. Managed to right herself.

Jason wasn't all that certain Tessa would make it to her room. He could keep her here. What possible good would that do? He couldn't make her talk. Despite his misgivings, he watched her walk out the door.

Not only did he hurt her feelings this evening, he humiliated her when he stopped her from giving herself to him. She reached out to him. In the process, he felt as if he slapped her in the face by denying her what she tried to gift him with. If he believed this was her idea, he might have given it consideration.

Frustrated, desperate to learn why, he threw the glass at the fireplace. The delicate crystal shattered into tiny shards clattering to the hearth then the floor. He set his forearm on the brick mantel before burying his head on his arm. Long rasps of air filled his lungs while he searched his head for some way he could have proceeded in a different manner.

~ * ~

For Tessa her evening went from good to bad then moved on to very, very bad. Sitting on her bed after her mortification at Jason's behalf, she allowed her mind to travel over the events of the day. No, Jason wasn't at fault. She gambled on one last fleeting hope then lost. If given a chance, there was so much she would do different. First and foremost, she would never have gone to see her mother if she'd known Anice's plans for her.

People always spoke of hindsight. She made the worst decision of her life. Now, she would pay. Her mother would wring her dry. She could never fall into her mother's plans. How to avoid doing that Tessa was unable to grasp.

Back to the good part of the last ten hours. The beginning of her day brought light to her eyes coupled with joy to her heart. She laughed. Felt carefree. For now, she didn't intend to do any more thinking about her mother along with all she told her. Recalling the good parts was her intention.

Her sisters were in her bedroom with her, chatting nonstop about whatever popped into their heads. They all enjoyed the debutant scene. The dancing. The men all decked out in their best finery. Both loved flirting with the line of men seeking a wife. Neither planned on making a choice any day soon. The time was nearing the dinner hour. They each had a small glass of sherry in hand. Tessa added a log to the cheery fire.

Standing back, hands clasped in front of her, her thoughts were on Jason. The red-gold flames danced in the hearth. She was in love with the man. Had been since the moment she saw him. True, she told him no to the proposal. True, doing so was more difficult than she expected. She wanted what their oldest sister had…love. Jason didn't seem ready or willing to give his love, only his protection. She couldn't live with that. In Tessa's mind, a marriage would never last without love. She could site her mother and father's marriage as an example. There was no love between the two, only bitter hatred.

"The Laughton's ball is coming up next week. Do you think we'll be going?" Nellie asked as she concentrated her attention on Tessa then her sherry. "I've a new gown being made for the occasion. The green silk brings out the color of my eyes. That's what Maggie told me. I for one am excited. Hope we don't move to the country before then."

Move to the country? She hadn't heard about a departure from the city. Tessa felt a dreamy wave pass through her at the prospect of the ball. "I'd like to dance with Jason," Tessa said as she wove dreams in her head. Wanted to feel his arms around her. Sway to the music with him. Needed to feel the warmth of his body while he twirled her around the dance floor. Didn't intend going down the marriage path unless the man loved her. From what little Maggie told her when she wasn't busy with her husband and now her baby, love was something to hold out for. Maggie told them all she'd loved Jasper almost from the first time she buried her nose against his shoulder then felt the heat of his body, knew his protection would be strong. Would last a lifetime. Protection was nice. She needed love to sustain her.

"Jason this…Jason that," Fannie said laughing as she spoke. "One would think you didn't have a coherent thought in your brain unless it revolved around Jason. He's all you ever talk about." Fannie was putting finishing touches on her needlework. She let her work rest in her lap. "I would that I had that problem."

"True. I do think about him most every second of every day." Tessa would go only so far in her thoughts about the man who stole her heart over a year ago. She was so ignorant of what went on between a man and a woman. Maggie told her she was innocent and that wasn't a bad way to be. In time, Jason would teach her what she needed to learn. She was eager. Impatient. Before she committed, needing everything to be perfect.

"True?" Nellie laughed again. "Is that all you can say?" She leaned forward her glass resting in a precarious manner between her fingers. "What I don't understand is why that besotted man…he is besotted with you… has not asked you to marry him. Thought he would have done so by now. We all know he's wanted you for more than a year…the way he looks at you tells the story. Still, he goes to see his lover in the evenings leaving you here."

Lover? Goes to see her in the evenings?

"He has. Twice. Asked me to marry him. What's that about a lover he is seeing?" Tessa cringed at the reaction of her sisters. Before this afternoon, she'd never told her favorite people in the entire world that truth. Now, they told her, Jason went to see a woman in the evenings. That was where he was off to when she couldn't find him.

When she began recounting her day, she never intended to dwell on anything that made her unhappy. That was unfortunate part about today. Bad news thrived.

Fannie rose, took the glass from her hand. "Then why aren't we planning a wedding? If he's asked, we should be picking out gowns, planning the wedding, deciding on the colors and everything else that needs to be done beforehand. The two of you are not running off to Gretna Green… Are you?" She refilled the glass. Handed it back to her. "Would like to understand the truth here."

"Jason doesn't love me. What did you say about a lover?" Her voice cracked with the seeds of humiliation. That couldn't be true. He would never ask her to marry him then keep a mistress on the side. Would he? She was far too uncertain of the ways of men. Her mother always was off seeing people. Was he seeing another woman? Now, the fact seemed obvious to her.

"Of course he loves you. We shouldn't have said anything," this from Nellie who sounded indignant. She was waving her hand in the air. "That man dotes on you. When the two of you are in the same room, he never takes his gaze away from you. If that's not love, I don't know what is. As to his lover, a man has needs. I've heard talk about that at some of the galas we've been to."

She huffed out a breath of air. "Staring at a person does not translate to love. What do you know about this lover of his?" Tessa said, her voice soft. The hurt she felt was tangible. Jason treated her with care along with consideration as to her feelings. When he asked for her hand in marriage, he never got down on one knee. She didn't understand why that was important to her. What she did comprehend was that love was the single most important factor in deciding to marry. So far, the words were not said. Now her sisters spouted about a lover. She didn't intend to let this go. She wasn't going to have a life such as the one her mother had.

"True. Lord Abernathy stares at all of us when we are in the same room. He makes my skin crawl. Never fails to raise goose bumps on my arms. Jasper says we still need to take care that we don't put ourselves in a precarious position where that man is concerned," Fanny said while she shot a look at her. Sipped her drink. "Might as well tell you what you want to know. We heard Jasper arguing with Jason about the woman. Jasper told him he needed to let her go. Said she wouldn't mind."

"Yes, Jasper told his twin he should end the affair," Nellie continued the conversation. "He should end it if he truly wants you. Can't have a lover along with a wife at the same time. Not right. Not right a'tall. Is what Jasper said."

"I wouldn't stand for it," Fannie spoke up with a small giggle. "Not that a wife ever has much of a say in matters of the heart where the husband is concerned. We all *ken* mother wasn't faithful. Father never seemed to care. He seemed happy to be well rid of mother. She is difficult to get along with."

With those words, Tessa found herself rubbing her arms where goose bumps appeared out of nowhere. Both conversations sent shivers down her spine. She didn't wish to think of Jason with another woman. Couldn't stand to think of Lord Abernathy at all. "Me too. My skin does react when I'm around Lord Abernathy. The small hairs at the nape of my neck stand on end. No matter how hard I try, I cannot forget how close Maggie came to being wed to that man. If not for Jasper…" Her voice trailed off. Abernathy wanted her a year ago. Now, from what she heard, he no longer wished to marry her. He wanted her as a mistress. That would never happen. Jason wouldn't allow something so dreadful even if he didn't love her.

"Neither can any of us…forget. Jasper saved Maggie's life by stepping into a situation fraught with danger. When he reached out to help Maggie, he didn't know who she was. Believed her to be homeless. That night changed all our lives," Tessa relived those terrifying days when they didn't know if Maggie was alive or dead. Didn't know if Lord Abernathy found her then hid her away somewhere. Jasper spirited her out of the country to keep her away from Lord Abernathy along with his disgusting plans to marry her. The couple fell in love.

"Let's get back to something more enjoyable," Nellie said interrupting the next wave of nostalgia. "Thoughts of Lord Abernathy leaves my stomach churning. Don't need that to ruin my dinner. You danced with the viscount more than once," she looked to Fannie, grinning at her sister's look of discomfiture. Tilting her head a bit, she asked "Do you have a *tendre* for the man? What's his name? Leo?"

"Heavens no, no *tendre* for me. This man didn't step on me feet, that's why I danced with him more than once. Yes, his name is Leonard. His friends called him Leo. All the other hopefuls bruised my toes. Left me with the feeling they wanted just one thing from me, my body," Fannie laughed while she stuck her bare feet in the air to wiggle her toes. "The man is too old for…" she stopped seeming to realize the huge differences in ages between Tessa and Jason.

Tessa waved her arm in the air to silence any further comments before she could say anything. "Age doesn't matter if the two involved in the relationship love each other. Like Maggie and Jason," she finished then needing reassurance from her sisters as well as her best friends, "Do you think age makes that much difference? I don't feel the difference so much with Jason." the question erupted on a weak thread. If Jason was seeing another woman, he didn't love her. She understood that for a fact.

In unison the two sisters blurted. "Of course not!"

"Love is the important factor, you're right," Nellie added in agreement then finished her sherry. She set the glass down with an emphatic bang. "I'm not going to settle for anything less than love. Neither should the rest of you."

"Love is all important," Fannie granted in compliance with her two sisters.

"Love…" Tessa sighed wishing for something that wasn't going to happen. Her hands were clasped beneath her chin. Jason was never going to fall in love with her even though it was obvious even to her the man wanted her. His eyes blazed, changed colors when he looked at her. The way he gazed on her warmed her until she burned. Her blood rushed through her at blinding speed. Tessa in her unworldliness didn't understand what that entailed. She was willing to learn even though she'd been taught from the cradle a woman shouldn't give her body to a man before she wed.

The missive requiring her presence at her mother's home came ten minutes after her sisters left to dress for dinner. What she should have done was toss the letter into the fire. Instead, she wrote a quick note to her sisters telling them she was fine. Afraid of a lecture when she returned, she didn't tell them where she was going. Told them she would be home as soon as possible. They would guess though. Where else would she go? If confronted, she would never be able to lie.

The ride in the carriage seemed to take an eternity, her mind racing with the potential reasons for her summons. Tessa was aware of the sounds flitting along the streets. Saw the fires from the homeless who milled around the flames attempting to warm themselves. Couldn't help but think back on the night Maggie met Jasper. Hacks driven recklessly passed by them. Young men out for a good time walked the streets in search of whatever entertainment they could find. The shivering response to her thoughts set her nerves blazing. Understood from gossip more than one woman found herself enceinte after these young men found their amusement from some unlucky woman.

After the carriage stopped in front of the MacRae townhouse, she swallowed several gulps of air. The lump in her throat didn't vanish. She told herself the breaths of air were for courage. They didn't help. True, she needed to pull whatever bravery she could find from herself to tackle this issue with her mother. She didn't wish to be anywhere near her mother. Had to find out what Anice wanted. For several minutes she sat, frozen. This was...

For the benefit of your sisters.

That's what the note said. Tessa didn't have any idea how this meeting would benefit any of them. For over a year they had no correspondence with Anice. Now, she wanted to see the youngest. The one she believed to be the most vulnerable. Their mother tended to bring chaos into their lives whenever she entered into it. She almost told the footman to take her back after he opened the door then placed the steps for her.

With a disapproving look, he held out his hand to help her down. Cleared his throat. "You shouldn't be here without Lord Kenworthy's permission. Without him. I'm not liking this a'tall. Can you reconsider?"

Weak was not going to be the way people described her character. *I'm not weak. I've a mind of my own. Opinions that don't need to be changed.*

"No, nothing to change my plans."

She found herself shaking her head. Lord Abernathy wanted her because he believed he could mold her into a proper wife. Thought she was someone who would jump to do his bidding. Whatever that might be. Weak willed. Spineless. She was not that person. Jason understood her true nature. Letting Jason mold her was also not part of the plan for herself. He would need to come to understand her way of thinking. Tessa stiffened her spine before tilting her chin higher. She could do this.

"Are you certain you want to be here?" her driver asked again while he escorted her to the steps. "I should insist on taking you home."

No. *I'm not certain.* "I'll be fine. Wait for me, please. Don't intend to spend a moment longer than necessary with my mother. Need to find out what she is after." The man was right to worry. Tessa knew she had no business walking into her mother's home without protection.

He cleared his throat before he gave her one more reason to hesitate.

Her hand was at the knocker. "Can't say Lord Kenworthy will be pleased when he discovers where I've taken you. He might…"

Startled by his words, she was quick to reassure. She'd not thought beyond her needs. "Don't fret. I'll make certain Jason understands I pleaded with you to bring me here. I'm safe with my mother. No harm will come from this visit. You'll see." Tessa didn't believe anything she told the driver was true. Her mother could turn on her with a blink of an eye. She was crazy to answer the note. Crazy to arrive on her doorstep without Jason or her sisters. A damn fool for not telling Nellie where she was going. Should have tossed the damn thing into the fire. Should be sitting down to dinner with my sisters.

"Could lose my job," he grumbled.

"You know that won't happen. How long have you been working for the Kenworthy's?" Tessa asked feeling more than a little responsible for this man's fears. "I'm sorry if I've made your life difficult."

"Longer than you've been alive. Longer than Lord Kenworthy too."

After she made up her mind a second time to stay, she patted his hand. "I promise nothing will happen to your job." The promise was made with sheer bravado. Tessa understood she had no clout with the Kenworthy twins when it came to hiring and firing employees. She did think that this time her reasoning might prevail if this situation came to the possible termination of his job.

"I'll be here waiting for you, Miss MacRae. Don't think I won't. Not going anywhere without you inside. Not without you tucked safe into the carriage. Won't let you down."

Standing on the tips of her toes, she kissed the elderly man on the cheek before she opened the door. The foyer was empty when she took off her cape to hang it on the coat stand. The scent of fresh picked roses clung to the air. Tessa expected someone to appear soon even though she didn't knock. She wiped her sweating hands on the fabric of her dress. Wished she wasn't so nervous.

"Mother, I'm here." Tessa called out then smoothed the cloth of her gown shaking out a few creases from her stint in the carriage. She walked the length of the foyer, peering into several rooms before she satisfied herself that her mother was nowhere to be found. Anice wouldn't appear until she wished. Her mother would play a waiting game with her, stretching her nerves with the insecurities Anice would know she was feeling.

"Mother?" A few thoughts of disgust fluttered through her head. She came all this way to be welcomed to an empty house. Did her mother think she wouldn't come? Perhaps. With no purpose in her head as to what she was going to do, she wandered into the drawing room. Noted the fire burning in the hearth. A somber glow illuminated the room, bathing the furniture. Lights had been lit in preparation for her visit. Her mother was expecting her.

She always loved this room. As she looked around, she imagined her sisters sitting around the fire chatting. Her mother rarely disturbed them in the evenings. The times together, here, were fond memories.

A tray was set out with refreshments. A teapot with two dainty cups. Small plates at the ready. The sugar bowl along with several slices of lemon. A pitcher with milk. Napkins.

So, mother did expect her most obedient daughter to do her bidding. It was obvious Anice was confident that she would comply to the command. She would give her credit for reading her mind. Had to since she fell into her hands by following her directives. Tessa realized her acquiesce in this matter wasn't caused by obedience. It was due to curiosity. For all her sisters, Tessa wanted to learn what it was that their mother expected of them even though she put herself in a precarious situation.

Tessa poured herself a cup of tea. Bit into a spice cake. Savored the taste. Anice did employ the best cook. She closed her eyes, enjoying.

"Ah, the little mouse has come home." The grating voice of her mother startled her out of her revery.

Choked by the sound behind her, Tessa dropped the cake on the small bone China plate. She coughed trying to clear her throat of the tiny obstacle that was lodged half way down her throat.

"Drink some tea, dear," Anice encouraged while she fixed herself a cup. "Wasn't certain you would show up. Was your handsome protector not at home to end your venture into the evening by yourself. I would have expected your protector, Lord Kenworthy, to put a stop to this excursion."

She cleared her throat, the last remnants of spice cake slipping downward. "What do you want, Mother? I'd like to hear you out then leave." Tessa didn't want to stay here a moment longer than necessary. Seeing her mother again brought back memories she'd rather forget. To dwell on whether or not she should be here was a moot point. She shouldn't have responded to the summons.

"So brusque. I would have thought your manners would be better. A year ago, you would never have cut to the point of a requested visit in such a curt manner. You are becoming more like your sisters." Anice sat back, one hand holding the saucer, the other the cup. Her eyes narrowed while she studied her youngest daughter.

"Why don't you have another cake? Had the cook bake your favorite." Anice nodded her head toward the plate of delicacies.

"You were so certain I would come?" Of course, Anice was certain. She never defied her mother. Anice would never believe she would start now.

"Once a mouse, always a mouse. I suppose Lord Kenworthy appreciates the fact you fail to have an opinion. Such an easy girl to mold to his way of thinking. Have you slept with the man? Of course, you have. When I last saw the two of you together, you were smitten by that man."

Tessa had enough. Anice was rude beyond anything she expected. What she did or didn't do with Jason Kenworthy was none of her mother's business. "I should go."

She motioned to the now empty chair. "Oh, do sit down. A snit will not get us anywhere. I've important information for you. Don't wish for you to leave until you understand."

"My driver is waiting for me. Get to the point, Mother." Her anger rose not so much at her mother but at herself. Anice was acting true to form. She expected as much. If she still thought to harbor a few soft sentiments for Anice, they vanished the moment she asked if she'd slept with Jason.

"Sit. Not speaking with you if you're standing in front of me with that horrid glare on your delicate features. You will get wrinkles sooner than later. Can't imagine how you came to be so fragile considering who your father is." Anice took a cake from the tray. Bit with delicate precision.

Anice wasn't going to get to the point of the visit any time soon. With a heavy sigh, Tessa sat. Waited for her mother to get through playing with her prey. Anice spoke about her father without mentioning a name. She'd always been certain her father was not the same as her siblings. Her sire was a different man. She wondered what it would have been like to grow up in a different home. If she had, she would not have come to care so much for her sisters. She might have been loved.

Would the man who is her father be nice? Would he have cared about her? Too many questions to count. What she needed now was to stick this out. She was here for a reason. The intent of her mother would not bode well for her.

"What do you want, mother?" Tessa found she was exhausted as well as frustrated with the cat and mouse game Anice played. "Tell me now, so I can leave."

By the time Anice finished explaining her plans for the two of them, Tessa was sick to her stomach. She couldn't ignore what her mother wanted. Had to find some way to play the game long enough so she might find the means to win. Enlisting Jason's help was out of the question.

Heart-sick, Tessa welcomed the friendly presence of her driver after she left her mother's home. He gave her a fatherly pat on her hand as if he sensed her disillusionment. Tessa understood whether she came to visit tonight or tomorrow or even the next week, Anice would have found a way to put her disgusting threat in front of her.

When she walked into the library of the Kenworthy home, she felt dirty. She needed to wash the filth from herself. No amount of scrubbing would make her clean again. Her mother used her. Did that surprise her? No! Anice used everyone she could. All she needed was to find a weakness. As she discovered visiting with her mother, she had more than one weakness.

So unlike her, she grabbed Jason glass of brandy and downed the contents. Almost laughed at his stunned look of surprise. The fiery liquid sliding down her throat did nothing for her disposition. Her confusion must have shown through her bravado. She splashed more brandy into Jason glass then poured herself a drink.

She was confused as well as frightened. Proceeding with the plan was difficult. She didn't wish to be part of this. Didn't know what to do.

As she began to fiddle with her buttons, she understood she exploded into dangerous territory. Having Jason make love to her wouldn't solve problems. No, doing this would create more than she had any idea how to deal with.

When he rejected her ill-thought out advances, her cheeks flamed. Heated. She wished there was some hole she could climb into then hide from him forever. He learned that she visited her mother. How, she had no idea.

Jason demanded answers. She had nothing to give him that would subdue his burgeoning anger with her. When they spoke of the woman he was seeing, she wished she dared slap him. He couldn't ask her to marry him in one breath then run off to warm himself in the bed of his mistress. The woman wasn't his mistress. He told her as much. After the brief meeting, she raced to her room. To seek solace by herself was her motivation.

Still feeling the filth from her mother coupled with the humiliation from Jason, she pulled the bell cord for a bath. Not much later the heated water arrived. She poured scented oil into the steaming liquid before she stripped then settled into the hot bath.

To cease thinking about this day would be her dream. To have had the day never happen would be a miracle. She soaked until the water turned tepid. Washed. Finally stepping from the water, she wrapped a towel around her hair then one around herself.

She placed another log on the fire. Watched the flames leap into the air. Tears slid from her eyes. She pushed them away with the backs of her hands. Tessa didn't know how she was going to face Jason tomorrow morning. If she got lucky, he wouldn't be around. Sometimes he left early to ride. She could hope.

The knock on her door startled her. The person on the other side could be one of her sisters. Who else would it be? She didn't want to see them. They would take one look at her then ask a wealth of questions she didn't dare respond to.

"Tessa!"

The devil, no!

"I don't wish to see you!" The panic she heard in her voice would also be heard by Jason. He would insist on entry. He'd not given up on finding out why she set out to see her mother or what her mother wanted from her. She wouldn't be able to withstand his gentle persuasion. He had that way about him.

"You've no choice," Jason spoke with a calming voice. His words though, did nothing to calm her. "One way or the other I'm coming into your room. Have to speak with you about tonight. You ran off before I could get a few answers from you. Need to get a few things understood before I sleep tonight."

"No!"

"As I just said, you've no choice." Jason persisted on this theme. His voice was gentle. While he wasn't giving her a choice, he was using tactics that would subdue someone with greater strength than she possessed. "I'd like you to open the door for me. Now."

"I'm not decent." She groped for one excuse after another. "I've…"

"Put a robe on," he said as he turned the handle. "I'll give you to the count of ten." Jason began to count. "One…two…"

Tessa didn't have time to find the lock to the door. She would look for the key afterward. This wasn't going to happen again. She raced to the armoire. Dropped both towels before opening the doors. Where was her nightgown? Her robe? She was such a bundle of nerves. Her fingers fumbled while she searched in desperation. She didn't recall where she saw them last.

"Ten…"

"Oh, no…no…"

Wide eyed, she turned to see Jason open the door then step into the room. With haste, she reached for the first thing she could find. Air was what she found. Saw one of the towels lying a few feet from her. Dashed for it. In a moment, she had the towel wrapped around her, her blood rushing through her.

"Jason…" she breathed out his name. "You shouldn't be here. I…" He saw her naked. without a stitch.

With his hands behind his back, he rocked on his heels. With deep husky words, he spoke. "I see that. Go on. Find your nightgown and robe. I'll turn my back while you look. Need for you to calm down."

"Calm down?" she parroted, panicked. "How can I calm down when you're in my room and I'm na…naked?"

The throaty chuckle following her statement did nothing to relax her. "If I recall a little while ago, you were undressing yourself in front of me. What am I supposed to think? Seems you're running a bit hot and cold. You don't seem to know your own mind."

"I…can't we talk in the morning?" Even while she uttered the question, Tessa comprehended what his answer would be.

"No."

That was what she thought. She gulped down a smidgeon of air. "I'm not going to be telling you anything about my visit to my mother. I won't. If that's why you are here then you're wasting your time."

"Find the robe, Tessa. If you don't, I will. My patience is running thin."

By the sound of his voice, what he told her held the ring of truth. "Oh!" She dropped the towel. Searched. Found a gown that would never do. The fabric was gossamer, silky meant to… She didn't know what it was meant for. Not warmth that was for certain. Nonetheless, this piece of silken fabric her mother gave her before the sisters had a falling out was better than nothing. She slipped the gown over her head just as he was turning around again.

His eyes darkened. He stepped toward her. His hand outstretched. "Your hair is all a tangle. Still wet. Go sit by the fire. I'll comb it for you."

"That's not why you're here. What do you want?" Frantic she searched her mind for some tidbit she could tell him. Something that might ease his mind. "Why are you here where you've no business?"

"We will be married. You need to get used to me seeing you with little to nothing on."

"I said no." She backed up a step for each one he took toward her.

"Yes. A man needs to know where his woman is as well as why she put her life at risk. Don't you think? Give me a reason I can't refute."

"Not your woman." She wished she was his. Needed him to love her the way his twin loved her sister.

"You are. I've waited far too long for you to figure it out. Tonight put a period to the waiting. If you won't say yes…well, there are other ways to get a reluctant woman to the alter."

"What are you talking about?"

"Sit on the hearth. I'll comb your hair.

Dazed, Tessa obeyed without further argument.

I am a mouse.

~ * ~

"You know Tessa went to see mother. What do you suppose she wanted?" Nellie asked, her voice growing paper thin with the question. They were all afraid Anice would find some means to make the youngest sibling do her dirty work. They both understood Anice would blackmail if she got the chance. She'd always been underhanded in her dealings. Nothing would have changed in the year since Maggie's wedding.

"What does she have to hold over Tessa's head? There is nothing that I can think of." Fannie asked while she watched the door for movement. "I'd like to learn what it is. We need to speak with our sister so she can tell us what Anice wants. Do you think she would be forthcoming with us?"

"No, not if the threat included us. In that case she would tell us nothing. Tessa was out late with mother. I would suspect Jason saw her before she went to bed. She won't be down yet. It's far too early. We need to be patient with our little sister. There is a lot of pressure on her. I'm certain Jason has been applying thumb screws to get her to talk to him. We need to make certain she understands she can count on us to protect her best interests."

"Do you think our talk about his mistress shook her so much she gave into whatever mother wanted?" Fannie was drumming her fingers on the armrest of her chair. It was a nervous habit that drove Nellie half crazy. "If mother summoned her, Anice would be confident that Tessa would have no choice in the matter."

"There is no mistress…no other woman in my life. I'd appreciate for the rumors along with the gossip would stop." The gruff voice brought both girls to attention. They both groaned, felt heat flush their faces. "What goes on between Tessa and myself needs to be between the two of us. I've explained to Tessa what she needs to know. She understands that the woman is in my past not our future. A man cannot be expected to be celibate."

"It can't be just between the two of you," Nellie said quite frankly finding the need to lecture this man surfacing. "We all share everything. We are as close as sisters can be. That's not going to change."

"No longer. What goes on between Tessa and myself is private." He poured himself a cup of tea then set about dishing up a plate of food. He sat down before speaking again, "Tessa won't be down for another hour or more. She's exhausted from the evening. There was a great deal that happened that was out of her control."

"What about your mistress…Sarah," Fannie blurted with angry words while she persevered on the topic Jason just told them was not their business. Fannie folded her hands together. "If Tessa is going to shed tears over your lovers, past or present, she needs to be able to confide in us."

Jason didn't seem to understand how best to deal with Tessa's siblings. He pinched the bridge of his nose before clearing his throat to move on to a new topic. "As I just mentioned, I have no mistress or lover. There is nothing to share. Tessa doesn't need to confide in her sisters. She has me to confide in now." Without giving them more attention, he thumped the egg he was about to eat then carefully peeled the shell away.

"Jason is right." Tessa made her way into the room. Beneath her eyes were dark shadows giving testimony to a sleepless night. Jason was right. She was exhausted. "I will…confide in Jason. No one else. He's made himself clear on that matter to the two of you this morning as well as to me last evening. There will be no arguments or persuasive lectures. What is between Jason and myself stays between us."

"You should still be in bed," Jason said as he stared pointedly at Tessa. "Last night was too much for you."

Nellie and Fanny shared the direction of their gazes. Both were concerned for their little sister. She looked as if she'd been run over, trampled by a speeding carriage.

"I couldn't sleep. Under the circumstances, no point in staying in bed," Tessa murmured as she sat down at the breakfast table.

"Eat…" He waved his arm to the sideboard where platters of food abounded. "We are traveling to the country today. There you will find some rest. You can sleep as long as you wish. Anice will not be allowed to bother you. The butler has been given the direction that whatever missives come to you they must go through me first." He turned his attention to the sisters. "You will follow after the Laughton ball if you would like to join us. As you all can see, Tessa needs a change of scenery. I'm worried about her. We are all concerned for her health."

What he wasn't saying was that she needed to be away from Anice. Nellie closed her eyes, understanding Tessa was their mother's latest victim. Jason would do all in his power to protect her. He loved her even though Tessa didn't realize that yet.

Nellie wanted to be loved. The rakes she met so far were not ready to find a wife. She realized she needed to look for an older man. A twenty something young pup, as Jasper called the men who were eager to find wives at the debutant balls, wouldn't do unless they were closer to the thirty mark. Younger men seemed to need to figure things out. Nellie wasn't at all certain what needed to be figured out. That was the only logical explanation she could think of; the need to bed as many different women as possible before turning thirty.

Jason turned thirty a couple of years ago. He must have everything all figured out. Tessa was lucky his roving eye landed on her.

Don't Hustle Letty
Good Girls Book One

She's a good girl...

As tempted as Scarlett was, she had too many secrets to let someone enter her world—secrets that would send any reasonable man to the farthest ends of the earth. Bobby was far from reasonable and despite her desperate attempts to hold him at bay, he would not let her past destroy their future. With her escort service, Scarlett used men and their insatiable lust for women to capitalize on the means to survive and prosper. She vowed to never wed, to never put herself in the control of a man.

...nonetheless he has other ideas.

Lord Robert Munroe, with his newly acquired title of marquis goes to Scarlett's for training on how to comport himself. The marquis, better known as Bobby, knows how to pick a pocket as well as get into a bloke's home to steal them blind. What he doesn't know is how to be a gentleman. When he sets his sights on the prim Miss Scarlet, Letty, to his way of thinking, he decides she is the woman he wants to call his wife. He tempts all that she is with sweet words and tender coaxing until she is unable to refuse all he hopes to give her.

Only Caro's Baby
Good Girls Book Two

The Scheme

Genius botanist with theories of inherited traits, Caroline Kenworth desperately wants a baby. Finding a suitable father won't be easy. Caroline's super-intelligence makes her feel pushed aside, unwanted as a woman. As a bluestocking she is determined to spare her child the suffering that plagues her life. Which means she must find someone very special to father her child. A person very...well...ignorant.

The Target.

Duncan Murray, the Earl of Downsberry, well known for his lack of intelligence as well as his rakish ways with women, seems as if he is the flawless man to fulfill the role. His amazing good looks and Scottish brogue are misleading. Caro learns too late that this debonair earl is a lot smarter than she first thought—in addition he's not about to be used then abandoned by any woman who has schemed to steal his sperm.

The Detonation

A dazzling solitary woman whose desires to learn what it would be like to become a mother... A man who is in control of all he does never allowing anyone to usurp his role will settle for nothing less than surrender... Can lust coupled with physical attraction drive two strong-minded yet vulnerable people to a completely unforeseen love?

Honey
Good Girls Book Three

She's a good girl...

Born a bastard, Honey McRae is taunted and bullied by her half-brother most of her life. Branded with a tattoo of the Saber and the Rose by the men's association, she is desperate to be free and escapes the country estate where she was held prisoner. Resigned to a passionless life devoid of men, she fights the nightmares that haunt her. Despite her past fears, she accepts the fact she will never be able to give herself wholly to the man she loves. Until that man, bold and breathtaking, decides he will find a means to woo her into his arms.

Nonetheless...

Stolen at birth and sent to live in the bowels of London, Billy– once a pickpocket and thief–discovers he is actually the Duke of St. Aubries. He is determined to win the woman he fell in love with the first time he saw her, the lady with a tattoo on her breast, a woman who has been cruelly used. He disputes her notion that men are only capable of inflicting pain...instead he binds her to his heart with his gentle and patient loving.

Betsy Be Good
Good Girls Book Four

AN ENGLISH ROSE

Sweet Betsy Darling, the oh-so-prim and innocent tutor for children born of rich aristocrats, is a woman on a mission—she has but a short time to lose her standing as a respectable spinster. Arriving in Glasgow with skirts flying, parasol pointing, and plump mouth issuing demands, she understands only one thing will save her form losing all she holds dear: complete and utter disgrace.

A BRAW HIGHLANDER

Known throughout the city as a bad boy with more money than he needs, Evan Murray has lost his temper one too many times, and now he's suspended from teaching at the university he loves as well as Halstead & Family the financial firm owned by his family. An apology which he refuses to issue is one of two things that will restore his career. The second is his complete and utter respectability! Now he's been coerced into escorting the bossy, parasol toting Miss Betsy Darling, and she's hell-bent on chasing down a tattoo parlor, dressing in skimpy clothing and worse...lots worse.

Gracie
Good Girls Book Five

She's a good girl...

During a tempest, Gracie Seymor flees the hands of an abusive fiancé to find herself tossed from her horse. The blow to her head causes the loss of her memory. In the shelter of a wayside inn, she meets a man who steals her heart. From the moment the handsome man, Gordan Murray, lifts his dark brown eyes to meet hers, they are drawn together, spellbound, into each other's arms then into the night of passion that claims her innocence sending her on a course that will change her life forever.

...Nonetheless he steals her heart

So dependent on the man who claims her virginity, Gracie becomes his mistress even though she understands she should refuse. She's a good girl. Good girls don't become men's playthings. After the night spent with Gracie in his arms, Gordan takes her to a cottage near his home. Here they will confront the specter of her past and discover Gracie's identity. It revolves around a tangled web of secrets coupled with a magical love that cannot be denied.

Dawn
Good Girls Book Six

Dawn Callahan's dream of freedom and a life of independence is shattered. After she realizes she somehow stepped through a portal into a different century all she has left to fight for is her sanity along with a way to return to the time of her birth. To do that she has to give up her autonomy. With no money to her name or a roof over her head, she needs Gordan Murray's help. In return she refuses to give him what he wants the most. Answers to his questions.

On first sight, Gordan means to take her into his home. Intends to give her everything she wants. When she refuses his sincere offers, he withdraws into himself searching for a means to convince her he has only good intentions toward her.

On that sunny day in July when Dawn tumbles from a whorehouse to land on her delectable little butt a woman was the last thing in the world he was looking for. He has a fine life. Finds willing women with a smile coupled with a nod.

Love has a way of changing the rules.

www.ingramcontent.com/pod-product-compliance
Lightning Source LLC
Chambersburg PA
CBHW060352260626
47160CB00006B/2288